BREWER AND THE PORTUGUESE GOLD

BREWER AND THE PORTUGUESE GOLD

BY

JAMES KEFFER

www.penmorepress.com

Brewer and The Portuguese Gold by James Keffer

ISBN-13: 978-1-950586-47-9(Paperback)
ISBN—978-1-950586-46-2(E-book)

BISAC Subject Headings:
FIC014000FICTION / Historical
FIC032000FICTION / War & Military
FIC047000FICTION / Sea Stories

Editing: Chris Wozney
Cover Illustration by Christine Horner

Address all correspondence to:
Michael James
Penmore Press LLC
920 N Javelina Pl
Tucson, AZ 85748

DEDICATION

To Christine—For all the love and support I didn't deserve.

CHAPTER ONE

The garden of the residence of the governor of St. Kitts was a beautiful place, renowned throughout the neighboring islands for the serenity it inspired in those fortunate enough to visit. On this spring morning it was especially beautiful. The expected rain had passed north of the island, leaving a whisper of sea breeze to carry the myriad fragrances to those who sat nearby.

Standing at one end of the garden, Commander William Brewer fought to control his nerves. He looked around him as casually as he could without drawing attention to himself. He was standing in front of a large crowd, between a priest of the Church of England on his right hand and Admiral Lord Horatio Hornblower on his left, and he was there to be married. He glanced down the aisle that divided the crowd, but there was no sign of the bride.

Brewer had never given much thought to having a large wedding; he would have been content with a small service attended by close friends. But Elizabeth had insisted. She had dreamed of this day all her life, she said, and he had gone along for her sake. Any moment now, she would appear at the far end of the center aisle on her father's arm. Brewer had seen her dress once—a beautiful white gown with accents of handmade lace and a train fully ten feet in length—but he had yet to see her in it, and it was all he could do not to crane his neck and stare.

"Not having second thoughts, are you, William?" a voice said at his shoulder. He glanced to his left to the smiling face of his mentor.

"Never, my lord," he said. "Did you, when you married Lady Barbara?"

"No," Hornblower confided, "but I must confess that, even if I had, Bush would have firmly dispelled them."

Brewer smiled at the inside joke and said, "I wish he could be here."

Hornblower looked steadily over the crowd. "As do I."

Brewer looked at the assembly and allowed his eyes to fall on Lady Barbara Hornblower stationed serenely in the first chair. She had travelled to Jamaica to visit her husband.

Next, Brewer's gaze fell on his men in the third row. Lieutenant Greene was seated on the aisle seat, with Dr. Spinelli next to him. Both men were watching his interactions with the admiral with interest. Mac, his coxswain, was seated on the Doctor's other side; he'd come along more to see that Brewer stayed out of trouble than anything else. In fact, he had been going to wait outside for them to come out; Brewer had had to insist he come inside for the ceremony. Next to Mac sat Mr. Sweeney, sailing master and substitute mentor. Brewer knew he was lucky to have him. The last was Commander Gerard, his old friend from the *Lydia* and the admiral's aide.

A change in music caught his attention, signaling to everyone the momentous arrival of the bride. Now he saw Elizabeth in a beautiful cloud of white, standing with her father, and the two began their slow march to join him at the altar. The crowd stood as the bride came forward. She halted just before the altar and knelt in prayer. Brewer felt his heart pounding; she was even more beautiful than he'd ever imagined she could be. After a few moments in prayer, she stood again, and her father presented her to her intended.

Afterward, Brewer would confide to his close friends that he had no memory of the ceremony itself. He could not remember saying his vows or pledging his troth, and he only vaguely remembered the admiral handing him the ring and the act of putting it on her finger. The only words he remembered hearing were "You may kiss the bride." At that point he turned toward her and kissed her tenderly, and when they parted he knew his heart was hers.

The minister presented them to the assembly as "Commander and Mrs. William Brewer," and Brewer walked his bride down the aisle to the thunderous applause of all. The couple made their way to the residence's main hall, where they waited to receive their guests at the traditional wedding breakfast.

Brewer's bride hung on his arm and buried her face in his chest. "Husband and wife," she said. "I can scarcely believe it."

"Believe it," he said, as he kissed her head. "You're stuck with me now, Mrs. Brewer."

"Mmm," she murmured as he squeezed his arm. "That's just the way I want it, Commander."

He smiled at her as the guests began to file in. They greeted each in turn and thanked them for coming. When the last guests had made their way to the tables and found their places, the happy couple proceeded to the table at the head of the room and took their seats.

The Admiral rose and raised his glass.

"Ladies and gentlemen," he said, "I ask you to join me as we drink the health of the happy couple." He cleared his throat loudly. "Ha-h'm! May they never know sorrow. May health and prosperity be their constant companions. May the wife find comfort in the knowledge that her husband is doing his duty for King and Country, and may the husband be supported in his duty by the loyalty and devotion of his wife. May they be blessed with sons who will wear the King's uniform and follow their father's example, and daughters to be the mothers of young gentlemen. I give you the bride and groom!"

The room erupted with cheering and acclamation.

Lord and Lady Hornblower approached the newlyweds, and Lord Hornblower bowed over the new bride's hand.

"If I may impose," he said, "I should like to borrow the Commander for a few minutes."

"Of course, my lord," she said sweetly, handing over her husband.

"I shan't be long," Brewer said quietly before following his admiral from the room.

"See that you aren't," Elizabeth replied.

The two ladies watched the gentlemen walk away. Elizabeth sighed.

"Milady," she said softly, "will I ever get used to it?"

"Used to what, my dear?"

Elizabeth stared at the door. "Watching him leave."

Barbara smiled and put her arm around her new friend. "I'm afraid not. At least, I never have. Keep yourself busy while he is gone, or you will go mad with worry."

"And if he doesn't return?"

"Some things are in God's hands," Barbara answered. "Cherish your time with him. And remember, you are always welcome at Smallbridge."

Brewer followed Hornblower into an empty office and closed the door behind them.

"Yes, my lord?"

"William," Hornblower said, "I have called you here to say goodbye."

"My lord?"

"I have reached the end of my three-year term and am returning to Smallbridge. Barbara came out on the West Indies packet to help me pack up and to accompany me home." Hornblower sat in a chair and directed Brewer to the one opposite it.

"My lord," Brewer said, "I don't know what to say. I am very happy for you both."

"Then just listen. I have decided to take advantage of the tradition that a relieved station chief can make two promotions, one to lieutenant and the other to post captain. I have my eye on a midshipman in *Clorinda* for the promotion to lieutenant, and I have decided to promote you to post captain."

Brewer stared at his mentor, wide-eyed and with his mouth hanging open. Hornblower laughed.

"That's the same look I had on my face when old Cornwallis did the same for me!"

Brewer blushed in embarrassment and closed his mouth. "My apologies, my lord. I don't know how to thank you."

"Keep doing what you have been, and that will be thanks enough. You've earned this, William, never doubt it. I was just fortunate to help with the timing, that's all."

Hornblower crossed his arms over his chest. "And, in light of your recent promotion, *Captain*, it is my duty to relieve you of command of HMS *Revenge*."

Brewer was dumbfounded. "My lord?"

The admiral smiled. "William, you know as well as I do that a post captain cannot command a sixth-rate like *Revenge*."

"Oh," Brewer said, ceding his admiral's point. "Yes, I see, my lord."

Hornblower smiled cryptically. "What you do not know, Captain, is that HMS *Phoebe* is scheduled for a refit as soon as *Revenge* clears the dock. She's yours when you return to Port Royal."

Brewer's spirits recovered immediately. "Thank you, my lord!"

"You're welcome. You may take your officers with you to your new command."

"You are too kind, my lord," Brewer said. "Pardon me, but you said my officers?"

Hornblower nodded, knowing what his friend was hinting at. "Yes, William. With all due respect to Mr. Greene, I have decided to give HMS *Revenge* to Commander Gerard. He deserves a chance at some good prize money, and I think he's earned a command of his own, don't you?"

"Undoubtedly," Brewer said. He felt disappointed for Greene, but on the other hand he was happy to be keeping his first officer by his side. "My lord, I don't know how to thank you for all you have done."

Hornblower waved it away. "I'm glad for the chance to help a promising young officer. I had officers who aided me in my career—Cornwallis and Pellew, for example—and I'm happy to pass it along. Just promise me you will do the same if you are ever in a position to do so."

"I promise, my lord," he said, and the two men shook hands.

The two men returned to the wedding breakfast and found their wives deep in conversation.

"My lord?" Brewer said as they approached the pair, "Should I be concerned?"

"Yes," Hornblower deadpanned in return. "You should."

"Now, Horatio," his wife scolded, "don't be poisoning the young groom's mind before I've even had a chance to train his bride."

"My apologies, my dear. I had no idea you weren't finished."

"Did your meeting go well?" Elizabeth asked her husband.

"Oh, very well indeed," Hornblower interrupted. "Ladies, may I introduce to you the newly-promoted *Captain* William Brewer, now commanding His Majesty's frigate *Phoebe*."

"Oh, William!" his bride jumped out of her chair and kissed him on the cheek.

Brewer's father-in-law now leaned forward over the table. "Congratulations, Captain. Forgive me, but I couldn't help but overhear the joyous news."

"Thank you, sir," Brewer said. Elizabeth glowed with joy.

Hornblower smiled. "I shall write out the orders giving you command of *Phoebe* before I leave, William. I pray your father-in-law will loan me a clerk to make copies?"

The governor bowed. "At your service, my lord."

"Excellent. Captain, your orders will include a paragraph authorizing you to sleep out of your ship for thirty days. I suggest you send Mr. Greene and the rest back immediately to oversee *Phoebe*'s refit."

"Yes, my lord," Brewer said. "Request permission for Dr. Spinelli to remain, my lord. I would prefer to travel with him on my way back to Jamaica."

Hornblower nodded. "I'll see to it. In the meantime, Captain, I suggest you enjoy yourself; your thirty days begin tomorrow. Report to me when you return to Jamaica."

Brewer bowed. "Thank you, my lord."

They enjoyed the wedding breakfast, feasting on the delicacies that came from the governor's kitchen. Brewer gazed in wonder at his new bride beside him, talking to one of her friends. Hornblower and Lady Barbara were on his other side, sitting silently and watching.

The following morning, Brewer and Elizabeth set off for their honeymoon. The governor and several friends came down to the jetty to see them off. Brewer raised the sail on the skiff he had rented, and they sailed away. Once outside the harbor entrance, Brewer turned north and sailed up the western side of the island to a secluded little cove just east of its northern tip. He lowered the sail as they entered the cove, and the skiff slid in to shore. At the far end of the cove, out of sight of the entrance, was a small cottage. Brewer jumped out and ran the skiff up onto the shore before helping Elizabeth out.

"I first came here not long after my father and I arrived on the island," she said, as they walked hand-in-hand up the beach. "I decided right away that if I got married while we were here, this was where I wanted to spend my honeymoon."

He opened the door for her and closed it behind them. The he put his arms around her and kissed her with all the passion he possessed. She returned his passion, nearly overwhelming him in the process. They looked at each other, words lost in the moment.

"Well," he said breathlessly, "I'd better go unload the skiff."

She grabbed him by the arm. He turned and noticed a devilish look in her eyes.

"I think that can wait, Captain," she said, and she led him to the bedroom.

The sun was low in the sky when they emerged and began to set up house. He made the trips to the skiff to bring their belongings and food to the cottage alone, she being busy inside the dwelling. There was a roaring fire going when he stepped inside from his final trip.

"Well!" he said. "Could it be that you were telling me the truth about your domestic abilities?"

"Captain," she said coyly, "see for yourself."

As pleasant days went by he did see, and he saw more than he ever expected to see. She kept house, cooked, and made coffee (nearly as good as Alfred's). He, too, was used to working in the kitchen and around the house, and cheerfully joined her in domestic bliss.

The two weeks flew by. It seemed to both of them that they had hardly arrived before it was time to return. They cleaned the cottage and took their possessions to the skiff. Brewer helped her in and then shoved off. He paddled the craft to the entrance of the cove before raising the sail. They sailed south without incident, with him sitting at the tiller and her beside him, leaning back on his chest and enjoying the sea breeze.

They arrived before the noonday sun beat hot upon the waters. Brewer returned the skiff, and the couple left their possessions at the dock office for servants to retrieve later.

On their way to Governor's House, they stopped at the inn where the good Dr. Spinelli was staying. They found him engaged in a game of chess with another resident.

"Ah!" he said when he saw them enter. "The happy couple appears. Well, my dear, I see you haven't thrown him overboard yet. So, do you still think him worth keeping?"

"Oh, Doctor," she said smiling, "I think he has great possibilities!"

Spinelli laughed as Elizabeth kissed her husband on the cheek.

"Doctor," Brewer said, "can you be ready to sail in the morning?"

"Aye, but I heard a couple of merchant captains talking, and they feared that bad weather was closing in."

Brewer frowned at the news. "Well, book us passage on the first available shipping to Port Royal, and we'll see what happens."

"You can sup with us tonight, Doctor," Elizabeth said. "Eight o'clock."

"Thank you, fair lady. I shall be there."

The weather did indeed close in and kept the two officers virtual prisoners for three days. Elizabeth watched her husband grow more and more restless with each passing day, and she herself began to fret. Dr. Spinelli noticed and asked her to take a walk through the garden with him during a break in the rain.

He addressed her as as they walked side by side. "I see you are troubled, my lady."

"I apologize, doctor," she replied. "It's just that I'm not used to seeing this side of my husband."

"What do you mean?"

"He is becoming restless, and I know not how to help him."

Spinelli smiled. "I'm afraid you cannot."

She stopped for a moment, but he gestured for her to move again.

"You will learn in time that his heart may be yours, but his mind and soul belong to his ship. He has a new command that he has yet to see. By this time, Mr. Greene and McCleary should be back and getting *Phoebe* ready for his arrival, but to him that's not nearly enough."

He stopped and faced her. "You must never doubt his love for you, but you must resign yourself to the fact that he is being called away by forces he cannot resist."

She sighed and looked down the pathway. "Lady Barbara said something similar when we spoke at the wedding breakfast, but I didn't realize it would be so hard."

The doctor nodded sympathetically. "He will come back to you, my dear; never doubt it. When all is finally said and done, he will be yours."

The next morning, Brewer was up early. He checked the weather and decided that there was a good chance they could make the morning tide. He quickly woke Elizabeth and rang for the servants to bring their tea. He dressed hurriedly, hardly paying attention to the cup of tea cooling on the dresser. He turned to find his bride standing at the end of the bed, watching him, herself still in her nightgown.

"You aren't going to get dressed?" he asked as he pulled on his boot.

"No," she said, sitting down on the bed beside him, "I believe I'd rather say goodbye to you here, where it's just the two of us." She rested her head on his shoulder, and he put his arms around her. "I wish you didn't have to go."

He closed his eyes; he'd hoped to avoid this. He took a deep breath and kissed her on the head. "I know. I wish it, too, but you know I have to go."

He felt her head nod against his chest, and he patted her shoulder. After a few moments, he heard her sniff back tears, and she sat up. He pulled on his other boot, and she stood and got his coat. She helped him into it, then turned him around and straightened his lapels. She smiled and pulled a piece of lint off one of his epaulettes.

"Now," she said, "you are ready to assume your new command."

"Aye aye, sir," he said. He took her in his arms and kissed her. "Goodbye for a little while, Mrs. Brewer."

"Goodbye for a little while, my love."

Brewer sent his sea chest to the ship and walked to the inn to collect the doctor. The two men hurried to the wharf and boarded a schooner bound for Jamaica. Despite his rank, Brewer found himself sharing a cabin with the doctor.

"Sorry about the accommodations," Spinelli said, "but this was the first available ship departing St. Kitts, and I thought you'd rather put up with me and leave sooner."

"You thought right," Brewer said. He tossed his coat onto his hammock and looked around. The cabin was barely big enough for their two hammocks to be strung comfortably. There was a small table under the porthole. "Did the captain say how long a passage?"

"He said he hoped for a fast passage. Perhaps a week, if we're lucky."

Brewer shrugged. "Shall we take a turn on the deck?"

The two officers went up on deck. They spoke briefly with the ship's master and observed the sailors. There wasn't much to else to see, only crates of excess cargo, and animals penned or tied up toward the forecastle. Brewer looked at the Doctor and shook his head, then started pacing across the deck, just aft of the mainmast. Dr. Spinelli fell into step beside him. For a while, neither of them spoke. They just paced back and forth, port to starboard to port to starboard. Brewer's eyes were focused on the deck eighteen inches in front of him. Finally, the doctor had had enough.

"William," he whispered as he leaned in close, "if we keep this up much longer, the ship will break in two and we shall fall into the sea."

That did the trick. The lunacy of the statement pulled Brewer up short.

"What?"

"Good," Spinelli said as he faced his captain and crossed his arms over his chest. "If you're trying to kill me, *sir*, might I request you use a pistol? It would be quicker."

Brewer looked around and realized what he had been doing. He shrugged his shoulders and sighed. "Sorry. It's just that my mind is torn in two. Every time I try to think about the ship and what's got to be done when we get there, I can concentrate only a few minutes before thoughts of Elizabeth break in, and I find myself missing her. So then I scold myself and try to concentrate on the ship, and there she is again."

Spinelli laughed as he took his friend by the arm, and they resumed their trek, only this time at a much more relaxed pace.

"Oh, William, did you really think you could leave a woman like Elizabeth after only a two-week honeymoon and simply put her out of your mind? No, no, no, my captain, it doesn't work that way. You see, now you have *two* wives, and they are fighting for your heart. Eventually, one will win, and only you will know which it will be. After that, you'll have a wife and a mistress, and only you will know which is which. You will spend the rest of your lives together leaving the one and coming home to the other, and you will feel guilty about it every time."

"You're not doing much to cheer me up," Brewer grumped.

Spinelli patted him on the shoulder. "My apologies, Captain." They came to the starboard rail and made their turn. "Just remember, Elizabeth will always wait for you to come home to her."

Brewer lifted his head and sighed. "Thank you, Adam."

The remainder of the journey passed quickly. The master invited them to dine with him almost every night. The food was nowhere near Alfred's standards, but it was good nonetheless. Brewer was grateful that the questions the master and his mate peppered them with were all about the pirates El Diabolito and Cofrese and not about Bonaparte. They walked the deck every day there was good weather, and they played many games of chess, either on deck or in their cabin.

They also discussed the new ship. One evening, a day or so out from Port Royal, they were enjoying the evening breeze, leaning on the rail at the port quarter, when Spinelli suddenly turned to his friend.

"What was that, Captain?" he asked.

"I was saying I hope they were able to replace all her copper," Brewer repeated. "I neglected to ask Mr. Greene to insist upon it."

CHAPTER TWO

Captain Brewer and Dr. Spinelli were standing by the entry port as the packet was tied up at the dock. They bid the master and his mate farewell and thanked them for a safe voyage. They walked down the gangplank and made their way to the end of the wharf before stopping to get their bearings.

"Well, Captain," Spinelli said, "where to first?"

Brewer looked around the harbor, trying and failing to spot *Phoebe*. "We divide forces here, I think," he said with a frown. "Make arrangements to have our dunnage forwarded to the ship, if you please. Report to Mr. Greene as soon as you can; that will let him know we have arrived. I am going to see the admiral."

"Aye aye, sir," the doctor said, knuckling his head for good measure.

Brewer acknowledged the salute and began his walk to the admiral's house. Along the way, he turned over in his mind what commanding a frigate would be like, compared to HMS *Revenge*, and whether he was really ready for it. Obviously, the admiral thought he was; he knew that Hornblower would not give him a command he had not earned. Therefore, what he was feeling boiled down to a question of self-confidence. His thoughts flitted to the Corsican and his advice about being ready to seize opportunity by the throat and make it his. He set his jaw and nodded to himself; ready or not, opportunity had arrived, and he had to seize it by the throat.

He arrived at the Admiral's house and knocked at the door. He was admitted by a servant and shown to the small library off the foyer to await his Lordship's convenience. He studied the titles of books until the door opened and Lieutenant Phillips swept in.

"Captain!" he said as he reached out and shook Brewer's hand. "Allow me to congratulate you on your promotion! Mr. Gerard sends his congratulations as well; he has already left to take command of HMS *Revenge*."

"Thank you, Mr. Phillips," Brewer said. "Tell me, do you have plans, now that the admiral is being relieved?"

Phillips looked simultaneously pleased and embarassed. "His lordship has been kind enough to invite me back to Smallbridge, where I shall join Brown in running his lordship's household. As a lieutenant on the beach, I shall continue to draw my half pay, and his lordship says that should supply my needs nicely."

"Congratulations! Tell me, will you be leaving with his lordship and Lady Barbara?"

"Yes, before much longer."

"May I prevail upon you to carry a letter back for me? My old captain has taken up residence in Smallbridge now, with his sister."

"Captain Bush, sir?"

"Yes," Brewer said. "Do you know him?"

"Haven't had the pleasure yet, but I expect to, soon after we arrive. I shall be happy to carry the letter for you."

"Thank you. I am in your debt."

Phillips smiled. "Let's call it even. Now, if you please, the Admiral is waiting for you in his study."

Brewer followed the aide to Hornblower's study and waited patiently as Phillips knocked and announced his arrival, then stepped aside to allow him to enter.

The admiral turned away from his desk and rose to greet his visitor. Brewer noted that the study was considerably more spartan than the last time he'd been there.

Hornblower admitted as much. "Yes, much of it has been packed away already and is on its way back to England. I hope your honeymoon went well?"

"Yes, but it was harder than I ever imagined to say goodbye to Elizabeth. Does it ever get any easier?"

Hornblower smiled and shook his head. "Not in my experience. I think in that one respect Captain Bush has the advantage of us."

Brewer nodded, Bush being a lifelong bachelor.

"Please, William, be seated," the admiral said, leading the way to the chairs before the window. He rang the bell and ordered refreshment for two from the servant who answered.

"Mr. Phillips told me of your offer to him," Brewer said. "That was awfully kind of you. I was thinking of him on the passage here, and I thought it would be very hard for him to get a ship in his condition."

"Indeed," Hornblower acknowledged, "but, truth be told, William, I find that I have grown accustomed to him. He has run my office here nearly as well as you did when we were on St. Helena, and having one arm will in no wise stop him from handling my correspondence and schedule when we get back to Smallbridge. Brown has occasionally expressed a dislike for paperwork, not to me directly, of course, but one does hear, so I think he will be glad to have that taken off his hands."

"I imagine he will, my lord."

The servant returned with two glasses of wine. Hornblower waited until he was gone before proceeding.

"Now, Captain," he said in an official voice, "to business. Mr. Phillips is putting the finishing touches on your orders, and I shall sign them in the next day or so. HMS *Phoebe* is being detached to the South American squadron. The Admiralty is increasingly concerned by rumors of a Brazilian push for independence. There are also rumors of a possible revolution stirring in Portugal itself, which may require Portugal's king to return to Lisbon. I don't know if you are aware, but the Portugese court was able to escape to Brazil along with their national treasury as Bonaparte's forces were invading from Spain. The king raised Brazil to nation status from being a colony and stayed in Brazil, making Rio his new capital. I'm afraid many back in Portugal did not like Brazil's rival status."

"I see, my lord. Who is in command?"

Hornblower looked into his protégé's eyes. "Commodore Hardy."

Brewer could not help reacting to the name. Hardy had been Nelson's flag captain on HMS *Victory* when Nelson was killed at Trafalgar, and it had been Hardy who mistakenly identified James Norman as the man who had taken revenge and shot down Nelson's killer, launching Norman on a career founded upon a lie and that eventually drove him insane, to the point where he would have shot Brewer down in cold blood on the deck of HMS *Defiant*. Brewer looked at his admiral with concern.

"How much does he know, my lord?" he asked.

"Impossible to say," the admiral replied, as he looked out the window at a passing bird. "This much I can tell you, William; Hardy is a straightforward, honest officer, dedicated to his duty. I do not think he could hold any ill will toward you in the matter of James Norman. Just be honest and factual in answering any questions, and you will be fine."

Brewer sat back and frowned, seeing all the trouble that might lie ahead. He took a breath and determined not to borrow trouble. His eyes came up to meet Hornblower's, and the admiral nodded.

"Good. Now on to *Phoebe*. Have you heard anything about her?"

Brewer shook his head. "Not really, my lord. Dr. Spinelli told me on our return trip that he had heard a rumor of a mutiny, or near-mutiny, on board a short time back."

Hornblower sighed. "That is true, I'm afraid. There was a near mutiny, brought on by the amount of flogging imposed by a former captain. I have seen the ship's punishment book, and the number of lashes given would have been deemed excessive even at the height of the Napoleonic wars. There was an attempt to take the ship—all reports indicate it was more just an effort to present grievances than an actual mutiny. When they saw that the marines were solidly behind the captain and ready for any trouble, they dispersed of their own accord. However, that wasn't good enough for the captain, one Miles Judah; he executed two hands he considered ringleaders by hanging them from the yardarm.

"When they arrived in Port Royal, I relieved the captain and first lieutenant immediately. The captain was court-martialed and cashiered, and the first lieutenant was sent home in disgrace."

The admiral paused to take a drink of his wine. Brewer wondered what the crew would think of their new captain.

"After consulting with the remaining officers," Hornblower continued, "I have transferred about thirty men off the ship and scattered them throughout the squadron. They have been replaced by volunteers from your old command." The admiral smiled. "I can tell you that Mr. Gerard was none too happy to lose thirty trained seamen. In fact, he asked that it be considered his wedding gift to you."

Brewer had to chuckle at that. Only Gerard would think to suggest such a thing.

Hornblower placed his glass on the table, then sat forward, resting his elbows on his knees. His hands were clasped in front of his face, and his index fingers were steepled. His face was extremely serious.

"I wish to warn you, Captain," he said, choosing his words with utmost care. "Merely removing two officers and transferring the most outspoken will not win you the hearts of the remaining crew." He looked out the window for a moment before turning back. "On both *Defiant* and *Revenge*, you have had crews who knew you and loved you. You are walking into a situation very much the opposite. Have you ever ordered a flogging? No, I thought not. I warn you, it may prove necessary aboard *Phoebe*."

Brewer could not bring himself to speak.

Hornblower rose and walked to his desk, returning with a paper. "You are keeping two of *Phoebe's* officers; Lieutenant

Hobbs will be your second, and Lieutenant Rivkins will be your third. Mr. Reed was put through a commissioning board last week, and I am pleased to report that they passed him and confirmed his commission."

"I am vary glad to hear it, my lord."

"You are also inheriting the ship's standing officers, as well as the captain of marines and captain's clerk."

Hornblower sat back and looked out the window again. Brewer wondered what he would say if he were not so careful in picking his words.

"You must be firm, William," he said slowly. "I know you, that you will be fair in your dealings, but you must rule with an iron hand." Another look out the window. "When a new captain takes over a ship like *Phoebe*, one of two things usually happens. One is for the new captain to be soft, intending to win the crew's regard by showing them he is not the terror their last captain was. This captain finds that the crew has no respect for him and simply ignores every order they can, the end result being the captain has to be even harder than the previous captain in order to regain control of the ship."

Brewer stared at his hands folded in his lap as he processed the information. Hornblower gave him a moment before proceeding.

"Another way is for the new captain to be even more tyrannical than the last, thinking he must be so in order to get control of the mutinous crew. The crew becomes convinced they've traded bad for worse, and the near-mutiny sometimes becomes the real thing."

Brewer's eyes darted to the empty corner of the room where the bust of Bonaparte had stood and wondered what advice the Corsican would have for him. Hornblower saw where the other's eyes had gone and smiled.

"Do you wonder what our friend would say?" he asked.

Brewer blushed and shrugged.

"Yes, my lord."

"I don't blame you," the admiral said. "While I cannot say for certain, I imagine he would say something along the lines of the following: seek out achievement and reward it. He did something similar when he created the Legion of Honor. This way, the crew will see that while you punish them when necessary, you are also willing to reward them when able. You have a good moral code, Mr. Brewer. Be sure you live by it, and all on *Phoebe* will see that it is so. Will you win over everyone on board? No, of course not; there will always be the diehard malcontents who say that no captain can be trusted and that you will end up as bad as the last tyrant. Unfortunately, there is nothing you can do about hands like that. You must stay your course, and the vast majority of the crew will see you for what you are."

"I understand," Brewer said. "Thank you, my lord."

Hornblower stood, and Brewer rose as well. The admiral led the way to the door.

"Report aboard your ship, Captain," he said. "Report back to me in forty-eight hours on your readiness for sea. When you sail, you will report to Commodore Hardy aboard HMS *Superb* at Rio de Janeiro."

"Aye aye, my lord."

Hornblower shook the young captain's hand. "Good luck, William."

"Thank you, my lord," Brewer said. "Please convey my regards to Lady Barbara."

"I shall."

Brewer paused at the door. "If I have a chance, before I sail I shall endeavor to teach Mr. Phillips how to stroll to her ladyship's satisfaction."

Hornblower erupted in laughter. "I shall inform Lady Barbara. She will be pleased, I can assure you."

Brewer stepped out into the street and began to make his way to the pier. He strolled at his 'Lady Barbara pace,' and he chuckled when he caught himself in the act. He passed a pub like the one where he'd rescued the good doctor from the mob while they were on the island of St. Kitts, and he paused momentarily in front of the establishment, wondering if he would ever get a letter like the one that had driven the doctor to the bottle.

He cursed himself for allowing himself to dwell on such dark forebodings and started off for the dockside again. He found a boat available to take him out to his ship and was soon in the stern sheets, watching as the boatmen pulled around and between shipping in the harbor before setting course directly for their destination.

Brewer carefully studied the ship as they approached it. The ship was approximately 900 tons and carried twenty-six 18-pounders on her upper deck, along with long nines and 32-pound carronades on her main deck above. She carried a nearly full complement of 250 souls; Brewer wondered how many of them would be ready to mutiny at the first opportunity. The ship's main claim to fame was the destruction of the American frigate *Essex* in the Pacific during the war back in 1812.

As they closed on the frigate, Brewer heard the challenge issued from the deck. He stood and shrugged his boat cloak from his shoulders and cried, *"Phoebe!"* The frigate now knew her new master was coming.

Captain William Brewer stepped on the deck of his new command and was piped aboard with all the ceremony accorded his rank and position. He was greeted by Lieutenant Greene. The two men saluted and shook hands.

"Welcome aboard, sir," Greene said. "Will you follow me and allow me to present your officers?"

"Thank you," Brewer said. Greene led the way to the officers, standing at attention.

"Sir, I present Mr. Hobbs, the second lieutenant."

Hobbs saluted. "A pleasure, Captain."

Brewer nodded. "Thank you, Lieutenant."

They moved down the line to a familiar face.

"Sir, I present Mr. Rivkins, the third lieutenant."

Rivkins saluted. "A pleasure to see you again, Captain."

"For me as well, Lieutenant. I'm pleased to see you stuck with it."

"Thank you, sir."

Greene looked to his captain. "Do you know each other, sir?"

"Mr. Rivkins was a midshipman in my division on the old *Lydia* during her last commission in the Mediterranean."

"I see," Greene said, and he moved to the last in line. "I believe you already know Mr. Reed, sir."

"Indeed I do," Brewer said. "Congratulations on passing your board, Lieutenant."

"Thank you, sir!" Reed saluted.

Brewer turned and looked down the deck, and he saw the hands all looking at him.

"Well, let's get this over with, Mr. Greene. Call the hands aft, if you please."

"Aye, sir," Greene said. He picked up a speaking trumpet and cried, "All hands! All hands lay aft! All hands lay aft!"

The hands mustered aft, slowly and deliberately. Brewer awaited them patiently, and when they were all assembled he pulled his commission from his coat pocket and began to read. The document required William Brewer, Esquire, to take command of His Majesty's frigate *Phoebe*; it was nearly identical to the one he had read when he'd taken command of HMS *Revenge* the previous year. He watched the hands as he read; their eyes were dull and remained that way, almost as though they were half asleep at worst, woefully unconcerned at best. He wondered what he would have to do to get through to them.

He finished reading and refolded the letter before returning it to his pocket.

"Mr. Greene," he said, "dismiss the hands, if you please, and then would you please join me in my cabin? I want to see my officers there in one hour."

Greene saluted. "Aye aye, Captain." He turned to the assembly. "Hands dismissed!"

Brewer made his way below deck and then went aft. No sentry was posted at his cabin door, so he let himself in and closed the door softly behind him. The dining cabin was set up to his satisfaction—proof that Alfred was alive and well. He stuck his head inside his sleeping cabin and was pleased to find a bookshelf already put up on the outer bulkhead and his library set out in order. He stepped into the day cabin.

Light from the frigate's stern windows lit up the room. There was a desk off to the right with his portable writing desk upon it. He took two steps forward and looked around. It was not as large or opulent as the day cabin on HMS *Defiant*, but this one was his, and it would do fine.

He heard a throat being quietly cleared behind him, and he turned to see his servant, Alfred Thomas, standing in the doorway. He smiled at Alfred, not five feet tall but with skills in the use of arms that had saved Brewer's life on more than one occasion.

"Alfred," he said, holding his arms wide, "it's good to see you again. The quarters looks wonderful."

"Thank you, sir," the servant said, acknowledging the compliment. "Is there anything I can get you?"

"Do we have any coffee?"

"I believe so, sir."

"Mr. Greene is on his way. Coffee for two, please, Alfred. That bloody packet the doctor booked us passage on had not so much as a single bean aboard."

Brewer saw the slightest hint of a smile at the corner of Alfred's lips. "Right away, sir."

No sooner had he gone than McCleary appeared. Brewer had taken him on as his coxswain while in command of *Defiant*, and Mac had stayed with him ever since. Brewer found him to be a man of many talents—bodyguard, valet, and nurse; he had proven his loyalty to Brewer time and time again.

"Reporting for duty, sir," he said.

"Mac, it's good to see you," Brewer welcomed the big Cornishman. "So, tell me: what do you think of her?"

"A tad bigger than *Revenge*, sir, but we'll grow into her quick enough." He moved to the side to allow Brewer to see the man who was with him. "Begging your pardon, sir, but this is Henry Ball. He was the previous captain's clerk, sir, so I thought you'd want to be getting a look at him."

The captain nodded his thanks to the coxswain and looked the clerk over. Ball was a small, wiry man, only a bit taller than Alfred, and the glasses on his face and his hair pulled tight behind into a small thin ponytail gave him an intelligent look. He had a meek presence, but he stood quiet and respectful.

"Mr. Ball," Brewer said, "I'm pleased to make your acquaintance. I have not decided on a clerk as yet, so for now you may stay in your billet."

"Thank you, sir."

"We shall talk again after we have sailed."

The clerk heard the dismissal and came to attention. "Aye, sir."

After the clerk had left, Mac stepped into the day room. "Anything I can do, sir?"

"Yes. What do you think of Mr. Ball, Mac?"

Mac considered for a moment. "Can't say as yet, sir. I only met him a day or two ago; can't rightly read him yet."

Brewer nodded. There was a knock at the door. Mac went to open it and admitted Mr. Greene.

"I'll be going, sir," the Cornishman said, closing the door behind him.

"Thank you, Mac."

Greene watched the door close and turned back to his captain. "I'm glad he's here."

"As am I." Brewer paused while Alfred brought two cups of coffee. The two men sat beneath the stern window. "So, tell me, Benjamin, what's your first impression?"

Greene took a long sip of his coffee. Brewer couldn't tell if he was trying to choose his words, or figure out how to avoid the question altogether.

The first lieutenant finally put his cup down and sat back. "I've been on this ship for nearly ten days, Captain. Physically, she's ready; I mean, the ship itself is sound. I've been over every foot of rigging with the bosun, and I have to say Mr. Knight has done a marvelous job, sir. Every sail is new and ready for sea. One thing I'm particularly pleased with, Captain—we got one of those new metal water tanks installed during the refit. It can hold nearly 130 tons of water. They say the water stays fresher longer in these new-fangled tanks; I for one surely hope so." He sat forward and reached for his cup, but his hand stopped halfway there, and he sat back again. "But the men, sir, well, that's another story. I'm not quite sure what happened when their previous captain was in command, but it bothers the crew to this day. Many are angry, some are discouraged, and some whisper they wish the mutiny had succeeded. We've got our work cut out for us, if we can figure out what's behind it all."

Brewer sighed. "The admiral and I have discussed the matter. There was a near-mutiny on their last cruise. The marines on board broke it up before it got rolling; it seems the sight of the marines ready to fight took the wind right out of their sails. The captain wouldn't even wait until he got back into port to punish the ringleaders; he hung two crewmen on the way to Port Royal. I've seen the punishment book. I tell you, Benjamin, it was positively overflowing!

Thousands of lashes handed out! Lord Hornblower said that even during the Napoleonic wars that would have been regarded as excessive! It's no wonder they erupted."

The captain leaned forward, elbows on his knees, and stared into the coffee cup he held in both hands. "Our orders are to head south. We are being detached to the South American squadron temporarily. It seems the Admiralty is becoming concerned about the rumors of revolutions in South America spreading to Brazil. We are to report to Commodore Hardy at Rio de Janeiro."

"When do we sail?"

"I don't know," Brewer sat back and drained the dregs from his cup. He set it on the seat beside him. "I am to report back to the admiral in forty-eight hours. I expect we'll know more after that."

There was a knock at the door. Alfred opened it to admit the ship's officers, along with Dr. Spinelli.

Greene leaned toward his captain. "I took the liberty of inviting the doctor, sir. I thought you might want an independent viewpoint."

Brewer nodded. "Good idea. Thank you."

The two rose to greet the new arrivals. Brewer noticed that the doctor lingered at the rear of the group, making his way over to sit quietly in the corner so he could listen. Their eyes met for a moment.

Brewer addressed the group. "Gentlemen, thank you for coming. Let me be blunt. This ship is in trouble, and it is our job to fix it. Mr. Greene and Mr. Reed have sailed under my command before, and I'm sure Mr. Hobbs and Mr. Rivkins will learn my ways very quickly. I don't know what caused the crew of this ship to attempt a mutiny, but I have seen the punishment book. *Thousands* of lashes were handed out! Gentlemen, that is not leadership, that is brutality, and *it will stop!* Men who are driven that way and beaten mindlessly for minor infractions will cower and seek to save themselves in the face of the enemy. It will be our job to lead them, to show them how proper British officers behave and what they have a right to expect from their men. I believe the hands will respond positively to this. I realize it will take time for them to come around, and we shall try to make that time as short as possible. However, I am not saying there will be no floggings. Violations of the Articles of War will be met with appropriate punishments.

"As for each of you, what I require from you is your loyalty. Your loyalty should be to me, this ship, and to England—*in that order!* If you have a question or problem, bring it to the first lieutenant. If he can't help you, he will bring you to me if he deems it necessary. Keep your eyes and your ears open. Make note of what you see and hear, and report it immediately.

"I am not fool enough to believe that every hand on this ship will turn over a new leaf, as they say. But I do believe that the vast majority will come round, once they are convinced of our sincerity. Take it from me, they will be watching us closely to see whether or not we are genuine in our actions, whether or not we are trying to trap them in order to inflict a new round of floggings. Alfred!"

The servant appeared. "Yes, sir?"

"We'll have refreshments now, if you please."

"Very good, sir." The servant withdrew and reappeared a moment later, followed by McCleary, each of carrying a silver tray with glasses of wine on them. Brewer noticed that when they were done serving, Alfred departed with both trays while Mac stood beside the doctor—without a glass of wine.

Brewer raised his glass. "Mr. Vice, the King!"

All eyes turned to Reed—as the youngest in the room, the honor of drinking the King's health fell to him. He cleared his throat nervously and raised his glass.

"Gentlemen, the King!"

"Please, gentlemen, take your seats," Brewer said as he resumed his own, Mr. Greene sitting beside him. "Mr. Hobbs, how long have you been aboard *Phoebe*?"

"Two years, Captain," the lieutenant answered.

"And you, Mr. Rivkins?"

"Only two months, Captain. I only just passed my commissioning board a couple of months before, and I was put on a schooner from Port Royal to join *Phoebe* at Martinique."

"Just passed your board, did you say? Congratulations, sir! I say, Mr. Greene, it seems we have two brand new lieutenants on our hands! How shall we ever survive?"

Greene grinned. "I'm sure we'll manage, sir. If all else fails, we can send them to school with Mr. Sweeney."

Brewer laughed, remembering how Phillips—now the admiral's aide—had been put under the tutelage of the first lieutenant (then-Lieutenant Brewer) and sailing master, Mr. Sweeney on board HMS *Defiant*. Together, Brewer and Sweeney had taught Phillips everything he needed to know to be a King's officer.

"You three will be key to our winning the crew," Brewer said, addressing the junior lieutenants. "Your relationships with your divisions will be seminal to the success of our efforts. The first lieutenant will publish the watch bill tomorrow. Get to know your divisions and quietly mark any malcontents who need watching. Mr. Greene, questions, comments?"

Greene thought for a moment before shaking his head. "Not at the moment, Captain."

"Mr. Hobbs?"

"Sir," Hobbs said hesitantly, "I..."

"You may speak freely, Lieutenant," Brewer prompted.

"Thank you, sir," Hobbs said. "Sir, might the hands take this... 'new approach' to discipline to mean we are going soft on them? How are we to prove them wrong?"

Brewer leaned forward and rested his elbows on his knees. "There are a couple of ways we do that, Mr. Hobbs. The first is that we do not bring anyone to a Captain's Mast for a flogging who doesn't deserve one. I mean the charge has to be legitimate. We are not going to flog anyone for a minor infraction that could be handled in a different manner. This will lead us right into the second, which is that anyone with a set of honest eyes and ears will quickly see that punishments are only given out when they are deserved, and that these punishments are appropriate for the crime, so to speak."

Hobbs frowned slightly, but said nothing more. "Aye, sir."

"You'll see, Mr. Hobbs. Treat them like men and not criminals, and they'll notice. Mr. Rivkins?"

"Not at the moment, sir."

"Mr. Reed?"

"None, sir."

"Very well." Brewer stood, indicating the meeting was over. His officers stood as well. "Thank you, gentlemen."

The junior lieutenants filed out, leaving Greene, the Doctor, and Mac. Brewer and Greene resumed their seats, and Dr. Spinelli sat on the captain's left. Mac took up his usual station by the door. Alfred appeared with a decanter, which he used to refill their glasses.

"Well, gentlemen," Brewer said, "what do you think?"

Spinelli shrugged. "Hard to tell anything from a small sample like that, sir."

"What do your instincts say?"

The Doctor pursed his lips and sighed. "Mr. Reed we know. The only question about him is how he will react to any defiance from his division. I'm not worried about him; he was in *Clorinda* before coming to us in *Revenge*, so he's seen some things. He also had no trouble dealing with Simmons when he was abusing young Mr. Short."

"True," Brewer said, remembering how Reed as senior midshipman had discovered the abuse and dealt with it using the "justice of the lower deck"—meaning he had the bosun's mate give Simmons two dozen swats with his rattan while Simmons was stretched over a table in the midshipman's mess. It had been effective and appropriate.

The doctor continued. "I understand you know Mr. Rivkins?"

"Yes. He was on HMS *Lydia* with me on her last cruise. He was a midshipman in my division."

"I see," Spinelli said, as he thought for a moment. "What do you think of him, Captain? I mean, you seem to know him better than we do. What was he like then, and what is your impression of him now?"

Brewer looked at the deck beams overhead for a moment. "On *Lydia*, he was... conflicted. It seems he is distantly related to Nelson, and he was forced to sea to continue the family tradition of service as a King's officer. I helped him as much as I could, encouraged him to give it his best efforts, which he had not been doing up to that time. I also gave him a purpose, namely to keep me alive. I starting taking him with me whenever I was sent to board a Barbary ship; his orders were simply to make sure I came back alive." Brewer grinned. "I'm not sure, but I think I may have had him convinced that if I were killed, the captain would court-martial him for disobeying an order!"

They all laughed at that, then Brewer grew somber.

"Now? I'm not sure. There's something different in his eyes, and I am not sure what it means."

"Yes," murmured the doctor. "His body language is hard to figure out as well. You can tell he comes from minor nobility—that fits with what you said about his being distantly related to Nelson—but at the same time, I get the impression that there's something deeper. I think I will try to become his friend."

"A good idea, Doctor," Brewer said. "And Hobbs?"

The doctor sat back and folded his hands in his lap. He stared at them for several seconds before replying.

"I don't know about that one, Captain; I mean, it has been a very short period of observation, as I said, but I am afraid."

"Of him, or for him?" Greene asked.

"Both," Spinelli said emphatically. "Remember, he has been a lieutenant on this ship for the last two years, the time that led up to the attempted mutiny. He *saw* all those lashes you read about in the punishment book, Captain; God only knows how many he ordered personally. His question about appearing soft is particularly telling. Remember, too, that he is a relatively young man, younger than you, I believe, Captain. I think he bears watching."

"Agreed," Brewer said. "That will be your job, Benjamin."

"Aye, sir," Greene said.

Three days later, HMS *Phoebe* was ready for sea. Mr. Greene was proud to report to his captain that the lighters had topped off the new water tanks in the hold—125 tons of water, enough for six months if necessary! Stores were also loaded and secured: twenty-five barrels of beef, seventeen of pork, forty-five barrels of beer, two hundred bags of bread and 900 pounds of butter. There were also seventy-five bushels of oatmeal and sixty of pease. Flour was stored in fifteen barrels, the suet in one, the raisins in two, and to top it all off there were sixteen half-hogsheads of rum. Alfred saw to the cabin stores, including the coffee, tea, and the captain's favorite wines. Brewer wasn't exactly sure what Alfred had for him, but he'd learned to trust his servant not only with his life, but with his stomach.

His meeting with the admiral the day before had gone well. Brewer was to sail when ready for sea and report to Commodore Hardy aboard HMS *Superb* at Rio de Janeiro. He accepted an invitation to dine with Lord and Lady Hornblower, after which Lady Barbara persuaded him to accompany her on a stroll in the town before returning to his ship. He enjoyed it as much as he had enjoyed those walks years ago in Smallbridge.

Now he stood alone at the center of the quarterdeck, watching silently as his men went through their various tasks to get the ship ready for sea. His eyes were everywhere, missing nothing, and his men knew it.

"Mr. Henry," he said, "you are the midshipman in charge of signals, correct? Make this signal: *Phoebe to Flag, ready to proceed.*"

Mr. Greene approached him and saluted. "Anchor's hove short, sir. All stores secured."

"Thank you, Mr. Greene." He turned to watch young Henry studying the reply to his signal through a glass, pausing three times to check his book.

"Reply, sir!" he said. *"Good luck and Godspeed."*

"Very well!" He turned to his first lieutenant and smiled. "Get the ship underway, Mr. Greene."

"Aye, sir!"

Brewer stood and watched as chaos seemed to break out all around him. Officers bellowed orders that sent hands scurrying in several directions at once, one group climbing the shrouds to loose the topsails, another straining at the capstan to raise the anchor from the harbor floor, and a third preparing to man the braces when the ship began to move. Through it all, Brewer saw order, like a symphony being played.

He watched, saying nothing, until after the anchor was aweigh and the ship was moving towards the harbor entrance. His eyes narrowed as he watched the hands jump to their stations, loosing heads'ls or manning the braces, and he was not satisfied. They were going through the motions; there was no "speed" in their steps, none of the "spring" that he'd seen in the crews he'd commanded on *Defiant* and *Revenge. Of course,* he realized, *those crews knew me, and I knew them.*

Just then, the voice of Lieutenant Greene intruded upon his thoughts.

"Man the braces, you men! Look alive there!"

Brewer frowned and shook his head ever so slightly. *No,* he thought, *this will never do. I must watch for every opportunity to...* he paused, groping for the right word... *fix this, to build up their confidence in me as well as in themselves.*

Mr. Greene approached him and saluted. "We'll clear the harbor in the next ten minutes, sir. What course shall I set?"

Brewer looked out over the rail and saw that his premier was quite correct. "Set course for Barbados, if you please."

"Aye aye, sir," Greene saluted. "Mr. Sweeney! Make your course for Barbados, if you please!"

"Barbados! Aye, Mr. Greene!" the sailing master replied.

"Call all hands to make sail, Mr. Greene," Brewer said. "Let's see what our new ship can do, shall we?"

Greene smiled. "Aye, sir."

Again Brewer watched as his new crew went about their duties, and again he saw the same lack of urgency in their steps. He pursed his lips and wondered silently what these men had endured to make them so halfhearted in manner.

"On course for Barbados, Captain," Greene reported. "Ship is currently on the starboard tack."

"Very good, Mr. Greene," Brewer replied. "I am going to my cabin. Why don't you join me for dinner?"

"Thank you, sir."

Below, in his cabin, Captain Brewer took off his hat and coat and handed them to Alfred. The servant stowed them with care and returned.

"Anything I can get for you, Captain?" he asked.

"Hm...? What? Oh, no, thank you, Alfred," Brewer said. "There will be another officer for dinner today."

"Very good, sir."

Brewer sat down at his desk and began a long letter to Elizabeth. It was his first since they had parted, and he wanted to make it special. He told her about the ship and how he had been given the task of turning the crew around and making them act like proper sailors again. He set his pen down several times and crumpled the page twice; somehow letters had not been so hard before they were married. He judged the third try acceptable and quickly signed and sealed it before he discovered something wrong with it as well.

Just then there was a knock at the door, and the sentry opened it to announce the first lieutenant. Brewer knew from the first sight of him that something was wrong.

"Captain," he began, sounding slightly embarrassed, "I must report a defaulter, sir."

Brewer was grim. "Who?"

"Collins, sir. Topman."

"And what is he charged with?"

"Being drunk on duty, and pissing on the deck, sir."

The Captain was shocked. No one in his previous crews had ever done that.

"Any witnesses?"

"Aye, sir—he was caught in the act by Lieutenant Rivkins."

Brewer sat back in his chair and closed his eyes. He had hoped to have more time to make an impression on the crew before having to face something like this. Everyone would be watching him to see how he dealt with the offender. Would the new captain use the heavy hand so favored by his predecessor? Or would he let the offender off with a light sentence in an attempt to gain favor with the crew? He rubbed his nose to cover his indecision. His sense of outrage at the stupidity of the act was rising, but thoughts of Seaman Grant and her death on board *Revenge* due to his orders forced their way to the front of his mind, and he took a deep breath to calm himself. He realized he must not decide in anger, whatever his eventual decision might be. Suddenly, he heard a soft voice whispering in his ear, as if it were one come back from the dead.

Why do you hesitate, mon ami? the Corsican's voice said. *You command, do you not? Then command, I tell you! Do not make this harder than it need be. The man committed the crime, yes? He was caught in the act by one of your officers, yes? So you have the perfect case to show yourself to your crew! Judge rightly. I warn you, do not make an example of this man, as so many would want to do. Your men will tolerate discipline; what they will not tolerate is duplicity. This is not your previous command, mon ami, do not treat it as such. You must be their Captain.*

Brewer dropped his chin to his chest for a moment as he privately acknowledged the truth of what he had heard. He lifted his chin and opened his eyes, his decision made.

"You say this man was caught in the act?" he asked.

"Aye, Captain, by Lieutenant Rivkins."

"So there is no doubt of his guilt?"

"None, Captain."

"Very well. Defaulters at eight bells, Mr. Greene."

"Aye, Captain." Greene came to attention.

Captain Brewer came up on deck just as eight bells rang out. He took his place at the quarterdeck railing. "Call the hands, Mr. Greene," he said.

Greene picked up a speaking trumpet. "Hands lay aft to witness punishment!"

The bosun's mates rigged the grating as the hands gathered slowly. The sergeant at arms appeared, with Collins beside him in irons. The man looked pale and sick; Brewer wondered if that was from his hangover or shame for what he had done. The charges were read and Mr. Rivkins gave his evidence. No one spoke up in Collins' defense.

"Two dozen lashes!" Brewer called out, thankful that his voice did not crack.

It took all of his control to stand there, eyes straight ahead, never reacting to the guilty man's cries of pain.

"Punishment completed, sir!"

He saw the bosun was waiting for orders.

"Cut him down. Doctor, see to him, if you please."

Mr. Greene stepped over. "Shall I dismiss the hands, sir?"

"Yes—no, Mr. Greene. I shall address the men." He stepped forward and raised his voice. "Men of *Phoebe*! I hope you see now where I stand! This man violated the Articles of War, and he has been given a just punishment for his misdeeds. If you do your duty and stay out of trouble, no harm will come to you. We are all of us in the King's service. The press gangs are gone; we are all here of our own free will and are committed to serve in this ship through this commission. Do your duty well, and perhaps the good Lord will bless us with prize money or even head money to line our purses on the way home! Dismissed!"

Later on, seated with Mr. Greene at dinner, Brewer wondered how his speech had been received by the crew. He questioned Greene about it.

"I'm not sure, Captain," Greene said. Time will tell."

CHAPTER THREE

HMS *Phoebe* took nine days to reach Barbados. During the voyage, Brewer implemented his plan to begin turning the crew of his frigate into sailors worthy of Nelson or Hornblower. Mr. Greene ran the hands through sail drills. Brewer watched from the fantail as Greene ordered them aloft time after time, and he had to cover his mouth to hide his grin when he heard Mr. Greene chastise their lack of effort.

"Oh, for pity's sake, you've got to do better than that! Do you want the pirates to laugh at us as they sail right around us before getting away scot-free? Do you want to be feared, or a laughing stock, I wonder? You ought to climb as if your life depends upon it, because, believe me, it will! You do any less against pirates the likes of El Diabolito or Roberto Cofresi, and they will laugh while they pick you off as if you were so many grouse at a manor shoot! Or maybe you like watching prize money sail away from you?"

Near the end of this leg of their journey, Brewer thought he saw some improvement in their performance, more speed from some of the men. No, not speed—*urgency*. The need to obey as fast as they could. That was what he saw. That was what he needed to see.

When they reached Barbados, Brewer ordered a southwesterly course, to pass east of Ponta do Seixas, the easternmost tip of Brazil, without putting in at the port. There was a murmur amongst the crew, who may have been expecting shore leave, but nothing more, so Brewer overlooked it. The men were kept busy with sail drill followed by gun drill, and then doing it all over again; Brewer hoped that change would take hold.

Lieutenant Reed stepped into the wardroom and fell into the first available chair. It was the end of his watch, and he was exhausted after three days of relentless drill. The captain was drilling the men hard and taking his officers along for the ride.

Reed heard the grumblings at the heavy workload, but he also saw some grins at praise from the captain or Mr. Greene when the men met or exceeded an exercise goal. Thinking back, he also thought he noticed some of the hands—the younger ones, mainly—carry themselves a little differently, as if they were proud of who they were.

He sighed heavily and rested his head on the table.

"Tired, Mr. Reed?"

Reed's head came up, and he saw Lieutenant Hobbs sitting at the far end of the table, book in hand and a glass of wine on the table before him.

"I'm sorry, sir; I didn't see you when I came in."

"No need to apologize," Hobbs said as he closed the book on his finger and reached for his glass. "Good God, man, you look exhausted! Winfield!" he cried, calling for the steward. "A glass for Mr. Reed!"

A glass full of dark nectar appeared at Reed's elbow, and he drank it gratefully. He set the glass down and looked at his hands.

"My hands are raw from all the climbing I did today," he said ruefully.

Hobbs looked up from his reading. "More sail drill, eh?"

"Yes, but I think it's bearing fruit," Reed replied. "We've cut the time to loose topsails by fully fifteen seconds, and the men seem proud of it."

"Proud?" Hobbs closed his book and sat forward. "Proud, are they? Of what? Performing for the new captain? Wait until they show their true colors, Mr. Reed, then we'll see what the captain thinks of them."

Reed set his glass down. "What do you mean, 'true colors'?"

"I mean, Collins was just the tip of the iceberg," Hobbs said gloomily. "Giving that scum two dozen for what he did was the worst possible thing the captain could have done. Now they all think he's weak, and they can get away with anything. Mark my words, sir, we're going to have trouble."

Reed cocked an eyebrow in disbelief. "I'd hardly call two dozen lashes nothing. Have you seen the man's back? He'll be in pain for weeks. More, if any of those lashes get infected."

Hobbs shrugged and picked up his glass. "He deserved six dozen."

"In God's name, why? Are you trying to teach him a lesson or maim him for life?"

"They only respect strength," Hobbs insisted. "The captain looks weak now."

Just then the door opened and Mr. Rivkins came in. He nodded to the two officers sitting at opposite ends of the table.

"Good day, gentlemen," he said. "What goes on here?"

When Hobbs stayed silent, Reed answered. "The second lieutenant was just telling me how the captain is soft."

"Do tell!" Rivkins said. "And how is that, Mr. Hobbs?"

"He only gave Collins two dozen."

"That seems an appropriate sentence for the charge."

"Appropriate?" Hobbs cried. "Appropriate gets you nowhere. You have to crush that behavior, or it will spread like leprosy and eat away at the crew. Don't you see?"

Rivkins sat down at Reed's end of the table. "I suppose I don't, Paul. Tell me what I ought to see."

Hobbs waited while Winfield refilled their glasses and departed.

"Before Captain Judah took command of *Phoebe*, the ship was commanded by Lord John Clydesdale. Born into money and married still more of it. His lordship knew nothing about the navy or commanding ships, but as the wars were closing down he prevailed on some friends at the Admiralty to get command of a frigate. He thought it would help him look good in the House of Lords after the fighting was done. It turned out that his wealth made him indolent. I don't think he came out of his cabin if he could help it. He may have been a nice host at a dinner party, but he knew nothing about discipline aboard a King's ship or how to deal with the lower deck. As a result, the crew ran wild. The first lieutenant did not want to overstep his authority, so the lower deck had no fear.

"Fortunately, the ship was assigned to Sir Edward Pellew's squadron in January 1815, and Pellew saw at once what was going on. He tactfully convinced Lord Clydesdale that he had succeeded in his mission and even promised to sit beside him during the next session of the Parliament when they would discuss the rebuilding of Europe as a whole and England in particular." Hobbs scowled. "He succeeded in his mission if his mission was rendering one of his majesty's ships unfit for duty. Then Captain Judah came aboard. He saw at once the condition of the crew and set about to remedy it immediately."

"And just how did he set about doing that?" Rivkins asked.

"He ordered the officers, bosun's mates, and petty officers in charge of parties to carry starters and use them. There were three floggings in as many days for hands who made to strike a superior officer. The entire ship's grog was stopped for thirty days when one young hand appeared drunk on duty and cursed the captain. Someone reported it to the captain, and the next day we saw his backbone. He died two weeks later from infection in his back.

"You'd think the crew would have settled down after that, but they didn't have the sense to! No, they got up their mutiny." He paused for a drink. "That was just before you joined us, Percy. The mutineers gathered in the forecastle and armed themselves. Lieutenant Richards, the second lieutenant, had the watch, and somehow word drifted aft to him that they were coming. He quietly called out the marines. They formed a line just forward of the mizzenmast armed with muskets and fixed bayonets, and he stood in front of them. He also sent reinforcements to guard the captain's cabin and the wardroom. The mutineers came aft, and Richards met them as they approach the quarterdeck. I can still see it..."

"What can I do for you men?" Richards asked them.

"We've had it with the navy, Mr. Richards," one of those in front said. "We're sick of being beat like pack animals. We're going to take this ship and go follow the Bounty men."

"I don't think so," Richards calmly replied. "Disperse and get below."

"Careful, Mr. Richards, or you're first!" another in the front said.

Richards turned and shouted over his shoulder. "Captain! If I fall, take no prisoners!"

"Aye, sir!" The captain of marines drew his sword. "Aim!" he called, and every marine in line picked a target and prepared to fire.

Richards turned to face the hands. "Well? What's it going to be?"

Hobbs was smiling now. "When Richards gave them his ultimatum, the heart seemed to melt away from the traitors. Richards ordered the marines to hold the mutineers in seclusion, and he reported the incident to the captain.

"Captain Judah was furious, and rightly so! Richards and Markham, the first lieutenant, both told him to wait until they returned to Port Royal to court-martial the mutineers, but he held a Captain's Mast before dawn and hung the two who threatened Richards during the uprising. He left the bodies hanging from the yardarms all day for the crew to see. Rumors flew around the ship that the captain was going to begin executing all the mutineers the next morning, and it was then that Mr. Markham led the officers—including the captain of marines—to meet with the captain.

"Markham told him nobody else was going to die without a proper court-martial. He urged the captain to set course for Port Royal immediately. The captain said, 'And if I don't?', and Markham answered, 'Then we shall do it for you.' Well, the captain had no choice but to order the course change. It was just after that that we rendezvoused and you transferred aboard, Percy.

"As soon as we hit port, the captain, Markham, and Richards went ashore to see the admiral. None of them came back. Royal Marines came aboard and removed the remaining mutineers from the ship. The rest you know."

Reed said, "And after all that, you still don't think Captain Judah used too hard a hand?"

"I do not, sir!" Hobbs insisted. "The trouble was caused by Lord Clydesdale's inaction, and Captain Judah was unable to correct the situation. He deserved better from his officers, if you ask me."

"Give Brewer a chance, Paul," Rivkins said. "I've served with him before, in the Med. He was the second lieutenant then, and I was in his division. I soon learned that he honestly cares for his men, but he's not one to put up with foolishness. He's a good officer."

Hobbs shrugged. "Doesn't mean he'll do it as captain."

"You're wrong, Mr. Hobbs," Reed said. "I was with the Captain in HMS *Revenge*, his first command. He made mistakes, let me tell you, but he learned from them! I remember the captain was angry about something, and he ordered additional sail drill, overruling the first and second lieutenants, who said the wind was too dangerous for any more drill. A hand fell from the yardarm and died. The captain thought it was his fault for ordering the additional drill over his officers' objections. I tell you, Mr. Hobbs, *I saw his face!* He was devastated! Later, we learned that it wasn't an accident, that the hand had been pushed off the line deliberately. But even then, the captain didn't forget his lesson. He learned from it."

Greene entered the room and silence immediately descended. He stopped and looked around.

"Have I interrupted something?"

Hobbs went back to his book, so Rivkins spoke up.

"Not at all, sir. We were just discussing captains and how they deal with their crews."

"Ah," Greene said, "I see. And Mr. Hobbs thinks the captain was too soft today."

"More or less," Rivkins said with a smile as he looked at Hobbs, still ostensibly buried in his book.

"Is this true, Mr. Hobbs?" Greene asked as he sat down, diplomatically in the middle of the table. "Winfield! A glass, if you please! Well, Mr. Hobbs?"

"Aye, sir," Hobbs said.

"I see," Greene said. "Thank you, Winfield. Mr. Hobbs, let me tell you a story. This is my third ship with Captain Brewer. Mr. Reed can tell you of sailing under his command in HMS *Revenge*, and Mr. Rivkins can tell you about him as a second lieutenant, but I was with him in HMS *Defiant*, the frigate that brought us to the Caribbean. The captain's name was James Norman. Mr. Brewer was first lieutenant, and I was the second. Captain Norman flogged the crew incessantly, and he frequently picked out junior officers or one of the hands to play games with until they broke and he could flog them for disrespect. On our voyage, he chose a young lieutenant as his target, Mr. Phillips, a sixteen-year-old kid who had received his commission via special dispensation from the Admiralty. As a result, he did not have the knowledge that new lieutenants normally have.

"Captain Norman took to putting poor Phillips to various tests before the hands, which both he and Phillips knew were beyond him, all for the purpose of breaking him. Do you know, Mr. Hobbs, Lieutenant Brewer stood up for Phillips, on deck and before the hands? The captain was so incensed that he ordered Brewer to the tops for three days' extra duty! Can you image that? The *first lieutenant* ordered to the tops like a common landsman!

"Off the eastern coast of the United States we got caught in a hurricane, and Captain Norman got swept overboard. Brewer took over command for the remainder of the voyage.

"Listen to me, Mr. Hobbs—this is the point of my tale. The change in the crew was extraordinary. Much of the grumbling ceased with the change of command. The men moved faster; it was as if they wanted the new captain to succeed. Do you know why? Because they knew that Brewer cared. They knew he would treat them fairly.

"I believe this crew will come to the same conclusion once they get to know the captain. In the meantime, lawlessness will be met with *appropriate* discipline. No less, but no more, either. Give the Captain a chance, Mr. Hobbs."

Hobbs shrugged and drained his glass. "We'll see," he said. Then he took his book and went to bed.

The next day, Mr. Rivkins relieved Mr. Hobbs and took the afternoon watch. He checked the slate for any change in the standing orders and, finding none, walked over to join the first lieutenant, sailing master, and Mr. Reed.

"Mr. Rivkins," Reed said, "I was just telling these gentlemen about our conversation with Mr. Hobbs last night. Before you came in, sir."

Greene shook his head in disbelief. "Incredible."

"I was tempted to ask him if he was making it all up," Reed said.

"I doubt it," Greene said. "I know Richards; what you've told me sounds exactly like something he would do."

"I'm not sure what to make of Hobbs," Rivkins said. "On the one hand, he seems sure that Captain Judah did only what was necessary to keep order and discipline on board. Even when the crew was driven to mutiny, Hobbs blamed it on the previous captain. Granted, I agree he laid the foundation, but I think the punishment book bears out the fact that Judah went too far, too often."

"It looks to me as though the crew may be coming around a little," Mr. Sweeney commented, "in the last day or two."

"Agreed, Mr. Sweeney," Greene said. "Mr. Reed, I have a task for you. I want you to go and find Dr. Spinelli and tell him about your conversation of last night. Tell him I think today might be a good day to play chess with Mr. Hobbs."

"Aye, sir." Reed saluted the premier and was gone.

One hour later, Paul Hobbs was in his cabin reading when there came a knock at the door.

"Enter."

The door opened to reveal a lad named "Skimpy" by the crew. He was the smallest of the ship's boys, but he could climb and move as quickly as a monkey.

"Beggin' yer pardon, Mr. Hobbs," the boy said, "but the doctor wants to see you."

"The doctor? Whatever for?"

"Don't rightly know, sir."

Hobbs closed his book and got out of his bed. "Very well. Tell him I'll be down directly."

"Aye aye, sir." The boy darted from the cabin.

Hobbs made his way to the sickbay. He knocked and stepped inside.

"Doctor?" he called. "Oh, there you are. Skimpy said you wanted to see me."

"Yes, Mr. Hobbs. Thank you for coming. Sit down. I have it on good authority that you know how to play chess."

"Chess?" Hobbs seemed confused. "Why, yes, Doctor, I play. Why do you ask?"

"I need a partner," Spinelli said. "I was hoping to draft you."

"Really, Doctor, I hardly think I'm the right one—"

Spinelli cut him off. "I can always whisper in Mr. Greene's ear that I think you're a bit overworked and suggest he order you to relax by playing chess."

Hobbs just stared at him. "You wouldn't dare."

The doctor just sat there and smiled.

Hobbs sighed in surrender. "Very well, Doctor, you win. But I must warn you; I'm not very good. I doubt I shall provide much of a challenge for you."

"Quite all right, I assure you," Spinelli said. "I believe you will be challenge enough."

The doctor got his set out. Hobbs chose white, and the two men went to war. Spinelli quickly discovered that his opponent had lied about his skill, and settled himself to take the game more seriously. He took a knight with a bishop.

"Let me ask you something, Mr. Hobbs," he said. "You are in a unique position to tell me what I want to know, and that is, how are the crew reacting to their new captain?"

Hobbs shrugged without taking his eyes from the board. He reached out and took the bishop with a pawn. "Why ask me?"

Spinelli moved a knight. "Well, you have been on board for the past two captains before Captain Brewer. That means three different styles of command, although you may not be accustomed to that of Captain Brewer yet. I want to know your opinion of which works best on this crew."

"That would be a hard question to answer, Doctor," Hobbs said. He moved a pawn to expose a bishop's attack on Spinelli's king, while simultaneously threatening a rook. "Check. As you say, I am not really familiar with Captain Brewer yet. Besides, I was just a junior lieutenant during the previous commands."

"All the better to observe the men." Spinelli moved his king, and Hobbs took the rook. Spinelli frowned. "So, tell me."

"Well," Hobbs hesitated while he moved a knight, "my first captain was little more than a rich appointee. He wanted to command a frigate to advance his political career in the House of Lords after the wars. No discipline at all, and the crew ran wild. Captain Judah took command and tried to instill discipline, but the crew resisted."

Spinelli moved his pawn. "To the point of mutiny?"

"Unfortunately, yes."

The doctor looked up from the board and studied his opponent. Hobbs looked at the pieces, but his eyes were not focused. They were glassy and welling up with tears.

"Mr. Hobbs? Mr. Hobbs, are you all right?"

Hobbs blinked and sat back in his chair. "Fine, Doctor. Just got a bit of grit in my eye."

"Quite all right, Lieutenant. Tell me, where were you when the mutiny took place?"

Hobbs leaned forward to study the board again, and for a moment the doctor thought he wasn't going to answer the question.

"I was below, in my cabin. I had just gotten off watch, you see, and I had a glass of wine and lay down. I must have dozed off—never knew anything about it until it was all over and the captain began to take his revenge."

Spinelli looked up at that word, but Hobbs was concentrating on the game. *Perhaps that's why the word slipped out,* he thought.

"And what happened then?"

Hobbs rubbed his chin before taking a pawn. "The captain hung the two he considered leaders of the mutiny. He would have hung more, but the first and second lieutenants stopped him. We set course for Port Royal. The three of them went ashore to report to the admiral as soon as we made port, and they never came back."

Spinelli nodded and moved his knight. "Check. Do you think what the captain did was right? Not waiting for a court martial, I mean?"

Hobbs moved his king. "I don't know. Mr. Markham and Mr. Richards certainly didn't."

"Well," Spinelli said, "it hardly seems legal. Even a captain on a King's ship can't hang a man without a trial." He took a pawn with his bishop. "Check."

Hobbs took the bishop with a rook the doctor hadn't seen. "I suppose not, but he is the captain."

Spinelli moved a rook and sat back. "You sound as though you thought a great deal of Captain Judah."

Hobbs shrugged. "I think he had the chance to be a great captain." He moved his queen and took the Doctor's knight. "Checkmate."

CHAPTER FOUR

One of Lieutenant Rivkins' duties was that he was in charge of the thirteen 18-pounder cannons that made up HMS *Phoebe's* larboard battery. He was currently working with the forward five of those guns, and he wasn't particularly pleased with either the crews' accuracy or the speed of their reload.

"Right!" he said. "Let's do it again!"

His crews groaned.

"The standard is our firing two broadsides to the enemy's one," Rivkins said. "That means the reload for the entire battery must be complete by one minute, fifteen seconds. Our last reload was two minutes, three seconds. That barely matches the enemy one-for-one."

"It'll be easier when I gets Collins back," said the captain of Number 2 gun. "Say, Mr. Rivkins, any idea when he'll be released to duty again?"

"Any day now, so the doctor says."

"You know the captain from before, right, Mr. Rivkins?" a hand from Number 4 gun asked. "Is he soft?"

Rivkins leaned against a bulkhead. "What do you mean?"

"Well, I heard some of the blokes a mess or two down saying how Captain Judah would have given at least four dozen for it, so that must mean the new captain is soft."

Rivkins pushed himself to his feet. "I wouldn't call him soft. It's more as if he's giving Collins—and the rest of you—the chance to learn what's not acceptable behavior. Trust me, the next person who gets drunk on duty and pisses on the deck is going to have his back ripped open."

"So that means he's as cruel as old Judah?"—this from Number 1 gun.

Rivkins turned and walked toward Number 1 gun. "Are you daft? Would Judah have given you a chance to learn your lesson, or would he have had Collins' backbone exposed for all to see? Collins was drunk on duty. Should the captain just turn his back and let him go?" There was a murmur of disagreement. "Well, then." He pointed to the hand who had spoken up. "What would you have done with Collins if you'd been the captain?"

"I wouldn't give him the cat," the hand said. "I'd send him aloft for extra duty."

"I see," Rivkins shrugged. "And what would you do when the mates two messes or so down from yours decided that they could go ahead and get drunk on duty anytime they wanted, seeing they weren't going to get the cat for it?"

The man's eyes flew wide, as though he'd never considered that consequence. "The next ones would get four dozen!" he said.

Rivkins smiled. "Now you've got some disgruntled hands that are wondering why Collins was sent to the tops while they got four dozen for the same offense. Now they not only hate you as captain, but they probably hate Collins as well. And you can bet they'll be talking."

He walked back and forth before his men, knowing they were all listening to him now. "Better to be fair with the punishment. Every man on this ship now knows that he'll get the cat for being drunk on duty. If he's stupid enough to do it anyway, his punishment is on his own head, not the captain's."

The hand who'd asked the question nodded his head up and down slowly as he thought it over. "Sounds good. Where'd you learn all that, Mr. Rivkins?"

The lieutenant smiled. "From Captain Brewer, when he was my lieutenant on the old *Lydia*."

The captain of Number 5 gun stepped forward. "And what happens if one of the boys gets accused, but he didn't do it?"

"The captain would not convict an innocent man," Rivkins said firmly. "I promise you that. Now, once more on the timed reload. Ready, Mr. Drake?"

The midshipman had the watch before him. "Ready, sir!"

"Remember, men, when I give the order to fire, reload as fast as you can. Ready? Fire!"

The five guns belched flame and shot before bolting backward to the limit of their ropes, and the men jumped to action. The barrels were wormed and sponged out before cartridge, wadding, ball and wadding were rammed down and the gun captain cocked the flintlock and stood to the side, lanyard at the ready.

Rivkins' eyes flew over each gun to make sure no steps were skipped. When the last captain signaled his gun was ready, he turned to his midshipman.

"Time, Mr. Drake?"

"One minute and twenty seconds, sir!"

The men cheered the time, and Rivkins led the way. Not only was it the best time the division had produced, it was the best time in the ship in the last year.

"Good work, you men," Rivkins said when the cheers died down. "Now let's get these guns secured."

Captain Brewer came up on deck to find a warm, sunny morning and a brisk sea breeze on his face. He stood at the top of the companionway for a moment and took in the sight of his ship at sea. The sails overhead were full, and the log told him they were skimming over the waves at a clip of 6 knots under plain sail. At that rate, Rio was still three days away.

He strolled over to join Lieutenant Greene and Mr. Sweeney just aft of the wheel. The two men were about to greet him when the lookout interrupted.

"Deck there! Sail on the starboard bow!"

"Where away?" Greene called.

Brewer accepted a glass from a quartermaster's mate and went to the railing to search the direction indicated by the lookout. Soon his eyes settled on a tiny patch of white on the horizon.

"Mr. Sweeney! Alter course to intercept!" he called to the sailing master. He turned to Mr. Greene. "Let's get a second set of eyes in the tops. And send someone to act as a runner."

"Aye, sir," Greene said.

HMS *Phoebe* came around to her new course, and Brewer decided to go forward for a better view.

"Lookout," he cried, "let's hear you!"

"Still hull-down, sir!" came the reply. "Looks like it might be two ships!"

Brewer hurried forward to see for himself. On the way, he caught sight of Mr. Murdy, midshipman of the watch.

"Mr. Murdy," he said, "my compliments to Mr. Greene. Tell him to call the hands to make all sail. I want to close on those ships as fast as we can."

"Aye, sir!" The midshipman saluted and was gone.

Brewer went back to studying the approaching ships. He felt his ship lurch forward as the additional sails grabbed all the air they could, and soon their quarry was hull-up on the horizon and closing fast.

It was indeed two ships, at least one of which looked like a warship. He closed his telescope and made his way back to the quarterdeck. No sooner had he arrived than he was joined by young Skimpy.

The lad saluted. "Begging your pardon, sir," he croaked between gasps for air, "but the lookout told me to find you in a hurry. He says there's two ships out there. One is a British merchantman and the other appears to be a brig, and it's flying the Brazilian flag!"

Brewer looked at the ships again. "Brazilian?"

"Aye, sir."

Brewer looked back to his runner. "My compliments to the lookout. Mr. Greene! Beat to quarters, if you please!"

"Aye, Captain! Beat to quarters!"

The marine drummer boy began to play as the hands raced to their assigned stations. Brewer took a moment to watch them, and he was pleased with what he saw. The men were reacting as the crew of a King's ship should. In fact, they were almost the equal of *Revenge's* old crew. Almost. It was eleven minutes and forty seconds before Mr. Greene reported *Phoebe* ready for action.

"Well done, Benjamin," Brewer said.

"Getting better, sir," Greene said, standing with his hands clasped behind his back. "Not quite where we want them."

HMS *Phoebe* closed on her quarry quickly now. Brewer remained on the quarterdeck, awaiting a further report from the lookout."Can you see what's going on yet?"

The lookout studied the horizon through his glass. "Looks like the Brazilian is trying to make the British ship heave to, sir! She may intend to board her!"

Brewer's eyes were hooded as he considered the implications of the lookout's report. He turned to Mr. Greene.

"Go forward and get the long nines ready. I want to be able to put a warning shot off the Brazilian's beam as soon as we're close enough."

"Aye, sir." Greene saluted and went forward. Brewer turned to find young Skimpy awaiting orders, ready to deliver any message.

Just then the lookout called, "Deck ho! The Brazilian is a warship—a brig, sir—his guns are run out. Ours is a merchantman; she's not quite as big as an Indiaman."

Now Brewer could see the hulls through his glass. He turned to the messenger beside him. "Skimpy, I want you to go forward. You'll find Mr. Greene at the long nines. Tell him what you've just heard.Off with you, now!"

The boy scampered away, and Mr. Sweeney came over. "Orders, sir?"

"We need to close as fast as possible. Stand by for some quick maneuvers once we close on them."

"Aye, sir."

Brewer went forward and joined Greene. He found the premier with his glass to his eye, studying the two ships ahead. Brewer smiled as he saw Skimpy nudge him and whisper something before scampering to the other side of the gun. Greene lowered telescope and turned and saluted.

"Captain."

"Mr. Greene. I see you have a new warning system."

Greene looked over at Skimpy, leaning over the rail and studying the ships. "Seemed like a good idea. Worked pretty well, I'd say."

"How long till you can open fire?"

"Not more than another half-hour, sir," Greene said.

Suddenly Skimpy began to jump and point. "Lookee, sir! Is that a shot?"

Brewer and Greene got their telescopes up in time to see the last of the smoke from one of the brig's guns fade away.

"The merchie's heaving to, sir," Greene said.

"Aye, and the brig as well." Brewer lowered his telescope and thought for a minute. "Open fire as soon as possible. Keep it up until the brig notices. We'll heave to where we can keep the brig covered while we send a boat over to see what's going on."

"The brig's lowering a boat, sir."

"Skimpy," Brewer said, "back to the tops. Tell the lookout to watch for the long-nine's shot and report to me on the quarterdeck."

"Aye, sir!"

Brewer made his way aft, and he was walking up to Mr. Sweeney at the wheel when he heard the report of the first long-nine going off. The second came a second later.

"Mr. Sweeney," he said to the sailing master, "I want us to heave to with one broadside aimed squarely at the brig's stern windows. Get me to within a half-pistol shot."

"Aye, sir."

"Mr. Tyler," he said to the midshipman of the watch, "my compliments to Lieutenant Reed. He is to load the guns and run them out."

"Aye, sir."

Two more shots rang out. Three minutes later, Mr. Greene made his appearance on the quarterdeck.

"That second pair got their attention, sir," he said.

"Good," Brewer said. "Benjamin, I want you to take the boat over to the merchantman and see what's going on. Take eight marines with you, and Mac; he's big and ugly, should be intimidating in a fight."

Lieutenant Greene stepped up onto the deck of the merchantman, flanked by marines with muskets and Mac with a brace of pistols. He was immediately accosted by a man he presumed to be the captain.

"Thank heaven you've come, sir," the man exclaimed. "This bloke here"—he gestured at an approaching man with dark hair and an angry expression—"forced us to heave to. Now we've been boarded and he demands to see our manifests!"

Greene asked, "And you are, sir?"

The officer took a breath. "Forgive me. I am George Smalltree, captain of HMS *Camel.*"

"I am Lieutenant Greene of His Majesty's frigate *Phoebe,*" Greene announced. He turned to the other man in the argument. "And who are you?"

The man faced Greene, his hand conspicuously on the hilt of his sword. "I am Allejandro, first mate of *Gato*. We have a letter of marque from the government of the Empire of Brazil that allows us to seize ships that are carrying supplies to the Portuguese oppressors who are trying to make our country into a second rate colony again."

"So why have you stopped and boarded a British ship?" Greene asked.

"This ship was bound for Salvador," Allejandro said.

"With cargo for the British merchants there," protested Smalltree.

"Who will sell it to the Portuguese!" accused Allejandro.

"Enough!" Greene shouted. "Captain Smalltree, you will gather your manifests and return to the *Phoebe* with me. Sr. Allejandro, you have one minute to get yourself and your men off this ship."

"You have no right to do this!" the Brazilian exploded.

Greene calmly pointed to his ship. "The broadside ready to fire at your ship says that I do, señor. Get back to your ship and tell your captain that he has fifteen minutes to report to Captain Brewer on *Phoebe*. If he doesn't speak English, tell him to bring someone with him who does. And tell him to bring his letter of marque."

The Brazilian didn't move, and Greene looked over his shoulder.

"Mac!"

"Sir!" the coxswain pulled his pistol and aimed it at the Brazilian's head.

"My ship is only a half-pistol shot away," Greene explained. "My captain has given orders that on the first sound of a pistol going off on this ship, HMS *Phoebe* will fire into your ship. Doesn't matter if it is fired by your men or mine, or whether it is accidental or on purpose. If you don't move by the time I count three, my coxswain will fire his pistol into your head, and my ship will fire its broadside. Of course, you won't live to see it. If one of your men guns him down, he may save your life, but my ship will still open fire. One."

Allejandro's eyes narrowed as he stared at Greene. His eyes darted to several members of his crew.

"Two."

Allejandro turned to Mac when he heard the coxswain cock his pistol. He said something in his language, and his crew began to make their way back to their boat. Once they were all over the side, Greene sighed.

"Very well, Captain, get your manifests and let's get back to my ship."

"As soon as they were over the side and away, we came straight back here, sir," Greene finished his report.

Captain Brewer sat back in his chair, tapping the top of his desk as he considered what he had heard. He had scanned Captain Smalltree's manifests while listening to Mr. Greene's report; *Camel* was indeed taking her cargo of foodstuffs and wine to British merchants in Salvador, and he had to admit that they were such things as might end up in the hands of the Portuguese there, even if they were of no direct use in aiding the Portuguese to fight their war with the Brazilians.

Brewer pulled out his watch. "Mr. Greene, have someone check whether *Gato's* captain has arrived? He should have been here by now."

"I'll check myself, sir," Greene said. He came to attention and left the cabin. He had a bad feeling about this in the pit of his stomach, and he wanted to see for himself.

As he stepped up on deck, he was met by Mr. Henry.

"Sir!" he said as he stopped just short of knocking Greene from his feet. He turned and pointed toward the brig.

"The brig is making sail!"

Greene immediately ran to the waist railing.

"Mr. Reed! Fire at the Brazilian ship!"

Reed came into view. "Too late, sir! Our guns don't bear!" Greene turned to the midshipman. "My respects to the captain; ask him to come on deck now! I'm going forward to try to get the long nines to bear."

Ninety seconds later, Captain Brewer burst from the companionway and onto the quarterdeck.

"Report!" he cried.

Mr. Sweeney stepped forward. "Approximately three minutes ago we noticed the brig making sail. I immediately sent Mr. Henry for you, but he ran into Mr. Greene as he came up on deck. Greene ordered Mr. Reed to fire, but Reed told him the guns didn't bear. Greene sent the midshipman after you while he went forward to try the long nines."

Brewer saw the brig begin to pull away around the merchantman's bow. He grabbed a speaking trumpet and stepped forward.

"All hands make sail!" Brewer cried. "Mr. Sweeney, steer a course around the stern of the merchantman. Try to cut them off!"

"Aye, sir!"

Brewer went to the rail and watched as the Brazilian brig disappeared behind the merchantman. Forty-five seconds later, HMS *Phoebe* began to move. She picked up speed as she gave the merchant's stern a wide berth. As soon as they cleared the British ship, Brewer could see the brig heading away from them to the southeast.

"There they go!" he said. "Follow them, Mr. Sweeney!"

"Aye, sir!"

Phoebe swung around to port and settled down to pursue the brig. Brewer walked forward and found Mr. Greene standing behind the nines.

"We're closing, sir," Greene said as he lowered his glass, "but slowly."

Brewer glanced up and searched for the sun through the cloudy sky. "How much daylight do you think we have left?"

Greene glanced skyward. "Six hours at most."

Brewer studied the chase and lowered his telescope. "It's going to be close."

Greene nodded and raised his glass to his eye again. He could see the gap was indeed closing, but were they closing fast enough? He lowered the glass.

"I estimate it will be at least four hours before we can try with the long nines, sir," he said.

Brewer did some calculations in his head. In the end, he had to agree with his first lieutenant's assessment.

He turned and walked aft to the quarterdeck.

"Mr. Sweeney," he said, "we need more speed. Hang every stitch she'll carry."

"Aye, sir!"

Brewer stood back and watched his crew go through their tasks. Again, he was pleased to see that the men were moving more quickly than before. Within minutes, the great cloud of white over Brewer's head grew to the greatest area possible, and the captain felt the ship edge further ahead. He jumped to the mizzen shrouds and studied the chase, but he decided that it would still be on the order of three hours before they would be in range.

He jumped down to the deck. "Mr. Sweeney, I am going to my cabin. You have the deck until Mr. Greene comes aft. I want to be called if anything happens or when we get within range of the chase."

"Aye, Captain."

Brewer went below. He had discovered during his tenure as commander of HMS *Revenge* that he hated the waiting that was a part of chasing down the enemy. He vaguely remembered Bush commenting once that Lord Hornblower had sometimes filled such gaps by playing whist with his officers, but Brewer could not bring himself to try that. He briefly contemplated sending for the doctor to play chess, but dismissed the idea.

He allowed McCleary to take his hat and coat as he stepped into the room. He went to his desk and pulled paper, pen and ink from his writing set. He turned when he heard Alfred in the doorway.

"Is there anything you require, sir?" he asked.

"Coffee, if you please, Alfred."

"Aye, sir."

Brewer arranged his materials on the desk and took up the pen.

My Darling,

If I could change anything in the Navy, I would make it so the mail was more regular. I hate having to wait so long to get a letter from you! It's hard for me to conceive that we have been man and wife for nearly two months now, and for that time I have had but a fortnight in your arms. Oh, to be the master of an Indiaman and be able to take you with me to the far corners of the earth!

Our voyages take us south to Brazil. We are to join the South American squadron there under Commodore Hardy. The Brazilians are going to end up fighting the Portuguese for their independence very soon, if they haven't declared their intentions already. Our job is to protect British interests in the area, particularly our merchant fleet at sea. During the late American war of the last century, privateers by the hundreds set sail with letters of marque and preyed on British commerce; I can only imagine something similar will happen here. At this moment, we are in pursuit of a brig flying a Brazilian flag and claiming to have such a letter. We caught them trying to board a British merchantman.

Listen to me, giving you a briefing when I should be telling you how much I love you. I hope you can forgive me, my sweet Elizabeth. Your portrait is tucked inside my writing desk for safety, and I take it out every day to tell you how much I love you and how badly I miss you.

A knock at the door interrupted his thoughts.

"Enter."

The door opened to admit Mr. Murdy, the senior midshipman. "Mr. Greene's respects, Captain. He thinks we can reach the brig now."

"What, already?" Brewer pulled out his watch and was shocked to see that three hours had passed! He looked at his desk and noticed for the first time a cup of coffee, now grown cold, quietly placed there by Alfred two hours ago. "Yes, of course. My compliments to Mr. Greene. I shall be up directly."

Murdy smiled. "Aye, sir."

Brewer stowed the letter, ink, and pen, closed the letter box, and rose. He donned his coat, amazed that he could lose himself for so long in visions and words to his beloved so distant. What would it be like when they had the chance to be together?

He emerged from the companionway and walked over to Mr. Greene and Mr. Sweeney.

"Gentlemen," he said in acknowledgement to their salutes. "Are we ready, Mr. Greene?"

"I think so, sir," Greene said. "Definitely close enough to try."

"Good. Please pass the word for Mr. Rivkins. Gentlemen, we are going to open fire with the long nines. Sooner or later, he is going to try to turn to give us a broadside. Mr. Sweeney, when he does, I want you to change our course to cut across his stern."

"Aye, sir."

Lieutenant Rivkins arrived and saluted. "You sent for me, sir?"

"Yes, Mr. Rivkins. We are about to open fire with the long nines. Eventually, the brig will have to turn to fight. When he does, we are going to rake his stern, whatever way he turns. You need to have both batteries loaded. You have to get the battery run out and fire before we pass the brig."

"Aye, sir."

"Good luck. Mr. Greene, let us go forward and see what damage we can cause."

The two men made their way forward to find the crews of the long nines eager to get into action.

"Prepare to run out your guns!" Greene called.

The men cheered and went about their work with vigor.

"I want the first shot off their quarter," the captain said. "Let's give them a chance to surrender."

"Aye, sir," Greene replied. "Check your aim, gun captains! Ready?"

Two hands went up.

"Fire!"

Fire and smoke erupted from the two barrels. By the time they sailed through it, they could not see the fall of the shot.

"Lookout! What was the tale?" Brewer cried aloft.

"One shot off the larboard quarter, and the other short astern, sir!" came the reply.

Brewer and Greene studied the brig, but neither man saw any sign of it slowing down.

"Very well, Mr. Greene," Brewer said, "you may fire at will."

"Aye, sir!"

Brewer stepped off to the side, both to get out of the way and also to get a better view. The next volley went off, but he found he was still blinded by the smoke.

"Both short astern, sir, but not by much!" the lookout reported.

Frustrated, Brewer looked around before jumping to the foremast shrouds and hanging outward, his glass to his eye. When the next volley went off, he was rewarded by the sight of splinters springing from the brig's railings and upper works.

"Well done, Mr. Greene!" he cried. "At least one hit! Keep it up!"

The brig tried small adjustments to its course to throw off the guns, but Mr. Sweeney matched them change for change. Soon Brewer thought they were close enough to try something.

"Mr. Greene, load with chain!"

"Aye, sir!"

Brewer watched with anticipation as the next volley tore sails and rigging. He pulled his glass down to the deck in time to see an officer gesturing wildly.

"Mr. Tyler," he called to the midshipman on the deck "run aft to Mr. Sweeney! Tell him to be ready!"

"Aye, sir!"

Brewer jumped to the deck and squeezed Mr. Greene's arm. "Well done, Benjamin! Fire as long as your guns bear. I'm going aft."

Brewer arrived on the quarterdeck and tossed his glass to Mr. Tyler. "Get up on the mizzen shrouds there and tell me which way she turns!"

"Aye, sir!"

"Stand by, Mr. Sweeney!" The sailing master nodded, and Brewer went to the waist railing.

"Mr. Rivkins, stand by!"

The young lieutenant came into view. Mr. Reed stood beside him.

"Ready, sir!"

Now they waited, all eyes on Tyler in the larboard mizzen shrouds.

"Mr. Greene's chewing their rigging up, sir! Every shot is telling now! Wait a minute, wait..." Tyler pressed the instrument to his eye and called out, "Larboard, sir! He's turning to larboard!"

"Larboard battery, Mr. Rivkins!" Brewer called down to his lieutenant. "Run out and fire as your guns bear!"

"Aye, sir!"

Brewer stepped back from the railing to see what was happening. Mr. Sweeney had altered *Phoebe's* four points to starboard. Brewer judged they would be in a good position to rake the brig, if Mr. Rivkins could get his guns out fast enough.

The brig lost a great deal of speed when it made the hard turn, allowing HMS *Phoebe* to close. Brewer just had time to make it to the larboard railing before Rivkins' guns began going off. He watched as the brig's stern window shattered and the woodwork above and around it disintegrated, sending showers of deadly splinters into the bowels of the ship.

"Hard to starboard!" Brewer called. "Bring us around! Mr. Rivkins! Starboard battery, stand by!"

"Aye sir!" Rivkins shouted. Brewer could hear him shouting to the starboard battery even as he moved to the railing. He was looking to see if there was any sign of surrender. Sadly, he saw none. He turned to Sweeney.

"Take us past her stern again, Mr. Sweeney. Steady up on a southwestern course."

"Aye, sir," Sweeney said. He didn't like this any more than his captain did, but the young fools in the brig apparently weren't smart enough to know when they were outgunned, let alone outsailed.

Brewer went to the waist.

"Stand by, Mr. Rivkins."

"Ready, sir."

Brewer watched the activity on the brig's quarterdeck. He saw the captain desperately trying to organize a defense.

"Surrender, curse your hide!" Brewer said under his breath, knowing it was useless.

"Mr. Rivkins! Try to take out their rudder as we pass!"

"Aye, sir!"

Rivkins left the captain and moved to his battery.

"Listen, you men!" he called. "The captain wants us to take out her rudder on this pass! Stand by!"

A gun captain near Reed spoke quietly. "Take out his rudder? Who does the bleedin' captain think we are? HMS *Victory*? How are we supposed to do that?"

Reed turned to him. "Why can't you do it? What do you think we've been practicing for? I've seen your gun at work, Patrick; you can do it, I have no doubt. So can many others in the battery."

Patrick looked at him as if he'd grown a third eye.

"Have you lost your senses, Mr. Reed?"

"Look, Patrick," Reed said in voice with an edge like steel, "if you can't do it, say so now, and I'll get a captain for this gun who can. Decide now."

Patrick looked around and saw all the eyes that were on him. "I can do it, Mr. Reed."

Reed put his hand on the man's shoulder. "I know you can, Patrick. I've watched you practice. Your men can pick a swallow off a branch!"

Patrick nodded and turned back to his crew, who were smiling to a man. Reed stepped back and was met by Rivkins.

"Trouble?" the third lieutenant asked.

Reed grinned. "Not a bit, sir. Ready when you are."

Rivkins looked from Reed to Patrick's gun and back again before nodding.

"Stand by!" came the order from above.

"Captains," Rivkins called, "sight your shots carefully, just as we practiced! Do not fire until your guns bear!"

"Fire!"

"Fire!" Rivkins repeated. The guns went off singly or in pairs. Rivkins was proud of his men's discipline in waiting until they had a good shot before pulling on their lanyards. Now they waited for the word, and smiled when they heard the cheers from above.

Brewer watched the broadside pepper the area around the brig's rudder before he finally saw it disintegrate. The quarterdeck erupted in cheers! *Phoebe* pulled away from the brig.

"Reduce sail, Mr. Greene," Brewer said. "Bring us around to starboard, Quartermaster, make your course due west."

"Aye, sir, due west."

The Captain looked at Mr. Sweeney. "Think they'll surrender now?"

Sweeney shrugged. "If they do, it'll be the first smart thing they've done today."

HMS *Phoebe* settled on her westerly course and waited to see what her quarry would do. *Phoebe's* guns were loaded and run out, and his crew's confidence was riding high. Brewer was proud of his men.

Brewer joined Greene on the starboard to survey the damage to the privateer brig. It took a moment for him to focus his glass, but once he did he was able to see the brig's upper works were shredded, and their deck had taken a lot of damage. He could see some men milling about, but nothing more.

"Mr. Sweeney," he said, "I want you to take us in a wide loop around the brig so that we end up within half pistol shot of her stern."

"Aye, sir," Sweeney said. "You're giving them a chance to think it over, aren't you?"

Brewer nodded. "Precisely. I hope that staring at our broadside circling their ship will induce them to surrender."

Sweeney smiled his approval and turned to look at the brig. "Let's hope it works." He shook his head. "The alternative is for us to pound her or board her. Either way, good men will die for nothing."

"Not for nothing," Brewer said sternly. "Not if I can help it."

As they approached the brig's stern, Brewer turned to his first and said, "Benjamin, I am going to try to reason with them, talk them into surrendering. If I should fall, your orders are to blow them out of the water."

"Aye, sir."

"Heave to, Mr. Sweeney," Brewer said. He grabbed a speaking trumpet and went to the railing. "I am Captain William Brewer of His Majesty's Ship *Phoebe*. I order you to surrender!"

"Never!" came the reply.

"If you do not surrender within five minutes, we will open fire. Your men would die for nothing!"

"You have illegally attacked our ship when we were operating under a letter of marque from our government!"

"You were attacking an English ship. Surrender, or we shall open fire!"

There was silence from the brig. Brewer consulted his watch and raised the trumpet to his lips again.

"Two minutes!"

Finally, he saw a different officer come to the brig's fantail.

"Very well, Capitan! We surrender!"

"Stand by to receive our boat!" Brewer called. "Any mischief, and we shall open fire!"

The officer on the brig waved. "There will be no trouble. We shall await your boat."

Brewer handed the trumpet to a midshipman and turned to Mr. Greene. "Take the launch, Benjamin. Take extra marines. I want their captain brought back here, along with their letter of marque and any records of ships they've attacked."

"Aye, sir." Greene saluted and went off, bellowing orders for the launch and crew.

Greene stepped up to the deck of the brig and looked around. The marines had already secured the deck, and a nod from Greene to their sergeant sent teams below to search for cargo and papers. Greene, accompanied by two marines, walked over to a group of officers on the quarterdeck.

"I am Lieutenant Benjamin Greene of His Majesty's frigate Phoebe. Which of you is the captain?"

One of the men stepped forward. “The capitão and his mate perished in your attacks. I am in charge. Lieutenant José Perez.”

“You will return to my ship with me,” Greene said firmly. “My men are searching your ship for your letter of marque, any orders, reports, or other papers.”

“There is no need to search,” Perez said. “I will take you to the documents you seek.”

“Thank you. Michaels, Tibbets, go with him.” The two marines followed Perez below.

Greene looked around the deck. The damage from their broadsides was extensive, and he didn’t want to begin to count the bodies strewn about. A glance at the brig’s upper works showed that the three or four salvoes they’d fired with chain had been most effective; undoubtably, this was what made their captain decide to turn and fight rather than try to escape into the coming darkness.

Perez returned with a packet in his hand, which he gave over to Greene. “This contains the information you requested.”

“Thank you. Mr. Pulley,” Greene called to the senior petty officer, “this ship is impounded as a prize of war! You will remain here with the marines and prepare her to sail to Rio in company with *Phoebe*. A prize crew will be ferried over to you. Secure the brig’s crew below and get a detailed report of the ship’s cargo ready for the captain.”

“Aye, sir,” Pulley said.

“Now, sir,” Greene said to Perez, “if you’ll be so kind as to accompany me? By the way, is there anyone in your crew who can translate these for my captain?”

The prize crew was detailed and the repairs were made to the brig, which then sailed to Rio under *Phoebe's* lee. It took two days for Mr. Ball, the captain's clerk, to transcribe the translated papers Greene brought back for the captain.

Captain Brewer was going over the papers in his cabin. He had Lieutenants Greene and Rivkins with him, as well as Mr. Sweeney and the doctor. Mr. Hobbs had the deck, and Mr. Reed was sleeping in the wardroom.

Brewer passed the first paper to Greene. "Well, it looks like their letter of marque is legitimate, in any case," he said as he handed it over. "It's signed by the Brazilian Captain-General of Bahia."

"Does that mean we're in trouble?" Rivkins asked.

"Lieutenant, we shall never get into trouble protecting British ships from capture," Brewer said.

"Even if it's a frigate of the Portuguese navy?"

Brewer smiled. "Even so."

"At least *Camel* wasn't carrying guns or powder to the Portuguese garrison," Spinelli said.

"It's only going to get worse as the fighting increases," Sweeney added. "What do we do if we find a Brazilian—warship or privateer—stopping a Portuguese merchantman? Or what about a neutral?"

Brewer handed Greene another page. "I have no orders about that as yet. I'm sure that will be part of my briefing when we meet Commodore Hardy at Rio."

"The good news is that we caught the brig right at the start of her voyage," Greene said, looking up from the reports. "It seems *Camel* was the first ship she stopped."

"And the last!" Sweeney grinned.

Brewer smiled. "The men did well. How long to Rio?"

"Three days," Sweeney said.

CHAPTER FIVE

Captain Brewer was finishing his breakfast on the morning of the third day when Mr. Drake, the junior midshipman, knocked and was admitted by the sentry.

"Mr. Sweeney's respects, Captain," he said. "We've sighted Cape Frio."

The captain stood. "My compliments to Mr. Sweeney. Please tell him I shall be up directly, Mr. Drake."

"Aye, sir."

Brewer made his way to the deck and was pleased to find the Brazilian sunshine warm on his face. Mr. Sweeney awaited him.

"Good morning, Captain," said the sailing master.

"Been here before, Mr. Sweeney?" the Captain asked.

"Aye," Sweeney replied. "Me favorite spot in South America."

Brewer smiled. "Take her in, if you please, Sailing Master."

Mr. Sweeney saluted before turning and bellowing out his orders. The crew rushed skyward to reduce sail and allow *Phoebe* to glide into the harbor. The ship passed into the Bay of Guanabara and then between the Sugar Loaf and the Fort of Santa Cruz to enter the enormous bay. The brig followed close behind.

"Aye," Sweeney said from a few feet away, "'tis good to see the old gentleman again."

"And who is that, Mr. Sweeney?" Brewer asked.

"Oh, begging your pardon, Captain," Sweeney said. He pointed to the peaks on the far side of the bay. "Do you see that mountain range there, Captain? The dominant peak—yes, that crooked-looking one—that is Corcovado, commonly known to British sailors as 'Lord Hood's nose.'"

Brewer stared at the rock until all of a sudden he saw it and laughed. "Yes, I see what you mean."

Sweeney shrugged.

HMS *Phoebe* passed wooded islands, several rocky outcroppings with either white churches, or forts, or both, before finally coming abreast of the heavily fortified island of Villegagnon. Only after skirting the island did the city of Rio de Janeiro come into view. The ships slid past a multitude of shipping before heaving to and dropping anchor off the island of Ratos near the naval arsenal. Captain Brewer took in the shoreline while his officers surveyed the bay.

"Sir," Greene called, "no sign of HMS *Superb*!"

"Mr. Tyler," the captain called, "take a glass and get up to the main top! I want to know if *Superb* is in port or not."

"Aye, sir!"

"I'll be in my cabin," Brewer said to Greene. "If the commodore is not here, I'll need to go ashore and see the British consul. Let me know what Tyler finds."

"Aye aye, sir."

Brewer went below, conscious of a dull ache in the back of his head that he took as a warning of danger. When the door was safely closed behind him, he took off his hat and coat and tossed them on the table for now. He turned and saw Alfred appear in the doorway.

"Anything I can do for you, Captain?" he asked.

"Yes, Alfred. A glass of port, if you please, and pass the word for Mac."

"Aye, Captain."

He went into the day room and sat beneath the stern windows, sighing as he took off his shoes. Alfred brought his drink and then Mac arrived.

"Gentlemen," Brewer told them, "my best uniform, please."

Alfred began laying out a clean shirt along with the captain's best breeches and stockings. Mac got his hanger and sword out and made sure the hilt was polished, then he went to work polishing the captain's shoes and making sure the buckle shone. In ten minutes, Brewer was ready.

Mr. Greene arrived. "Mr. Tyler reports HMS *Superb* is not in the harbor, sir."

"I thought as much," Brewer said. "Call the gig, Benjamin; we go to the consul, then."

"Aye, sir." Greene came to attention and left the room. Mac silently followed him out.

Brewer sat beside Mac in the stern sheets of the gig as he was rowed ashore to meet with the British consul. Hopefully, the gentleman would have some instructions for him from Commodore Hardy. When they reached shore, he left Mac in charge of the gig and made his way to the consul's residence.

He was shown immediately into the consul's presence. Sir Henry Chamberlain was a tall, sturdy man with dark curly hair and dark eyes. He came across the study and shook hands with the young captain.

"Very pleased to meet you, Captain," he said. "George, pour us some wine. Come, sit over here, Captain. Thank you, George." The servant set their glasses on a low table between the chairs and withdrew silently. Chamberlain picked up one glass and handed it to Brewer before raising the other one in a toast.

"Now, Captain," he said after they'd drunk, "what can I do for you?"

"I was ordered to meet Commodore Hardy here, sir. When he was not here, I came to see you. I hope you have instructions for me."

"Indeed I have," he said, rising to retrieve an envelope from the drawer of his desk. He handed it to Brewer. "Orders from the commodore, although I do not know what they say. He asked me to hand them to you when you arrived. Yes, please, go ahead and open it."

Brewer broke the seal and read the letter. It was short and to the point, ordering HMS *Phoebe* to join him on the Pacific coast at Valparaiso. He was to sail as soon as his ship was provisioned.

"I was informed you brought in a Brazilian ship as a prize," Chamberlain said.

"We came across her firing upon and boarding a British ship, sir," Brewer explained. "When we tried to speak to her, she ran. When we caught her, she turned to fight rather than surrender. We put two broadsides into her before she lowered her colors."

"I see," the Consul said. He rose and began to pace, his head lowered in thought. It struck Brewer how much the gesture reminded him of Hornblower or Bush, so he decided to quietly wait the consul out. It was a matter of minutes before the gentleman sat down again.

"Captain," he said slowly, "I'm afraid you've caused a bit of trouble for both of us. I'm sorry to tell you that your prize will be turned back over to the Brazilian government and most likely repaired at British expense. Less than two weeks ago, the Portuguese garrison of Rio—known as the Legion—under General Jorge de Avilez, surrendered to Brazilian forces loyal to Crown Prince Pedro. They have withdrawn to a location up the coast where they will be transported back to Portugal. The Brazilians now have control of the city." He took in a slow, deep breath and expelled it slowly and loudly. "Are you aware of the history of the present conflict? No? You need to know; it will help you understand the restrictions under which we operate.

"Brazil was the richest colony of the nation of Portugal. When Bonaparte invaded the Iberian Peninsula in 1808, the Portuguese had enough notice to move their entire government, lock, stock and treasury, to Brazil. King João VI declared Rio to be the capital of his empire. Bonaparte was reportedly none too happy to discover that not only had the government of Portugal escaped his clutches, but they also managed to take their national treasury with them! All of it safely transported across the oceans—thanks in part to the Royal Navy—and beyond his greedy reach.

"King João—which is Portuguese for John, by the way—I hope you won't mind if I call him that; it's just easier for me to say." The Consul continued. "After Bonaparte was finally beaten at Waterloo, calls came from what government officials remained in Lisbon for the king and government to return home. King John was so impressed with Rio and the Brazilian people that he raised Brazil from a colony to kingdom status, equal with Portugal in the Kingdom. He combined the two lands into a single country, which he named *The United Kingdom of Portugal, Brazil, and the Algarves*. Naturally, this did not make the courtiers in Lisbon very happy. In 1820, the Liberal Revolution broke out in several cities in northern Portugal. They had two major planks in their platform—the return of the King and government from Rio, and the return of Brazil to colony status. In other words, a return to the prewar status quo."

Brewer shook his head. "I can't imagine that idea went over well in Rio."

Chamberlain smiled. "That would be an understatement, let me assure you. Soon the king realized he had no choice but to return. Before he left, however, he did something that many said guaranteed war. He left his son and heir, Pedro, behind in Brazil, and gave him the title of 'Regent of Brazil.'"

Brewer's eyes widened.

Chamberlain shrugged. "Personally, I think there would have been war whether Pedro had remained or not. Had Pedro returned to Lisbon with his father, I cannot believe Brazil would meekly have submitted to the imposition of colony status. Portugal would have had to re-conquer the country. And now that Pedro has stayed as Brazil's 'regent', there will surely be a war, started by Brazil for their independence. Either way, Britain remains stuck in the middle."

Brewer looked up. "How so?"

"While Brazil was a colony, the only country she was allowed to trade with was the mother country. When she was elevated to kingdom status, that allowed trade with Britain and several other countries, and because of that Brazil is on her way to becoming a very wealthy nation. If she were forced to return to colony status, that wealth of trade would be lost. The effect on our economy alone would be staggering. British exports to South America totaled £3.5 million in 1820."

Brewer frowned. Hardy's task of protecting British interests was vital indeed.

"I can't just sit back and allow Brazilian ships to attack British shipping," he said. "Did the commodore happen to tell you what he would do in such an event?"

"Not even a hint, I'm sorry to say," the consul answered. "You shall have to ask him when you find him. Is there anything else I can do for you?"

Brewer shook his head. "I think not, thank you. I shall sail as soon as I have completed stowing our provisions for the trip round the Horn."

The two men rose, and Chamberlain shook his guest's hand warmly.

"I wish you Godspeed and safe passage, Captain," he said.

Brewer thanked his host and returned to his ship.

Brewer sat in his cabin with Mr. Greene, listening to the purser's report of what he'd obtained ashore.

"We should be well stocked for the trip, Captain," Mr. Tenpenny said. "I was able to get beef, pork, bread, flour, tobacco, butter, raisins, sugar, cocoa, peas, oatmeal, limes, lemons, red wine, brandy, and rum. I was also able to lay hold of more than a ton of coffee at a very good price, as well as a half-ton of tea." He looked up from his book. "I was informed ashore that we were authorized additional meat, bread, and rum for the trip round the Horn. I'll be going ashore tomorrow to secure it."

"Thank you, Mr. Tenpenny," Brewer said. "Just make sure we're not buying old meat that's already rotted in the cask." The purser came to attention and departed. Brewer turned to Greene. "I wonder if it would be possible to preserve meat longer if we put it in metal casks, sort of like we have with our water on board."

Greene was intrigued by the thought. "The water certainly is staying fresh longer. I heard that the army is beginning to look into sending its field rations in metal cans. If that's so, perhaps it'll bleed over into the Navy."

Brewer was about to speak when the voice of the sentry broke in.

"Third Lieutenant, sah!"

"Enter!"

Lieutenant Rivkins entered the room.

"What can I do for you, Mr. Rivkins?" Brewer asked.

Greene interrupted. "I sent Mr. Rivkins ashore, sir, when a French squadron entered the harbor. I thought we might like to know who our neighbors are."

"Quite right," Brewer said. "Well, Mr. Rivkins?"

"French frigate *Amazone*, sir, along with a brig and corvette. Commanded by a commodore, sir, name of Roussin."

Brewer and Greene stared.

"Are you sure, Mr. Rivkins?" Greene spoke first.

"Aye, sir. Is anything wrong?"

Brewer and Greene looked at each other, and both smiled. For some reason, Rivkins did not think that was a good sign.

"Lieutenant," Brewer said, "I have a message for you to take to the commodore. Please invite him and one other officer to dine with me. Tell him my chef is still alive."

Rivkins was now thoroughly confused. "Your chef is still alive, sir?"

"That's correct, Mr. Rivkins. Ask them to please arrive at sundown."

Rivkins hesitated a moment, but it was clear that his instructions were complete. He nodded and turned to go.

"Mr. Rivkins," Brewer said, "you are to give him no other information. Is that understood?"

"Aye aye, sir. No other information."

By the time Rivkins stepped up on the deck of the French frigate, he was sure he was missing out on some sort of inside joke between the captain and Mr. Greene. He was met by a French officer and saluted smartly.

"I am Lieutenant Rivkins, of His Majesty's frigate *Phoebe*. My captain has sent me with a message for your commodore."

He waited while the officer went away. He returned within minutes and asked Rivkins to follow him.

He was admitted to the commodore's day cabin and found it furnished in a much more resplendent manner than Brewer's aboard the *Phoebe*. There were two officers drinking wine sitting beneath the stern window. Neither had his coat on, so Rivkins did not know whom to address. One of the officers rose.

"I am Commodore Roussin," he said. "I understand you have a message for me?"

Rivkins bowed by way of paying his respects. "Sir, my captain has asked me to extend to you and one other officer an invitation to dine with him aboard HMS *Phoebe* at sundown tonight."

"A generous offer," the Commodore said. "And what is your captain's name?"

"Well, sir, you see," Rivkins was embarrassed to say it, "he, er, asked me not to tell you."

Roussin's brows shot skyward at that. "Really? Is there anything he said you *could* tell me?"

Rivkins cleared his throat. "Aye, sir. He said to tell you that his chef is still alive."

The look on the commodore's face told Rivkins that he was as baffled as Rivkins himself. The commodore turned to his compatriot for help, but the poor man was just as puzzled as everyone else. The Commodore's lips moved as though he were repeating the phrase to himself, and suddenly a look of understanding dawned on his face, and he smiled.

"This chef," he asked, "is he a man of small stature who can work magic in a galley?"

"Aye, Commodore."

"And he has a great reputation with the sword?"

"Aye, Commodore."

"Your captain's name, it is Brewer."

"Aye, Commodore."

The commodore turned and looked at his companion, who now understood the joke as well. He turned back to Rivkins.

"You may tell your captain that Lieutenant de Robespierre and I will be honored to attend. We shall call upon him and his marvelous chef at sundown."

They sat around the table in Captain Brewer's cabin, stuffed from the feast that Alfred had prepared. Brewer had barely had time to send his servant ashore for certain items he needed for the feast. In fact, the meal had been thirty minutes late, but the result had been well worth the delay. Brewer and Greene watched their guests lean back in their chairs and sigh in satisfaction.

"As good as I remember," de Robespierre said.

"Do you know, Captain," Roussin said, "if I came upon you and your ship, and the ship was sinking, I believe the only man of your crew I would save would be your tiny chef."

Brewer raised his glass. "The only one worth saving!"

The four men cheered and drank the toast. Alfred was summoned and congratulated on his skill, much to his embarrassment and his captain's delight. The party adjourned to the day room, where cigars were handed out and Mac brought in a silver tray with four glasses of brandy. The four men sat and drank.

"Tell me, Captain," Roussin said, "what happened to you after we parted company? I presume that your renegade admiral followed you, as we never saw him again."

"Yes, he did. We were only saved by the timely intervention of Admiral Lord Hornblower with two additional frigates. Cochrane turned tail as soon as he saw them coming. Have you run into him again?"

"No. Why? Is he in these waters?"

"We believe so," Greene said. "Our last information was that he was still in command of the Chilean Navy."

"We have been in these waters for three weeks," de Robespierre said. "We have seen nothing of the Chileans."

Brewer went on to tell his guests about his wedding and the admiral's subsequent gift of his promotion to post captain and getting command of *Phoebe*. The Frenchmen offered their felicitations.

"May one ask who is the bride?" de Robespierre asked.

"Her name is Elizabeth," Brewer said. "She is the daughter of the governor of St. Kitts."

"I have met her, *mon ami*," Roussin said, "when I called on her father the governor on a visit to the island. I congratulate you, sir; your bride is a beautiful woman."

Brewer raised his glass. "Thank you, my friend."

The others joined him in raising their glasses, and they drank to the captain's new bride. Brewer looked to his guests.

"Have you seen any action, Commodore?" he asked.

"What do you mean?"

"On our way here, we intercepted a Brazilian brig with a letter of marque attempting to stop and board a British merchantman. We forced her surrender, but when we got to Rio, the British Consul denied our prize and gave the ship back to the Brazilians."

Roussin nodded. "I see what you mean, Captain. To answer your question, we have not encountered any such happenings. My admiral was somewhat... evasive when I requested instructions on such matters when we arrived." He shook his head disapprovingly. "It seems France does not have quite the economic interest that you British have in the area."

Brewer sat back. "My orders are to sail as soon as we are ready. We go around the Horn to meet Commodore Hardy at Valparaiso."

Roussin brightened and said, "Then you must come and dine with me at noon tomorrow, Captain, before you depart. Bring Mr. Greene with you, of course! Please, you must allow me to show you my ship, Captain. It is the best and most modern France has to offer."

"Commodore, we shall be honored," Brewer answered. He called for Alfred to refill their glasses.

The hot Brazilian sun was high in the sky the next day when Brewer and Greene were rowed over to *Amazone*. Soon they found themselves feasting on French delicacies in Commodore Roussin's cabin on the *Amazone*. Brewer sat back in his chair, feeling well satisfied, and took an appreciative swallow of very fine cognac.

"So, Commodore," he said, "yesterday I filled you in on our adventures since we parted ways after leaving San Andres. Now, I believe, it is your turn."

"So it is, *mon ami*," Roussin said with a smile, "so it is." He paused while his steward brought out cigars. "Ah, Brewer, these are the last of the batch you gave me." He puffed one to life and blew a glorious cloud of smoke toward the deck above them. "I have never found their equal. Well, after we left you, we had an uneventful journey back to Martinique. You should have seen the governor's face when we sailed into the harbor with two of his luggers under our lee and presented them to him as prize ships! I was sure that

Donzelot was going to challenge me to a duel. Fortunately, he controlled himself and told me he could not accept the luggers. However, he did allow me to sell them to local merchants, so at least my crew got some money in their pockets.

"The governor was able to have me relieved of the *Semillante* on some pretext, but within a month I received orders to Guadeloupe to join Admiral Jurien and was given command of *Amazone*. We sailed south with vague orders to show the flag and protect what little trade France is beginning to develop in the region. After only a couple of weeks, the good admiral announced he was returning to France. He wrote me orders granting me the temporary rank of commodore and leaving me a brig and corvette along with my frigate, to impose the will of the king on South America."

De Robespierre made an exaggerated sweeping gesture with his cigar and grinned. Brewer and Greene laughed and raised their glasses in a toast.

"And how is that going for you?" Greene asked.

The lieutenant sank as though someone had let the air out of his balloon. "Not so well. What commercial interests we have are mainly on the Pacific coast, in Chile and Peru. In Brazil? Not so much."

Brewer leaned in. "And you say you haven't had any run-ins with Brazilian navy or any of their privateers? What about the Portuguese?"

Roussin shook his head and took a drink from his glass. Brewer shared a look with his premier as the commodore set his glass on the table and rose.

"I promised you a tour, did I not, *mon ami*?" he said. "I will warn you—we have finally found the perfect inducement to steal prime British seaman from the Royal Navy."

As they rose to follow the commodore out of the cabin, Greene leaned in and spoke softly in his captain's ear. "This should be good."

They toured the upper deck and noted the armament of the French ship.

"Eighteen-pounders, Commodore?" Brewer said. "I'd have thought a new ship like this would have twenty-fours at least."

"There was some discussion, Captain, but arming the ship with twenty-fours would mean carrying six fewer guns. It was decided to keep the number of guns. The weight of the broadside is nearly the same."

They went below to the gun deck, and the Commodore turned and smiled.

"Gentlemen," he said, "here is the greatest advancement in French warship design in more than fifty years!" He pointed proudly to a new model galley stove.

"Looks like an oven to me," Greene said.

"Oui," de Robespierre said, "but not just any oven. This oven not only is able to provide a regular supply of fresh bread and baguettes, but it also serves to keep the entire ship dry."

Brewer and Greene stared. Here indeed was a wonder, if it could do everything the Frenchmen claimed. Among the greatest complaints of the typical British tar was the wetness of the lower deck. At times and in certain climates, it had been a major contributor to the sick list on many ships. Now the British officers could only wish this oven were theirs. The galley stove aboard *Phoebe* could do little more than boil meat, peas, and duff.

In the stern sheet of the gig, on their way back to the ship, Greene leaned over to his captain. “Sir, request permission to form a cutting out expedition.”

Brewer grinned. “Do you want to steal their ship, Benjamin?”

“No, sir,” came the reply. “Just their oven.”

Brewer laughed and wished it could be so.

CHAPTER SIX

HMS *Phoebe* weighed anchor and made her way slowly through the inner harbor. Water had been topped off at 110 tons, and the extra bread, meat, and rum authorized to the ship brought aboard and stowed. The ensign was dipped in salute to the fort at Santa Cruz. When *Phoebe* made her way out into the Bay of Guanabara, she was brought to a halt by a seventy-four flying a Portuguese flag signaling for her to heave to. Behind the seventy-four were three frigates and what looked to be three corvettes or sloops of war leading a dozen transports. Brewer ordered Mr. Sweeney to heave to as he watched the battleship lower a boat.

The officer who stepped up on *Phoebe's* deck was smartly dressed. He marched right up to Brewer and saluted.

"Capitão," he said formally, "I am Lieutenant Alvarez, flag lieutenant to Admiral of the Blue Diogo de Almeida, commander of the Portuguese Navy. I bring an invitation from my admiral for you to join him for drinks. He also has some questions you may be able to answer."

Brewer saluted his guest as he considered what kind of questions a Portuguese admiral might want him to answer. A glance at Mr. Greene showed the same concern in his eyes. Brewer smiled at his visitor.

"And when does your admiral propose we meet?"

"In one hour's time, sir," Alvarez bowed.

Brewer looked over to Greene and then to Sweeney; both men shrugged.

"Very well," he said. "Please convey my respects to Admiral de Almeida and tell him I shall be honored to be at his service."

"Ah, thank you, *Capitão,*" Alvarez said as he bowed again. He saluted smartly and left the ship.

"Well," Sweeney said, his fists resting on his hips, "what do we make of that?"

Greene looked at the seventy-four. "I'd say they're hoping for the latest intelligence on what's going on in Rio. Those ships in the outer harbor look for all the world like a troop convoy, probably bringing reinforcements for the garrison."

"They're too late," Brewer said. "The British Consul, Sir Henry Chamberlain, told me that the Portuguese garrison surrendered to Brazilian forces less than two weeks ago."

"In that case," Sweeney said, "it may be a short conversation."

"Be that as it may," Brewer said, "pass the word for Mac, if you please, Benjamin. Launch's crew, all smartly turned out. We have an admiral to impress."

Brewer stepped through the entry port of the Portuguese flagship to be greeted with all the ceremony due a visiting captain. Lieutenant Alvarez awaited him and saluted.

Brewer returned the salute smartly. "At your service, sir."

"Thank you, *Capitão*," the lieutenant answered. "If you would please follow me? The admiral awaits us."

Brewer followed the younger man aft and then up to the quarterdeck and the admiral's cabin under the poop. Alvarez hesitated when he got to the door and turned to his guest.

"I hope you will not be offended, Captain," he said, "but my admiral does not speak English. I shall be acting as his interpreter."

"Thank you."

The lieutenant smiled before knocking once on the door and opening it. He marched in, stood aside to admit the admiral's guest, and closed the door behind him. Brewer stood at attention while Alvarez made the introductions.

"Captain, may I present to you Admiral of the Blue Diogo de Almeida, Commander of the Portuguese Navy?"

Brewer bowed and then remained at attention while Alvarez presented him to his admiral. The admiral bowed and shook hands warmly with his guest. He turned and indicated the table.

"Sit, please," Alvarez translated the admiral's invitation.

The admiral's servant appeared and set glasses before the three men before departing. Admiral de Almeida raised his glass in a silent toast. Brewer and Alvarez did the same. Brewer was surprised at the dark liquid.

"Cognac?" he asked.

"I was forced to sail many times with the French during the wars," the admiral said through his interpreter. "I have developed a fondness for cognac as a result. Perhaps the only good thing to come out of that experience!" The admiral chuckled, and Brewer smiled. "Captain Brewer," he continued, "you have just come from Rio. What can you tell me of the conditions there? I have just arrived with a relief garrison for the city, but I must know the situation—both political and military—before entering the inner harbor and landing my troops."

Brewer tossed back his cognac and sat back comfortably in his chair. "I regret to say that I can give you naught but bad news. I have just spoken with the British Consul, Sir Henry Chamberlain. He told me that less than two weeks ago, the Portuguese garrison under General Jorge de Avilez surrendered to forces loyal to the Prince Regent and have evacuated the city for a port from which they may embark for Portugal. The Brazilians have taken control of the city."

Brewer sat back and watched as the devastated lieutenant translated his report for the admiral. The old man's face went from shock to anger, and he demanded to know how Brewer knew this to be true.

"I captured a Brazilian brig," the captain explained. "It was acting as a privateer and attempting to board an English merchantman. I brought the ship into Rio as a prize, but the consul said that it had to be given back to the Brazilians and most likely repaired at British expense."

The admiral listened to the translation, all the while staring at Brewer with eyes so hard that they would surely have broken down any walls hiding concealed intentions. As the lieutenant finished, the admiral blinked and looked away. He called for his servant to refill their glasses. After this, he seemed to think quietly. Brewer looked at Alvarez, but the flag lieutenant only shrugged. It was apparent they would simply have to wait the admiral out.

Finally, de Almeida bestirred himself and spoke to Alvarez. The lieutenant turned to Brewer.

"Do you know the port from which the garrison was to embark?"

Brewer shook his head. "No, I'm sorry. I do not."

The admiral nodded his understanding even before the response was translated for him. He thought for a moment or two more before rising and speaking to Alvarez.

Alvarez and Brewer rose as well. The lieutenant turned to the Englishman.

"The admiral thanks you for your time and wishes you a successful voyage."

Brewer came to attention. He started to make his farewells to his host through the good lieutenant, but the admiral had already turned away from them and gone into his day cabin. Alvarez shrugged by way of a weak apology and led his guest back to the entry port.

Brewer returned the lieutenant's salute. "A man of few words, your admiral."

Alvarez just smiled. "Good luck, Captain."

HMS *Phoebe* slipped past the Portuguese fleet and made her way out to sea. She set her course SSW toward the Horn, the easterly breezes pushing the frigate along at a little better than four knots under all plain sail. Due to the stifling heat and humidity, Captain Brewer gave special dispensation for officers to appear on deck without their coats.

Lieutenant Hobbs, for one, was grateful for the dispensation. Even without his coat, his shirt was nearly soaked through, and his watch was only half over. The good news was that the cool of the evening was waiting to greet him when he got off watch, and he intended to find a spot where the delicious evening breezes could give him their undivided attention.

Hobbs stood to the side as Mr. O'Reilly, the midshipman of the watch, made his way to the fantail to cast the log. He made ready and looked over his shoulder at Mr. Henry, who was ready at the glass. Henry nodded.

"Now!"

O'Reilly heaved the triangle overboard and watched the rope as it fed out. Henry flipped the glass and watched the sand flow through the waist and shouted the word when the last grain had drained to the bottom. O'Reilly clamped down on the rope and began to pull it in, counting the knots as he did so.

"Well?" Hobbs asked.

"Not quite five, sir," O'Reilly called.

Hobbs sighed. "Very well. Record it, if you please, Mr. O'Reilly."

"Aye, sir."

Hobbs was lost in thought. He was still not sure of the new captain, and it bothered him greatly. Part of him could see the improvement in the crew's performance since the new captain and premier had come aboard, but then he felt frustrated and angry that they had not given the same dedication and performance to Captain Judah.

He strolled over to the lee rail and stood with his hands behind his back, turning the problem over in his mind. It wasn't as if Captain Judah had turned the crew into mutinous filth; he inherited the lot when he took command from that pompous imposter. He'd dealt out the punishment they'd deserved, but somehow they'd only gotten worse. And now, here comes bloody Captain Brewer, who doesn't give out a tenth the punishment for the same offense, and the crew love him! Hobbs scowled. It just didn't make sense.

He made his way forward, walking with his head down, studying the deck planking before him and paying no attention to the world outside his thoughts. As he approached the forecastle, he didn't see one of the hands working on the starboard 32-lb carronade rise and begin to back up. Nor did he see that same hand trip over the gun carriage. Hobbs' first reminder of the outside world was when the seaman fell into him and nearly knocked him down.

"Here now," Hobbs said, "get off!" He was angry and not thinking, or he probably wouldn't have done it, but he shoved the seaman away from him without so much as seeing who it was. The seaman, not knowing who was shoving him away, quite naturally spun around with his fists raised. He dropped them as soon as he saw who it was who had shoved him, but by then it was too late.

Hobbs stood before him, wide-eyed and with a tiny smile beginning to show at the corners of his mouth. He knew this man, and knew him well. Ferguson. Topman and troublemaker, a thorn in the side of Captain Judah almost from the day he'd come aboard.

"I'm sorry, sir," Ferguson said.

"Oh, it's too late for that," Hobbs cooed. "Sergeant-at-arms! Clap this man in irons! The charge is making to strike an officer. That'll get you six dozen, Ferguson! I knew that the captain's soft ways wouldn't change a scum like you!"

The Sergeant-at-arms took Ferguson below, despite the seaman's protestations of innocence. Hobbs looked around at the growing crowd.

"What're you all standing around for?" he bellowed at them. "Get back to work! Mr. O'Reilly! You have the deck. I have to report to the captain."

The captain was not in a very good mood himself. He had just lost his third game in a row to the doctor.

"It just isn't your night, is it, Captain?" the doctor crowed, trying but failing miserably to be magnanimous in victory. "Would you prefer to try poker? At least then you could blame a loss on the luck of the draw."

Brewer was spared having to reply by a knock at the door. The sentry opened it and announced the second lieutenant. Mr. Hobbs marched in, looking rather pleased with himself, and came to attention.

"Yes?" Brewer asked. "What can I do for you, Mr. Hobbs?"

"I need to report a defaulter, Captain," the lieutenant said. "Making to strike an officer, sir."

Brewer looked to the doctor. "Pass the word for Mr. Greene." The surgeon got up and went to the door.

The captain turned back to Hobbs. "Who is the seaman?"

"Ferguson, sir. Topman."

Brewer got out the watch bill and found the name. "Here he is. He's in Mr. Rivkins' division. Sentry! Pass the word for Mr. Rivkins."

"Aye, sir!"

The doctor returned, and Brewer rose.

"Let us move into the day cabin." He led the way in and sat under the stern window. Mr. Greene arrived with Mac right behind him.

"Mac," the captain said, "we shall require a few more chairs."

"Aye, sir." He moved two chairs in and set them to the side.

"What's going on, sir?" Greene asked.

"Mr. Hobbs is reporting a defaulter. We're waiting for Mr. Rivkins."

Rivkins arrived and took a seat off to the side, beside Hobbs.

"Very well," Brewer said. "Mr. Hobbs, you may begin."

Hobbs rose and cleared his throat. "I was walking on deck, Captain, seeing to the general tidiness of the deck, when all of a sudden this big oaf crashes into me with no warning whatsoever. I pushed him off, and he turned with fists raised to strike me."

"I see," Brewer said. "And you said this was Ferguson, a topman?"

"Aye, sir."

"Mr. Rivkins, the watch bill says this man is in your division."

"That's correct, sir."

"What can you tell us about him?"

"He does his work well enough. I've never had a problem with him, sir."

"He has a long history as a troublemaker, Captain," Hobbs insisted. "He gave Captain Judah no end of trouble."

Brewer's eyes flashed to the doctor, sitting silently in the corner, but Spinelli was looking at the deck.

"Were there any witnesses?" Greene asked.

"I don't know, sir," Hobbs answered. "What difference does that make? He made to strike me!"

Brewer rose. The rest of the room followed.

"Mr. Rivkins," he said, "you are excused. Mr. Hobbs, you may return to the deck. We shall reconvene when you come off watch."

Both officers came to attention and left the cabin.

"Mac," Brewer said, "ask around quietly. See if there were any eyewitnesses. Get their stories."

"Aye, sir."

After Mac was gone, he turned to Spinelli. "Doctor?"

The doctor pursed his lips and thought for a moment before giving his input. "I'm not sure what to say, Captain. This goes back to the previous administration, obviously. Pending any eyewitness accounts, I think we need to give weight to Mr. Rivkins' words."

Brewer looked to his premier.

"I agree with the doctor, sir," Greene said.

Brewer thought it over for a moment more before sitting back down again.

"While we're waiting for Mac to return, why don't we hear from the accused? Doctor, please pass the word for the sergeant-at-arms to bring the prisoner."

While they waited, Alfred brought them coffee. The doctor made a particular show of inhaling the aroma and delighting in his first taste.

"I think Brazilian coffee is better than that from the Caribbean," he said. "What about you gentlemen?"

"This is the first time for me," Greene said. He took a tentative sip, and then a deeper drink. "I think you may be on to something, Doctor. What say you, Captain?"

The captain was just about to reply when a knock was heard at the door. The sentry announced the sergeant-at-arms. The prisoner was marched into the room and stood before them, manacled hand and foot. At a signal from the Captain, he sat in one of the chairs off to the side. Brewer recognized the face now and could not recall him causing or being involved in any trouble since they'd sailed from Jamaica.

"Mr. Ferguson," he said formally, "you are aware that the second lieutenant is having you charged with the crime of making to strike an officer. I have brought you here now to hear your side of the story. I will warn you, we are searching for eyewitnesses to what happened, and it will go badly for you if you lie in what you are about to say. Do you understand?"

"Aye, Captain," Ferguson answered miserably.

"Very well, then; tell me your story, Mr. Ferguson."

"I was on duty," he began slowly, "checking to make sure the starboard carronade on the fo'c'sle was secure. I retied one of the knots and stood up with the extra rope in my hands. I started to back out onto the deck, but I tripped over the gun carriage. All I knew was that I fell into someone who angrily cried for me to get off him and shoved me hard back into the gun carriage. Sir, I confess that I was overcome with a moment of anger, during which I turned and raised my fists. But I swear I wouldn't have struck out, sir—I swear I wouldn't! I've learned that much since we sailed. I dropped my hands as soon as I saw it was Mr. Hobbs and apologized, but he said it was too late and I was going to get six dozen for making to strike an officer."

Three sets of eyes snapped up at the prisoner's words. For most men, six dozen lashes meant a death sentence.

"I see," Brewer said. "Do you have anything to add, Ferguson?"

"No, sir, 'cept that I would never strike an officer, sir!"

Greene leaned forward. "Why did you confess the way you did?"

"That were Mr. Rivkins' advice, sir," Ferguson said. To Brewer, "He said that if we were ever in trouble with you, the best thing we could do was to come clean and not hide anything, so that's what I did."

Brewer looked hard at him, then said, "Sergeant-at-arms, return the prisoner to the cable tier. I will send for him again after the turn of watch."

"Aye, sir. Up, you!" The sergeant marched Ferguson out of the cabin, and the sentry closed the door behind them.

"Six dozen!" Greene breathed out. "Obviously, Hobbs wanted more than just punishment."

"So it would seem," Brewer said over his cup. "Doctor, does Ferguson's statement seem plausible to you?"

The doctor shrugged. "Certainly plausible. Maybe even true. It does sound like something that Hobbs would do, especially if he was distracted and not paying attention to his surroundings."

"Did you notice his remark about Ferguson and Captain Judah?" Greene asked.

"Yes," the captain replied, but made no further comment.

There was a knock at the door, and McCleary was admitted.

"Well, Mac?" Brewer said.

"I talked to several of the hands who were on deck and forward of the foremast at the time, sir," the big Cornishman said. "A lot of them turned to watch when they heard Mr.

Hobbs yell "Get off!" and saw him shove Ferguson back into the gun. They all agree that Ferguson jumped up and turned with his fists raised, but that he dropped them immediately once he saw who it was."

Brewer considered this as the doctor stepped up.

"Mac, did anyone see what happened *before* Mr. Hobbs yelled?"

Mac smiled. "One. Skimpy. He was leaning against the portside carronade—says he saw the whole thing. He said Ferguson was working on the gun's tackles. He picked up some extra rope and went to step back, but he tripped over the gun carriage and fell into Mr. Hobbs. The rest you know."

The Captain nodded as he drank his coffee, and Mr. Greene heaved a sigh.

"Ferguson was telling the truth," he said.

"Yes, but what good will it do him?" Brewer wondered aloud. "Every man on the fo'c'sle saw him raise his fists to an officer."

Mr. Greene hung his head at the pronouncement, while the doctor stared at the ceiling. Brewer began to pace back and forth across the breadth of the cabin, wracking his brain for some way to spare Ferguson without destroying the authority of his second lieutenant among the crew. Mr. Greene and the doctor sat over in the corner and talked quietly.

Finally, Brewer stopped his pacing and sat down. "Looks like we're going to have to do this the hard way," was all he said. Eight bells were heard from the deck above.

"Doctor," he said, "will you please pass the word for Mr. Hobbs."

Dr. Spinelli rose and went to the cabin door to have the sentry pass the word. When he returned, he saw a look on his captain's face he had not seen since the death of the seaman Grant on the *Revenge*.

Hobbs arrived. Brewer wasted no time.

"Mr. Hobbs," he said, "we have interviewed witnesses to the event in question. Most were alerted after your shout and so only saw you push Ferguson away. They confirmed your report that he did turn on you with his fists raised. They also reported he dropped them immediately and tried to apologize. Is that so?"

Hobbs could only gape at his captain for several moments, so stunned was he by Brewer's question. He struggled to regain his composure.

"I... don't recall, sir," he stammered. "He may have, but surely that's irrelevant when you have witnesses who verify that he raised his fists to me?"

Brewer crossed his legs and folded his hands in his lap. "Mr. Hobbs, I told you *most* of the witnesses were alerted by your shout when Ferguson collided with you, but there was one witness who saw what happened before that collision. Are you interested?"

Hobbs stood there silently; the only evidence of his growing anger was in his eyes. Brewer looked at his hands as he continued.

"Ferguson was working on the tackles of the carronade. He rose and went to step back but tripped over the gun carriage and subsequently fell into you."

"I hardly see how that matters," Hobbs said, his voice obviously under tight control. "You have the witnesses."

Brewer looked up at him. “It hardly sounds like the actions of a man who was planning on striking an officer to me. Taken together with the fact that he immediately lowered his hands and attempted to apologize to you, it sounds like an unthinking reaction that could have been overlooked.”

Hobbs was fuming. “Ferguson has a long history of rebellious behavior. I’ve told you how he was a constant thorn in Captain’s Judah’s side.”

“Yes, it’s interesting that you should mention that. And yet, you heard the testimony of the man’s divisional officer that he has performed his duties well and has given that officer no trouble whatsoever. How do you explain that?”

“I cannot, nor will I attempt to,” Hobbs said testily. “I know this man—“

“Apparently not, Mr. Hobbs; you know who this man *was*, not who he *is*.” Brewer rose and stood before his second. “Do you know what I think, Mr. Hobbs? I think you were walking and thinking as we all do. Your head was down. Suddenly, Ferguson collides with you, and you react in shock and anger, shouting at him and pushing him away and back into the carronade. Just as you did, he reacted without thinking and rose, ready to defend himself. Upon seeing who it was who’d pushed him, he immediately dropped his hands and apologized.” Brewer began to pace. “But you, you realized who it was in front of you, and you were having none of his apology. Here was the proof you have been seeking, that the crew were just as rebellious now as they were for your previous captain. And you decided to make him pay.”

"I told him he was going to get six dozen lashes," Hobbs said, obviously beginning to lose control of himself. "It was the least Captain Judah would do under the circumstances."

"Yes," Brewer said, still pacing, "so I heard. The only problem with that is that it was not your decision to make." He stopped pacing and stood eye-to-eye with his second. "And I am not Captain Judah."

"What would have had me do, sir?" Hobbs asked.

Brewer stepped back and began to pace again. "Do, Mr. Hobbs? I would rather you had bothered to investigate *why* the man collided with you! Perhaps you might have set an example and simply caught him, rather than throwing him back against the gun! Or you might have asked him if he was hurt when you caught him!" He stopped pacing and stood nose-to-nose with Hobbs, no longer making any attempt to hide his anger. "But none of that even occurred to you, did it, Mr. Hobbs? And do you know why? Because this crew—those who served under the previous captain, at least—will never be anything more to you than mutinous scum. You cannot believe that they could do better under a different command, because you cannot."

Brewer's gaze bore into his second's eyes for several moments, searching for any sort of challenge and finding none. He stepped back and inhaled deeply to calm himself, exhaling slowly and loudly as he began to pace again.

"However, be that as it may, I am bound to uphold my officers' authority in front of the men," he said as he stepped back and forth before the second. "Now I find myself forced to flog a man who is guilty of nothing more than common clumsiness!"

He ceased his pacing, head down, eyes darting from point to point as he cudgeled his brain for a way to spare Ferguson, but he came up empty. He sighed loudly in exasperation.

"Mr. Greene," he said, "Ferguson is to receive one dozen lashes for making to strike an officer. Defaulters at four bells."

"Aye, Captain."

Brewer turned to his second lieutenant. "You are dismissed, Mr. Hobbs."

"Sir!" Hobbs came to attention before turning smartly and marching out of the cabin. Outside the door, he made for the gun room.

There's got to be something better than this, he thought to himself. *And when I find it, I'm going to take it.*

CHAPTER SEVEN

HMS *Phoebe* continued SSW on her way to the Horn. Unfortunately, the winds did not seem to be in a hurry; during the first week they only made 700 miles. The good thing about heading south was the change in temperature. It was 92°F on the day they sailed from Rio de Janeiro. Now, barely a week later, they were off the River Plate and the mercury read 68°F. Dr. Spinelli was able to report to the captain that the sick list was back to a normal size now that they had left the heat behind.

The captain and doctor were enjoying the break from the heat in their usual way—playing chess in the captain's cabin. Suddenly, the ship rolled in an unexpected way.

"What's that?" the doctor asked.

There was a knock at the door, and the sentry admitted Mr. Drake, HMS *Phoebe's* youngest midshipman.

"Mr. Reed's respects, Captain," he said, "but the wind is shifting, and he asks that you come up on deck."

"My compliments to Mr. Reed," Brewer said as he studied the board and frowned. "You may tell him I shall be up directly."

"Aye, sir." The midshipman snapped to attention and was gone.

"So," the doctor murmured smugly as he sat back, crossing his arms over his chest, "you are saved by duty from an ignominious defeat."

Brewer shrugged as he picked up his hat and stepped toward the door. "Are you sure about that, Doctor?"

"Yes!" he called after the retreating form of his friend, but after the door was closed, he reluctantly studied the board again. Ten minutes later, his eyebrow rose as he spotted the captain's trap.

Brewer stepped up on deck and was staggered by the force of gales out of the east. He quickly got his balance and made his way to the wheel. Mr. Sweeney was already on deck and in conversation with Mr. Reed when the captain joined them.

"Mr. Sweeney?" he asked, "Your opinion?"

"Not unusual for gales to pop up south of the Plate, Captain," Sweeney said. "The bad news is that we won't be able to hold this course much longer. These gales will end up driving us due south, and very soon, too."

Brewer surveyed the deck and the cloud of sail above his head as he considered his sailing master's words.

"Mr. Reed," he said, "get some hands and make sure everything is tied down securely."

"Aye, Captain."

"Alright, Mr. Sweeney," he said, "where are we exactly?"

"I place us about 150 miles ESE of the River Plate, Captain," Sweeney said. "I can work you up an exact position in the chart room, if you like."

Brewer shook his head and leaned into the wind as it shifted slightly to their port quarter.

"Let's ride it out while we can, Mr. Sweeney!" he said, shouting to be heard over the wind. "Call the hands to reduce sail. I want reefed courses and a jib. I am to be called if the wind shifts."

"Aye, sir!"

Despite the reduction in sail, the frigate leapt forward. Over the next few days, as long as the wind held on the port quarter, she averaged seven knots, with a high day of eight-and-a-half, during which they covered over 200 miles on that day alone.

Two days later, Brewer was on deck talking to Mr. Sweeney and Lieutenant Greene. Neither of the officers had been round the Horn before, so the captain was leaning on his sailing master for advice during the dangerous end run around the tip of South America. Mr. Sweeney reported the change in the wind.

"It started about three hours ago, Captain," Sweeney shouted to be heard over the roar of the wind. "The shift to the southwest is making it almost impossible to hold this course, sir!"

"Due south, do you think?" Brewer asked.

Sweeney grimaced before finally nodding. "Unavoidable, sir."

Brewer shook his head; he didn't like the idea any more than his sailing master did. The change would push them far to the east of their planned course and potentially add weeks to their sailing time. Still, there was no arguing it. He took a deep breath, his resolve set.

"Due south, Mr. Sweeney," he said. "Set whatever sail she'll take."

"Aye, sir."

Brewer turned to his premier. It was clear that Greene didn't like the change of course, either.

"No way around it, Benjamin," Brewer said.

"I know," Greene said privately. "I just don't like it."

Brewer smiled. He turned when Mr. Sweeney returned.

"I recommend riding close hauled on the starboard tack for now, sir," he said. "I'll make sure you're called if we have to change it."

The captain considered. "Make it so."

"Aye, Captain!"

Several days later, the captain sat in his cabin beneath the stern windows, sipping a cup of wonderfully hot coffee. He had called Lieutenant Greene, Mr. Sweeney, and the doctor to share a drink and talk about the next few days and weeks.

"Captain," Greene said, "there's something we need to deal with. The temperature is continuing to drop. We need to do something now, or the crew will begin to suffer very soon."

"Issue the clothing we took on at Rio," Brewer said. "Felt-lined gloves and coats, is that correct? Very well, let's get them issued at once. What else?"

"I recommend caulking the lower haves of the gun ports," Sweeney said. "We should also put deadlights over all windows."

"I agree, sir," Greene said. "I will speak to the carpenter immediately. Mr. Sweeney, can we expect the winds to get worse as we go farther south?"

Sweeney nodded emphatically.

Greene turned back to his captain. "Sir, I would also suggest that we rig extra preventer stays on all the masts to help them against the winds."

Brewer nodded. "Do it."

The doctor sat forward. "Something else, Captain. The rough seas are making it harder and harder to feed the crew. A lot of food is already ending up in the scuppers. Also, soon we will have to look at rigging portable stoves on the gun deck."

The captain rose. "Thank you all. Keep me informed."

The portable stoves were rigged on the gun deck and also in the sick bay. The captain and his premier watched them being installed, and both men were struck by the same thought. Brewer leaned over.

"Are you thinking what I'm thinking?"

"Unfortunately, sir, yes."

Brewer considered, then leaned in again.

"Lieutenant Greene, I approve your request to cut out the stove from the *Amazone*. You may leave immediately."

Greene shook his head. "We should have offered to trade Alfred for the stove."

Brewer grinned. "I think Roussin might have gone for that. For now, let's get these going and keep a fire going in the fore cabin."

HMS *Phoebe* continued to claw her way south on her way around the Horn. Within a week, she passed to the east of the Falkland Islands, the winds still forcing the ship and her crew south. This caused the temperature to continue to drop precipitously. Soon ice and snow blanketed the deck and froze the rigging and sails. One hand slipped on the frozen deck when he was caught by a gust of wind and broke three ribs when he was thrown against a gun.

Spinelli was concerned enough to go to the captain.

"I'm very worried, sir," he said on a visit to the captain's cabin. "The sick list is growing almost every day."

"I didn't notice that many in the sickbay when I was there yesterday," Brewer said.

"I have discovered that most on the list have cold-related ailments. Their favorite place to recuperate is the fore cabin where you ordered a fire to be kept going. By the way, the midshipmen have taken a liking to it as well."

A knock at the door heralded the entrance of the midshipman of the watch, Mr. Tyler.

"Mr. Rivkins' respects, Captain. He requests you come up on deck. The wind appears to be shifting."

Brewer jumped out of his chair. "I'm on my way," he said. "This could be the best news we've had in weeks!"

Lieutenant Rivkins saluted as his captain appeared on deck. "The wind is shifting to the south, sir! We may be able to change course soon!"

Brewer made a quick survey of the sail and the waves. "It appears so, Lieutenant. Is Mr. Sweeney on deck? No? Pass the word for him, please."

But the sailing master had felt the change and was already striding towards the helm.

"Mr. Sweeney," Brewer said, "I want to change course to the southwest for Staten Island and the Horn. Any objections?"

Sweeney squinted, searching his memory for anything unusual about the winds south of the Falklands. Finding nothing, he turned to his captain.

"None at all, Captain."

The hopes of the entire crew raised when they felt the ship change course, and when the confirmation filtered below decks, they cheered and drank toasts with their grog.

Mac was with his mess when the word reached them, and he smiled as he watched his messmates cheer and bob their heads in delight. It was still colder than a witch's elbow, but now they could see the light at the end of the tunnel.

Pudge came up to him, shivering as he held his cup and biscuit in his hands. Mac set his own biscuit on the table and turned so he straddled the bench. He picked the youngster up and sat him on the bench in front of him, then he opened his coat and pulled the shivering Pudge to him back first and closed his coat around the boy. Within a few minutes, his shivering had subsided and he was leaning back into the big Cornishman while he nibbled his biscuit.

Pudge looked up at him. "Is it true that we'll be warm again soon?"

Mac laughed. "Not yet, but we're closer now that we've turned. Besides, you've got *me* to keep you warm, you little squirt!" He tickled the boy and then hugged him close.

"Closer?" said Yank from the other end of the table. "Closer to what, I'd like to know. The South Pole? We'll be lucky if we're not frozen solid before we see the sun again!"

"Why don't you be quiet?" Mac said. "There's no reason to be scaring the kid like that."

"Why shouldn't he know the truth?" Yank challenged. "You, Hudson, did you not install deadlights in the captain's cabin yesterday? He's nice and warm, I'll wager!"

Mac pointed his finger at Hudson. "Didn't he also tell you to caulk the gun ports and set up the extra stoves to try to keep us warm and dry?"

"True," Hudson admitted.

"Don't seem to be doing much good," Sparrow griped. "Still bloody freezing down here."

Mac shrugged. "Don't think the Captain has it any better. Believe me, I've been there; he don't have no stoves in his cabin to keep him warm."

"How do we know you're not lying to us, eh?" Yank challenged him.

Mac held his tongue and then hugged Pudge tight. "Why don't you go get warm, little man? You can come back in a while when you feel better."

"Okay, Mac." Pudge slid off the bench and trotted off in the direction of the fore cabin.

Mac looked hard at Yank. "I suggest you think first before making accusations, mate. You might not like the storm it will bring down on yer ears."

Yank scoffed. "You mean you and yer officer friends?"

Mac shook his head menacingly. "I don't need no help."

Yank's face went deadly serious. "Whenever you're ready."

Mac met his eye and held it. "You know where to find me. But, for now, why don't you do your whining somewhere else? That's a good boy."

Yank looked at the others around the table and found no support. "So," he said, "that's how it is? You all knuckle under and throw your support to the captain, when we're freezing like this? Fine, if that's the way you want it, so be it. I thought you was men, that's all."

He stood and gave each one of them a look of disdain and contempt. When he reached Mac, the look changed to pure hatred.

"I won't forget this," he said, and he stomped off forward.

"Don't worry about him," Mac said. "Some people just don't know when they've got it good. Believe me, mates, as long as we have Captain Brewer, we've got it good."

The next day the sun broke through the cloud cover. Nearly every man spent all of his off duty hours on deck basking in its warmth. For two days *Phoebe* sailed through beautiful white-crested waves while the warmth of the sun allowed the men to dry out. The crew saw penguins, and porpoises and whales broke the surface to blow. They were also cheered by the sudden appearance of a flight of stormy petrels along with a couple of albatrosses. The appearance of the latter brought Captain Enfield of the marines on deck with his musket. He stood next to the main mast and waited for one of them to fly over the ship, and as soon as one swooped in low over the quarterdeck, he brought his musket to his shoulder and fired. The big bird dropped to the deck with a thud that brought the captain up on deck.

"What's going on, Captain?" he said to Enfield. "It sounded like a meteor was trying to crash through the deck into my cabin."

Enfield held up the carcass. "I'm sorry about the noise, Captain," he said, "but I thought you might like a roast bird for supper tonight. I imagine Alfred could do wonders with a beauty this size!"

"Capital idea, Enfield!" Brewer said. "Let's go and put it to him, shall we?"

They went below and found Alfred in his pantry polishing the silver platter.

Brewer called him out. “Alfred, what can you do with this?”

Enfield showed him the albatross. Alfred took it by the legs and looked it over.

“I can do a great sea-pie with this, Captain,” he said. “I have some very good vegetables left that would do nicely for the purpose.”

“Good. Can you have it ready for supper tonight?” Brewer asked.

Alfred pursed his lips and looked the bird over again as he considered the request.

“I can do it, Captain, but it would be better if you allowed me to soak it overnight before it’s cooked. It takes any fishy taste out of the meat.”

Brewer raised his eyebrow as he debated within himself whether the delay would be worth the better taste. He looked over to Enfield, who quietly nodded his agreement.

“Very well, Alfred,” Brewer said, “we shall delay the feast until tomorrow. We’ll have the officers, Mr. Sweeney, the doctor, Mr. Murdy, and you, my dear Captain,” he clapped Enfield on the shoulder, “shall be the guest of honor! Will the pie be big enough, Alfred?”

“Oh, yes, sir, with some left over.”

“Good! Until tomorrow night, then.” They left the bird with Alfred.

Brewer spent much of his time on the quarterdeck, watching the grandeur of nature just like anyone else. On the morning of the second day, he stepped up on deck and found Mr. Sweeney talking with the quartermaster.

"Good morning, Captain," Sweeney said.

"Good morning." Brewer turned his face toward the sun and inhaled deeply. "You know, Mr. Sweeney, when I left my father's farm behind, determined to become a King's officer and stand on his quarterdeck, *this* is what was going through my mind. Sailing just like this."

Sweeney rubbed his ear. "Captain Cook had a saying that unfortunately comes to my mind just now: 'Enjoy the weather while it lasts. I guarantee it will change before you know it.' Somehow, it seems appropriate."

The captain's face wore a grim smile. "I hope he's wrong this time. I'd rather not go back to what we've just sailed through."

"I'm not disagreeing with you, Captain," the Sailing Master said, "but I don't think we're done freezing just yet."

Sadly, Mr. Sweeney's prophecy was fulfilled during the night. The wind shifted again, this time turning westerly and bringing driving rain that quickly turned to sleet and snow. The dinner party huddled close, each man wearing his overcoat and wishing the candles on the table put out more heat. Thankfully, the pie was hot and delicious, and the wine helped warm them on the inside. Everyone noticed, but nobody commented on, the absence of one of the portable stoves in the captain's cabin. The day after Mac had it out in his mess with Yank over how warm the captain was, Brewer had gone to the sick bay to check on the doctor and noticed how cold it was down there despite the presence of one of the stoves. When he got back to his cabin, he ordered Mac to move a stove from his cabin to the sick bay. Mac put the fire out, and as soon as the stove had cooled he moved it. On the way, he stopped at his mess to show his mates what he was doing and why. Somehow he wasn't surprised when Yank transferred to another mess on the first of the next month.

When the dinner party finally broke up, the men filed out, thanking Captain Enfield for the unexpected feast. Mr. Greene lingered a moment.

"Mr. Sweeney and I are going to check the deck before we turn in, sir," he said.

"Very good," the Captain replied. "Call me if I'm needed."

Even so, Brewer was surprised when the knock came at his door a few minutes later. The sentry admitted Mr. Tyler.

"Mr. Greene sends his respects, sir," he said, "and would you please come up on deck?"

Brewer sighed and rose. "My compliments to Mr. Greene. I shall be up presently."

He donned all the cold weather gear he could find but was still cold when he stepped up on deck and was hit by the winds. It was with difficulty that he joined Greene and Sweeney at the wheel.

"Sir," Greene shouted in his ear, "Mr. Sweeney and I agree that this wind will not allow us to make our turn to the west! We recommend that we hold this course SW for another day or two!"

Brewer looked at the seas and raised his eyes aloft to verify the close-reefed foresail and topsails. "Very well, maintain course." There was nothing more to be said. Brewer turned and retreated to his cabin. The hopelessness was beginning to eat into him as well.

The very next day, Brewer came on deck and was astonished. The weather had suddenly cleared, and the sun was shining down on them through a clear blue sky.. Just as Mr. Sweeney was about to greet him, Brewer saw the sailing master look past him and stare, his mouth hanging open in awe. Brewer quickly turned to see what was the cause, and when he saw it, he could only agree with Sweeney's reaction.

Off their port bow, at a distance of about two miles, was what could only be described as a solid wall of ice rising from the ocean surface. Almost perfectly smooth and unbroken, it was the most impressive sight Brewer had ever seen.

"Mr. Sweeney," he said, "what is *that?*"

"Looks like a wall of ice, Captain," Sweeney answered.

"I can see that, Mr. Sweeney," Brewer deadpanned. "Is it an iceberg?"

Sweeney shrugged. "If it is, sir, it's the straightest one I've ever seen."

Brewer looked over his shoulder at his sailing master. "Very funny. It has to be an iceberg. I mean, what else can it be? Although... I've heard rumors of a continent of ice somewhere hereabouts; could this be it? How high would you say the wall is?"

Sweeney considered for a moment before looking over to the quartermaster, who shrugged his ignorance.

"I honestly don't know, Captain," he said at last. "Four hundred feet, at least. As for the other, a year or two ago some Russians made some noise about discovering the ice continent, but I don't know if the scientific people in London believe them. I also heard that a few American whaler captains claim to have set foot on the continent, but to my knowledge nobody has brought back proof."

"It could be the South Shetland Islands, sir," Lieutenant Hobbs said. "I saw a copy of the *Times* before we left Jamaica, and it said that Captain Edward Bransfield of HMS *Andromache* discovered the islands south of the Falklands that he thought were very close to the ice continent. Perhaps those islands are what we see before us."

Brewer looked again to the ice wall. "Mr. Sweeney?"

The sailing master shook his head. "If the South Shetlands are south of the Falklands, as Mr. Hobbs says, we're too far west for these to be them."

"So we're back to an iceberg."

"Or the ice continent itself," Mr. Greene added.

"I don't think so, sir," Sweeney said, shaking his head in disbelief, "I just don't think we're that far south."

Brewer turned. "Did you sail these waters with Captain Cook?"

"No, sir. He was in these waters during his second voyage. I didn't join him until his third."

Mr. Hobbs was still staring at the ice wall, and Brewer could see that he was trying hard to come to a decision about it.

"Something wrong, Lieutenant?" he asked him.

Hobbs was startled by his captain's voice. "Oh, no, sir," he said. "I was just wondering about this great monstrosity." He gestured at the wall. "If Mr. Sweeney says these aren't the South Shetlands, well, he would know our position better than I do. But, sir, don't you think that the islands might look just like this? I've never read a description of them, but islands this far south, and in such proximity to the ice continent, well, they would naturally be covered by a great deal of ice and snow, wouldn't you think?"

Brewer looked at the ice wall and considered his lieutenant's words. "What you say makes a good deal of sense. Given the climate hereabouts, I shouldn't wonder that ice and snow might actually disguise an island and fool some poor tar into thinking it's a huge iceberg."

He turned toward the wheel. "Mr. Sweeney, the one thing I know about icebergs is that they are bigger under the water than they are on top. Put the wheel over to starboard, if you please. I don't want to get too close to this thing." Sweeney did so, and Brewer regarded the ice wall. "I wish there were some way to preserve this image. I can't draw, and it's much too cold to paint."

"I know what you mean, Captain," Hobbs said. "This is beautiful."

"It is indeed, Mr. Hobbs." Brewer took one last look joining Mr. Sweeney at the wheel. "Mr. Sweeney," he said, "call me when the wind allows us to turn north again."

Two days later, he got the call.

CHAPTER EIGHT

They sailed north, feeling warmer with every mile. It seemed to Brewer that his ship fairly flew towards the warmth. He was on deck for practically every daylight hour, enjoying every minute of it.

Four days after they made the turn north, and forty-eight days after leaving Rio de Janeiro, they finally sighted the peaks of the Chilean cordillera. Two days later they reached their destination.

HMS *Phoebe* slid into the great semicircular bay, the shores of which held the trade town of Valparaiso. The Spanish had arrived in 1536. The first pier had only been built in 1810 by a wealthy merchant, and the modernization of the city had continued apace. The expansion of trade brought more wealth to this city than most of the ports in South America.

Phoebe exchanged salutes with the fort on the southern end of the bay then dropped anchor. The harbor was teeming with shipping from many nations, both warships and merchant shipping. The U.S. Navy was represented by the 74-gun *Franklin* and the frigate *Constellation*. Mr. Greene and Mr. Rivkins noted merchant shipping from no less than eighteen different nations. Their cataloging was interrupted by the lookout.

"Deck, there! There's a British sloop-of-war in the harbor!"

"Where away?" Greene answered.

He pointed toward the ship. "Off the port bow, sir, maybe three hundred yards."

Greene put a glass to his eye and tried to focus past all the shipping in between, finally making out the sloop. *Definitely flying British colors,* he thought. *About the same size as* Revenge.

"Can you make out her name?" he called.

The lookout strained, trying to make out the lettering under the sloop's stern window. Finally, he lowered his telescope and called down to the deck.

"Looks like *Blossom*, sir!"

Greene lowered his telescope and sighed. He turned and saw Midshipman Henry.

"Mr. Henry, my respects to the captain. Inform him we've sighted a British sloop-of-war in the harbor."

"Aye, sir!"

Mr. Sweeney stepped up beside the first lieutenant and stood there, staring at the sloop with his hands on his hips. Greene noticed the way he jutted out his jaw and was about to ask whether the master knew the ship when the lookout spoke up again.

"Signal from the sloop, sir!"

Mr. Dye, the signals midshipman, leapt to the shrouds with a glass and studied the signal.

"Our number, sir! Signal reads, *Captain come on board.* Shall I alert him, sir?"

"Yes, Mr. Dye, if you please. Be sure to give my respects."

"Aye, sir."

Dye leapt down and made his way below to the captain's cabin. The sentry announced him, and he was granted entry. He found the captain at his desk, writing.

"Yes, Mr. Dye?" Brewer asked.

The midshipman came to attention. "Mr. Greene's respects, sir. We've received a signal from a British sloop. Our number, and it reads 'Captain come on board.'"

"Very well," Brewer said. "Tell Mr. Greene I shall come up on deck."

"Aye aye, Captain!" The midshipman came to attention again and was gone. Brewer wondered about the signal as he picked up his hat and followed Dye to the deck.

He joined Greene and Sweeney. "What's going on, Benjamin?" he asked, as he nodded his thanks to Dye for the loan of his glass.

"We sighted a British sloop-of-war in the harbor, Captain. The lookout identified her as HMS *Blossom*. The sloop hoisted a signal with our number, ordering the captain to report on board."

Brewer put the glass to his eye and studied the sloop. "Anyone know this *Blossom*?"

Mr. Sweeney cleared his throat. "I do, Captain. Not the ship, per se, but I know her captain well enough. The *Blossom's* commanded by Frederick Edward Venables Vernon. I sailed with him in HMS *Bumblebee* during the wars. He's about thirty-two. Son of the Archbishop of York, grandson of the Marquis of Stafford and related by marriage to five earls. His political connections got him a promotion to post-captain at twenty-four, and they are the only reason he still retains command of a ship in His Majesty's navy. He is... very precise and fussy, and he doesn't like to be kept waiting."

That last remark made Brewer look to his sailing master, but Sweeney looked straight ahead at the shipping in the distance. Brewer handed the glass back to Mr. Dye.

"In that case, I better get ready. Mr. Dye, please acknowledge the signal. Mr. Rivkins, call away the gig. Mr. Greene, Mr. Sweeney, will you join me in my cabin?"

The captain led the way below without waiting for an acknowledgement. The officers fell into step behind him. The sentry held the door for them and closed it gently behind them.

"My coat and sword, Alfred," Brewer said to his waiting servant. He turned and sat down on the desk. "Mr. Sweeney, would you mind explaining yourself?"

Sweeney halted mid-step at his captain's demand and looked quickly to Greene, who stood off to the side and out of the way. Sweeney looked back at the captain.

"What do you mean, sir?" he asked.

"You know very well what I mean," Brewer said, aware of the edge that was creeping into his voice. "Since when do you talk about a King's officer like that, let alone a captain?" Sweeney stood silently, and Brewer sighed. "I presume you have a history with this man? You said you sailed with him."

Sweeney looked at his feet. "I apologize for any disrespect, Captain. Yes, you could say we have history, he and I, although I doubt he would deign to remember my name."

"What did you mean when you said his political connections were the only reason he retains command of a ship in His Majesty's navy?"

Sweeney looked up to see Brewer donning his coat, the diminutive Alfred standing beside him, the Captain's sword in his hand. He shook his head and took a deep breath.

"I was there when his friends at the Admiralty handed him command of *Bumblebee*, sir. He had just been promoted to post-captain, although in my opinion he had done nothing to earn it. We were in the Caribbean at the time, and the admiral allowed him to take the ship out for a short training cruise, much like you were allowed to take *Revenge* out, sir. I was the master. We had been at sea for three days, sir, when the weather threatened to close in. We were in for a storm, and a bad one. Within two hours, I became convinced that we were sailing into a hurricane. I told the captain of my fears, and he rebuffed me. Told me he knew better than I did, and that we would stay on course for Barbados. The first lieutenant came on deck, took one look at the gathering clouds, and went to the captain. The captain ignored him as well, finally shouting the man down and throwing him out of his cabin." It wasn't but a few hours later that the storm broke on us. Only then Captain Vernon tried to change course, but it was too late, and we all knew it."

"My God," Greene whispered. "What happened?"

"The ship broke up and foundered," Sweeney said very matter-of-factly. "The first lieutenant was swept overboard, just like Captain Norman was, sir. I couldn't reach him, couldn't save him..." Sweeney had to pause to gather himself. "We had to abandon ship. The captain was nowhere to be found; we thought he had been swept overboard as well. We took to one of the boats, convinced that our lives would be counted in hours, if not minutes. Fortunately for us, that storm turned out to be one of the fastest moving storms I'd ever seen. We survived and were rescued by a merchantman who took us back to Port Royal. When we were put ashore, who do you suppose was there to greet us but Captain Vernon himself.

"We tried to ignore him, but he followed us to a pub and dared to try to sit with us! After what he did, all those good men he killed... the first lieutenant... God, I'll remember his face as the wave took him as long as I live. Vernon actually had the nerve to blame the loss of the ship on the first lieutenant! That was too much for me. I wrote a report and got the quartermaster's mate, who was in the boat with me, to attest that it was correct in every respect. The admiral read it and brought Vernon in for questioning. The fool contradicted himself in front of the admiral and totally fell on his face! The admiral—it wasn't Lord Hornblower, Captain—wrote a damning report to the Admiralty, recommending that Vernon be discharged from the navy for gross incompetence. His political and family connections forestalled that, and after a few months on the beach, he was given *Blossom* and sent to the South American squadron."

"Well," Brewer said as Alfred buckled on his sword, "I'll be sure not to invite him to dinner. You have the ship, Mr. Greene."

He led them back up on deck. Before he stepped down to the gig, he patted his sailing master on the arm.

Brewer stepped up to the deck of HMS *Blossom* to be greeted by a single lieutenant.

“Sir,” he said as he saluted, “I am David Berry, first lieutenant of HMS *Blossom*.”

Brewer returned the salute. “Captain William Brewer, HMS *Phoebe*.”

“If you will please follow me,” Berry said, “I’ll take you to Captain Vernon.”

Brewer followed the lieutenant below deck and aft, remembering to bend low to avoid striking his head. They found Vernon seated beneath the sloop’s stern windows, sipping a glass of wine. When the captain set his glass down and rose, Brewer saw he measured barely 5 feet, 5 inches in height; he could stand erect despite the low ceilings on the sloop. He was thin and carried himself with the air of one born to privilege, used to doing what he pleased and not being questioned about it. Brewer took an instant dislike to him.

“Sir,” Berry said to his captain, “may I present Captain William Brewer of His Majesty’s frigate *Phoebe*? Captain Brewer, may I present your host, Captain Frederick Vernon of HMS *Blossom*.”

“Sir!” Brewer came to attention. Vernon inclined his head in acknowledgement and shook hands with his guest.

“Please, Captain, sit down,” he said. “Would you care for a glass of wine? Simpkins, a glass for the captain. Thank you. Now, sir, tell me what you are doing in Valparaiso.”

“We were seconded from the West Indies Squadron to the South American. In accordance with our orders, we sailed from Port Royal to Rio de Janeiro to report to Commodore Hardy. When we arrived at Rio, we did not find the commodore there, so I reported to the British Consul. He delivered a letter from the commodore that ordered me to sail for Valparaiso and meet him here. So, here I am."

Vernon face bore a grim smile. "I'm afraid you must endure history repeating itself, Captain, for, once again, the commodore is not here, and I, too, have a letter from him to you."

He reached inside his coat and pulled out a letter, which he handed to Brewer.

"The commodore was ordered to return to the Atlantic," Vernon said. "He sailed for Rio about three weeks ago." He took a sip of his wine before gesturing to Brewer. "Yes, yes, Captain, by all means, open it."

Brewer did so and extracted a letter. He opened it and scanned it quickly. "I am ordered back to Rio with all speed."

Vernon sighed. "Yes, I thought it might say that. The Admiralty seem quite convinced that the fighting in the Pacific is all but over, and the main theatre of operations will be the Atlantic coast. However, Captain, I have a task for you before you leave. I want you to take *Phoebe* north and patrol the waters off Peru for a few days before you make your way back to the Atlantic."

"Sir, don't you think it would be best if I caught up with the commodore as soon as possible?"

"What I think, sir," Vernon raised his voice almost to a shout, "is that it would be better for you to obey the orders of those superior to you! That is, if you wish to continue as a King's officer."

Brewer sat perfectly still, struggling with all his might to keep control of his tongue and keep his mouth shut. He slowly and purposefully refolded the commodore's letter and put it in his coat pocket. "Captain Vernon," he said, slowly and carefully, "I should like those orders in writing, if you please."

Vernon sat back and sipped his wine again, basking in his victory. "Of course, Captain, of course. I wouldn't have it any other way."

Vernon rose and went to his desk. In ten minutes he had written and signed the document ordering Brewer to take his frigate north to ensure there was no danger either to British interests or to the lives of British citizens. The orders did not specify the amount of time Brewer was expected to remain in Peruvian waters, but as he left Vernon's cabin Brewer was determined to measure the time in hours, if not minutes.

Brewer returned to his ship and went directly to his cabin upon arriving. He was angry, and he didn't want to chance a slip of his tongue revealing this to the crew. He paced back and forth in his day room. He had not felt this way since his disastrous interview with Admiral Freemantle aboard HMS *Victory* at Gibraltar nearly two years ago. Captain Bush had talked him down that day. The sound of the ship's bell made him aware that he had been pacing for over an hour. He stopped and rubbed his eyes, feeling vaguely foolish for acting as he had.

"Alfred!" he called.

The servant appeared instantly. Brewer wondered how long he had been waiting by the door, but decided against asking.

"Do we have any coffee?" he asked. "Excellent. Make it for three, please. Pass the word for Mr. Greene and Mr. Sweeney."

Alfred bowed and withdrew. Brewer stretched and allowed his anger and embarrassment to drain away from him. His mood lightened immediately, and he sat beneath the stern windows and waited for his guests. In short order there was a knock at the door and his two officers were admitted. Brewer rose and greeted them, then led the way to the day room. They had barely taken their seats when Alfred arrived bearing three steaming cups on his silver platter.

"That man could earn thousands of pounds just making coffee in London," Greene said.

"Don't even suggest such a thing, Benjamin, or I'll have you flogged," Brewer said morosely. "Mr. Sweeney, you'll be pleased to know that your old captain is just the same as he always was and has learned no manners since you left him."

Sweeney heaved a sigh. "I'm sorry for that, Captain."

"What did he say, sir?" Greene asked.

Brewer pulled the commodore's letter from his pocket and handed it to his premier. "He had this letter for me from the commodore, ordering us back to Rio."

Greene began to read the letter, but Sweeney looked at his captain as though he was waiting for the other shoe to drop. Brewer smiled.

"Are you waiting for something, Mr. Sweeney?" he asked.

"Well, Captain," the sailing master said, "I'm just waiting for you to tell us the rest of the story."

The captain's brow rose. "And what makes you think you there is a 'rest of the story'?"

Sweeney shrugged. "There usually is."

Brewer pulled Vernon's orders from his pocket.

"What are those, sir?" Greene asked, as he handed the commodore's letter to Sweeney.

"Orders directing us to patrol off the coast of Peru before returning to the Atlantic."

Sweeney sat back in his seat and shook his head.

Brewer handed the orders to Greene. "How soon can we be ready to sail, Mr. Greene?"

"Well, sir," Greene said as he perused the orders, "there's a problem with that."

"What kind of problem?" the captain asked.

"It seems that there is no ship's bread in Valparaiso, sir."

"None at all?" Brewer was shocked.

"No, sir," Greene said. "We received the word while you were aboard *Blossom*. We're at the end of the queue for it. It may be a month before we can sail."

Brewer drew a long, deep breath and sat back before letting it out slowly. "Let's use the time as best we can. Benjamin, make sure we complete any repairs. I'll write a letter to Captain Vernon stating that we'll sail as soon as the bread crisis is resolved. Have Mr. Hobbs take it over to *Blossom* tomorrow."

Greene smiled. "Aye, sir. In the meantime, I shall arrange for a supply of bread from shore until our ship's bread can be obtained."

Three days later, the captain and Doctor Spinelli were trying their best to ignore the sweltering heat by playing chess. Neither was particularly able to concentrate, and the knock at the cabin door came as a relief to both of them.

"Enter," Brewer called.

Mr. Tyler was admitted by the sentry. "Begging your pardon, sir, but Mr. Peters sends his respects. He says there's a boat approaching. It appears to be from the American seventy-four."

"Really?" Brewer asked as he leaned back in his chair. He looked to the doctor, only to find him to be as surprised as he was. "Well, bring the messenger down when he arrives, Mr. Tyler."

"Aye, sir." The midshipman came to attention and left the room.

"Well," Brewer said again as he studied the board with renewed interest. He was disgusted to see that his attention had wandered enough to allow the doctor to gain the upper hand once again. "What do you suppose this means, Adam?"

The doctor moved a knight. "Time will tell, I'm sure. It probably means you get to go to another dinner party while the rest of us have to stay here and eat salt pork."

"Now, now, Doctor," Brewer scolded as he took the knight with a bishop, "jealousy does not become you."

Ten minutes later, Tyler was back with an American lieutenant. Brewer rose.

"Captain Brewer," Tyler said, "may I introduce Lieutenant David Farragut of the USS *Franklin*." Farragut snapped to attention.

"As you were, Lieutenant," Brewer said. "Allow me to present our ship's surgeon, Dr. Spinelli. What may I do for you?"

Farragut nodded to the doctor before turning back to his host. "Captain, I bring an invitation for you and your first officer to dine aboard *Franklin* with Admiral Hezekiah Albritton at the turn of the first dog watch this evening." He pulled a watch from his pocket. "I make it to be now going on 3 bells."

Brewer automatically pulled his watch out as well and confirmed the time. "Thank you, Lieutenant. Please tell your admiral that we gladly accept his kind invitation. Mr. Tyler."

Farragut came to attention again and followed Tyler out of the cabin. Spinelli watched them go and turned again, to see a strange look on his captain's face.

"Something amiss, Captain?"

Brewer looked at his surgeon. "Do you not recognize the name, Doctor? During our last war with the Americans, Albritton commanded the frigate *Constitution* and caused us a lot of trouble. He beat several of our frigates in single combat and took a score or more of our ships as prizes. He must have been a captain then. Can you excuse me, please, Adam? I have some work to do before the dinner party you so rightly predicted. Ask the sentry to pass the word for Mr. Greene, would you please?"

"Of course," Spinelli said as he rose. He nodded to his friend and went his way.

Lieutenant Greene came in. "You sent for me, sir?"

"Yes, Benjamin. It seems you and I have been invited to have dinner aboard the USS *Franklin* with none other than Hezekiah Albritton."

"Truly?" Greene said, his eyes lighting up. "Albritton himself? His cruises during the last American war made him a legend, even in our navy."

"The very same. We are to be there by the turn of the first dog watch; we don't want to keep Admiral Albritton waiting. Your best uniform, if you please, Benjamin. Warn Mac to have the gig's crew turned out smartly."

"Aye, sir. So he's an admiral now, is he? That's hardly a surprise."

The time flew by, and before he knew it, Brewer found himself seated in the stern sheets of the gig beside Mr.

Greene, listening to Mac give orders to the crew. The waters in the bay were calm, and the *Franklin* slowly grew in front of them. She was a big 74-gun line of battle ship, neat and clean and beautiful.

As soon as they were safely aboard, the British officers were met by Lieutenant Farragut, who introduced them to his captain.

"Captain Brewer, may I present Captain Washington of the USS *Franklin*? Captain Washington, this is Captain Brewer of HMS *Phoebe*."

The two officers saluted.

"A pleasure to make your acquaintance, sir," Washington said as the two shook hands.

"The pleasure is mine, sir," Brewer said. "May I present my first officer, Lieutenant Greene?"

"A pleasure, Lieutenant." The two saluted. "Now, if you gentlemen will follow me?"

They made their way aft, Brewer walking beside Washington, with Greene and Farragut two steps behind.

"Pardon me, Captain," Brewer said as they walked, "but would you be any relation to the president?"

"Unfortunately, no. I saw him once, when I attended his first inauguration in New York. For such a big man—he was six feet, four inches tall, and every inch of it muscle—he was very soft-spoken. I was about two-thirds of the way back in the crowd, and I could barely hear him take the oath or make his speech."

"I met the man who was his secretary during those years, and he said the president was a man of very forceful personality, " Brewer replied.

"I can well believe it, seeing what he managed to accomplish." Washington answered. They climbed the companionway steps to the quarterdeck, and Washington led them to the great cabin under the poop. "Here we are," he said as he opened the door and led them inside.

The great cabin was considerably bigger even than the captain's cabin on *Defiant*, and richly decorated. Washington led the British officers past a dinner table that displayed a fine china pattern set for four, into the admiral's day cabin. Brewer noticed that they had lost Lieutenant Farragut somewhere along the way. The admiral rose from his seat beneath the great stern windows, several of which were open to allow the sea breeze to cool the room.

"Sir," Washington began the introductions, "may I present Captain Brewer of His Britannic Majesty's frigate *Phoebe*, and his first officer, Lieutenant Greene? Gentlemen, this is your host, Admiral Hezekiah Albritton, commander of the South American squadron of the United States Navy."

Brewer studied the man before him. Albritton was an inch or so taller than Brewer, and though his body showed the usual signs of aging—such as the slight paunch in the middle—Brewer could easily see the barrel-chested, muscular figure of his younger years beneath. His dark hair was going grey at the temples, giving him a rather distinguished look, and his eyes were dark, close-set and piercing. His nose was hooked, with a great bridge set in it like the Duke of Wellington's. His voice was deep and commanding.

"Please, be seated, gentlemen. Dinner will be served shortly. Newby!"

A servant appeared at the door.

"Drinks for our guests."

"Aye, sir."

They were no sooner seated than the faithful Newby appeared and held a silver platter low so they could take their drinks. He withdrew afterward without a sound.

"Your health, Captain." Albritton raised his glass and toasted his guests. Brewer returned the compliment and inhaled over the glass before taking a sip. He was surprised by the taste.

"Excuse me, Admiral," he said, "but isn't this bourbon?"

"Yes, sir, the best Kentucky has to offer. I take it this is a rarity for an Englishman?"

"Yes, sir. I've only had it once before," Brewer said. "I was first lieutenant on HMS *Defiant* when she stopped off at Boston. I went ashore to find a bookstore. I wanted to purchase a new biography of your President Washington that I'd heard about, and in the store I met a kindly old man. We struck up a conversation, and he invited me back to his inn for supper. That's where I first tasted bourbon."

"Now, there's a coincidence for you," Albritton said. "I'm from Boston. May I ask the name of the old man? I wonder if I know him."

Brewer smiled over his glass. "John Adams."

"The *President*?" Washington asked.

"The same. He told me a great deal about your first president, General George Washington. I wish I could have known him."

Albritton smiled. "As it happens, I know President Adams well. He lives in Quincy, just south of the city, but he often comes to town for books or just to visit with folks in the local taverns."

"An interesting man," Brewer said. "I hope one day to return and visit with him again."

"You won't be sorry for it," Albritton agreed. "Tell me a little about your career, Captain. Did you fight in the wars?"

"Against the French, yes, sir, but not against your navy. After the wars, I spent a year on St. Helena as aide and secretary to Governor Horatio Lord Hornblower. Then it was a cruise in the Mediterranean to fight the Barbary Pirates. After that, I was sent to the Caribbean, and now here I am."

Albritton set his drink down and looked at Brewer. "Captain, it seems we have much in common, you and I. You were on St. Helena? So I suppose you made Bonaparte's acquaintance? I met him in 1803 when my ship docked at Boulogne. He was still First Consul then. His army was camped outside the city, and he sent an invitation for me and my first officer to dine with him." He shook his head at the memory. "The most extraordinary night of my life. Then you said you fought the Barbary Pirates? I was there two different times, first in 1801 and then again in 1815. The second time I was sent home with a head wound and another in my thigh. That one still bothers me occasionally. Well, hopefully, they finally learned their lesson."

Brewer raised his glass. "Here's hoping."

Albritton's brow furled as a memory struck him. "Brewer? You wouldn't happen to be the one who killed the pirate El Diabolito and sank his ship, would you?"

"Yes," Greene spoke up with a smile on his face, "he would." Brewer shot him a look, which Albritton ignored.

"I owed him," Brewer said. "He ambushed my ship when I first arrived in the Caribbean."

"Damn shame that happened." Albritton shook his head sadly. "Good riddance, say I; but I did hope to be the one to put him in the grave."

"Tell me, Admiral," Brewer said, "have you been in these waters long?"

"Nearly a year, I think. Why do you ask?"

"I was wondering if you had had the pleasure of meeting Admiral Cochrane?"

The Admiral set his drink down and sat back. Brewer thought the older man's defenses had gone up. "As a matter of fact, I have. The last time was three weeks ago in Peru. Why do you ask?"

"I had some dealings with him in the Caribbean last year," Brewer said. "He tried to sink my ship in retaliation for El Diabolito. It is only through the timely arrival of Lord Hornblower with two frigates that I am able to sit before you today."

"So that's where he was," Albritton muttered as he shared a look with Washington. "He disappeared for several months; I always wondered where he went to. Now rumors are rife that he will leave O'Higgins' service to take over the navy of Brazil. It seems that Dom Pedro pays better."

"I don't look forward to meeting him again," Brewer said.

Just then Newby appeared and announced that dinner was served. The four men made their way to the table; Brewer was given the place on the admiral's right.

"I will confess that I have heard your name, Captain Brewer," Albritton said, "and when I heard that you might be in command of the British frigate, I did not want to miss the opportunity of meeting you."

"Thank you for the invitation, Admiral," Brewer said. "Lieutenant Greene and I are grateful for the chance to make your acquaintance as well. Your exploits command the respect of every naval officer."

The stewards appeared with a feast. Roast fowl was followed by a platter of mutton chops, fresh broccoli, carrots, fresh bread with butter and marmalade, tarts and shepherd's pie, with apple pie for desert. The four men ate heartily, and the conversation grew animated as they discussed old campaigns and former ships. Mr. Greene looked almost sheepish as he claimed the last slice of the apple pie. His companions chuckled.

"Please, Lieutenant, help yourself," Albritton said. "Newby! We'll have cigars and brandy in the day room."

"Aye, sir," the servant replied as the four officers stood from the table.

Albritton led his guests aft to seats under the stern windows. Newby passed out the brandy and cigars, which were fresh and wonderfully flavorful. Brewer began to suspect that the tobacco trade accounted for a significant portion of the shipping he'd previously seen.

"Tell me, Admiral," Brewer said after he had puffed his cigar into life, "what am I likely to find when I head north? I have been ordered to patrol the waters off Peru before returning to the Atlantic."

Albritton shrugged. "Hard to say. There are still many privateers operating in the area, even though Peru has won its independence from Spain. Most of the Peruvian Navy, such as it is, is made up of vessels taken from the Spanish by Cochrane back in the days when O'Higgins helped them win the war. Now the Peruvians find themselves hemmed in by

Gran Colombia to their north, Brazil to their west, and Chile to their south. They're feeling out their place in the world."

Brewer thought for a moment. "Have they interfered with any foreign trade or citizens?"

The Admiral shook his head. "Only if by foreign trade you mean Spain's efforts to reclaim former territories. The Peruvians seem determined to interfere with those efforts."

Albritton drained his glass and rose, so Brewer followed suit. The two men shook hands.

"It has been an honor to make your acquaintance, Captain," the Admiral said warmly. "And yours as well, Lieutenant. I hope we shall meet again in the Atlantic."

"When that happens, sir," Brewer said, "you must dine with us on *Phoebe*. I have an excellent chef."

"I look forward to it, Captain." The Admiral led the way to the cabin door. "Captain Washington will see you to the entry port. Good luck, gentlemen, and safe journeys."

CHAPTER NINE

Day blended into day as HMS *Phoebe* endured her imprisonment in the gilded cage that was Valparaiso. Soon Brewer began to notice an increase in the number of men who were brought before him for relatively minor infractions, followed a few days later by some slightly more serious ones. It was clear that the men were becoming bored and were getting themselves into trouble. He had to figure out a way to stem the tide before he had a serious problem on his hands.

He sat at his desk trying to work through his problem by describing it in a letter to Lord Hornblower. Suddenly, Alfred —who had come to know him so well—appeared at his side with a cup of steaming hot coffee.

"I thought you might need one just about now, sir," he said.

"Thank you, Alfred," Brewer said as he inhaled the rich aroma. He blew on the lip of the cup and took a sip. He leaned back in his chair and sighed. "You know, I *was* just about to call you and ask for a cup."

Alfred nodded and turned back to his pantry. Brewer recognized it as a favorite gesture of his, used only when they were alone, and an idea began to form in his mind.

"Alfred," he called, and the servant reappeared in the doorway. "Sit down, if you please. I have a question to ask you."

"How may I assist you, sir?" the servant asked as he sat on the other side of the desk.

"It's funny that you should ask, Alfred, because I believe I do need your assistance. You are aware that we are stuck here in this port by the lack of ship's bread. Now the men are becoming bored, and as a result they are getting into trouble. We need to engage them in something, and that is where you might be of service."

"Shall I teach them how to make coffee?"

Brewer smiled. "No, actually I was hoping you would teach them to fight."

The diminutive servant was very still, looking at his captain and saying nothing.

"I know this is not *Revenge*," Brewer hurried on, "but I need you to do the same thing you did then with this crew. I am convinced, that, without your training, the crew would not have fought as well as they did against the pirates. Very probably, El Diabolito and Cofrese would be alive right now, and we should be dead." Brewer leaned forward intently. "I do not have the same confidence in this crew as I had with that of the *Revenge*," he said bluntly. "They need to be honed to a fine edge, and I am asking you to teach them as you did the crew of our last ship. Make no mistake, I am not *ordering* you to give them lessons. I know how personal this is for you. If you refuse, the gunner and the bosun will teach them, and I will think nothing less of you. You proved yourself in my eyes long ago."

He sat back in his chair and let Alfred think about it. The little man's eyes held his for a few moments before closing. When they opened again, he turned his head and looked out through the stern windows before turning back to the captain. When he did, Brewer thought there was a different look in his eyes.

"Will you excuse me for a moment, sir?" he asked.

"Of course, Alfred," Brewer replied. He watched as the servant rose and left the cabin. He was back three minutes later. In his hand he held two wooden swords, nothing more than three-foot-long poles with a circle of wood attached six inches from one end, to simulate a hilt.

"While you were gone for your wedding," Alfred explained as he handed the 'sword' to his captain, "I asked the carpenter on *Revenge* to make me five sets of these practice swords. They are the same weight as a real sword, so practice can be as realistic as possible."

"Alfred," Brewer said as he tested it, "this was well thought out." He looked to the servant, who was holding the other instrument in his hand and smiling. "When do we start, sir?"

The next morning Brewer passed the word for Lieutenant Rivkins.

"You sent for me, sir?" the Lieutenant said when he arrived.

"Yes, Mr. Rivkins. I want you to assemble your division before the foremast for training."

"Training, sir? Aye, sir."

"Ten minutes, Mr. Rivkins."

"Aye, sir."

Ten minutes later, Brewer and Alfred were waiting on deck as Rivkins' division gathered. The Lieutenant watched and counted, and finally turned to the captain. "All present and accounted for, sir."

"Thank you, Lieutenant." Brewer stepped forward and addressed the men. "Men, I am willing to grant an extra ration of grog for the best swordsman here. Who is it?"

The men looked to each other and then to their lieutenant, who was staring at the captain.

"How shall we know who is best, sir?" he asked.

"By combat, of course," Brewer replied.

"Against you, sir?" one of the hands spoke up.

"No," the Captain said. "Against him." He motioned to Alfred, standing beside him.

Murmuring began at once amongst Rivkins' men, and Brewer smiled. He was well aware of the rumors that had been flying around the lower decks about how Alfred had killed the pirate Roberto Cofrese, and now they were debating whether or not it was really true. For his part, Alfred stood there, beside his captain, hands clasped behind his back, and waited for an opponent.

Finally, a big man pushed his way to the front and stepped forward.

"I accept the challenge, sir," he said.

"What's your name?" Brewer asked.

"They call me Jersey, sir."

"Best be careful, Jersey," the tar next to him whispered loudly. "You know what we heard about that bloke."

"C'mon," Jersey said disdainfully "he's barely bigger than a sword!"

"Step forward, Jersey," Brewer called. He picked up two of Alfred's practice swords and handed one to each man.

"Toy swords, sir?" Jersey said. "Why not the real thing?"

"Because I don't want him to kill you today," Brewer said with a smile.

Jersey stared at his captain as though he'd grown a second head before taking his position ten feet in front of Alfred.

"Ready?" Brewer asked. "Begin!"

Jersey raised his sword and charged his smaller opponent with a great yell. He slashed wildly at Alfred's head. Alfred easily ducked beneath the attack and stabbed Jersey in the chest with his sword's blunt end.

"See, Jersey?" Brewer said. "You're dead."

"Dumb luck, that's all," he said. He retreated to his starting point and readied for another go. This time he charged in and tried to take Alfred's sword from his hand. The smaller man parried two thrusts before dodging to his left and bringing his wooden blade down hard on his opponent's wrist. Jersey howled in pain as his sword dropped to the deck.

"You're not in some tavern brawl," Alfred said to him. "You charge in like that and you're only running to an early grave. Now, are you ready to listen?"

Jersey stared at him, holding his injured wrist and saying nothing.

Alfred stepped toward him and spoke so all could hear. "You've got to use your strengths. Jersey, you want to try to work in close to your opponent and pin his sword so you can get hold of him and use your strength against him. Now pick up your sword and we'll try it again. Slowly."

Jersey took his place again and advanced slowly this time. On the second thrust, he stepped in close when Alfred parried and managed to grab him by the front of the shirt and lift him from the deck.

"Oh," he crowed, "like this, you mean?"

"Just so," Alfred gasped. Suddenly he kicked Jersey in the groin. The big man howled in pain, letting Alfred go and dropping to the deck in pain. Alfred walked up to him and laid his sword on his opponent's neck.

"You're next," Alfred said as he picked up Jersey's sword and tossed it to another man. The man reluctantly stepped forward and took his position. This time, when the captain said "Begin", Alfred produced a pistol from behind his back, pointed it at the man and pulled the trigger. The click from the empty pan seemed to echo across the deck. Alfred smiled at his opponent's outrage.

"That's not fair!" the man raged.

"You're not in some bloody duel, mate," Alfred said loudly. "There are no rules. The only thing that matters is that you kill your opponent before he kills you. Use any advantage at hand to win. The captain has asked me to instruct you in the use of the sword. I want nine men to step forward."

When the men hesitated a moment, Rivkins stepped forward.

"You two," Rivkins said, pointing at two men in the front of the crowd and nodding to Jersey, still lying on the deck, "drag this boastful mess out of the way. I shall be your first volunteer, sir."

"You, Mr. Rivkins?" one of the men asked.

"Have you ever been in a boarding action, Reese?" Rivkins asked the man. "No? Well, I have, in the Mediterranean with the captain when he was a lieutenant. We barely escaped with our lives. I wish I knew then what I've seen Alfred do already this morning. There's one thing I know: when we board and enemy ship, I want the man who has my back to know what he's doing. Eight more, step up now. That includes you, Reese."

Brewer smiled and turned to his servant. "I leave this in your capable hands, sir." He turned to the men. "Gentlemen, I strongly urge you to listen to what he has to say. I went through these same lessons myself on our last ship, and I can tell you it has saved my life more than once."

He went aft, smiling as he listened to Alfred begin the training he hoped would turn his crew into a fighting machine to be feared.

Two weeks later, thirty-seven days after entering the harbor, HMS *Phoebe* was finally able to sail out of it. The bread crisis had been resolved, and Brewer took his ship northwards to complete the pointless sideshow Captain Vernon had imposed upon him. His men were anxious to be free of the land in order to hunt for prizes.

On the morning of the second day at sea Brewer came up on deck to a beautiful morning with the warmth of a rising sun on his face and a stiff breeze driving them northwards. Mr. Greene, who had the watch, came over to greet him.

"Good morning, Captain," he greeted his captain with a salute.

"Good morning," Brewer returned. "Anything to report?"

"Mr. Sweeney said he doesn't like the look of the sky ahead," Greene said. Brewer turned and thought he could just make out some dark clouds above the horizon. Greene continued, "He thinks we'd better prepare for a strong squall at least, and perhaps a gale storm."

"Is that all?" Brewer asked as he studied the set of their sail.

"Oh, ah," Greene added. "Mac had to take four men to the sickbay."

"What? Why?"

"Well, sir," Greene had to look at the deck to regain his composure, "it seems Alfred was instructing the men of Mr. Hobbs' division when he began teaching them how to deal with more than one adversary simultaneously. Rather than watching and learning, there was a group who heckled their comrades who lost to Alfred, and remarks were made about Alfred's stature."

"Oh, no," Brewer whispered. He closed his eyes, knowing what was coming.

"Exactly, sir."

Brewer sighed. "Go on."

"It seems Alfred gave four of the wooden swords to four of the hecklers, keeping the last for himself." Greene shrugged. "You can imagine what followed."

"Yes, but tell me anyway."

Greene shrugged. "The biggest talker of the group has a broken rib and a rather large lump on the side of his skull. A second has a broken arm, while the third may have a broken femur—Dr. Spinelli isn't sure about that one yet. The fourth dropped his sword and ran. All are covered with bruises."

Brewer shook his head. "Why didn't Mac stop him?"

Greene shrugged again. "Don't know, sir, but I imagine he didn't want to get hit."

"Well, what did Alfred say?"

Greene smiled. "He picked up the sword that had been thrown down and called the coward back. He said to him and the group, 'The next man who runs, in practice or in battle, I swear I'll bend him over the nearest gun and whip him with this (he held up the sword) like he was a disobedient son.' And he threw the sword at the coward and made him his practice dummy for the remainder of the lesson."

Brewer grunted and looked at the sails again, trying but failing to suppress a smile of his own. "Well," he said, "at least it was only four."

Mr. Sweeney joined them now, and Brewer nodded at the horizon to the north.

"How bad do you think it will be?"

"Nothing like we endured rounding the Horn, Captain, but I guess we are in for a blow."

Brewer looked at the horizon and felt a knot beginning to grow in the pit of his stomach. He had learned by now to trust Mr. Sweeney's "guesses" when it came to the weather.

"Benjamin," he said, "make sure everything is tired down securely."

"Aye, sir."

He turned to Sweeney. "How long do we have?"

The sailing master pursed his lips and squinted at the horizon as he ran the calculations in his head. "We'll be in it before the end of the day."

As it was, Mr. Sweeney's estimate proved generous. Six bells of the afternoon watch saw them enter the leading edge of the squall. Brewer reduced sail and went below to ride it out.

HMS *Phoebe* fought her way north through the squall for three straight days. The cloud cover made the daily sightings impossible, so, just to be safe, on the morning of the second day Brewer altered their course three points to port. He knew the island of San Lorenzo was out there somewhere to the north, and he wanted to make sure they passed it to the west.

The weather finally broke at about two bells on the forenoon watch of the morning of the fourth day. As soon as he noticed the sun shining on the sea, Brewer left his cabin and went up on deck. The sea breeze was delicious on his face, and the sun was busily drying the crew out after the soaking they had endured. Brewer was just about to ask Mr. Sweeney about their position when the lookout made himself heard.

"Land ho!"

"Where away?" Brewer asked as he nodded his thanks to a midshipman for handing him a glass.

The lookout pointed. "Off the starboard bow, sir!"

He met Mr. Sweeney at the starboard rail and put the telescope to his eye. He quickly spotted the trace of brown upon the blue of the sea, just under the horizon.

He lowered his telescope and turned to the sailing master. "What do you think, Mr. Sweeney?"

"Captain, that can only be the northern tip of San Lorenzo," Sweeney said. He looked skyward. "More than three hours until the noon reading. Unless, of course, you want to head east and see if we run into Callao."

Brewer considered for a moment before deciding the sailing master's idea was a good one. He was just about to issue the order when the lookout cried out again.

"Sail ho!"

"Where away?" Brewer asked.

"Four points off the port bow, sir!"

"Pass the word for Mr. Greene," Brewer said. "I'm going forward for a better look."

"Aye, sir," the sailing master answered.

Brewer turned to go and found himself face to face with his first lieutenant.

Greene hastily saluted. "Pardon me, Captain. You sent for me, sir?"

"Yes, Mr. Greene. Follow me."

The two men made their way forward, Brewer explaining the situation as they went. A midshipman handed Greene a telescope when they arrived, and both studied the strange sail. Brewer lowered his glass and frowned.

"Is it me," he muttered, "or is something wrong here?"

Greene lowered his glass. "What do you mean, sir?"

Brewer ignored him, instead frowning at the speck of white on the horizon. He looked up to the foretop.

"Lookout!" he cried. "Report on the sail approaching! What do you see?"

The lookout studied the horizon for a full minute before lowering his telescope and looking down to his captain.

"Sir! Looks like two sails now!"

"I knew it!" Brewer turned back to the rail and studied the horizon. "Looks like we'll run right into them if we hold this course. I love it when the prey comes to you."

"Sir!" It was the lookout again. "I can see it better now, sir! There're definitely more than two ships, sir. The closest one looks like a brig!"

Brewer turned and looked forward.

"Benjamin," he said softly, "kindly pass the word for the midshipman of the watch, if you please."

"Aye, sir," Greene said. He went aft on his mission.

"You sent for me, sir?" Mr. Lee said as he saluted.

"Yes, Mr. Lee. I want a second set of eyes on the sail ahead. Get a glass and take your station at the foretop. Take Skimpy with you as a runner."

"Aye, sir! Come along, Skimpy!"

Brewer took one final look forward before returning to the quarterdeck. Mr. Sweeney was waiting for him, along with the quartermaster and his mates.

"Call the hands, Mr. Sweeney," Brewer said. "Make sail."

"Aye, sir."

HMS *Phoebe* came alive with activity. The hands jumped to the shrouds and climbed for the yards. Canvas obscured the sky, and *Phoebe* leapt forward.

Mr. Greene approached. "Awaiting orders, sir."

"Thank you, Mr. Greene." Brewer thought for a moment. "I'm concerned about what we are getting into, Benjamin. There are at least three ships up ahead, with one possibly a brig."

"You're thinking she's a privateer?" Greene asked. "Or a pirate?"

Brewer shrugged. "Good possibility. I'm hoping Skimpy will show up any minute with the answer."

He looked back over the starboard quarter at the rapidly fading island of San Lorenzo. His attention was drawn forward again by the sound of a child's bare feet running on his deck. He turned in time to see young Skimpy skid to a halt three feet in front of him.

"Captain, sir," he gasped as he tried to salute, "the lookout says there's *four* ships out there! The brig's flying a strange flag, and there's two luggers with him. But sir, the fourth ship looks like an English whaler!"

Brewer's eyes snapped forward at that. He rushed to the rail and snapped the glass to his eye. He lowered it and looked at Skimpy.

"The whaler's at the rear of the formation?"

"Farthest away from us," the boy said, still gasping for air. "Yes, sir."

He looked once more, but couldn't see what he wanted. He snapped the glass shut in frustration.

"I'm going forward," he called over his shoulder to Greene. "Come along, Skimpy."

"Aye, sir!" The boy trotted forward after his captain. He had nearly caught up with him when they neared the foremast. He was surprised to see his captain mount the mizzen shrouds and climb for the foretop.

"Are you coming, Skimpy?" Brewer called. Skimpy was standing on the deck staring up at his captain. He smiled and reached for the shrouds and began climbing.

Skimpy's surprise at the captain's actions was nothing compared to the lookout's reaction when he realized it was the captain himself who was coming over the foretop railing.

"Captain?" he said.

"Easy, Christian, easy," Brewer said as he moved into a place beside the lookout. He took his glass from where he had slung it over his shoulder and put it to his eye. "Report, Mr. Christian."

"Captain, we have a brig and two luggers between us, and what appears to be a captured English whaler. The brig is flying a flag that's strange to me, the other ships aren't flying any flags at all. About two minutes ago, it looked like they split into two groups. The brig and one lugger are turning toward us, while the other lugger and the whaler are now heading due east for the coast."

Everything Brewer saw confirmed his lookout's report. The brig and one lugger were heading almost due south while the other two ships had turned due east and were crowding on sail. He lowered the glass and thought for a moment.

"Skimpy," he said, "I want you to run to the quarterdeck. My compliments to Mr. Greene, and would he please meet me at the long nines? Go on, now."

"Aye, sir!"

"Christian, keep your eye on that whaler. I want to know if she changes course. I'll send Skimpy back to be your runner."

"Aye, sir."

Brewer made his way down from the tops, his feet touching the deck just in time to greet his first lieutenant.

He led Greene to the bow chasers.

"The brig and one lugger are trying to keep us busy while the other lugger gets the whaler safely to the shore. We'll be on them in less than an hour, I should think. As soon as you are in range, I want you to open up on the two in front of us with the long nines. Keep firing as long as you can. At some point, I will veer off to starboard to go after the whaler, and I will warn you before I make the turn. I intend to put a broadside into each of them with the larboard battery as we sweep past. I am hoping that between us, we can put them out of action. The second lugger should be no match for us, if we are careful with our distances. Then we can take back the whaler and escort her back to Valparaiso."

"Sounds good to me, sir," Greene agreed.

"I'm going to the quarterdeck," Brewer said. "Let me know when you're ready to open fire. Skimpy's in the foretop if you need him."

"Aye, sir."

Brewer returned to the quarterdeck, his mind racing with plans for taking the strange ships out there as prizes.

"Mr. Sweeney," he said when he arrived, "it looks as though our friends up ahead are splitting up. The brig and one lugger are heading this way, presumably to keep us busy while the second lugger takes their prize to the east and the Peruvian coast. Mr. Greene is up with the long nines. He has orders to open fire when he is within range of the approaching ships. Once we get within pistol shot, I intend to alter our course to starboard and head to cut off the lugger and the whaler. We will pay our respects to the brig and lugger with the larboard battery as we pass them. Questions?"

The sailing master smiled and shook his head. "Nary a one, Captain."

Brewer nodded. "I have the deck!" he announced. "Clear for action!"

He watched silently as the bosun and his party put the boats over the side, rigged for towing during the coming battle. Below, Mac, Alfred, and several hands were breaking down the walls of his cabin and laying them down; the idea was to minimize the chance of their being damaged if *Phoebe* were raked through the stern.

Lieutenant Hobbs appeared—Mr. Greene being at his post with the long nines—to report that the ship was cleared for action and await his commands.

"Thank you, Mr. Hobbs," he said. "Kindly load the guns, but don't run them out yet."

"Aye, sir," Hobbs saluted and left.

Ten minutes later, Skimpy appeared and saluted.

"Mr. Greene's respects, sir, and he thinks he can reach the brig now."

"My compliments to Mr. Greene. He may open fire at his discretion. He is to keep firing as long as his guns bear."

"Aye, sir." A quick salute, and the lad was off.

"Beat to quarters!" he called.

The marine drummer played his tune, sending the hands to their action stations. The marines also jumped to their posts: sharpshooters with rifles to the tops, others to their stations around the ship.

Three minutes after Skimpy headed forward, the long nines erupted. Brewer was at the larboard rail, but he couldn't see the fall of the shot.

"Mr. Sweeney, I'm going forward."

He made his way swiftly to the bow, arriving just as the second salvo was fired.

"Report, Mr. Greene," he called out.

Greene emerged from the smoke. "I am concentrating on the brig. The first salvo fell twenty yards short and slightly to starboard. Lookout! Report on second salvo!"

"Dead on, but ten yards short of the brig, sir!" the lookout replied.

Greene looked at his captain. "At the rate we're closing, he'll feel them from now on."

Brewer eyed the distance. "Carry on, Mr. Greene."

Greene sighted down each barrel before stepping back beside his captain.

"Fire!" he cried.

Both guns spewed flame and smoke. The smoke from the salvo blinded them on the deck, so Brewer looked up to the lookout.

"Two hits, sir!" he shouted down to the deck. "I see splinters flying!"

"Well done, men!" the captain said. "Benjamin, fire at will. You should be able to get two or three more salvoes in before we veer off to starboard. Once that happens, hold your fire for the moment. Your next target will be the second lugger, but don't fire if there's a danger of hitting the whaler."

"Aye, sir."

Brewer returned to the quarterdeck. When he got to the waist, he paused.

"Mr. Rivkins!" he called. The lieutenant appeared.

"Sir!"

"Soon I shall veer to starboard. As soon as we come out of the turn, run out the larboard battery. I want one broadside put into the brig and another for the lugger, if you can reload fast enough."

"Aye, sir," Rivkins replied. "Fire on your order, sir?"

Brewer didn't want any delay. "You may fire as your guns bear, Lieutenant. Both salvoes."

Rivkins smiled and saluted. "Thank you, sir!"

Lieutenant Percy Rivkins rushed back to his gun crews.

"Alright, you men!" he called loudly in order to be heard over the THUMP-THUMP of the long nines. "Larboard battery, be ready to run out as soon as we make the turn. Gun captains! Be ready to fire as you bear, then reload and run out again, double quick! We'll have to move smartly if we're to give the lugger a bellyache as well! Stand by!"

The ship heeled over to port, and as soon as she came out of it, Rivkins called, "Run out! Run out! Captains! Fire as you bear!"

The broadside walked down the battery, the guns going off in twos or threes as his men showed the fruit of countless hours of practice. They jumped to the reload without waiting for his word and ran the guns back out as soon as they were ready. Rivkins was standing behind the two most forward guns in the battery. He pushed past his men and stuck his head out of the gun port and saw they were just coming up on the lugger. He managed to turn aft in time to see the battered wreck of the brig limping off to port.

He quickly jumped back. "The brig's a wreck, men! Stand by for the lugger, now! Fire as you bear!"

Again, the broadside seemed to walk down the side of the frigate. Rivkins looked out a gunport again and whooped for joy!

"The lugger's broke in half and sinking!" he called to the battery, and the men cheered.

"Mr. Rivkins!" the captain called down from the deck above. "Well done! My congratulations to your crews!"

"Thank you, sir!" Rivkins called. When he turned back to his crews, he didn't have to say a word. They had heard the captain. Rivkins was impressed with his men that day, and they were pleased with themselves, as professionals would be. He marveled at the difference in them since he'd come aboard after all the trouble under Captain Judah.

Brewer turned from the waist and walked to the larboard rail. He could easily see the second lugger and the whale about five miles or so distant on an easterly course. He smiled when he saw them trying to crowd on more sail. *Go ahead,* he thought, *for all the good it will do you.*

He looked over his head, reassured to see *Phoebe's* sails filling the sky. He handed his telescope to a waiting midshipman and walked to the wheel to confer with Mr. Sweeney.

"Steady as she goes, Mr. Sweeney," he said.

"Aye, sir, steady as she goes. What do you think, Captain? Two hours or three?"

"Closer to three, I should think. How much daylight do we have?"

Sweeney studied the sun for a moment and ran some equations in his head. "Maybe five hours, probably less."

"Let's not waste any time, then," the Captain said. "I'm going forward."

He found the first lieutenant standing beside the long nines, studying the chase. Brewer smiled when he saw Skimpy—standing beside Greene but facing aft—discreetly reach over and tug on the Premier's sleeve and alert him to the approach. Greene turned and saluted as his captain neared.

"Captain," Greene greeted him as he approached.

"I see you've improved your security," Brewer said, nodding toward young Skimpy, now standing off to the side.

Greene shrugged. "Seemed like a good idea."

Brewer smiled before turning his attention to the two ships ahead of them. "How long before you can open fire?"

"At least an hour, I should think," Greene replied. "We are closing the gap."

"Captain, look!" Skimpy cried from the rail. He was pointing forward.

Brewer and Greene both spun to see the two ships ahead of them separating. The lugger was still heading due east for the coast, but the whaler was turning to port and settling on a course of northeast, showing *Phoebe* her stern.

Both men studied the scene for a moment, then Greene lowered his glass and turned to his captain.

"Sir?"

Brewer lowered his glass and sighed. "There's no question, is there? We go after the whaler. Let me know when you want to try putting a ball off her quarter."

"Aye, sir."

He turned to go aft again, and, as he did so, he saw Skimpy standing by the railing, watching the whaler. He paused, which got the lad's attention.

"Well done, *Mister* Skimpy," he said proudly. He playfully mussed the boy's hair a little and went aft.

The boy stared at the retreating form of his captain in awe. He turned and saw the first lieutenant, who had observed the whole scene.

"Did you *hear* that, Mr. Greene?" he said. "The captain called me *Mister*."

Greene smiled. "I sure did, Skimp."

He watched as the lad went to get himself a glass and jump up into the foremast shrouds to keep a better eye on the whaler, all the while carrying himself a little taller and his head a little higher.

When Brewer got back to the quarterdeck, he found Mac there waiting for him. One of the ship's boys was standing beside him.

"What's this?" he asked Mac.

The big Cornishman shrugged. "I'm not really sure yet, sir. He just seems to have adopted me."

Brewer looked down at the boy, standing as still as he could beside the coxswain, arms at his side. He looked to Mac and raised his brows in question.

Mac tapped the boy on the shoulder. "Salute the captain, just like I showed you."

Brewer watched as the lad's right hand literally flew from his side, his knuckles striking his forehead, nearly knocking himself backwards. Mac saluted as well. Brewer returned the salute.

"Ow," the boy whispered as he rubbed his head.

"What's your name, lad?" Brewer asked.

"Pudge," he answered.

"Sir," Mac whispered out the side of his mouth.

"Oh, sorry, Mac," he said. "Pudge, sir."

The captain looked him over. "And what can I do for you, Pudge?"

"I want to be your coxswain when Mac is done," he said proudly. He caught the look Mac threw at him and turned back to the captain. "Sir," he added.

"Well," Brewer said, "I shall keep that in mind, Pudge. You listen to Mac and learn from him. Mac," Brewer motioned for his coxswain to step off with him, "what's his story?"

"The lad's in my mess, sir," the coxswain explained. "I guess he's taken a shine to me."

"Detail him as my cabin boy and have him report to Alfred. I'm afraid his battle station will have to stay the same."

"Understood, sir," Mac grinned. "Thank you, sir!"

Brewer watched them go below after returning an exaggerated salute from Pudge. He smiled to himself as he turned to Mr. Sweeney.

"The two ships we're chasing have split up," he explained. "We're going after the whaler. Steady as you go."

Half an hour later, Skimpy arrived on the quarterdeck and presented himself to the captain.

"Begging your pardon, sir," he said as he saluted. "Mr. Greene sends his respects. He says he thinks he can reach her now."

"Very well, Mr. Skimpy," Brewer said formally, "let's go see."

The captain followed the boy forward. "I've brought the captain, sir!" he shouted to Greene as they approached.

The first lieutenant turned and saluted. Brewer quickly raised his glass to his eye and observed the whaler.

"You may fire when ready, Mr. Greene."

"Aye, sir." He checked the sighting of the left gun first, and then the right, before standing back.

"Fire!" he shouted.

The two long nines belched out smoke and flame. As soon as the din died down, Brewer looked to the foretop for a report from the lookout.

"Both shells landed about twenty yards short, sir!" the lookout shouted to the deck below.

"Well done, Mr. Greene," Brewer said.

"Sir!" It was Skimpy from the foremast shrouds. "She's changing course!"

Brewer and Greene spun around and saw the whaler had altered course two or three points to starboard.

"Trying to throw off our aim," Greene said.

"Yes," Brewer said. "Let's show him how well he succeeded. Lay one off his starboard beam. Close."

Greene smiled. "Aye, sir."

The right hand gun was loaded, and Greene verified the aim before standing back. He offered Brewer the lanyard, but the captain refused. Greene did the honors. Brewer felt the force buffet his body. A beautiful geyser signaled the ball hitting the water not fifteen yards off the whaler's starboard beam. Two minutes later, a white flag was flown up from the whaler's quarterdeck. A cheer arose from the *Phoebe's* forecastle.

Brewer lowered his telescope and felt satisfied. He was grateful that the chase had not forced them to open fire. He turned to the guns' crews.

"Well done, men!" he congratulated them. "Mr. Greene, an extra ration of rum for these men!"

"Aye, sir," Greene acknowledged the order as the men cheered.

"Mr. Greene," Brewer said as he walked aft with his premier, "take a boat and board the whaler. Release the crew and put any prize crew in irons. Take Mr. Reed with you. I want to know what happened. Report when you can."

"Aye, sir," Greene saluted and went to gather his crew.

Brewer went aft and found Mr. Sweeney awaiting him on the quarterdeck.

"Bring us within pistol shot and heave to, Mr. Sweeney," he said. "Mr. Greene is going to board the whaler."

"Aye, Captain."

Lieutenant Greene sat erect in the stern sheets next to Lieutenant Reed. He wanted the prize crew on the whaler to see him coming, and he wanted them to be afraid. He wasn't sure it would work, but he wanted to try.

They lay alongside the whaler's port side. Greene looked to the sergeant of marines.

"Secure the deck, Sergeant," he said.

"Aye, sir." The sergeant rose. "Up, you men! Up the side! Establish a perimeter!"

Greene watched the six marines follow their sergeant up and onto the deck of the whaler. It was only a matter of minutes before the sergeant looked down over the railing and told Greene all was secure.

Greene and Reed climbed up to the deck and looked around. A dozen men were huddled together on the quarterdeck, looking at the British crew with a mixture of curiosity and loathing. The rest of the deck was clear. Greene turned to Reed.

"Take four men, two of them marines," he said. "Go below. Find the whaler's crew and set them free. Send them to the deck. Then set two men to search the hold while you take the other two and search the captain's cabin."

"Aye, sir," Reed said. He pointed to four men and told them to follow him below.

Greene turned to the group on the quarterdeck. "I am Lieutenant Greene of His Majesty's frigate *Phoebe*. Who is in command?"

The men looked at each other for nearly a minute before a small man stepped forward.

"I am Geraldo Hernández," he said in good English. "I am the prize master."

Greene was not impressed. "And why should I not call you a pirate and hang you and your men?"

"Your men will find a letter of marque in the captain's cabin."

That caught Greene's interest. "Signed by whom?"

"Admiral Cochrane."

Greene looked at the prize master with hooded eyes but said nothing. If Cochrane was in the area, the Captain needed to be told immediately. A noise forward drew his attention, and he turned to see the whaler's crew appear on the forecastle. One of them walked up to him.

"I am John Wyatt, master of the *Syren*," he said. "Thank you for setting us free."

"Lieutenant Benjamin Greene of HMS *Phoebe*. What happened?"

"We were approaching the Galapagos Islands when we ran into a brig and two luggers. The brig put a ball across our bow, and we hove to right away. We were on our way home with our hold full of prime whale oil. They put a prize crew aboard and locked us up below. That's all I know, until you came aboard and set us free."

Greene nodded. He saw Reed and his four men appear on deck.

Reed came over to report. "Hold's full of whale oil, sir." He saluted. "Otherwise nothing unusual. I found this in the captain's quarters." He handed over a packet. "Letter of marque and a set of orders to head to Callao."

Greene scanned the letter of marque and recognized the signature at the bottom. He tapped the paper and gazed at *Phoebe*, standing off the port quarter. He thought he recognized the captain himself standing on the quarterdeck. He turned back to Wyatt.

"Please take fifteen minutes to send your crew below decks to inspect the ship and cargo. Report any discrepancies to me."

"Yes, sir." Wyatt turned and issued orders to his crew. The twenty men scattered and disappeared below. Wyatt and his mate made an inspection of the deck, and then Wyatt went below to check out his quarters. Greene looked to Reed.

"Is there somewhere below where we can secure the prize crew?" he asked.

"Aye, sir," Reed said, "where the crew were being held. But I'd recommend leaving the marines to guard them."

Greene nodded. "See to it, if you please."

"Aye, sir." Reed saluted before instructing the sergeant of marines to take the prisoners below.

Wyatt came back on deck. "Nothing seems to be disturbed in the hold, Lieutenant. Some wine is missing from my cabin, but I can guess where that went. Otherwise, *Syren* seems shipshape."

"Good. I will return to *Phoebe* and brief my captain. Mr. Reed will remain aboard along with the marines to guard the prize crew. You should hear from us soon. Please remain hove to for the time being."

The two men shook hands. Greene briefed Reed and then took the boat back to *Phoebe*. When he arrived, he went directly to the captain's cabin to give his report. Brewer listened closely until his first lieutenant was finished.

"So," he said slowly, "we now know the Peruvians have privateers at the Galapagos Islands, preying on our whalers. Alfred!"

The servant appeared. Brewer noticed that Pudge stood silently beside him.

"Sir?" the servant asked.

"Coffee for two, please."

"Very good, sir," Alfred said. Pudge followed him back into the pantry.

"We need to head south for Valparaiso," Brewer went on. "That is where the nearest British authorities are located. We'll drop the whaler and the prize crew there and continue on, back to Rio. We must find Commodore Hardy and report this to him."

Greene waited while Alfred and Pudge brought in their coffee. "How are you going to avoid Captain Vernon once we get to Valparaiso?"

He saw his captain smile through the steam over his coffee.

"Who said we were going to enter the harbor?" the captain said quietly.

Greene stared in disbelief before a smile crept over his face. He sipped his coffee in silence.

Two hours later, HMS *Phoebe* was leading *Syren* south toward Valparaiso. As he had done coming north, Brewer set his course to the west of San Lorenzo to avoid any coastal trouble. He had sent Lieutenant Greene back to the whaler with instructions for the journey south and also to retrieve Mr. Reed. The ships sailed southward through generally calm seas; the bright sunlight and blue skies made for perfect conditions.

They had just passed the southern tip of San Lorenzo when the mizzen lookout made himself heard.

"Sail ho!"

"Where away?" cried Mr. Hobbs, who was officer of the deck.

"Port quarter!"

Hobbs went to the rail and raised the glass to his eye. He only needed a moment for his fears to be confirmed.

"Midshipman of the watch!" he called.

"Aye, sir?" Mr. Lee replied.

"My respects to the captain," Hobbs said. "Tell him we've sighted a frigate on our port quarter, and she seems to be on an intercept course."

"Aye aye!" Lee saluted and was gone.

Hobbs went back to studying the newcomer. He thought she was a forty-four gunner, which would make her superior to *Phoebe* in number of guns. He was so lost in contemplation that the arrival of the captain and Mr. Greene took him by surprise.

"Report, Mr. Hobbs," Brewer said.

Hobbs recovered quickly. "Frigate approaching on the port quarter, sir. Apparently came from the eastern side of

San Lorenzo. We didn't sight her until she cleared the island."

Brewer studied the approaching vessel. "Hm... What do you think, Mr. Greene? Forty? No, I think she's a forty-four gunner. Probably 18-pounders, wouldn't you think?"

"Captain?" Greene said. "Am I mistaken, or is that our old friend the *Valdivia*? Do you think Lord Cochrane's still aboard?"

"I don't see his pennant," Brewer said, "but I think you're right. It probably is the *Valdivia*. Offhand, I'd say the lugger found some help, and she's here to reclaim her prize. Let's not give her the chance. Mr. Sweeney, bring us about. Mr. Hobbs, beat to quarters. Mr. Greene, go forward and direct the long nines. Open fire as soon as you are within range. Mr. Dye, raise the blue pennant, if you please."

"Aye, sir" and "Aye aye, sir" echoed on the quarterdeck as his officers went about their duties. Hobbs' announcement sent the crew into action; Brewer listened to the drummer beat out the rhythm that heralded a coming battle. Mr. Sweeney called for hands to bring the ship about and steer her into danger. Brewer turned and watched the signals midshipman go aft and raise the blue pennant, the prearranged signal for *Syren* to make her way south to Valparaiso with all speed. Nine minutes, thirty-seven seconds later, Mr. Hobbs reported that HMS *Phoebe* was cleared for action.

"Well done, Mr. Hobbs," Brewer said. "Report to your guns. Load with canister and run out both sides. Be ready; I have not yet decided what we shall do, so be alert."

"Aye, sir." The lieutenant saluted and made his way to the carronades on the fo'c'sle.

"Deck, there!" the lookout called from above. "The frigate's altered course to go after the whaler!"

"Well," Brewer said, to no one in particular, "now we know."

Lieutenant Reed arrived to take command of the carronades on the quarterdeck. Brewer gave him the same instructions he'd given Hobbs and left him to his work.

"Mr. Sweeney," he said, turning to the sailing master at the wheel, "in a few moments, Mr. Greene is going to open up on the *Valdivia* with the long nines. What she does shall determine what I will do. I am going forward. I shall send a runner with instructions. Mr. Dye, Mr. Drake, you're with me."

"Aye, sir," Sweeney replied calmly.

"Have the mizzen lookout keep an eye on the *Syren*. Just in case *Valdivia's* job is to distract us."

"Aye, sir."

Brewer made his way forward. Hands manning their guns gazed at him as he swept past, his face and eyes fixed forward. He was The Captain, about to lead them into a battle in which some of them might die. He had ascended to Mount Olympus—as they expected him to—and he would not return until the battle was over.

He stepped onto the fo'c'sle just as the first volley was fired. By the time he reached the guns, the reload was well underway.

"Report, Mr. Greene," he said without ceremony.

"It seems our first attempt went straight over the deck, Captain," he said. "Slight damage, but nothing like it should have been. The second volley is just about ready."

"Proceed."

The second volley erupted. Brewer and Greene braced themselves against the wall of sound and turned to the man in the foretop for his report.

"Two solid hits, sir!" he called down.

"Well done!" Greene commended his crews.

Brewer turned to his premier. "Continue to fire as long as your guns bear. I am going to turn to port and put a broadside into her with the starboard battery. After that, we will circle around *Valdivia* and put a broadside of chain into her rigging to slow her down. Report to me when your guns no longer bear." It was important that his officers knew his plans. If harm befell him, they could carry on.

"Aye aye, sir."

Brewer made his way aft, his plans still evolving in his mind. He stopped at the waist.

"Mr. Rivkins!" he called down. The lieutenant appeared.

"Sir!"

"We are about to turn to port. Ready the starboard battery to put a broadside into that frigate as she passes. Reload as quickly as you can with chain and elevate your guns. I intend to swing around her stern and put another into her rigging. I want to slow her down so the *Syren* has the best chance to escape."

"Aye, sir!"

"Wait for my command to fire."

"Aye, sir!"

Brewer turned from the waist and hurried aft to the wheel. Sweeney and the quartermaster were there, looking past him, trying to watch Mr. Greene's progress.

"It looks like Mr. Greene's going for her rigging," Sweeney commented.

"So will we in just a few minutes," Brewer replied. "Mr. Drake, my compliments to Mr. Hobbs. Tell him to ready his starboard battery. He may fire with the broadside. I want him to reload with ball and rake her stern when we cross it."

"Aye, Captain." The midshipman saluted and scampered forward.

"Mr. Reed, you heard the orders," Brewer called without turning.

"Aye, Captain," the lieutenant replied.

Mr. Sweeney walked over to where Brewer was standing.

"How close do you want us after the turn?"

"Half pistol-shot," the captain replied. "When I order the turn, bring us out parallel to her course. Once we are past her, put the wheel over hard to starboard. Straighten out just long enough for Mr. Hobbs and Mr. Reed to rake her stern, then hard to starboard again so Mr. Rivkins can have a go at her rigging."

Sweeney looked at him, but the captain's face betrayed nothing of what was going on inside his head. He acknowledged the order and returned to the wheel.

Brewer focused on the gap that was rapidly closing between the two ships. He noticed that *Valdivia* was trying to return fire with her bow chasers and the first couple guns from her starboard battery, but he couldn't worry about that now. He had to time this turn just right. Steady... Just another moment...

"Now, Mr. Sweeney!" he called.

The sailing master grabbed a speaking trumpet and began bellowing orders. The hands aloft reacted like the well-trained crew they had become, and *Phoebe* turned smartly. Sweeney watched the turn, calculating its progress in order to straighten them out in order to be where the captain wanted them. Brewer watched him in silence, his confidence in Mr. Sweeney's abilities being such that he would not think to interfere. Finally the sailing master raised the trumpet to his lips again, and the ship steadied up on her new course.

Brewer stepped over to the waist and waited before looking down to see Mr. Rivkins awaiting his orders.

"Fire as you bear, Mr. Rivkins," he said calmly.

"Aye, sir," Rivkins ran to his guns and waited until all had a target. "Fire!" he roared.

The battery went off as a unit, followed a split-second later by the carronades on the fo'c'sle and the quarterdeck. Brewer felt the impact of *Valdivia's* broadside, which was fired at almost the same instant. He heard the cries of the wounded and the dying. One carronade on the quarterdeck was hit squarely and put out of action, its crew killed. Lieutenant Reed began shouting at his men to reload with ball and not to miss their chance to pay the *Valdivia* back in spades.

The captain turned to Mr. Dye. "Go below and get me a damage report from Mr. Rivkins."

The midshipman disappeared below. Brewer turned to see Mr. Sweeney pick up his speaking trumpet and order the turn to starboard. He looked to the quarterdeck carronades and was pleased to see the last one being run out.

As *Valdivia* swept past them, *Phoebe* swung hard to starboard across her opponent's unprotected stern. For a moment, Brewer locked eyes with Captain Turrado on *Valdivia's* quarterdeck; the man looked very angry. *You don't like this, do you?* Brewer thought, *Now that I have more than a twenty-gun sloop. Well, you've earned this, my friend, and I hope—as my old friend Bush would say—you'll be truly grateful.* He smiled as he saw Turrado dive when he realized what was coming. Brewer turned to Mr. Reed.

"Fire!"

The quarterdeck carronades belched fire, smoke and destruction into *Valdivia*. Lieutenant Hobbs' guns on the fo'c'sle had gone off a split second after Reed's, and Brewer made a mental note to congratulate his second lieutenant on being ready.

Mr. Sweeney came over. "Orders, sir? Shall we put the wheel over to starboard and give her another one?"

Brewer shook his head. "Depends on how ready she is." He moved a few steps to get a better view of *Valdivia's* now-visible port side. Just as he feared; her guns were loaded and run out. He turned back to his sailing master.

"Swing us forty-five degrees to starboard and hold it just long enough for Mr. Rivkins to unload his broadside into their rigging. Then put the wheel hard over to port and take us across their stern again."

Sweeney turned to put the captain's plan into action. Brewer went to the waist.

"Mr. Rivkins!" he called. The lieutenant appeared. "Stand by to fire your starboard battery. Is the larboard battery loaded?"

"With ball, sir."

"Good. After you fire, we shall come around to port. Fire the larboard guns as they bear on *Valdivia's* stern."

"Aye, sir!"

"Mr. Reed!" Brewer turned to his fourth lieutenant. "How are your larboard guns loaded?"

"Canister, sir," Reed said.

"Sweep her deck as we pass astern."

"Aye, sir!"

"Mr. Lee! My compliments to Mr. Hobbs. Tell him if his larboard guns are loaded with canister, he is to sweep *Valdivia's* deck as we pass astern. If they're loaded with ball, his target is her mizzenmast."

"Aye, sir," the lad squeaked, his voice breaking in the excitement.

Brewer felt *Phoebe* swing to starboard and straighten up almost immediately.

"Now, Mr. Rivkins," Brewer said calmly.

"Fire!" the lieutenant shouted to his men. The guns went off as one, and *Valdivia's* upper works tore and snapped. A lucky shot took the mizzen topmast away cleanly. Brewer watched it tumble to the deck and over the side, dragging the damaged frigate off course.

Brewer looked down to see Mr. Rivkins already hurrying his men to the larboard battery so as to be ready to fire when the moment came. *Phoebe* heeled to starboard as the wheel was put hard over to port and she came around behind her foe.

"Fire as you bear, Mr. Rivkins," he ordered.

He heard a muted "Aye, sir," come from below, and when he looked he saw Rivkins already squatted beside the captain of the forward gun of the battery. He worked his way down the line, speaking with each captain to ensure they knew their orders. When he reached the last gun, he ran forward, shouting for them to stand by.

Suddenly, Lieutenant Greene appeared on the quarterdeck.

"Helping Mr. Hobbs?" Brewer asked.

Greene shook his head. "I was going to, but he has everything well in hand. In fact, I was just leaving when Mr. Lee arrived with your orders. I turned and saw Mr. Hobbs nod to himself and say, 'It's the mizzen, then.'" Greene looked at the damage their guns had done to *Valdivia*. "Too bad Cochrane's not over there. He deserves it."

Privately, Brewer agreed with him. "Stay alert. Turrado knows his business. Let's not give him the chance."

"Aye, sir," Greene said.

HMS *Phoebe* sailed across the unprotected stern of the wounded enemy frigate. Rivkins' guns opened up as they bore, going off in twos and threes. Brewer watched grimly as the *Valdivia's* stern windows and the captain's quarters disintegrated, and he was thankful that the roar of his own guns prevented him from hearing the cries of the wounded and dying. He turned to watch across the deck as Lieutenant Hobbs sighted each of his carronades personally. The second shot took a piece out of the enemy mizzenmast, and the fifth shot brought the mast down completely. Lieutenant Reed joined the fray as his quarterdeck carronades came to bear. The canister they unleashed across the *Valdivia's* exposed decks tore through the flesh of everyone unlucky enough to be in their way.

Brewer turned away from the slaughter and walked over to the wheel.

"Steady as you go, Mr. Sweeney," he said. "I want some distance. Let's see if she has the stomach for any more fighting. Where's the whaler?"

"Safely away to the south, Captain," Sweeney replied. "No sign of pursuit."

"Very good. Let's go forward, Mr. Greene."

Greene duly fell into step behind his captain as they made their way toward the fo'c'sle.

"Mr. Hobbs," Brewer said as he acknowledged the younger man's salute, "you and your men did sterling work against the *Valdivia*. Superb work, you men!"

Hobbs looked about him, as if seeing the men of his commend in a new light.

"And I shall be sure to note in my report to the Admiralty your accuracy of fire. When I told your division officer to take out the enemy's mizzenmast, you delivered! Gentlemen, I salute you, one and all!" He doffed his hat to them, and the men cheered wildly. He turned to his second lieutenant.

"Well done, Mr. Hobbs."

"Thank you, sir."

As they made their way aft again, Brewer turned to his premier.

"Tell me, Benjamin," he said softly, "do you think Mr. Hobbs has come around? Or is he still under the 'spell' of his old captain?"

Greene glanced over his shoulder before replying. "I couldn't say, sir. He does his job well enough—we've just seen proof of that, haven't we?—but he rarely says anything. Hardly opens his mouth any more in the gun room. I can ask Rivkins or Reed—perhaps he says more to them."

Brewer stared at the deck for a moment as they walked. "Keep me informed. Keep your eye on him, Benjamin."

"Aye, sir."

They arrived on the quarterdeck.

"Where's *Valdivia*?" Brewer asked.

"There, sir," Sweeney answered, handing him a glass and pointing aft. "Three points to larboard."

Brewer walked to the fantail and raised the telescope to his eye. He saw men on the *Valdivia* working to clear the wreckage of the fallen mizzenmast. There appeared to be a great deal of destruction on the deck, but at this distance he couldn't be sure. He lowered the glass and shook his head.

"She's finished," he said. "Hard to port, Quartermaster; let's catch up with the *Syren*."

HMS *Phoebe* swiftly caught up with the *Syren* and escorted her toward the safety of Valparaiso. The day before they arrived at the city Brewer ordered both ships to heave to and invited the *Syren*'s master, John Wyatt, to join him for supper.

After the meal was over, the two captains adjourned to sit on the day cabin for cigars and Port.

"So, Captain," Wyatt said as he blew a cloud of smoke heavenward, "tomorrow it's Valparaiso for us. Where will you be off to next?"

Brewer smiled. "I'm afraid *Phoebe* will not be entering Valparaiso with you tomorrow."

"Oh?"

"No, for I am under orders from Commodore Hardy to meet up with him at Rio as soon as possible, so I cannot spare the time. Before you leave, I will give you a copy of my report on your rescue for you to deliver to Captain Vernon aboard HMS *Blossom*."

Wyatt raised his glass in salute. "'Twill be an honor, sir."

Later that evening, Brewer stood on the quarterdeck beside his sailing master and watched as the *Syren* disappeared into the darkness toward the port and safety.

"What do you think Captain Vernon will say when Wyatt hands him your report?" Sweeney asked.

Brewer shrugged. "Perhaps we'll find out in six or seven months, if he ever shows up in the Atlantic again."

Sweeney turned away and looked at the stars, grateful for the darkness that hid the grin he wasn't entirely sure his captain would approve of.

CHAPTER TEN

HMS *Phoebe* glided gently into the harbor at Rio as the pilot guided her to a berth in the harbor. Captain Brewer and Lieutenant Greene stood patiently on the quarterdeck until the pilot indicated he was finished and departed the ship. Brewer picked up a glass from the rack and had just begun to survey the harbor when he heard Mr. Murdy, the senior midshipman, call out.

"Commodore's broad pennant off the starboard beam, sir!"

"That's *Superb* all right, sir!" Greene said.

"Signal from *Superb,* sir," called Mr. Dye, midshipman in charge of signals. *"Captain to come aboard."*

"Very well," Brewer said. "Acknowledge the signal, Mr. Dye."

"Aye, sir!"

"Mr. Greene," Brewer said calmly, "please call for my gig. Mac, I'll join you at the entry port."

"Aye, sir," the coxswain said, and headed forward.

"I'll be in my cabin. You have the deck, Mr. Greene," Brewer said. "Please let me know when all is ready."

Brewer headed to his cabin, only to find that Alfred had already laid out his best uniform and was now polishing his sword.

"Alfred?" he asked.

The servant shrugged. "I thought you'd be needing them to go see the commodore, sir."

Brewer grinned. "You're right, as usual. Help me get changed."

He pulled off his clothes and threw them on his cot. Then he put on a clean shirt and his best duck trousers. He washed his face and shaved while Alfred polished his shoes. He was running a comb through his hair when there was a knock at the door. It was the first lieutenant announcing the gig was ready to go.

The captain took a deep breath as he gathered his reports to carry to the flagship. He was not looking forward to this interview.

Brewer sat in the stern sheets of the gig and tried to enjoy the sun on his face as he was rowed through the crowded harbor. He had tried to think of how he would handle the subject of James Norman, should the commodore bring it up. He finally decided that honesty was still the best policy, he prayed fervently that the subject did not come up.

He was met at *Superb*'s entry port by Captain Jonathan Lee, the ship's captain.

"Welcome aboard, Captain," Lee said. "The commodore's waiting for you. If you'll please follow me?"

Brewer obediently fell into step and followed his host through the bowels of the seventy-four to the door of the great cabin. The sentry knocked and opened the door. Lee led Brewer into the day cabin.

"Commodore," he said formally, "may I present Captain William Brewer of HMS *Phoebe*? Captain, this is Commodore Sir Thomas Hardy."

Brewer came to attention and nodded. "How do you do, sir?"

The commodore turned from the stern windows and set his glass on the table. In Hardy's eyes and the set of his jaw Brewer saw at once the strength of character he was know for. He was not a tall man—possibly five feet, eight or nine inches—but he was broad-shouldered and thick in the chest. He also carried an aura of authority about him. Brewer wondered how much of that he'd gained or learned from Nelson.

The commodore stepped toward his guest and extended his hand. Brewer shook it heartily.

"Pleased to meet you, Captain," Hardy said. "Julius! Refreshments for my guests! Now, then, Captain Brewer, please sit down. Ah, that's better! Thank you, Julius." Hardy took two glasses from the tray his servant held and handed the first to Lee and the second to Brewer.

"Now, then," Hardy repeated as he settled himself, "I'm glad you have finally caught up with us, Captain."

"We have been chasing you for some weeks, Commodore," Brewer said.

"Yes, I imagine so."

Brewer noticed the commodore was staring at him.

"Brewer? Where do I know your name from, sir? By chance, were you the young man who was on St. Helena with Lord Hornblower when he was governor?"

Brewer smiled and bowed his head. “Guilty as charged, Commodore.”

Hardy nodded. “I thought as much. What postings have you had since you left the island?”

Brewer hesitated before deciding to go ahead and be done with it. “I was first lieutenant of HMS *Defiant* and assumed command when the captain was lost in a storm. After that I was given command of HMS *Revenge*, a sloop of war, and now I command *Phoebe*.”

“I see,” Hardy said. “Tell me, was James Norman still captain of HMS *Defiant* when you were there?”

“Yes, sir,” Brewer said. “’Twas he that was swept overboard. Allow me to offer my condolences, Commodore; I believe you knew him from HMS *Victory*.”

Hardy’s eyes snapped, and Brewer thought for a moment that he had said the wrong thing. Then the commodore looked down at his glass and sighed.

“You know about that, do you?”

Brewer didn’t know what to say, so he said nothing.

“It’s alright, Captain. I know all about him.” Hardy drew a deep breath and let it out slowly while his glass was being refilled. “Not one of my finer moments. I didn’t find out about my error until 1809, when two officers and a marine who had been on the poop when Nelson died told me what happened *before* I turned around and saw Norman holding that musket.” Hardy took a drink and shook his head sadly. “I wish to heaven that Norman had come to me back then and told me of the mistake. Anyway, after I found out, I kept my eye on his career. As long as the war was on, he was fine. He did well in his frigate and took a few prizes. What he didn't do was something that would eclipse the false reputation he was already famous for."

Hardy rose and began to pace back and forth across the cabin. "Then the wars ended, and the mistake was all he had left. You might think that he would have retired with his prize money and have done with it. The problem with that was, it was worse ashore when people realized who he was. So, that left the sea and the loneliness of the captain's cabin." Hardy stopped pacing and turned to Brewer. "I hope he didn't kill anyone while you were with him in *Defiant*?"

Brewer studied his hands and said quietly, "One hand died under punishment."

Hardy closed his eyes and dropped his chin to his breast for a moment. "Another. More blood on his hands, and on mine as well. I tried to fix the problem, Captain. When I found the truth, I went to the publishers of the *Gazette*. Just as I got there, a report came in that Norman had taken three French merchant ships. As you can imagine, they didn't want to hear anything I had to say."

"I am sorry, sir," Brewer said softly.

Hardy looked at him for a moment before sighing.

"All that is in the past, Captain," he said, "and I prefer to leave it there. James Norman was a tragedy, but he was one of my making, not yours. One day I may have to atone for the excesses to which I inadvertently drove him, but they have nothing to do with you, my dear Captain. Do we understand each other?"

"Aye, Commodore."

"Good. Now, to the matter at hand. The Brazilians are fighting for their independence from the Portuguese. I'm sure this is not news to you. What may be news is that His

Majesty's government wants them to succeed. The Prime Minister sees huge new markets opening up, not only in Brazil but also all across a South America newly freed from Spanish—and Portuguese—domination. The idea is that the Brazilians will be ready to do business as soon as the Portuguese give up and go home. Our orders from the Admiralty are to preserve British interests in the region. However, we are do so while interfering as little as possible in the war itself. The king has developed a certain fondness for the Portuguese king, Don John VI, you see. So the PM wants the trade with Brazil, but our king wants good relations with Don John. Bit tricky, that." He paused for a drink. "So, Captain, tell me of your adventures since you came south."

Brewer did so.

Hardy listened intently, then said. "It sounds like you acted properly, Captain. Our orders are to protect British interests, not take prizes, so securing the whaler was the best course. I only ask that you be careful, should you run into any ships of the Portuguese Royal Navy."

Brewer shifted in his seat. "Just how far *can* I go with them, sir?"

Hardy smiled at his guest over his glass. "Captain Brewer, you are ordered to do *whatever you must* in order to protect British interests, property, and lives."

Now it was Brewer's turn to smile. "Aye aye, Commodore."

Hardy stood up and began to pace. "There is an additional piece of news. A long-standing rumor has recently been confirmed. It seems that Lord Cochrane is leaving the Chilean Navy to take command of the Brazilian."

Brewer's glass froze on its way to his lips, and his eyes met his host's. "Cochrane? Here?"

"Yes. What do you know of him?"

Brewer drained his glass. "I ran into him while tracking the pirate El Diabolito in the Caribbean. It turned out that Cochrane had just hired the pirate to help him take the Spanish Treasure Fleet that sailed from Panama last year, and he asked me to leave off my search. I refused. Later, with the help of a French frigate, we damaged the pirate's ship and then tracked him down and boarded him. We had just taken the ship when it caught fire and we had to abandon it. It exploded a short time later. Lord Cochrane was furious when he found out what we had done and swore revenge. Sir, the frigate we recently fought in the Pacific was the *Valdivia*, the same one Cochrane had in the Caribbean."

"Was Cochrane aboard?"

"I doubt it, sir; there was no pennant flying, and there had been when we met him previously."

Hardy frowned. "This could complicate matters. Cochrane is famous for holding grudges." He rubbed his chin as he turned various scenarios over in his mind.

"We shall cross that bridge when we come to it," the commodore decided. "Let us hope he has better things to do than settle old scores with you."

"Indeed, sir," Brewer said.

Hardy called for their glasses to be refilled. "Now, Captain, on to business. As I have told you, the king is leaning toward Portugal in Brazil's war for independence. He recently summoned the First Sea Lord and First Lord of the Admiralty for an audience, during which His Majesty expressed his wish that the Royal Navy do what it can to aid the few Portuguese outposts left along the Brazilian coastline. To that end, the squadron has been ordered to take up position in the harbor at Salvador, ostensibly to protect British interests, but in reality to give Cochrane pause before he launches an all-out attack on the port by sea."

The commodore took a long drink of his wine. Brewer drank his own and wondered where he and *Phoebe* fit into Hardy's plans.

The commodore set down his glass and sat back, stretching his arm out along the back of the long settee. He seemed to consider for a moment, then continued.

"As Salvador is presently under siege from a Brazilian army, the only way to bring in supplies is by sea. I am ordering every British ship to load as many extra supplies as she can carry."

"Have we an estimate of how long the Portuguese can hold the city?" Brewer asked.

Hardy shrugged. "I believe it's only a matter of time before Salvador falls. The Brazilians have cut off every land route into the city, and the Portuguese Royal Navy is not strong enough to supply it—not if Cochrane can create a navy for Dom Pedro like he did for Bernard O'Higgins."

Brewer nodded his agreement. "When I arrived in Brazil I was told by our consul general in Rio that Dom Pedro had authorized any regional governor or garrison commander to sign, on behalf of his government, letters of marque that allow for attacks on any Portuguese vessel or any vessel bound for a Portuguese-held port."

Hardy pursed his lips as he thought. "I think we can expect those attacks to intensify after Cochrane takes full control. He'll use them to try to keep both the Portuguese navy and our ships too busy to interfere with his plans. He knows we shall always go to the aide of a British ship, no matter who is attacking. Curse the man."

Hardy's eyes narrowed, and Brewer could see them darting from side to side, exploring options as quickly as they entered his mind, discarding each in turn as its flaws were made evident. Finally, he closed his eyes and leaned his head back on the settee, taking deep, slow breaths and expelling them just as slowly; Brewer himself sometimes did something similar to calm himself and bring order to his thoughts.

Hardy opened his eyes and sat up. "Captain, I'm sending you south. Stick your nose into every port you come to, including the River Plate and Montevideo. Under no circumstances are you to round the Horn. Get back here as quickly as you can. By the time you return, a convoy should be assembled, bound for Cape Town. You shall be the escort. In Cape Town you will pick up ships for a second leg, after which you are to return to Rio and resupply before joining me at Salvador. Don't forget to overstock for the squadron."

"Aye, sir," Brewer said. "When do I sail?"

"As soon as you're provisioned for sea. And, Captain, I don't need to tell you, but I will anyway: should you run into Lord Cochrane, please give him my regards."

Lieutenant Greene paced the quarterdeck as HMS *Phoebe* navigated the channel prior to anchoring in the bay at Rio de Janeiro. The captain was below, putting the finishing touches on his report before sending it ashore. Greene accepted a glass from a hand nearby and began scanning the harbor. There was no sign of HMS *Superb* or any other British warship. Panning to his right, he spotted five merchant ships anchored near the entrance to the channel; these could only be the convoy they were to escort to the tip of the African continent. As soon as the anchor dropped, Greene dispatched Lieutenant Hobbs to go ashore with the purser, Alfred, and the gunroom steward to arrange resupply for the ship. It was fortunate that they did not have to take on water. Greene shook his head in amazement at the thought; the new tanks *Phoebe* had received during her last refit kept the water fresh far longer than the old casks had. They also allowed them to carry 18% more water than before.

The captain wasted no time in heading ashore, stopping just long enough to give Greene instructions in case of an emergency before stepping over the side.

As he watched the gig row toward the shore, Greene became aware that he was no longer alone. He turned to see Mr. Rivkins.

"Something I can do for you, Mr. Rivkins?"

"No, sir," he replied, but he did not move off, and he looked troubled. A moment later, he asked, "Sir, may I ask a question?"

"You may ask," Greene said.

"I have heard rumors below deck, sir," Rivkins began, "concerning the frigate we fought in the Pacific. Some of the old *Revenge* hands said you had run into her before, in the Caribbean, and that Lord Cochrane had been aboard."

"That's correct."

"I see." Rivkins crossed his arms over his chest.

"Is there something you wish to ask me, Mr. Rivkins?" Greene said.

"Well, sir, it's just that I was surprised at the time that the captain didn't take the frigate as a prize. The frigate being Peruvian, sir, I thought we might not have to give it back this time."

"We are not at war with Peru, Lieutenant. Our main priority was to escort the whaler to safety at Valparaiso."

"I see, sir." Rivkins considered for a moment. "Mr. Greene, have you ever met Lord Cochrane?"

"I have had the honor," Greene said, still studying the harbor. "Why do you ask?"

"I was wondering if you considered him the type to hold a grudge."

Greene lowered his glass and looked at the third lieutenant for a moment before raising his glass again. Rivkins thought the premier was simply going to ignore him, and he made to turn and walk away when he heard the first lieutenant speak up.

"Mr. Rivkins, I absolutely do."

Captain Brewer came back aboard with orders to sail on the morning tide for Cape Town, escorting the five merchantmen anchored near the harbor mouth. Brewer called the five captains to come aboard *Phoebe* for a quick conference on organization and signaling during the journey to the South African cape. In the morning, the frigate led the merchantmen down the channel and into the South Atlantic waters.

"Set extra lookouts, Mr. Greene," Brewer said as they set their course ESE for Cape Town. "Mr. Sweeney estimates three weeks for us to get there, if we don't run into any unexpected company along the way."

"We can only hope, sir," Greene said.

Brewer looked up. "That we do or that we don't?"

Greene just smiled. "Aye, sir."

Down in the gunroom, Mr. Reed entered to find Lieutenant Hobbs sitting at the table reading a poster of some sort.

"Hello, Paul," he said. "What are you doing?"

"Hello, Jonathan," Hobbs said without looking up. "I'm looking over an advertisement I saw in town today. The Brazilian Imperial Navy is attempting to recruit British officers to man their ships."

Reed snorted in disgust. "Good luck with that! Why would any respectable British officer do such a thing?"

Hobbs looked up. "Have you seen what the Brazilians are paying?"

"No. What are they offerng?"

"With a five-year contract, first lieutenants get 8 pounds per month. Sub-lieutenants get £5 per month."

"What?" Reed demanded, amazed. "That's half again what we get paid!"

"Exactly! The poster also mentions an added incentive for Englishmen: Lord Cochrane is going to take command of the Brazilian Imperial Navy."

Reed dropped into a chair. "Oh, God. That's going to tempt a lot of men."

Hobbs grunted. "You bet it will. Since the wars ended, fewer than one in five lieutenants can find a post on a warship. And those on the beach don't qualify for the half-pay post captains get. Do you know what else this poster says? At the end of one's five-year contract with their navy, one has a choice: either re-enlist and get a *fifty percent increase in pay*, or retire and get half-pay for life!"

"What! As a lieutenant? Are you serious? Let me see that!"

Hobbs slid the poster over. Reed snapped it up and read it eagerly.

"You're right! They're even offering seamen two pounds sixty per month! That's a whole pound more per month than we pay. Do you think a lot of men will try to take advantage?"

"Wouldn't you?"

"No," Reed said firmly. "I serve the king."

The ship's bell struck seven times, and Hobbs rose from his seat. He took back his poster.

"I'd wager they still remember what it's like to have discipline on a ship. I'll talk to you later, Jonathan; I'm on duty in thirty minutes." Hobbs retired, still studying the paper.

Reed stared at the closed door for several moments before going in search of Lieutenant Rivkins. He found him sitting by one of the forward long nines, enjoying the breeze and reading a book.

"Hello, Jonathan," Rivkins said. "Looking for me?"

"Yes, Percy," Reed said as he squatted down beside him. "I have just had the most interesting conversation with Mr. Hobbs."

"Really? What about?"

"The Brazilian Imperial Navy is recruiting British officers and sailors to man their ships."

Rivkins closed his book and sighed. "Yes, I heard that. I hope it won't become a problem for us."

"Have you seen what they're paying, Percy?"

"Yes. Quite tempting, I must say."

"Would you take it?"

Rivkins shrugged. "Not if I had a berth on a king's ship. But if I was on the beach...?" He he looked over the water. "I think it would be very hard to resist."

"Do you think they're recruiting in England, too?"

Rivkins looked at him and grunted. "Wouldn't you be? Where else are you going to find the officers and men you need, practically standing about, just looking for a chance to go back to sea? And for that pay? They'll be jumping at the chance by the hundreds in Plymouth and Southampton alone."

Reed sat back on his heels and thought about it for a while. "Percy," he said quietly, "I think he's going to do it."

Rivkins looked up from his book. "Who?"

"Hobbs."

Rivkins leaned his head back against the gun and closed his eyes. "Are you sure?"

"Well, no—he didn't say as much. But he did make a comment about how they might at least have discipline on board ship."

Rivkins' eyes snapped open at that. "So, he's still got that bee in his bonnet, does he? I thought he'd learned better. Well, I just hope he remembers to resign his commission first. Otherwise, he'll be a deserter."

"Well, do you think we should report it? Let Mr. Greene know about our suspicions?"

Rivkins thought it over. He sighed and rose to his feet.

"I suppose you're right, Jonathan. Best to make sure we don't get into trouble. Let's go find Mr. Greene. He can decide whether to tell the captain."

They finally found the first lieutenant in the gunroom, enjoying a snack of wine and cheese and looking at a poster like the one Hobbs had shown to Reed. He looked up when they came in.

"Have you two seen this?" he asked, holding up the poster.

"Not I, sir," Rivkins said, "but Hobbs was showing one to Jonathan earlier."

"Really?" Greene looked to Reed, who was speaking to Winfield. The fourth lieutenant sat across from the premier.

"Jonathan," Rivkins said after he, too, placed an order with the Winfield, "tell Mr. Greene what you told me up on deck."

Reed thanked Winfield as he set a plate of cheese and goblet of wine on the table, and then told Lieutenant Greene about his conversation with the second lieutenant. Greene listened, occasionally sipping his wine, interrupting only when Reed repeated Hobbs' statement about discipline.

"Excuse me, Lieutenant," he said, "repeat that for me, if you please."

Reed did so. And a third time, also at Greene's request. The first lieutenant's brows furled deeply as he thought. He leaned forward and placed his elbows on the table, resting his forehead in his hands.

"Why do I have the dread feeling that he's going to jump ship the next time we're in Rio?" he asked nobody in particular.

"Because he is," Rivkins said.

Greene looked up at him. "You know that for sure?"

Rivkins shook his head. "Gut feeling."

"That helps me not at all." Greene leaned back again and looked at the ceiling. He pursed his lips in thought, and Reed thought he heard a very quiet *tsk-tsk*. Greene shook his head. "It seems to me there's nothing we can do about this now. Hobbs isn't going anywhere, at least not until we get back to Rio. I'll let the captain know. Thank you, gentlemen."

Reed wandered out of the gunroom, and Rivkins sat next to the first lieutenant.

Greene set the poster down and sighed. "It is not against the law if Hobbs wants to resign his commission and join the Brazilian Navy."

Rivkins grunted. "The captain will be angry"

"Will he?" Greene wondered aloud. "He may not like it, but I'm not sure he would be angry or that he would feel betrayed. It's not as it was during the wars, Percy. Not everyone is motivated solely by love of king and country anymore. Frankly, I'm more concerned about losing crew than losing a problematic lieutenant."

Rivkins nodded glumly.

"One more thing," Greene said as he rose, "I don't want you or Reed bringing this up to Hobbs. Engage normal conversation, but do not ask him about his plans or pester him. I don't want him thinking we're watching him. We'll see what the captain wants to do."

"Aye, sir."

The convoy enjoyed fair weather for most of the crossing to Cape Town. HMS *Phoebe* spent much of the voyage in the lead, occasionally making a sweep around the convoy to check for stragglers or any strange sail on the horizon. It was on one of these sweeps that the only excitement during the entire voyage happened.

It was coming on to dusk. HMS *Phoebe* had just rounded the rear of the convoy and was sailing along the port sides of the merchant ships to regain its forward position. Mr. Reed had the deck. Mr. Greene was asleep in his cabin and the captain was playing chess with Dr. Spinelli when the mizzen lookout made himself heard.

"Sail ho!"

Reed grabbed a glass. "Where away?"

The lookout pointed. "Off the larboard quarter, sir!"

Reed made his way to the rail and searched the horizon. He saw the unmistakable white dot that seemed to float on the water. "What do you make of it, lookout?"

"Can't rightly say yet, sir!"

"Mr. Henry!" Reed called to the midshipman of the watch. "My respects to the captain. Tell him we've sighted a sail on the northern horizon."

"Aye, Mr. Reed." The midshipman saluted and disappeared.

Reed called up to the lookout, "Can you make her out now?"

"No, sir!" was the reply. "She's still hull down."

"Report, Mr. Reed."

Reed was startled by his captain's arrival and fumbled his salute. "I beg your pardon, sir." He handed the captain his glass and nodded a quick greeting to the doctor. "The mizzen lookout sighted a sail to our north. Request permission to alter course to investigate."

Brewer raised the glass and quickly found their quarry. The spot of white seemed to be stationary, getting neither bigger nor smaller, which meant she was on a parallel course and keeping pace with them. He lowered the glass and considered before turning to Reed.

"Who's the lookout?"

"Moresby, sir."

Brewer nodded. Moresby was an old hand and a good one. "Let's hear you, Mr. Moresby!" he called.

Moresby looked down, surprised at hearing his name until he saw it was the captain who had called him. "Still the same, Captain!" he called back. "She seems to be pacing us, sir!"

"As I thought," Brewer muttered as he stared at the horizon, the stranger barely visible without the aid of the telescope. "Oh, no, my friend—not this time."

He looked around the quarterdeck. "Quartermaster, hold our position here relative to the convoy. Keep us between that ship and the convoy. Mr. Reed, keep your eye on that ship. Let me know if she moves in or disappears over the horizon. Signal the convoy that a strange sail is in sight to the north. All ships post extra lookouts and watch all points of the compass."

"Aye, sir!"

He handed the glass back to the fourth lieutenant. "I shall be in my cabin. You have the deck. Doctor, shall we continue our game?"

Spinelli was surprised by his captain's actions but knew better than to question him in front of the crew. Instead, he merely smiled. "At your command, sir."

The two men returned to the day cabin and resumed their game.

"Now," the doctor said, "would you mind explaining why we are not going to investigate?"

Brewer studied the board and frowned. He moved a knight. "I refuse to be fooled twice, Doctor."

Spinelli quickly moved a pawn and looked to his captain. "Excuse me?"

Brewer took the doctor's bishop. "Check. I was second officer on the *Lydia* in the Med when the Barbary pirates used this same trick on us. A strange sail at dusk. The captain took the bait and went off in pursuit. We lost them in the darkness, and they doubled back and took the brig we were escorting, complete with the new British consul taking passage in her."

"Your decision?" Spinelli asked as he moved his king.

"No, Captain Bush was in command, but I agreed with his decision at the time." He advanced a pawn.

"I see. Yes, I remember now." The doctor studied the board before moving his queen. "Checkmate."

"You heard about it?"

Spinelli looked up. "Your Lieutenant Gerard told me about the misadventure during his recovery."

Brewer began moving the chess pieces back into their box. "I'd forgotten Gerard was transferred to the naval hospital ashore at Gibraltar. I'm glad you were there for him."

"Yes, I should have taught him to play chess."

Brewer suddenly remembered the question he had intended to ask weeks ago. "Doctor, do you know why you're here?"

"You would miss my company?"

Brewer laughed in spite of himself. "That, certainly! But the Admiral said that if I wanted command of HMS *Phoebe*, I had to take you with me. He did not explain why. Care to enlighten me?"

Now it was the good doctor's turn to laugh. "It appears, my good Captain, that I committed the unpardonable sin in the Admiral's presence."

"And that would be?"

"I beat him at whist."

Brewer started, his eyebrows arching high in disbelief. "You *what?*"

"I beat him at whist."

"You mean your team won the rubber."

"No," Spinelli picked one of the bishops up from the board, flipped it in the air, caught it, and placed it into the box "*I* beat *him*. We both had incompetent novices for partners. It was me against him, and I won. Dramatically, as it happened; I took the last three tricks and the rubber. Lord Hornblower actually stared at the cards dumbfounded. It was quite something to behold; I'm afraid I lost control and smiled."

Brewer sat back in his seat, shaking his head in disbelief. He had *never* known the admiral to lose at whist. Neither Bush nor Gerard had ever related a story of Hornblower's losing. He must have lost sometimes, being human, but Brewer had never heard tell of it.

There was a knock at the door, and the sentry admitted Mr. Reed.

"Sir, that strange sail disappeared over the horizon about fifteen minutes ago and has not reappeared."

"Thank you, Mr. Reed," the captain said. "You are off duty now, I take it?"

"Aye, sir. Mr. Rivkins has relieved me. I passed on your instructions about positioning and lookouts."

"Thank you, Mr. Reed. Dismissed."

"Aye, sir." Reed came to attention and left.

Brewer rose and headed for the door. "Come with me, Doctor."

The two men went up on deck and found Rivkins talking to the quartermaster's mate at the wheel.

Rivkins saluted. "Captain. Doctor."

"Did Mr. Reed brief you, Lieutenant?" Brewer asked.

"Aye, sir. We are to watch for a strange sail on the horizon to the north."

"Correct. Does this remind you of anything?"

Rivkins' brows furled as he tried to remember whatever it was his captain was hinting at. He looked out over the rail toward the north. Suddenly Brewer and the doctor noticed Rivkins' shoulders tense. When he turned again, his eyes were wide.

"The British Consul?"

"Exactly. We are not going to fall into that trap again, Lieutenant."

"No," Rivkins said firmly. "I should say not, sir."

"Good. You know what to watch for."

"Aye, sir."

As they were walking away, Spinelli leaned in and said, "I take it Rivkins was on the *Lydia*?"

Brewer nodded. "He was the midshipman in my division."

The strange sail appeared a total of five times over the next seven days, but Brewer resisted the temptation to take his ship and leave the convoy. Finally, two days from Cape Town, the sightings ceased, telling Brewer he had been right all along. The night before they entered the harbor, Brewer sat alone in his cabin, writing a letter to his old captain, William Bush. He was just beginning the closing paragraph when he suddenly felt what could only be described as deeply ashamed. He re-read the letter closely and saw clearly that it would make Bush feel embarrassed or ashamed, or both, due to his mistake. He felt the blush creep across his face as he hurriedly wadded up the letter and destroyed it. He took a deep breath and thanked the Almighty for catching his error. Brewer knew he owed far too much to his old captain to ever risk hurting him or damaging their friendship in any way. He ordered a cup of coffee and took out a new sheet of paper.

The next morning, Brewer went ashore to visit the British consul and receive his orders for the next leg of his trip. The consul was very polite, congratulating Brewer for bringing in his ship without loss. The man remarked that there had been some pirate activity in the past few months, and Brewer was fortunate to have avoided it. Brewer merely nodded his head in agreement.

The consul handed him his orders and informed him the new convoy was assembled and ready to leave at the captain's discretion. Brewer thanked the man warmly, and the two shook hands in parting. It wasn't until he was back on board HMS *Phoebe*, relaxing in his cabin, that he broke the seal on his orders and saw his destination. He stared at the paper in his hands and fought down the conflicting emotions that threatened to overwhelm him. His destination was the island of St. Helena.

HMS *Phoebe* crawled into the harbor at Jamestown on the island of St. Helena under a calm wind and a pleasant mid-morning sun. Brewer stood still in the middle of the quarterdeck and allowed Mr. Greene to deal with the release of the convoy and the pilot. His eyes were on the harbor and waterfront. Very little had changed in the years since he had left. He could still see the café where he had taken the maid for a quiet drink. What was her name? *Ah, yes,* he remembered suddenly, *Claudette.* She had returned to France after Bonaparte's death; he hoped she was happy.

Mr. Greene approached and saluted. "The convoy has been released, sir. Will you be going ashore?"

"Yes," Brewer said. "Do we need anything?"

"No, sir. We can sail for Rio whenever you're ready."

Brewer nodded. "Good. We'll sail on the morning tide. Call away the gig, if you please, Benjamin."

"Aye, sir."

Crisp orders sent the crew into action, and in less than thirty minutes Brewer found himself being rowed toward the familiar shore. He wondered idly what might have gone through Lord Hornblower's mind as he'd approached this same shore for the first time. It was one subject they never discussed; Brewer made a mental note to ask his lordship in the letter he intended to write him during the voyage to Rio.

Brewer stepped from the gig and walked down the wharf. He was met by a man who emerged from what he remembered to be the dock office.

"Morning, Captain," the man said. "I'm Deacon Jones, harbormaster. Can I be of service to you?"

Brewer shook his head. "I don't think so, Mr. Jones. I just came ashore to pay my respects."

"Would you like an escort to the governor's office, Captain?"

Brewer looked at him. "Who is the governor?"

"Sir Hudson Lowe."

Brewer swallowed hard. "No, I don't think so. Tell me, Mr. Jones, where is Bonaparte buried?"

The harbormaster lowered his voice. "I'm afraid the gravesite is restricted, sir. No visitors without authorization from the governor."

"Interesting," Brewer said. "Still, I intend to pay my respects. Where is it?"

"Geranium Valley, near Longwood. That was his house. Do you need directions?"

"No, thank you, I remember the way."

He left the harbormaster behind and walked up the main street of the capitol and headed for Longwood. He found the grave in the valley, shaded by willows and near a spring of cool water. He kept a respectful distance and removed his hat. He bowed his head for a moment.

"So," he said quietly, "this is what they did to you. Buried in an unmarked grave." He grunted and shook his head. "Didn't even return your body to France. Were they still so afraid of you? Even in death?"

Brewer was not sure how long he stood there, remembering the man and the conversations they'd shared. Eventually he became aware that he was no longer alone.

"Excuse me, sir," a voice said from behind him, "may I ask what you are doing here?"

"Just paying my respects," he replied without turning around.

"I'm afraid this area is off limits, sir, by order of the governor."

"Really? After all this time?"

"The governor would like to see you, Captain."

Brewer turned around to find an officer standing thirty paces away, holding a horse. He recognized the man instantly.

"And what if I do not wish to see him, Colonel?"

The officer looked shocked. "Mr. Brewer? Is it really you?" He stepped forward and shook Brewer's hand heartily. "I'm sorry, I had no idea it was you, or I should have stood by until you were finished."

"That's quite all right, Colonel," Brewer reassured him. They turned back to the grave. "So, Lowe is still keeping him a prisoner?"

Colonel Patterson sighed and nodded. "Practically. The site is restricted. Someone reported your presence to the governor, and he sent me up here to fetch you."

Brewer pointed to the grave. "No name?"

Patterson looked embarrassed. "That was the compromise. The governor wanted it to say 'Napoleon Bonaparte,' while the French wanted just the imperial 'Napoleon' or 'Napoleon I'—I don't remember which. In the end, it was left blank."

Brewer's eyes narrowed in anger. "The man I knew when I was here didn't deserve this."

"Privately, I agree with you, Captain. But there's nothing either of us can do about that now."

"Why wasn't he returned to France?"

Patterson shrugged. "Louis XIII didn't want him. Even if he had allowed it, I doubt Lowe would have allowed the remains to leave the island. They were at war with each other after you left, Captain. The governor ordered 'General Bonaparte' to present himself daily, or he would have him arrested. In retaliation, Boney said he'd shoot the first British officer who entered his door. Shortly thereafter, Lowe took away his freedom of the island and restricted him to the plain around Longwood. I don't think he left the house the last few years he was alive."

Brewer flinched. "And all our projects? All we had accomplished for him?"

"Cancelled or allowed to fall into disrepair."

Brewer looked heavenward and sighed, trying to control his anger. Beside him, Patterson cleared his throat.

"Captain, I am still under orders to bring you to the governor."

Brewer considered for a moment simply returning to his ship, but he realized the gravity of the situation for Patterson. "Very well, Colonel. I have no wish to make trouble for you."

"Thank you, Captain."

The two men walked back to town, Patterson leading his horse by the reins. Brewer talked about his adventures in the Mediterranean and Caribbean since he had left the island. Patterson replied that he was looking forward to returning to England in the fall when he retired from the army.

"I'm thinking of writing a book," the colonel said, "about everything that went on here after you left." He looked grim. "The world should know the truth."

Brewer paused and turned to his companion. "Colonel, was Bonaparte murdered by the governor?"

Patterson hesitated before answering, but his eyes never left Brewer's.

"I don't know."

Brewer held his eyes long enough to satisfy himself that Patterson was telling him the truth, then the two continued their journey to the governor's office in silence. Patterson led him to the office door Brewer knew so well and knocked once before opening it.

"Governor, Captain William Brewer of His Majesty's frigate *Phoebe*."

Brewer marched into the office and stood at attention for a moment, his hat beneath his left arm. Behind him, he heard Patterson exit the room and close the door behind him. His eyes studied Lowe, standing behind the desk, and he saw the look on Lowe's face change as he recognized his visitor.

"Brewer?" he said. "Hornblower's secretary?"

"That's right, Governor," Brewer said.

"Well, Captain, why did you not report to this office first, upon arrival?"

"I'm glad I didn't," Brewer said matter-of-factly. "I wanted to see Bonaparte's grave."

"That site is off limits."

Brewer watched as the governor sat down behind his desk. He despised this wretched excuse for a governor, and he feared it showed on his face. "So I've been told."

Lowe sneered at him. "Of course, I suppose that wouldn't matter to you, Captain, just as it wouldn't to that traitor you worked for—"

Brewer drew his sword as he stepped to the desk and slapped it down, broadside, hard on the surface. The governor jumped back in terror.

"One more word like that from you, *Governor*, and I shall demand satisfaction from you. That is, if I don't run you through first."

"That would be murder!" Lowe cried, his voice quavering.

"Some things are worth the gallows," Brewer growled. "Anyway, isn't that what you did to him?"

Lowe's eyes widened in surprise, and Brewer wondered if he'd hit a nerve.

"No!" Lowe cried again. "Bonaparte was killed by a cancer of his stomach. You should read the autopsy report, Captain."

Brewer leaned in close and spoke in a low, menacing voice. "You'd better hope so, sir, because if I find out otherwise, I shall resign my commission and hunt you down like the mongrel you are."

"You cannot talk to me that way, sir! I am the governor! I shall report your conduct to the Admiralty, sir!"

"Go right ahead, sir. And when I have been stripped of my commission, there will be no reason for me not to do what I must to set things right."

"What do you mean by that?" the governor whined.

Brewer made a show of putting his sword back in its scabbard. Then he picked up his hat and marched out of the office without looking back. He walked back to the wharf and stepped into the gig without a word. Mac noticed that something was wrong, but he knew enough not to ask. They returned to the ship in silence, and Brewer went straight to his cabin.

He removed his hat, coat, and sword and left them on the desk. He went into his day cabin and fell into the settee beneath the stern windows. He heard Mac enter the cabin and put his things away. A few moments later, Alfred appeared in the doorway.

"May I get you anything, sir?" he asked.

"Not right now, thank you," Brewer said. "What is on the menu for supper?"

"I was going to cook you the last ham from Cape Town, sir, along with stewed potatoes and carrots."

"Enough for two?"

"Yes, sir."

"Mac?"

The coxswain appeared. "Sir?"

"Please find the doctor and ask him if he would care to join me at the turn of the first dog watch for supper and cigars."

"Oh, aye, sir!"

The coxswain departed, and Brewer looked to his faithful servant.

"Will that be enough time, Alfred?"

"Yes, sir. Would you like something to drink, sir?"

"No, thank you."

Alfred withdrew and Brewer went to his desk and pulled out pen and paper.

Your Lordship,

I know it has been far too long since I have written you, and I pray you will forgive me. Right now I am quite unsettled by some recent events, and I feel that you are the only one who can understand what I am going through.

I am writing you from the harbor at St. Helena, where we have just delivered a convoy. I went ashore, but when I discovered that Lowe was still the governor, I decided not to pay him a visit and went instead to find the grave of Napoleon Bonaparte. Yes, he is still here on the island; it seems that Louis XIII did not want him back in France, even as a corpse. He is buried in an unmarked grave in Geranium Valley near Longwood. The grave is in the shade of some willow trees near a spring.

As soon as he was told of my presence, Lowe sent Colonel Patterson out to bring me to him. Patterson told me the grave is restricted; the governor denies all access. Apparently, Bonaparte is still his prisoner, even in death. Patterson also explained to me why the grave is unmarked. Lowe and the French disagreed over how it should be inscribed. The French wanted him remembered as the emperor, but Lowe would not allow it. So, he lies beneath a plain slab of stone, unvisited and unremembered. It troubled me no end; regardless of what happened prior to 1815, I believe the man we knew deserved better.

I went with Colonel Patterson and allowed him to present me to the governor so he could not be accused of disobeying his orders. I must say the colonel was a gentleman throughout the entire incident. It may interest you to know that he will be returning to England when he retires later this year. He told me he is thinking of writing a book about what happened on the island after we left. I believe his words were, 'The world should know the truth.' I pray he does do so.

I shall not bore you with the details of my interview with the governor. You knew the man, so you can well imagine the sequence of events. Should you hear of my resigning my commission, you will know why.

Your Obedient Servant,
William Brewer

Brewer sat back in his chair and reread the letter, wondering if he should change some of the wording but in the end leaving it as written. He folded it and sealed it with wax.

"Mac!"

The coxswain appeared.

"Ask Mr. Reed to announce that mail will be collected, and put this in the bag. Have him put the bag on the next Indiaman bound for England."

"Aye, sir."

Brewer worked on reports until the doctor arrived, his spirit still very heavy, so much so that his visitor took note.

"Sir, would you rather I left?" he asked.

"What?" Brewer said, startled out of his thoughts. "What? No, no, Adam. I apologize for my bad mood. I went ashore today."

"I see, sir."

"No, I don't think you do," Brewer said, "but that's alright. I had to see the governor, and now I am in this mood. A drink? Alfred! We'll have coffee before we dine, I think. Bring it to the day room, will you? Thank you. What say you, Doctor? A game before we dine?"

Dr. Spinelli followed his captain into the day room and sat down across from him. He noticed that Brewer made no move to get his chess set; instead, he leaned his head back and closed his eyes until Alfred arrived with the coffee.

"Thank you, Alfred," the captain said wearily as he took his cup from his servant's silver platter. Alfred turned to give the doctor his cup, pausing long enough to be sure Spinelli saw the look of concern in his eyes. Spinelli nodded subtly, and the servant withdrew.

"I went to visit his grave today," Brewer said without preamble, as though he expected this to explain everything. Spinelli sipped his coffee thoughtfully; it very nearly did.

"Bonaparte?" he asked. His captain nodded and took a drink.

"The governor has placed his gravesite off limits," Brewer went on. "He's the one who relieved Lord Hornblower back in 1818." He set his cup on the table and smiled grimly. "Let us just say he was not a friend of ours—or of Bonaparte's. He got us off the island as quickly as he could, and within three years Bonaparte was dead."

"What happened during your visit?"

Brewer sighed and sat back. “I went ashore. When I discovered Lowe was still the governor, I decided not to pay the customary call on him and went straight to the grave. The gravesite is quite beautiful, actually, nestled beneath some willows, with a spring nearby providing soothing music. When the governor discovered I was there, he sent the garrison commander to fetch me to him. The man’s name is Colonel Patterson; he was the garrison commander under Lord Hornblower, so I knew him well.”

Greene sat silent as he listened to his commander’s tale. He could hear the edge, the raw emotion creeping into Brewer’s voice the further along he got.

Brewer took a gulp of coffee before continuing. “The governor remembered me. And he was every bit as surly and ill-mannered as I remembered him to be. I actually drew my sword on him when he called Hornblower a traitor. I threatened to run him through if he said another word like that. Can you believe it?”

Actually, Spinelli could not, and he quickly took a long drink of his now-tepid coffee to hide his surprise. Obviously, the subject of Napoleon Bonaparte was much touchier than he’d realized.

“You will be glad to know,” Brewer said, “that I managed to return to the ship without spilling any blood.”

“Thank heaven for that, sir,” the doctor said. “He meant a lot to you, didn’t he?”

“Whom do you mean?”

Spinelli just stared at him, one eyebrow arching off his forehead.

“Oh, Bonaparte? I don’t know; sometimes I think...” Brewer stopped mid-sentence. He stared into space, then at the ceiling, and finally at his desk. He rose and went to his desk. He pulled out his writing set and opened it, reaching deep inside and pulling out a decoration of some sort. From the way the Captain held it, Spinelli could see it obviously meant a lot to him. He lightly brushed it with his fingertips, and the doctor heard him sigh. The captain returned and sat down again, holding it out for his friend to examine.

"Do you know what this is?" he asked.

Brewer handed Spinelli a military decoration. It was a small five-pointed Maltese Cross attached to a short ribbon of rich red cloth. There was a disc in the center which held the head of a woman set in blue, surrounded by what appeared to be two French phrases. He turned it over, and saw that the reverse showed two crossed French flags, and a phrase or motto in French along with a date. Spinelli nodded in appreciation and handed the medallion back.

"Impressive," he said. "What is it?"

Brewer stared at him for a moment. "This, my dear Doctor, is the Grand Cross of the *Légion d'honneur*. That is the highest decoration given by the French Empire. The one in your hand is the personal medallion of the Grand Master of the Order."

Suddenly, it all made sense to the doctor. "Napoleon Bonaparte gave this to you," he said softly, "while you were on St. Helena."

The captain's face was very somber as he looked down at the trinket in his hands. "It was the last time he came to see me, just a day or so before we left the island. The governor was at his house, supervising the packing of the last of his belongings to be shipped back to England. I was working on reports, trying to get everything in line so the transition to the new administration would go smoothly. The office door opened, and Bonaparte came in. He was in uniform, as he usually was when he came to the governor's office, but he was not wearing his greatcoat; I don't know why, but that point sticks out in my mind. I rose to my feet as he approached and explained to him that the governor was not there. That was when he told me that he had come to see me."

Brewer shook his head in disbelief. "Can you imagine how I felt, Doctor? Napoleon Bonaparte coming to see *me*? He was quick to reassure me that the governor knew of his visit and had approved it in advance, but that did little to calm my nerves. We sat together in the office, and he gave me advice... about life, and seizing opportunity when it shows itself. Appropriate, don't you think, coming from him? I have no idea how long we spoke, but when he rose to take his leave of me, he hesitated for a moment before turning to me.

"'*M. Brewer,*' he said somewhat sadly, 'I wish in my heart that I had some substantial way to reward you for your faithful service to your governor and also your kindness to me in my exile.' He removed this from his own uniform and pinned it to my coat. 'What I give you now, I can never again give to another. You, *mon ami*, are the final person I shall ever induct into the *Légion d'honneur*. I present you with the Grand Cross of the Order. There is only one in the world, and it is worn by the Grand Master. I no longer have need of it, but I desire that it be held by one who has earned it by deeds and shall wear it with honor.'"

Brewer stared at the medal. "I didn't know what to say, Adam. I also didn't know what to do with it—it wasn't exactly something one could wear on one's uniform, or even display openly. Bonaparte noticed my hesitation, and he smiled at me. 'Fear not, M. Brewer,' he said. 'I know this must be our secret, and in truth I prefer it that way. I know you will cherish it as I have, and that is all I require of you.' He stepped up and kissed me on both cheeks. I tell you, Adam, I was so caught up in the moment that I could think of nothing else to do. I came to attention and snapped off a perfect salute. I did it to honor the man, not his nation or his history, but the man I knew. If that makes me a traitor, so be it."

Spinelli smiled. "I hardly think it does, William. What did Bonaparte do when you saluted him?"

Brewer stood, still looking at the medallion. "He was surprised that I did it—I could see it on his face. He came to attention and returned the salute. He said, *'Bonne chance, mon ami. Adieu.'* Then he left without looking back. I will always remember those last words to me—'Good luck, my friend. Farewell.'"

Brewer returned the medal to its hiding place and returned again to sit down beside his friend. "You are the first person I have shown that to since that day. Hornblower and Bush have no idea that I have it. I would appreciate it if this remained in confidence."

"Have no fear," Spinelli said, "my lips are sealed."

At that moment, Alfred appeared to announce that supper was ready, and the two men made their way to the table. Spinelli was concerned about his friend, but he had no idea how to help him.

Alfred brought out the ham, while Mac took up his usual place just inside the door. The servant left and returned with the potatoes and carrots, and then did so again to bring the wine. Spinelli took note of all this; a quick look at his captain told him he was oblivious. The doctor admired the way Mac and Alfred were protecting their captain—they obviously didn't want any of the crew to see him this way. He made a mental note to thank them both later.

The ham was extraordinary. The doctor was slicing a piece on his plate when an idea hit him.

"Tell me, Captain," he said nonchalantly, "did Bonaparte ever share any stories?"

Brewer looked up. "Stories?"

"Yes, war stories, strange things that happened to him, that sort of thing. I should think a man who'd gone through what he did in his life would have thousands. Did he ever share any?"

Brewer smiled and sat back in his chair. "Oh, one or two. I remember he told the governor and me about a rabbit hunt."

"Rabbits?"

"Yes. It seems they were on a campaign in... let me see, Glacia, I think it was. Anyway, the Army was resting for the day, so the emperor asked his chief of staff to organize a rabbit hunt as a diversion for his staff and senior commanders."

Spinelli chewed a piece of ham as he listened and wondered where the captain was going with this.

"The chief-of-staff's name was Berthier," Brewer continued, "and he was the best in the world at what he did. In fact, it has been said that the reason Bonaparte lost Waterloo was that Berthier was not there."

"Fascinating."

"It seems Berthier did his usual good job in organizing the hunt, and by the time Bonaparte and his guests were notified the hunt was ready, Berthier had over 3,000 rabbits ready to be hunted."

Spinelli's fork stopped halfway to his mouth. "Good Lord."

"Yes. So Bonaparte and his guests arrive, expecting to enjoy an afternoon's hunt followed by a delicious meal cooked from what they would bag during the afternoon. The trouble was—according to Bonaparte—nobody had told the rabbits they were supposed to be the prey. When the rabbits were released, they didn't run—instead they charged the hunters en masse! Bonaparte, his marshals, and all their combined staff were forced to flee for their lives!"

Both officers erupted with laughter. The very thought of the great Napoleon fleeing before a horde of rabbits very nearly left them hysterical. By the time they'd calmed down, both could hardly breathe. They resumed their meal, and then Spinelli looked up.

"By the way, did Boney say what they ended up eating that night?"

Brewer smiled as he helped himself to the carrots. "I believe he ordered his cook to make a soup."

The doctor laughed again and lifted his drink in a toast.

"Vive les Rabbits!"

After the meal, they retired to the day cabin for wine and cigars. Spinelli selected a cigar, bit off the end, lit it, and inhaled deeply.

"I envy you, William."

"How so?"

"Your time with Bonaparte. What I would give to have had the chance!"

Brewer nodded as he drew deeply on his cigar. "I can imagine. I cherish the memories. I rarely speak of him, you know? Too many people have accused me—along with Lord Hornblower—of being a traitor and giving aid and comfort to the most dangerous enemy in England's history."

Spinelli took a sip of wine. "And how did you respond to that?"

The captain thought for a while before answering. "Lord Hornblower's mandate was to put Bonaparte in his place, but quietly and man-to-man. He succeeded brilliantly. As a result, Bonaparte would come to the governor's office frequently to converse with him about whatever interested either of them. This was exactly what his Lordship was instructed to do—keep Bonaparte occupied so he didn't cause England international embarrassment before the Allied Commissioners. His Lordship came to an agreement with Bonaparte that if he would behave, the governor would do all in his power to make the ex-emperor as comfortable as possible by improving his living conditions. Again, this was entirely within his instructions."

The captain paused to take a drag of his cigar and blow a cloud toward the deck beams above. Spinelli could see the somber look on his face. "The problem was, there were forces both in His Majesty's Government and at several of the European courts that were against what we were trying to do, because they wanted to humiliate Bonaparte. Lord Hornblower told me an interesting fact once. Did you know, Adam, that when he escaped Elba, the European powers declared war on him?"

"Well, of course they did."

"No," Brewer said, perhaps a bit forcefully. "You don't understand. Austria, Russia, Prussia, and England did not declare war on *France*, they declared war on *Napoleon Bonaparte*."

Spinelli just stared at him as the full weight of what he had heard registered.

"They declared *war* on a *person*?" he asked.

Brewer nodded behind his cigar, and Spinelli sat back in awe at the implications. The captain continued.

"When he was defeated at Waterloo, he sought sanctuary with the British fleet. It probably saved his life. The Prussians were openly calling for his execution, and the Austrians and the Russians probably would not have stood in their way. The British refused to turn him over and took him to St. Helena.

"You must understand, Adam: the Napoleon Bonaparte I knew was not the despot who overran Europe. By the time Lord Hornblower and I arrived, he had been on the island going on two years, and he was beginning to accept that his destiny was to die on the island."

The doctor blew smoke at the deck beams above and looked to his friend.

"You should write a book about him."

"Who?"

"Bonaparte. Tell the truth about Hornblower's mission and his interaction with Bonaparte. The world deserves to know the truth."

Brewer's eyes snapped to his companion.

"What?" Spinelli asked.

His captain blinked and shook his head. “Nothing. It’s that phrase you used. Colonel Patterson said something similar when he told me he was going to write a book about events on the island after Hornblower and I left.”

Spinelli took a long drag on his cigar. “Interesting. Still, I urge you to consider writing your own memoirs. You can leave the manuscript with a solicitor with orders to publish after all parties are dead, if you want.” Spinelli sat forward. “If nothing else, do it for his lordship.”

“His lordship?”

“Yes!” the doctor puffed his cigar into life again. “He will need someone to vouch for his character during that time, and as I read the man, I don’t think he is going to do it himself, do you?”

Brewer thought for a moment before shaking his head. “No, he would not.”

Spinelli gestured with his hands, his cigar leaving a trail of smoke. “There you have it. If he won’t do it, it falls to you. Otherwise, history will be written by the forces that sent Lowe to relieve you. It’s up to you to put the truth out there so the public will know.”

Brewer liked the doctor’s idea, but he was unsure what was the right thing to do. “I’ll ask Lord Hornblower—”

“No!” Spinelli nearly jumped out of his chair. “William, if you do that, Hornblower will very likely order you never to put pen to paper! Or, worse yet, he would ask you as a personal favor to keep all such knowledge to yourself.”

Brewer stared at Adam, knowing in his heart that he had spoken the truth. Hornblower would never allow him to do anything that smacked of defending his reputation. Yet Brewer knew that it would need defending. Bonaparte’s life story would begin to appear in print in the next several years, and Hornblower's part in the emperor's stay on St. Helena—along with his own—was doomed to be mischaracterized, at best, and falsified outright, at worst. *Someone* was going to have to step up and set the record straight, and he was the obvious choice. He frowned at the thought of keeping it a secret from Hornblower and Bush, but he smiled when he considered that Lady Barbara would enthusiastically endorse the project. Finally, he set his cigar in the ashtray and called to Alfred for more coffee.

He turned to the doctor. "I'll think about it."

Spinelli smiled behind his cigar. "That's all I ask."

CHAPTER ELEVEN

Captain Brewer stood in the midst of the quarterdeck with his premier at his side as HMS *Phoebe* sailed down the channel and anchored in the harbor at Rio de Janeiro. Lieutenant Rivkins was the officer of the watch and he had successfully conned the frigate down the channel. Mr. Sweeney came and stood on the other side of Mr. Greene with a smile on his face.

"What's so funny?" Greene asked.

"Oh" Sweeney said, pointing off their starboard bow. "I just enjoy greeting his lordship every time I sail into this harbor."

Brewer overheard the exchange and turned his head in the direction of the rock formation colloquially known to British seamen as "Lord Hood's Nose." Brewer had to admit privately, having met the famous admiral many years ago, when he'd been a brand new midshipman, that the formation did indeed bear a resemblance to the old man.

He grunted. "Too bad we can't wake the old boy and get him to settle all our problems with the Brazilians."

Sweeney and Greene chuckled softly and stepped away toward the wheel.

"Commodore's broad pennant on the larboard beam, Captain!" It was Mr. Drake, *Phoebe's* youngest and newest midshipman.

"What? The commodore's still here? He was supposed to be in Salvador by this time."

Greene had grabbed a glass and was already at the rail. "That's *Superb* all right, sir!"

Mr. Drake raised his voice again. "There's another seventy-four past *Superb*, Captain! Can't make out the flag yet!"

"Doesn't look like one of ours, sir!" Greene added.

Brewer took a glass and jumped up the mizzen shrouds for a better look at the new ship. He had to agree with Mr. Greene—it wasn't a British ship. He could see a couple of officers on the poop, and they were not wearing British uniforms, or French either, for that matter. He did not think the ship was Portuguese, not in Rio, and it did not show any damage that might say it had been taken by the Brazilians as a prize after a battle. That left one option—the Brazilian Navy had Lord Cochrane and a brand new seventy-four at their disposal. Brewer lowered his glass and swallowed hard as he climbed back down to the deck; the British squadron's mission had just become that much more difficult.

Brewer no sooner set foot on the deck than Mr. Dye presented himself and saluted.

"Beg your pardon, Captain," he said, "but we've received a signal from the flagship. Our number. *'Captain come on board.'*"

"Thank you, Mr. Dye," he said. "Mr. Greene, call away the gig."

"Already done, sir," Greene said. "Mac's waiting for you."

Brewer smiled. "Thank you, Benjamin. I shall go change and then see what the Commodore wants."

Brewer stepped through the entry port of HMS *Superb* after a swift transit and was greeted by Captain Lee. The two officers saluted and shook hands.

"It's good to see you again, Captain," Lee said.

"And you. Here are my reports," Brewer handed the packet to Lee, who turned them over to his flag lieutenant. "Who's the new boy next door?"

Lee turned to lead his guest to the commodore's cabin. "You noticed that, did you? Brazilian, the *Dom Pedro I.*"

"Where did the Brazilians get a seventy-four?"

Lee smiled ruefully. "From the Chileans. They contracted for it to be built in the United States, then sold it to the Brazilians just before completion. She arrived here two days ago."

They arrived at the door. Lee nodded to the sentry and opened the door to admit Brewer and himself. Commodore Hardy himself met them inside.

"Captain Brewer!" he said, shaking the newcomer's hand. "Good to see you again, sir."

"And you, Commodore. I must confess, I did not expect to find you here."

"Yes, well, we got word that our friend next door was coming, and I decided it was best to delay my move to Salvador. Come, let me introduce you to her commander."

They walked into the commodore's day cabin, and Brewer came to a halt as the officer turned around. "Captain Brewer," he nodded. "Good to see you again."

Brewer swallowed and bowed. "And you, Lord Cochrane."

"The *admiral*," Hardy stressed, correcting Brewer's address, "and I were just discussing the strategic situation and Britain's place in it."

Hardy was treating Cochrane as a foreign admiral; his status as a member of the English nobility would not be taken into account.

"Indeed," Cochrane said.

Brewer turned back to Hardy. "And?"

"The admiral was just suggesting that we may wish to abandon our base at Salvador."

"Really?" Brewer looked back to the admiral.

Cochrane shrugged. "That was just a courtesy, Commodore. My fleet is about to tighten the blockade about Salvador to cut it off entirely from Lisbon."

"And the British ships?" Brewer asked.

"Any ship attempting to run the blockade would be subject to seizure as a prize of war, of course" Cochrane said.

Brewer's brows rose at the admiral's willingness to cross the country of his birth. He turned to Hardy, who hardly looked any happier at the turn of events.

"That may be considered an act of war against His Majesty's government, Admiral," he said coldly.

"Which is why the Emperor Dom Pedro I has granted my request to give the British six months to evacuate Salvador completely."

"You mean sell out and leave?" Brewer said incredulously. "Give up their livelihood, their businesses? And what about British merchantmen who try to enter the port?"

"They will be warned away," Cochrane said. "If they fail to heed the warning, they shall be considered blockade runners and seized."

"It is unlikely that the Royal Navy will allow British shipping to be taken by anyone," Hardy said.

Hardy's servant brought them each a glass of wine.

"Thank you," Hardy said. "I hope you enjoy this, gentlemen. It's the last of some excellent Boudreaux I got from the commander of the French squadron, Admiral Roussin, a few months ago."

"Roussin has been made admiral? Good for him."

"Do you know him?" Hardy asked.

"Yes," Brewer said. "We met when I visited Martinique last year."

Cochrane rose. "If I may, Commodore?"

Hardy nodded.

Cochrane raised his glass. "A toast, gentlemen. To the Emperor Dom Pedro I—long may he reign."

They sipped their wine, and Hardy raised his glass. "And a speedy end to the war."

"Here, here," Brewer echoed. Cochrane remained silent.

"I must say," the Brazilian admiral commented, "this wine is as good as advertised, Commodore."

The three stood in silence for a moment while they drank their wine before Cochrane remarked, "Tell me, Captain Brewer," he said, "do you remember Captain Turrado?"

"Turrado?" Brewer feigned confusion. "I don't believe I do. Should I?"

"Yes," Cochrane said. "You met in the Caribbean."

"Ah," Brewer said. "You mean the captain of the *Valdivia*. Yes, I believe I do remember him. In fact, I met him again just recently, off the Peruvian coast in the Pacific."

"Captain?" Hardy asked, clearly wishing for Brewer to repeat the story for Cochrane's benefit.

"Sir, we were dispatched under orders by Captain Vernon of HMS *Blossom* to patrol north as far as Peru before joining you at Rio. As we passed the northern tip of San Lorenzo, we discovered a captured English whaler, the *Syren*, taken by pirates and obviously on course to enter Callao."

"Strength?" Hardy demanded.

"A brig and two luggers. The pirates sent the brig and one lugger to keep us busy while the second lugger escorted the whaler eastward. We put a broadside into each of the pirates as we passed, disabling the brig and sinking the lugger, and then headed straight for the whaler. The second lugger abandoned their prize and headed for the coastline at full sail. We retook the whaler and escorted her south to Valparaiso. We made our course down the west side of San Lorenzo. As we cleared the island, we spotted the *Valdivia* closing on us from the other side of the island. I ordered the whaler to sail south as I turned *Phoebe* eastwards; my intention was to establish whether the newcomer wanted to talk or go after the whaler."

Cochrane bristled a bit, but Hardy signaled for Brewer to continue.

"*Valdivia* altered course to pursue the whaler. I fired a warning shot, but she refused to alter course so we engaged. We managed to fire two broadsides into her stern and also take down her mizzenmast. She was disabled when we left to escort the whaler to Valparaiso."

Cochrane jumped. "Don't you think you acted a bit precipitously?"

Brewer glanced at Hardy before answering. "Not at all, sir. The *Valdivia* was warned off, but she chose to ignore that warning. I did what was necessary to ensure the safety of an unarmed English whaler."

"Are you sure it was necessary, Captain?" Cochrane pressed.

There was steel in Brewer's voice when he answered. . "Oh, it was necessary on several fronts, Admiral. First, as I have already said, Turrado was attempting to capture an English vessel. I stopped him. Second, we taught him a lesson about challenging the Royal Navy."

Cochrane bristled. "Commodore, are you going to tolerate such behavior?"

"Tolerate it? My dear Admiral," Hardy said, "I intend to commend it in my report to the Admiralty."

Cochrane rose. "I shall report this to my emperor. I doubt it will do anything to improve England's standing at his court or in his new nation. I shall now deliver a message I was asked to convey. Captain Turrado has asked me to tell you, Captain Brewer, that there will be a reckoning."

"If he insists," Brewer said, "I shall certainly oblige him. Only please tell him this, sir: if there is a next time, I shall not show him any mercy."

Cochrane smiled. "My dear Captain, I should be very surprised if Captain Turrado were not of the same opinion."

The English officers stood to bid the admiral goodbye, and Captain Lee escorted the Brazilian admiral to the entry port. As soon as they were gone, Brewer breathed a low sigh of relief.

Hardy called for more wine before sitting down. "I believe you have now officially made an enemy."

Brewer shrugged. "Did you notice that he called Dom Pedro 'my emperor'?"

Hardy nodded. "Yes, I caught that."

Brewer chuckled. "I wonder if Pedro knows that Cochrane would leave his service if someone offered him a bigger purse?"

"Take care, Captain," Hardy said. "Cochrane is still an English earl, and he still has one or two friends in London."

Brewer took the hint. "Aye, sir." Brewer sighed. "Is he the reason you're still here?"

"Yes," Hardy said. "I heard rumors that Cochrane was in possession of a seventy-four and was headed this way, so I decided to wait for him and hear him out. When he arrived, I invited him to dine so I could ask his intentions. He was quite open. You heard him yourself—he intends to take his fleet and blockade Salvador. That city is the last remaining stronghold for the Portuguese in Brazil, and its surrender will all but guarantee Brazilian independence."

"But what about the English presence there? Do you think he will really stop English merchantmen from sailing into port to supply them?"

Hardy remained silent, but it was clear to Brewer that he considered it entirely possible.

Brewer shook his head in disgust and disbelief. "And how long will it be until he declares medicines a war material? Or boots? Or *food,* for that matter?" Brewer stewed. "What about the squadron? Are you still planning to base it there and have our ships carry in supplies?"

"The admiral has told me they will not be stopped, providing the supplies brought by our ships do not go ashore. I gave him my word that nothing would, and I expect you to honor that, Captain."

"Aye, sir."

Hardy took a long drink of his Bordeaux and set his glass down. "For all his bluster, Cochrane is not stupid. He knows he cannot win if the Royal Navy comes in on the side of the Portuguese. Therefore he will do his utmost to avoid antagonizing His Majesty's Government."

Brewer looked at him over his glass. "Do you really believe that?"

Hardy looked at him and smiled. "Oh, I think you gave him sufficient evidence of our resolve in the Pacific, don't you?"

"We did our best, sir."

"You may be wondering what it is that is making Cochrane play his waiting game—other than our squadron, that is. He has heard a rumor, and he is after a prize. He has heard that when the Portuguese king returned to his country he left behind the Portuguese national treasury."

Brewer was astonished. "You mean the actual national treasury?"

"I'm afraid so," the Commodore said. "You may remember that the Portuguese, alone of all the courts of Europe, had sufficient warning that Bonaparte was coming to be able to make arrangements for their king and court. They barely escaped Lisbon ahead of the French army and crossed to Brazil in a convoy of merchant ships, escorted by the Royal Navy. The convoy dropped the court off at Rio and afterwards quietly transported the gold and jewels to

Salvador, Portugal's strongest base in South America. When the king was forced to return to Europe, he hid the fact that the treasury was remaining behind. Presumably, he didn't want it to fall into the hands of the Junta."

Brewer was thinking furiously. "And you think Cochrane is after the Portuguese gold?"

Hardy looked bemused. "Wouldn't you be, if you were he?"

Brewer shook his head at the wonder of it all. Taking the Portuguese treasury would tilt the war conclusively in Brazil's favor, not to mention crippling Portugal's capability to make war at all. He looked back at the commodore.

"And what do we do?"

Hardy shrugged uneasily. "I do not know yet how the Admiralty will order us to act."

Brewer persisted. "But if he tries, do we stop him?"

Hardy managed a small smile. "Not unless the gold is being carried on English ships."

Brewer was amazed. The Portuguese national treasury had to be worth several kings' ransoms! Portugal had held an overseas empire, and for more than a century, gold and other resources had been sent back to Lisbon free from the molestation that English commanders, from Drake to Nelson, had inflicted on the Spanish treasure galleons. Add to that the fact that, unlike their Spanish neighbors, the Portuguese did not spend their wealth profligately. *If Cochrane is successful in getting his hands on even a portion of such a sum, he would immediately become the wealthiest person in England! He could buy his way to the Admiralty any time he wished, and nobody would dare to stand in his way.*

His eyes met the Commodore's. "We can't let him get his hands on it."

"I just told you, Captain, I don't know –"

"Begging your pardon, sir," Brewer interrupted, "you're not understanding me. I don't care about the Brazilians—we can't let *him* get his hands on one coin of that treasure."

Hardy's eyes narrowed. "You mean Cochrane?"

"Aye, sir. Can you imagine what Cochrane would do with that much money? He would return to England and buy whatever he wants, starting with the Admiralty and possibly moving on to the government itself."

Hardy stared at the young captain for several seconds through hooded eyes, digesting what he had heard and considering it from all angles.

Finally, Hardy tossed back the last of his wine. "Well, Mr. Brewer," he said, "try as I might, I can't find a hole in your logic." He moved towards the door, and Brewer followed suit. Hardy said, "I will send new sailing orders to you tomorrow. I am leaving for Salvador on the morning tide. I want you to wait two weeks, then follow me there. Your orders will contain a list of additional supplies you are to bring for the squadron. Captain," he paused to make sure he had Brewer's full attention, "I am trusting you not to create an international incident while I'm gone."

Brewer fought down a smile. "Aye, sir."

Captain Brewer sat erect and silent on his way back to the *Phoebe*, but his mind was racing with the implications of the Portuguese national treasure still being on Brazilian soil. He was trying to come up with a plan to safeguard the bullion without drawing England into a war with either Brazil or

Portugal, but for the life of him, he could not see a way. The Brazilian army had Salvador surrounded and under siege, while the emperor had bought Admiral Cochrane a navy powerful enough to blockade the port and make sure the treasure didn't leave via the sea. Sailing the gold out and back to Lisbon in English ships would be a direct provocation, and no matter how much the king hoped the Portuguese would win, Brewer doubted he was willing to go that far.

The captain's mind was so occupied that his body moved of its own accord after his gig reached his ship. Brewer was startled when Mr. Greene spoke to him.

"Welcome back, sir," Greene said. "I trust your visit with the commodore went well?"

Brewer recovered quickly. "As well as it could with Admiral Cochrane there."

Greene whistled in surprise. "Cochrane here? He must have brought in that spanking new seventy-four." The premier smiled. "Was he glad to see you?"

"About as much as you might expect, especially after he told me he'd heard from Captain Turrado about our meeting in the Pacific. Follow me, Mr. Greene." He looked to the quartermaster. "You have the deck. I shall be in my cabin. Have Dr. Spinelli join me there."

"Aye, sir."

"So, he wasn't pleased?" Greene clasped his hands behind his back as he followed his captain below. "By the way, did you notice that the *Amazone* is now flying an admiral's broad pennant?"

Brewer led the way aft, nodding to the sentry as he entered his cabin and began shedding his hat, coat, and sword.

"Yes," he said, "the commodore informed me of Roussin's promotion. I Say!" Brewer turned to his guest, "Shall we send Mr. Reed over with an invitation to dine? We'll help him celebrate." He went to his desk and quickly wrote out the invitation. Greene passed the word for the fourth lieutenant. When he turned back again, the captain was sealing the invitation with wax.

"I made it simple," he said. "It says, *'My cook is in good health. The usual time?'*

There was a knock at the door, and the sentry admitted Mr. Reed. Brewer gave him his instructions and dispatched him with the invitation. As Reed was heading out, he paused to allow the doctor to come in.

"You sent for me, sir?" the doctor asked.

"Yes, Adam, come in. Gentlemen, shall we sit in the day cabin? Alfred!" Brewer called. "Wine, if you please. Now, gentlemen, I have just come back from the flagship. Oh, thank you, Alfred." Brewer paused while his Alfred poured each of them a drink before leaving the decanter. Alfred bowed and left the cabin.

"I believe I need some counsel on how I should proceed. Lord Cochrane, now the commanding admiral of the new Brazilian Navy, was there as well. In fact, he brought us greetings from our old friend Captain Turrado, along with that worthy's promise that our next encounter will end very differently."

Greene sipped his wine. "I don't think it will."

Brewer smiled. "Nor I. However, the admiral intends to take his ships to Salvador and blockade the port. After the admiral had left, the commodore told me something extraordinary. It seems that the Portuguese national treasury is at this moment hidden somewhere ashore at Salvador."

Brewer drank of his wine as his companions stared at him.

"Excuse me," the doctor said as he set his glass down, "I want to make sure I heard you correctly. You said the *Portuguese national treasure* is at Salvador?"

"Yes."

"The same Salvador that is under siege and soon will be blockaded?"

"Yes."

The doctor rubbed his hands. "Oh, yes, that's much clearer now. You're saying the Brazilians are going to try to take the treasure."

"Worse," Brewer said, "Cochrane will." He spent the next half-hour reprising his conversation with Commodore Hardy on the danger Cochrane would pose should he manage to hang on to even ten percent of a treasure of that size. When he was finished, his companions were as dazed by the implications as he had been.

"So," Spinelli said, "as far as we are concerned, what is the question? How do we safeguard the treasure, or how do we keep it out of Cochrane's hands?"

Brewer sighed. "I don't know. The commodore is considering his options. I think we have to come up with a plan to keep it out of Brazilian hands altogether."

"Agreed," Greene said firmly.

Brewer looked to Spinelli. "Doctor?"

Spinelli rubbed his chin. "May I suggest we wait until Admiral Roussin arrives and seek his advice?"

The sentry knocked at the door and admitted Mr. Reed.

"Captain," he said, "the admiral says he and his flag captain will gladly accept your invitation. He also told me to warn you that he has not given up hope that Mr. Thomas will defect to the French Navy."

At the turn of the second dog watch, Captain Brewer stood at HMS *Phoebe's* entry port to welcome aboard Admiral Roussin and his flag captain, the newly-promoted Captain de Robespierre. He escorted them to his cabin, where Lieutenant Greene and the doctor awaited them. Mac met them inside the door to take their hats and coats.

"Well," Brewer said, "congratulations to both of you on your promotions!"

"Here, here!" cried Spinelli.

"Well deserved!" echoed Greene.

"Gentlemen, won't you follow me to the day cabin?"

The five officers moved aft and settled themselves comfortably. Moments later, Alfred arrived bearing his silver platter laden with glasses of wine.

"Ah, *mon ami*," Roussin exclaimed, "there you are! Thank you. Monsieur de Robespierre and I are looking forward to another of your fabulous meals! Is there *any way* I can persuade you to leave these barbaric conditions under which you labor, and persuade you to come to cook for me?"

Greene looked at Spinelli. "This is barbaric?"

Spinelli shrugged.

Alfred blushed and bowed to their guests. "That is very generous of you, Admiral, but Captain Brewer needs me."

"Bah!" Robespierre said. "You can train a monkey to cook for an Englishman. He'd never know the difference!"

Greene looked to Brewer. "Is that true, sir?"

Brewer shrugged. "I suppose it depends on how well Alfred teaches the monkey."

"At least the cook would be the same size," Mac said from the doorway.

Alfred gave Mac a later-for-you look as he left the room, and Brewer laughed when he saw Mac swallow hard.

Brewer addressed his guest. "Allowing you to tempt my servant was only half the reason I invited you here tonight, my dear Admiral. I was called aboard the commodore's flagship this afternoon, and I ran into an old friend of ours."

"Monsieur Cochrane?"

"Now *Admiral* Cochrane, commanding the Navy of the Brazilian Emperor."

"So *he* is the one who brought in the new seventy-four," Robespierre said. "I wonder how well trained they are?"

"Well," Greene mused out loud, "Cochrane can teach them, but how well these Brazilians will fight is an open question. Don't forget, he's also trying to recruit English officers and men to man his ships."

Alfred stepped into the room and announced that dinner was served. The five men rose made their way to the table. Brewer turned to his coxswain.

"Mac," he said in mock severity, "I want you stationed by the door. Every time one of our distinguished guests leaves this cabin, you are to search him first. Understood?"

The big Cornishman grinned broadly. "Aye, sir."

Brewer nodded before looking back to his guests. "I'm sorry, gentlemen; *Alfred stays.*"

De Robespierre shook his head sadly and patted his admiral on the shoulder—an obvious gesture of comfort.

"Another cross we must bear in the service of our king, my Admiral," he said sadly.

Roussin sighed and looked like he would weep.

Brewer watched the play-acting unfold before him and could barely contain himself. The doctor began to snicker before losing all control and laughing uproariously. The rest joined him with relish, and, when they were done and Alfred served them, Brewer thought he recognized the compliment in the Frenchmen's jesting.

Brewer went to bed that night with mounting concerns about what Admiral Cochrane might do once Commodore Hardy left for Salvador. When he rose in the morning, he was still worried. However, when he stepped up on deck, the *Dom Pedro I* was nowhere to be seen.

"Good morning, sir," Greene said. "I was just coming to tell you, Admiral Cochrane sailed as soon as the tides allowed. He was free of the harbor before the commodore."

"Let's hope he won't be back," Brewer said.

HMS *Phoebe's* two-week stay in Rio harbor went by swiftly and uneventfully, save for the defection of Lieutenant Hobbs. Every few days or so, Brewer had taken to sending a boatful of men who had earned privileges into Rio, accompanied by an officer, for a few hours of shore leave. Eight days after Commodore Hardy left in *Superb*, Brewer sent the launch ashore with Hobbs, Mac, and twenty hands. At the scheduled end of their leave, the boat returned. Mac led the men back on deck.

Mr. Reed was standing by the railing, taking in the sea breeze. “Hello, Mac! Where’s Lieutenant Hobbs?”

“Stayed ashore, sir,” Mac said. He handed a sealed letter to Reed. “He said to give this to the captain when we returned.”

Reed stared at the letter. “I believe the captain is in his cabin. You had better take it to him, Mac. I’m certain he’ll have questions for you.”

“Aye, sir.” Mac made his way below and the sentry admitted him. He found the captain playing chess with the doctor, with Mr. Greene observing.

Brewer looked up when the coxswain entered. “Yes, Mac?”

Mac held out the letter. “Mr. Hobbs said to give this to you, sir.”

Brewer broke the seal, unfolded the paper and scanned its contents.

“William?” Spinelli said.

Brewer sighed and handed the letter over. “Just as we feared. Hobbs has resigned his commission to join the Brazilian navy. Better pay, he says, and more room for advancement. Mac, did he seem different to you on the way in?”

The coxswain shook his head. “No, sir. He seemed his normal self. I had no idea anything was wrong until he handed me the letter.”

Brewer nodded thoughtfully. “What happened after he gave it to you?”

Mac shrugged. “Nothing, sir; he just handed me the letter, said goodbye and left.”

Greene felt a pang. As the Captain had said, it was not unexpected, but that didn't make it hurt any less. Spinelli finished reading and passed the letter on without comment. He returned his attention to the chess match and studied the board.

"Doctor?" the captain prompted.

"Good riddance, I say," Spinelli said, and he moved a knight.

Greene and Mac smiled, and the captain sat back down to the game, moving his rook out of danger.

"Do you suppose we'll meet him on a Brazilian ship?" Greene asked.

"If we do," Brewer said as he moved his king's pawn, "he'll be treated as any other Brazilian officer."

"And if his ship tries to take an English ship?" Spinelli asked.

"He'll be treated like any other person," Brewer said, quietly but firmly.

Spinelli held his captain's eyes long enough to ensure he had not misunderstood before shifting his attention back to the board. Behind him, Mr. Greene sighed heavily and crossed his hands across his chest. His narrowed eyes and compressed lips showed he was under no misunderstanding as to his captain's meaning.

The day came when *Phoebe* began to take aboard the additional provisions for transfer to the squadron at Salvador. Mr. Greene took charge of the provisioning. The captain and Mr. Sweeney watched from the quarterdeck as the first lieutenant supervised the placement of supplies that would keep the South American Squadron independent for weeks.

Boat after boat made its way to the frigate's side, and net after net hoisted cargo aboard. Mr. Greene, with the aid of the bosun and the purser, carefully stowed each load so as not to adversely affect the balance of the ship. Three times he had to stop the loading process to allow the weight to be redistributed. When all was said and done, 17,000 pounds of bread, 3,648 pounds of beef, 1,960 pounds of flour, 150 pounds of raisins, 1,850 pounds of sugar, 1,013 gallons of rum, 420 gallons of wine, 130 gallons of vinegar, and 45 gallons of lime juice were secured below for the squadron's use. The last item to be loaded was undoubtedly the most welcome—livestock, including twenty live oxen, along with fodder for each. *Phoebe's* water tanks were also topped off with an additional one hundred tons.

"Good God, Mr. Sweeney," Brewer said, "sounds and smells like that make me miss my family's farm."

"Aye, sir," came the reply. "Too bad none of those beasties ain't for us."

The captain turned and placed his hand on the sailing master's shoulder. "*Tsk-tsk*, Mr. Sweeney! Do you think I would neglect the chance to reward my officers? You are cordially invited to dine with me this evening, sir, along with my officers and the doctor. Alfred is already hard at work choosing and cooking the finest side of beef he could find. He has promised me the best steaks, ribs, and roasts I have ever tasted! Now, what do you think of that?!"

Sweeney grinned broadly. "Captain, I beg your forgiveness!"

Brewer laughed and slapped Sweeney on the shoulder. "Turn of the second dog watch, sir! Do not be late!"

"Even if I was dead, I'd still be early for Mr. Alfred's cooking!"

Both men laughed heartily, and Brewer went to speak to Mr. Greene.

"Captain," Greene saluted.

"Mr. Greene. How goes our loading?"

"Just completed, sir. I was about to take a boat and go round the ship to see how she lies."

Brewer smiled. "Good idea. We sail on the morning tide, so we'll get a sense of how she maneuvers up the channel before we hit the open sea."

Brewer went to his cabin and found Mac tidying up.

"Mac?" he said. "Where's Alfred?"

"Sir, he asked me to mind the cabin today so he could give his full attention to the meat."

"Ah," Brewer said. "Well then, a cup of coffee, if you please, Mac."

"Aye, sir." The big Cornishman disappeared to attend to his task.

Brewer went to his desk and got out his writing materials. He carefully laid out paper, inkwell, and pen before taking his seat and taking pen in hand. Mac appeared at his desk with a steaming cup. Brewer thanked him and blew carefully on the rim before taking a cautious sip. He was pleased by how good it was; either Alfred had made it before he left, or Mac had been taking lessons. He set the cup down and picked up his pen. He closed his eyes and thought for a moment, then he dipped pen in ink and began:

My Dearest Elizabeth,

I am writing to you from Rio de Janeiro. The beaches are beautiful and the sun is warm. The only thing missing to make it Eden for me is you. I wish I had you here, rather than your portrait. I cannot kiss it, I cannot hold it in my arms, and it cannot answer me with your wisdom and compassion. Still, I speak to it every night, wishing it were you, and it is before me as I write you now.

I have not had much success in the matter of prize money on this commission, at least not yet. Where do you want to settle when we finally look to purchase an estate for ourselves? We have our choice of anywhere in the world, you know. England, America, the Caribbean, Europe, anywhere your heart desires. We have been invited to settle at Smallbridge with Lord and Lady Hornblower and Captain Bush, but by no means are we under any compulsion to accept. I mention the subject only so that you can be thinking about it. We can discuss it the next time we are together.

We have fought two battles thus far, and I have come through unscathed. Please continue to pray for my protection and that of my ship and crew. Speaking of praying, I have written my mother and sisters about our marriage, so you may be receiving letters from them. Never fear; I have simply told them the truth, that you are the most beautiful woman God ever placed on this earth and that you have completely stolen my heart.

It was nearly two hours later when the sentry announced Lieutenant Greene. Brewer looked up from writing and set his pen aside, careful to wipe it off and close the cap on the bottle of ink.

"Well, Mr. Greene?"

"She looks good, Captain," Greene reported. "All that's left to be seen is how she handles in a seaway."

"Fine. Sit, if you please, Benjamin. Coffee? No? Very well. I wanted your opinion on the necessity of replacing Mr. Hobbs. Specifically, I have two questions: First, do we *need* to replace him right now, and second, if we do, is Mr. Murdy ready to be promoted to Acting Lieutenant?"

Greene leaned back in his chair, staring at the deck above, his arms crossed over his chest and one hand stroking his chin absentmindedly. Mac stuck his head in to see about refills, and Brewer signaled him. Mac brought his captain a fresh, steaming cup and left without a sound. Brewer made a mental note to congratulate Alfred on his teaching methods.

Finally, Greene sighed and lowered his gaze to his captain's. He did not look satisfied with his answers, Brewer thought.

"Captain," Greene hesitated, "I do believe it would be in our best interests to promote someone to replace Mr. Hobbs. However, I am not sure that Mr. Murdy is ready to be promoted to Acting Lieutenant. He only just took over as senior midshipman with our current commission, and I think he needs to gain more experience before we talk about promoting him."

Brewer sucked his teeth and nodded. "Is that your only reason?"

"Yes, sir. I think that one day he will make a fine officer. Just not yet."

"Very well. Whom does that leave us? Do we have any master's mates who have passed?"

"No, sir," Greene said. "May I speak to Mr. Sweeney and then report back to you, sir?"

"Of course, Benjamin. I would like to have the matter settled by the time we reach Salvador."

"Aye, sir."

"Now, Mr. Greene, if you will excuse me, I shall endeavor to finish this letter to my wife. I shall see you for dinner."

Greene smiled as he rose. He came briefly to attention and made his way from the cabin. Brewer watched him go and thought once again how lucky he was to have Benjamin Greene as his premier.

Brewer welcomed his company at the turn of the second dog watch. Mr. Greene led the way in, followed by Acting Second Lieutenant Rivkins and Acting Third Lieutenant Reed. The captain of marines came next. His name was Charles Enfield, and Brewer was ashamed to realize that he knew very little about the man, other than a rumor that he had fought at Waterloo with Wellington. Enfield was tall and thin to the point of looking emaciated, but Brewer had seen him exercising with his marines and knew that there was a strength underneath undreamt of by the casual observer. Dr. Spinelli came in with Mr. Sweeney to complete the assembly.

Mac was busy serving drinks. Brewer and Greene took glasses as he passed by.

"Pressed into service again, eh, Mac?" the captain said.

"Aye, sir."

"Well, remember, when the cannonballs begin to fly, you work for me."

Mac smiled. "Oh, aye, sir!"

Brewer mingled with his guests, mainly listening, trying to catch pieces of the various conversations. He smiled upon hearing Mr. Sweeney describe in great detail to Dr. Spinelli what he would like to do to one of the oxen that were even now tied up on *Phoebe's* deck, and he wondered idly what Alfred or the cook would say if Sweeney were allowed to try.

Brewer paused when he heard Mr. Greene address Captain Enfield.

"Pardon me, Captain," Greene said, "but is it true that you fought at Waterloo?"

"I did indeed, Lieutenant," the marine answered. "I was with Maitland's Guards Brigade. In fact, it was us that sent the Frenchies running. When the Imperial Guard made their charge, they came straight at us. I was lying on my belly with the rest of the lads when suddenly who should ride up behind us but the Duke himself, and Maitland. They surveyed the scene, and then the Duke said something to Maitland I didn't hear. Maitland told us to stand up and fire, and the effect on the Guard was devastating! Our first volley hit them like a hammer, and they faltered. The second brought them to a dead stop, and at the third they broke and ran."

Enfield shook his head at the sad memory. "Words cannot describe what happened next. I fought with Wellesley on the Peninsula—before he was the Duke, you understand—so I was no stranger to the French army, although I had never come up against the Imperial Guard before. I knew their reputation, of course; they were called the finest soldiers in any army in the world, and at one time that may have been true. But on that field in Flanders that day, when they broke and ran they took the entire French army with them." He turned and noticed Brewer listening. "Oh! I'm sorry, Captain; I didn't see you there."

"Quite all right, Captain. I was listening to your story."

At that time, Alfred appeared and announced that the meal was ready to be served. The men made their way to their places and sat down. While the trays were being brought in, Brewer turned to Enfield.

"Tell me, Captain, did you ever catch sight of Bonaparte across the battlefield?"

"No, Captain," Enfield actually sounded sorry. "We started out flat on the ground to protect ourselves from the French artillery. By the time we rose to repulse the Guard, the smoke was so thick that a body couldn't see across the battlefield with any clarity. We were concentrating on the enemy in front of us."

"Of course," Brewer said, and he turned his attention to the delicious meat pie Alfred had placed before him.

Enfield stirred. "Pardon me, Captain, but is it true you met Bonaparte?"

Brewer finished his mouthful and nodded. "It is, Captain. I had the honor to serve as Lord Hornblower's secretary when he was governor of St. Helena. I saw Bonaparte often when he came to see the governor."

"May I ask, sir, what was he like?"

Brewer took a long drink from his glass. He noticed Greene's eyes flash to him for a moment—of all the company present, Greene alone knew how he guarded his time with Bonaparte. Brewer set his glass down and sighed.

"The Bonaparte I knew was a different man from the victor at Austerlitz or even the foe you defeated at Waterloo, Captain," he said. "Remember, he had been on the island nearly two years by that time, and it was beginning to dawn on him that he would spend the rest of his life there. That... subdued him somewhat. Mind you, his mind and personality were as strong as they'd ever been. I believe that is one reason he got along so well with Lord Hornblower. Both rose from humble origins to nobility solely on the virtue of their military victories, and both were adored by their men."

Enfield snorted. "So he wasn't the despot who tried to conquer Europe? Is that what you're saying, Captain?"

Something in the man's tone generated an instantaneous reaction. Greene, Rivkins, and Reed all stared at the captain of marines, while Greene alone looked to Brewer for instructions. Brewer shifted his gaze from Enfield to Greene long enough to shake his head, a barely perceptible gesture.

"I am sure, Captain," Brewer said slowly, "that you realize that you misspoke just now, seeing how you never met the man, either as a despot or as the exile that I knew. I must ask you to guard your tongue, sir."

Enfield had the good sense to look chastised.

"I apologize if I have offended, Captain," he said. "People can change, I suppose."

Brewer nodded his head, accepting the marine's apology. "Thank you, Captain." He turned to Mr. Greene. "I, for one, am glad those days are behind us."

Greene frowned. "Captain, do you think the new regime in France can survive? I don't see anything that suggests the Bourbons have learned anything since the death of Louis XVI and his queen." He looked around the table. "If they don't change, what's to stop the same conditions from arising again, forcing the people to begin another revolution? And what if that revolution allows the rise of another like Bonaparte?"

"These are difficult questions, Mr. Greene," Brewer said. "We hope the Bourbons have learned something about the consequences of their actions. As for a second revolution, I imagine that the Austrian and Russian governments will be watching what goes on inside France with great attentiveness, and would not hesitate to send their armies into France if they thought an uprising might overthrow the king."

Greene considered. "If another revolution does come about, do you think one of Bonaparte's family will step forward?"

Brewer smiled. "Not if Bonaparte's descriptions of them were accurate. Apparently, there were times when he wondered if either he or they were adopted."

That brought smiles around the table.

"I take it he never asked?" Doctor Spinelli inquired.

"Doctor, there was one thing I was able to discover about Napoleon Bonaparte. Do you know who was the only person he feared on the Earth?"

The doctor shook his head.

Brewer looked at him. "His mother."

The men roared with laughter.

"Are you serious, sir?" Mr. Greene asked.

"Indeed! He told me the story of when his mother was presented to him for the first time after he was crowned emperor. He held out his hand for her to kiss, just as he had for everyone else in the reception line, only she rapped him across the knuckles with her fan!"

The laughter resounded again until there wasn't a dry eye in the room. Eventually, the room quieted down and the men returned to their meal. Meat pie and cutlets, stewed potatoes, carrots, peas, and pudding all disappeared in short order, and very soon Brewer's guests were sitting back in their chairs, satisfied as never before. Brewer took advantage of the lull in conversation to stand.

"Gentlemen," he said loudly so as to gain their attention, "since we embarked on this voyage, we have faced trials that I, for one, have never faced before. We have forged our frigate into what in my humble opinion can only be called the premier weapon in the South American Squadron!" Cheers went up around the room, quieting only when Brewer raised his hand for silence. "And I am well aware that this is due to *your* hard work! It is my honor to be able to reward your attention to duty and your care for this crew with this modest feast. Thank you, one and all!"

Applause and the stomping of boots echoed throughout the room. Brewer sat down. He was proud of these men; they were entitled to express themselves this way. He looked down the table and caught Mr. Sweeney's eye. The sailing master had a satisfied expression on his face. Brewer knew exactly how he felt.

CHAPTER TWELVE

Captain William Brewer was on deck at the break of day, not wanting to waste a single minute of daylight in leaving Rio de Janeiro behind and making their way to Salvador. He walked to the rail and paid his obeisance to Lord Hood's Nose. Mr. Sweeney joined him.

"Penny for your thoughts, Captain?" the sailing master asked.

Brewer nodded toward the famous rocks. "I was just wondering if the old boy knew he was being so honored."

Sweeney chuckled. "Not so far as I know. If he had, I imagine there would be a cemetery at its base."

The captain turned and smiled at that. "Right. Let's get underway, Mr. Sweeney."

At that moment, the First Lieutenant presented himself. "Ebb flow in fifteen minutes, sir. The anchor's hove short."

"Thank you, Mr. Greene. Take us out to sea, if you please."

"Aye, sir!" Greene picked up a speaking trumpet and stepped forward. "Stand by the capstan! Loose the heads'ls! Hands aloft to loose the tops'ls!"

The deck exploded with activity. Brewer stood his ground and took in every action, every movement. He had known for a long time that he could trust Greene's seamanship, and he never tired of seeing this symphony play out before him. The ship made her way slowly for the open sea. Brewer was careful to hold his place, feeling the movement of his ship as a doctor would feel a patient's pulse during an examination. He always marveled at how he could be "at one" with his ship. He never knew exactly when or how it had happened, but it had. It had been like that with *Revenge*, and now it was so with *Phoebe*.

When they entered the Bay of Guanabara, they found it empty, and Brewer decided to take advantage of the opportunity. "Mr. Rivkins!" Brewer called.

"Aye, sir?" The young lieutenant presented himself.

"You have the deck, Lieutenant," the Captain informed him. "Tack the ship, if you please."

"Aye, sir." Rivkins saluted and turned from his captain. "I have the deck! Ready about! Stations for stays!" He turned to the quartermaster at the wheel. "Keep a good full for stays!"

"Aye, sir!"

"Ease down your helm."

"Aye, sir."

Brewer and Greene watched as Rivkins looked about, timing his maneuver.

"Helm-a-lee!"

Rivkins kept one eye on the hands' actions and the other on the bracing. At the correct moment he shouted, "Raise tacks and sheets!" then later, "Mains'l haul!" This was the critical moment, and HMS *Phoebe* responded like a thoroughbred, straightening up on her new course without so much as a shudder.

Brewer smiled. Rivkins had timed the maneuver perfectly. Furthermore, Brewer had also verified that his premier knew very well how to pack a ship. Had *Phoebe* had too much weight forward, the bow would have dug into the water during the turn and put the ship in irons, necessitating a redistribution of weight aft. Brewer could not help a surge of pride in the seamanship of his officers as he turned to the quartermaster and called for a course for the open sea and Salvador.

When twilight fell, Brewer was in his cabin, enjoying a repast of eggs, ham, and toast. He turned the page of *Ivanhoe* as he reached for the butter. Suddenly, it occurred to him that Admiral Cochrane had not been at Rio when they'd left the harbor. He set the toast on his plate and wondered where Cochrane had taken the *Dom Pedro* and the rest of his new Brazilian Navy. The thought of meeting the renegade Englishman at sea made him wish that Admiral Roussin and the *Amazone* had sailed with him. His French ally had remained behind at Rio; Brewer had sent him a letter informing him of their plans and inviting him to Salvador if his orders permitted it.

The captain returned his attention to his toast. Meeting Cochrane on the open sea would almost surely mean a battle. Cochrane would not fail to take advantage of an opportunity to exact his revenge with no witnesses about. And while *Phoebe* could outrun *Dom Pedro*, Cochrane would certainly have one or two frigates at his disposal to engage his ship and slow it down, allowing Cochrane to arrive and deliver the *coup-de-grâce.* Brewer sighed and asked Alfred for coffee. He managed to read another two or three pages of his book, but he found that not even the jousts between Ivanhoe and the knights of Prince John at Ashby could hold his attention. He sighed and closed the book. He picked up his coffee and stepped into his day cabin, taking a seat on the settee beneath the great stern windows. He set his coffee down and leaned his head back, closing his eyes and letting the motion of the ship sooth him and calm his nerves. There was nothing to do but carry on, and it was foolish to worry about something that hadn't happened yet.

He sipped his coffee and was disagreeably surprised to discover he had allowed the brew to grow tepid. He briefly considered asking Alfred for another, but suspected he would not get through that one, either.

"Alfred!" he called.

Mac appeared in the doorway. "Can I help you, sir?"

"Mac? Oh, yes—pass the word for the doctor, if you please."

"The doctor? Aye, sir. Are you okay?"

"Fine, Mac. Just pass the word."

Fifteen minutes later, the sentry admitted Doctor Spinelli. He stumbled in, rubbing sleep from his eyes.

"You sent for me, Captain?" he asked as he leaned on the table.

"Yes, Adam. Did I wake you?"

The doctor shrugged. "Just a little nap, nothing I can't make up later. What can I do for you? Are you ill?"

Brewer sighed. "No, I'm not ill. In fact, I'm not anything. I was thinking about Cochrane being out to sea with his navy, and now I can't get it out of my mind. I was hoping you'd be up for a game to help me focus my mind on something else."

"My pleasure, Captain," Spinelli said. Mac retrieved the captain's chess set from storage, and while they were setting the board up the doctor said, "Of course, I'm not sure how much losing games to me will improve your disposition."

Brewer smiled but said nothing. They drew and the doctor chose white. For the first dozen moves or so, all was quiet. Spinelli knew his captain well enough to know that he would open up when he was ready, and nothing he could do or say would hasten the matter. About thirteen moves in, the doctor began harassing Brewer's queen with his knight and a bishop. The captain sat back in disgust.

"That's just how it would be," he said. "Now that Cochrane has a seventy-four and a few frigates and brigs he thinks he can rule Brazilian waters and bring about Brazil's independence from Portugal. Hardy won't put to sea to face him unless the Brazilians attack one of our warships, but I don't think Cochrane's that stupid."

"Unless the ship is the *Phoebe*," Spinelli said.

Brewer shrugged and took his opponent's bishop. The doctor responded by moving a rook and putting his captain in check. Brewer frowned.

Spinelli sat back. "Don't allow yourself to become fixated on Cochrane, William. You may miss something else entirely."

Brewer's frown deepened. Without a sound he tipped his king over, resigning the game, and began setting the board up for a new game. Spinelli smiled; he knew now that his captain would be all right.

Their voyage northward proceeded uneventfully. The animals on the deck, who objected loudly whenever the ship crested an unusually large swell, seemed to be the objects of the crew's desires. Lieutenant Rivkins entertained the wardroom one evening by repeating a one-sided conversation he'd heard, a quartermaster's mate telling one of the bovines—who remained totally oblivious—exactly how he would like to quarter and dress it before cooking it slowly on a well-greased spit over an open fire. The mate had even patted the creature on the side affectionately as he walked off.

Mac came on deck at the turn of the watch and found Pudge standing off, looking at the animals that were corralled on the deck. The boy wasn't approaching them at all; in fact, he looked rather confused by their presence.

"Hi, Pudge," he said. "What's going on here?"

"Hi, Mac," the lad said without looking up. "I'm just trying to figure out why we got all these animals with us while we're out to sea."

Mac grinned at that. "Don't you want them here?"

"Oh, I like them well enough," Pudge said quickly. "I mean, I love feeding and petting them and all, but what are they here for?"

"Lots of things," Mac said. "We get milk from the goats and eggs from the chickens. We cut up the cows when we get to Salvador and pass the sides of beef out to the other ships in the squadron. We might even fry up a chicken once in a while, just for a treat."

The boy's eyes went wide as saucers. "You mean you *eat them?*"

"Of course!" Mac could not believe what he was hearing. "Pudge, haven't you ever been on a farm?"

"Nope."

"Where do you come from?"

The boy names a village outside of Plymouth.

"Didn't your village have a slaughterhouse?"

"What's that?" he asked. Mac told him. Pudge shook his head emphatically. "Nope."

"Pudge," Mac asked, "do you like beef?"

The boy's face lit up. "Love it!"

Mac shook his head. "Pudge, beef comes from cows."

Pudge looked at Mac as though the big coxswain had grown a third eye. His mouth hung open in disbelief. His gaze shifted from Mac to the cows, calmly chewing, and then back again.

"You have a choice, Pudge," Mac said. "You can keep it as a pet, or you can eat. Which will it be?"

Mac sat back and watched the various emotions cross the boy's face. It was as if his heart was at war with his stomach. At the end, he saw Pudge sigh and pet the cow on the neck.

"We eat."

On the afternoon of the fourth day Mr. Reed was officer of the watch when a sail was sighted off the starboard beam. The captain was immediately notified and came up on deck. He took a glass and went to the rail. The small patch of white was clearly visible.

"Let's hear you, lookout!" he called. "What do you make of her?"

The lookout studied the strange sail before shouting down to the deck.

"Can't say, sir! She's still hull-down to me! She may be a frigate, judging by her sails."

"Shall I alter course to intercept, sir?" Mr. Reed asked him.

"For what reason, Mr. Reed?" Brewer asked. "What can we do if we do intercept him? Start a stampede as a boarding party?" He smiled as the young lieutenant went wide-eyed. "No, Mr. Reed," he said soothingly, "we shall do nothing. Keep a watch on the sail and let me know if she approaches."

Brewer continued to watch the patch of white for a while, wondering if it might indeed be Cochrane. He finally decided it wasn't and lowered his glass; Cochrane would have investigated a sighting by now, and this strange sail was about to disappear under the horizon. Brewer handed the glass to a midshipman and went below. Sooner or later, he would meet Cochrane again, and then accounts would be settled, one way or the other.

HMS Phoebe slid into the harbor at Salvador during the afternoon watch on the sixth day of their voyage. A small Brazilian squadron watched the port but made no attempt to stop *Phoebe*. A pilot came out and guided them to their berth. After he departed, Greene ordered lookouts into the shrouds to report on the shipping within the harbor.

"Sir?" Mr. Henry called, "I don't see *Superb* in the harbor!"

"I want eyes out for HMS *Superb*!" Greene shouted. "Now!"

Eyes up and down every shroud scanned the harbor to no avail.

Finally,Lieutenant Reed reported. “Sir, HMS *Superb* is not here.”

Brewer was just beginning to wonder what the absence of the flagship could mean when his thoughts were interrupted by a shout from the mainmast shrouds.

“Commodore’s broad pennant in sight, sir!” cried Mr. Dye, the midshipman in charge of signals. He jumped down and ran aft to his signal book. “The frigate is HMS *Creole,* sir —Captain Middleton!”

“Deck, there!” the mizzen lookout cried. “Boat pulling our way from the flagship.”

“Well,” Brewer said as he rocked back and forth on his heels, “hopefully, we shall find out what’s going on.”

“Aye, sir,” Greene said.

In short order, a lieutenant stepped up on deck and reported to the captain.

“Welcome to Salvador, Captain,” he said as he saluted. “I am Lieutenant Jonathan Dawson, Commodore Hardy’s new flag lieutenant.”

“Thank you, Lieutenant,” Brewer said. “What happened to HMS *Superb*?”

“Recalled to England on the normal rotation, Captain. The commodore’s transferred his flag temporarily to HMS *Creole* until his new flagship, HMS *Talavera,* arrives.” He dug into his satchel and pulled out a packet which he handed to Brewer.

“Here are your orders regarding distribution of the provisions you have brought with you, Captain,” he said. “In addition, Commodore Hardy invites you to dine with him this evening aboard HMS *Creole.* I shall return for you just after sundown, if that is convenient?”

"Indeed it is, Lieutenant. Now, if you will excuse me, I have work to do."

The flag lieutenant saluted and disappeared over the side.

Brewer watched him go before motioning for Mr. Greene to follow him below. Once they reached the confines of the captain's cabin, Brewer set the packet on his desk, took his coat off and tossed it on his bed before taking his seat at the desk. "Coffee, Benjamin?"

Greene declined the offer, so Brewer ordered coffee for one from Alfred. He returned his attention to the packet and verified that the seal was unbroken before opening it. He withdrew a sheaf of papers and scanned them. He frowned.

"We are to play the slaughterhouse, it seems," he said. "The beef is to be quartered here and then distributed, along with the other supplies, to *Creole, Beaver, Conway,* and *Doris*. Here are the quantities for each ship." He handed the papers to Greene, who skimmed them quickly before folding them away in his coat pocket. Brewer continued: "Get started on that at once, Benjamin; if you see to the slaughtering today, you may be able to begin distribution of the meat by morning."

At first Greene looked appalled, then he smiled.

"Sorry, sir; I forgot you were raised on a farm. Would you care to slaughter the first one, just for old time's sake?"

Brewer grinned. "No, thank you," he said sarcastically. "To be honest, I always hated slaughtering cattle. Except for one, that is—her name was Rose. She was the most bad-tempered cow I ever came across. She seemed to go out of her way to push me into the mud or chase me out of the pasture." He shook his head at the memory. "Best side of beef I ever ate."

Greene laughed and rose. "I'll get the men started at once, sir. If you'll excuse me?"

"Of course, Benjamin." Brewer watched his premier exit the cabin, and then he became aware that he was not alone. He turned to see the Alfred standing in the pantry doorway.

"Would you like more coffee, sir?" Alfred asked.

Brewer considered briefly before shaking his head. Alfred bowed and withdrew. Brewer raised his eyes to the deck above him as he heard the first of the cattle being led forward to the slaughter. A clearing of the throat let him know that Mac now stood in the doorway.

"Anything I can do for you, Captain?" he asked.

"I need my best uniform set out, Mac, complete with sword," he said. "I'm dining with the commodore aboard HMS *Creole* at dusk."

"Aye, sir. Shall I ready the gig, then?"

"No, the commodore is sending a boat for me. Just see to the uniform, if you please."

"Aye, sir."

Brewer smiled; he could tell Mac was disappointed at not being allowed to take his captain to his rendezvous.

"Of course, if you'd rather be up on deck slaughtering the cattle, I'm sure I could get Alfred to see to the clothes," the Captain offered.

"Oh, no, thank you, Captain," Mac stammered. "This will be just fine, thank you. Pudge! Come here and I'll show you how to take care of the Captain's clothes!"

The deck lamps were already lit when Captain William Brewer stepped up onto the deck of HMS *Creole*. She was actually smaller than Brewer's *Phoebe*, but with twenty-eight

32-pound carronades she would throw a devastating broadside at short range. Her captain met Brewer as he came aboard.

"Greetings, Captain Brewer," the man said. "I am Captain Clarence Middleton."

"An honor, sir," Brewer replied as he shook the man's hand.

Captain Middleton led Brewer below and to the captain's cabin, now occupied by Commodore Hardy. The sentry announced them formally and stood aside so they could enter. Brewer found Hardy in the day cabin, sipping wine from a crystal goblet. He stood as his guest appeared.

"Brewer!" he said. "Good to see you again! I trust you made it here without a visit from our friend in the Brazilian Navy?"

"Indeed, sir," Brewer replied. "We did sight a strange sail to the east about three days out from Rio, but I declined to investigate."

"Quite right, under the circumstances," Hardy said. "Jonathan, glass for Captain Brewer!"

The steward arrived with Brewer's port and the three officers toasted Brazilian independence.

"I've read your reports, which Lieutenant Dawson brought back earlier," Hardy said, "but I have some questions. Was Cochrane or the *Dom Pedro* at Rio when you left?"

"No, sir."

"And what was the strength of the Brazilian squadron outside Salvador when you entered?"

"A few brigs and sloops, sir, nothing more."

Hardy frowned at this intelligence. "Where has he gone?" he said, more or less under his breath. He looked up to Brewer. "My new flagship, HMS *Talavera*, is over a week late."

The implications were immediately apparent to Brewer. "You don't think Cochrane would be mad enough to attack a British seventy-four, do you? That would be insanity! Brazil has no chance if the Royal Navy entered the war on the side of the Portuguese."

Hardy chastened him with a look. "You've dealt with the man, Captain—what do you think?"

Brewer considered. "Yes, I suppose he could be so rash. But why would he chance it? He must realize we have no commitments at present that would prevent our concentrating overwhelming force if it were needed. It would be the end of him, and of the Brazilian Navy. Whereas if he leaves well enough alone, Britain's interests in Brazilian independence may be enough for us to remain effectively neutral."

"Indeed," Hardy mused. "But what do you think Cochrane would do if he decided that we were interfering with his plans for getting his hands on the Portuguese national treasury? We've already seen that he is not shy about taking vengeance—isn't that what he tried to do to you in the Caribbean? Would you put it past him to take the *Dom Pedro* and two or three frigates out to try to turn the *Talavera* around? What would he care about reprisals? By the time the Admiralty responded with force, he would have the treasure and be safely retired in Chile or Gran Colombia."

Brewer studied the dark liquid in his glass. The commodore's assessment was plausible; given the man's actions in the Caribbean, his loyalties no longer lay with the British crown.

"Should we send a ship out to look for the *Talavera*?" Middleton asked.

"It would take a frigate, and we didn't have one with enough supplies until *Phoebe* arrived," Hardy said. "I'll think about it."

"Aye, sir," Middleton replied, clearly disappointed with the commodore's answer.

The steward stepped in and announced that dinner was served, and the three men made their way to the table. They found their places and sat as the steward served the soup course.

Hardy paused between mouthfuls. "I recently received a letter, Captain Brewer. It was from Lord Hornblower, sent just before he returned to England. Is it true that you are newly married?"

"Aye, Commodore."

"Well, congratulations, man!" Hardy stood and picked up his glass. "Gentlemen, a toast to the new groom!"

Glasses were raised and the toast drunk.

"Who's the lucky girl, Captain?" Middleton asked.

"Her name is Elizabeth," Brewer said, "and she is the daughter of the governor of St. Kitts."

"Bless my soul!" Middleton exclaimed. "I met her a year ago when I stopped at the island for provisions and paid my respects to the governor!" He turned to the commodore. "A beautiful girl, sir—vivacious and possessing a quick wit. I recall wondering at the time what kind of man it would take for her to settle down, and now we know." He raised his glass to Brewer. "Congratulations, sir, and God's blessings on your union."

"Thank you, Captain."

The steward cleared their bowls and brought out plates for the main course. Brewer watched as a huge meat pie was placed before the commodore, along with young carrots and stewed potatoes.

"Middleton, would you please do the honors with regard to that meat pie?" Hardy said. "Brewer, help yourself to the rest."

The two captains readily obeyed.

"I must tell you, Brewer," the commodore continued, "that the situation in Salvador is getting worse by the day. Brazilian Army forces have made better progress than expected in the hills outside the city. Rumor has it that the Portuguese have a relief convoy on the way, bringing both supplies and reinforcements. Should they fail to appear soon, Governor General de Melo will be forced either to surrender or to evacuate the city, and if Admiral Cochrane arrives with his fleet first, evacuation may not be an option."

"So," Middleton said, "this is a race. If the Portuguese arrive here first, Salvador has a chance. But if Cochrane gets here first and blockades the port, the garrison and the Portuguese civilians are doomed."

"That about sums it up, sir," Hardy said. Brewer thought his words sounded like a death knell.

It was three days later that Hardy again called Brewer aboard the *Creole*.

"Thank you for coming so quickly, Captain," Hardy said when Brewer walked through the cabin door. "How goes the distribution of the provisions?"

"*HMS Doris* is the last, sir, and her boats are heading for *Phoebe* as we speak. We will be finished today."

"Well done," Hardy complimented his guest, genuinely impressed that the slaughter and distribution had been handled so quickly. "Now, to the reason I've summoned you, Captain. HMS *Creole* is scheduled to return to England in four days. Should *Talavera* not arrive by then, I shall have to transfer my flag to HMS *Phoebe*. Please make arrangements with Captain Middleton to have any sick or wounded men transferred aboard *Creole* and exchanged for any of her crew who wish to continue in His Majesty's service."

"Aye, sir," Brewer said. "Will we be going out in search of *Talavera*, sir?"

Hardy studied Brewer shrewdly.

"Not at this time," he replied at last. "I don't want to be away from Salvador if Cochrane should suddenly appear with his heavy units. However," Hardy tapped a heavy finger on his table, "if she does not appear in another week, we may well have to dispatch a ship to seek her out."

"As you say, sir."

"So," Hardy said, "return to your ship and make ready. I shall come aboard tomorrow by the end of the afternoon watch. Coordinate with Captain Middleton regarding any crew who need to be exchanged."

"Aye, sir." Brewer rose and came to attention before leaving the cabin. On his way to the entry port he spoke briefly with Middleton regarding the crew exchange.

Upon his return to HMS *Phoebe*, Brewer went directly to his cabin, pausing only long enough to instruct the petty officer in charge of the deck to pass the word for the first lieutenant and the doctor to join him. He had scarcely had time to remove his coat when the sentry announced their arrival.

"Gentlemen," the captain said without any preamble, "HMS *Creole* has been recalled to England on the normal rotation. She leaves in four days. Unless the new flagship, HMS *Talavera*, arrives by then, the commodore will be transferring his flag to HMS *Phoebe*. Mr. Greene, we shall need to move my things to the gunroom for the duration. Doctor, have we anyone who needs to be returned to England for medical reasons?"

"No, Captain," the doctor said. "I have a few names on the sick list, but none serious."

"If I may, sir," Greene interjected, "we could use a few replacements, if any of *Creole's* crew wished to stay."

"How many would you say?"

"About thirty men—and one officer, sir."

After the brief silence that followed, Brewer said, "Very well. I shall send a note over to Captain Middleton and make inquiries."

"Thank you, sir. We shall move your things in the morning."

"That will be fine. Thank you, gentlemen."

Brewer wrote his note and sent it to *Creole*. The next day, seventeen men volunteered to transfer to *Phoebe*, but unfortunately none was an officer. Brewer himself spent the day on deck; he was confident he could trust Alfred and Mac to shift his belongings into the gunroom, and he wished to oversee the final provisioning of HMS *Doris*. Late in the afternoon, a boat pulled alongside with the commodore's belongings. These were hastily brought aboard and stowed in the captain's cabin. An hour later, the commodore himself came aboard.

"Welcome to your new flagship, sir," Brewer said as he saluted.

"Thank you, Captain." Commodore Hardy looked around the deck. "A fine ship. Captain, I'm afraid I must impose upon you and request the loan of your servant. My own has come down with some sort of illness and will be going home with *Creole*."

"Of course, sir," Brewer said. "I hope it's nothing serious."

"The doctor thinks it's malaria. The trip will do him good."

Brewer led the way below and aft to the cabin. Once inside, he turned to the commodore with a smile on his face.

"About my servant, sir, I do have one condition."

"Which is?"

"He stays here when you leave."

Hardy chuckled. "Granted, Captain!"

Brewer sent for Alfred.

"I will admit to you that I have heard wondrous things about your servant," Hardy said. "I've been looking forward to discovering if his reputation is deserved."

"You shall not be disappointed, sir," Brewer started to say. He was interrupted by a knock at the door, followed by the sentry announcing Alfred's arrival.

"Just in time! Alfred, come over here, will you? Commodore Hardy, allow me to introduce Alfred Thomas. Mr. Thomas, Commodore Hardy. His own servant has taken ill and must return to England. I would like you to resume your normal duties here and care for him as you have for me."

"Aye, sir," the diminutive servant said. He turned to the commodore and bowed. "At your service, sir."

"Ah, thank you, Alfred."

Brewer smiled to himself at the commodore's reaction.

"May I get you anything, sir?"

"Coffee, please. Will you join me, Captain?"

"A pleasure, Commodore."

Alfred bowed and disappeared. Hardy watched him go and shook his head in disbelief.

"Not at all what I expected, Captain," he said quietly.

"Just wait until supper, sir; you'll be sorry you promised he would stay."

"Can he reach the stove?" Hardy asked with a mischievous grin.

Brewer lowered his voice. "I was advised when he first came aboard not to mention his stature, Commodore. My coxswain tried once and quickly found himself facing the point of Alfred's sword."

"Your coxswain? The big Cornishman?"

"Do not underestimate Mr. Thomas because of his size, sir. Do you remember the pirate Roberto Cofresi?" Hardy nodded. "It was Alfred who dispatched him."

Hardy's eyes went wide as saucers as they darted to the pantry door and back. "Are you joking?"

Brewer shook his head. "No, sir. I speak in most deadly earnest."

Hardy shook his head again, in wonder this time. "Extraordinary."

Alfred reappeared with two steaming cups on his silver platter. Each officer took one, and Brewer thanked him. Alfred nodded and withdrew. Hardy blew on the rim and took a careful sip.

"Delicious!" was all he could say.

Brewer smiled. "I told you."

Three days later, acting third lieutenant Jonathan Reed was making use of his time by making a detailed inventory of the provisions aboard *HMS Phoebe*. They had brought aboard so many unusual items not normally found on a ship of His Majesty's Navy that he wanted to go over the list and make sure every item was accounted for. He had noticed an unusual amount of traffic between the ship and the shore, and he had a feeling something wasn't right.

He worked his way through his lists, counting carefully and checking each item off in turn. *Let's see... five of dates, yes, that checks. Lime juice? Ten gallons? Yes, that's right.* He accounted for stores of ship's bread, flour, raisons, and sugar, working his way aft as he went. Behind the sugar he found bags of cocoa and frowned. He rechecked his manifest and finally found it on the last page, entered at the bottom, almost as an afterthought. Reed shrugged and counted. He rechecked the manifest and frowned again. The count was off. Not only that, it wasn't even close. The manifest said eighty bags, at seventy pounds weight each, were bought at Rio, and only two had been signed out to be opened. Yet when Reed counted again, he verified his earlier count of ten bags! Reed immediately thought of the excessive shore traffic and wondered if some had been stolen to be taken ashore and sold.

He went straight away to find the purser, Mr. Tenpenny, to put the question to him. He found him in the gunroom, reading a copy of the *Times* that was two months old.

"Yes, Mr. Reed?" he asked. "Something I can do for you?"

"Yes. I was checking stores, and I found something I can't explain. The manifest shows receipt of eighty bags of cocoa at Rio. But when I made the count, I could only account for twelve bags. Do you know anything about this?"

The purser cast a curious look at the lieutenant. "As a matter of fact, Lieutenant, I do, but only to a point. I purchased ten bags myself at Rio with my own money and sent them back to England for my family. As for the other bags, I have no idea; I can only say they were brought on board. Is there anything else?"

Reed was a bit put off by the purser's manner. The man did not appear surprised by Reed's discovery, nor did he seem interested in investigating the missing bags. Granted, it was only cocoa, but it wasn't as if someone had opened a barrel of apples and taken one out. Sixty-eight bags were missing!

"Will you at least investigate the disappearance of the bags?" he asked.

"Of course," Tenpenny said.

"Thank you." Reed turned and left the gunroom without looking back.

Tenpenny watched him go, his eyes narrowed and his lips set in a firm line.

Reed walked up on the deck and went forward. He leaned on the weather rail to get the full effect of the cool morning breeze on his face. He took off his coat and laid it neatly over the carronade beside him, then rested his forearms on the rail as he looked over the side and down at the calm harbor waters below. His interview with the purser was bothering him. He did not know Tenpenny very well, but it seemed to him that so large a discrepancy should have elicited a different response—more concern, perhaps, or outrage at the possibility of the theft of ship's stores. The purser's response had been anything *but* that. Not at all what Reed had expected.

He lifted his head and saw *HMS Creole* across the harbor making preparations to return to England. A pang of homesickness hit him; he had no idea when he would see his mother and father again, and there were never enough letters to satisfy him. He sighed and looked down at the waters again.

Suddenly, a thought struck him, and his eyes snapped up to *Creole* again. What was it the purser had said? He had purchased ten bags of cocoa for himself and sent them back to England for his family? Reed turned and scanned the deck but didn't find the man he was looking for.

"Mr. Tyler!" he called to a passing midshipman. "Can you please pass the word for Mr. McCleary?"

The midshipman saluted. "Aye, sir!"

Reed turned again to study *Creole* until he heard a throat being cleared behind him. He stood and turned to find the captain's coxswain.

"You sent for me, sir?" he asked.

"Yes, Mr. McCleary. I need your help. The purser says he purchased ten bags of cocoa with his own money in Rio. He says he is sending them home to England for his family. I want to know if you can discreetly make some enquiries and discover what ship he sent the cocoa to and how many bags he sent."

The big Cornishman nodded. "Leave it to me, Mr. Reed."

"Thank you, Mr. McCleary."

The coxswain saluted and left on his errand. Reed turned and leaned on the rail again, wondering what kind of trouble he was letting himself in for.

The cool of the evening fell, and Jonathan Reed was in the gunroom writing his parents a letter when a hand knocked at the door. He entered, came to attention, and handed Reed a note. Then he left without saying a word. Reed opened the note; it was from McCleary, asking him to meet him on deck.

Reed put away his letter and made his way up to the deck. He found McCleary at the fantail.

"You have something for me, Mr. McCleary?" Reed asked.

"Aye, sir," Mac said. He lowered his voice. "I asked around, just like you said, sir, and I found out that Mr. Tenpenny did indeed send ten bags of cocoa to the merchantman *Liverpool* for passage to England. The ship pulled out yesterday."

Reed's eyes narrowed at the news. "Ten bags? Then he told me the truth. But that leaves fifty-eight bags unaccounted for."

Mac looked around the deck before leaning in close. "Maybe he told you the truth, sir, but he didn't tell you all of it. I also discovered that he has been sending cocoa ashore, five or ten bags at a time. Not enough to make anyone question it, but it adds up, you see."

Reed stared at the coxswain. He opened his mouth and then shut it again. His mind was spinning at the implications. He looked back at McCleary.

"Enough bags to add up to fifty-eight?"

Mac shook his head. "Dunno, sir. I didn't get the exact count. I don't think the petty officers who conned the boats ashore bothered to count them."

Reed frowned. "Well, it can't be helped. Thank you, Mr. McCleary. It's time I went to see Mr. Greene."

Mac nodded. "Good luck, sir."

Reed found the first lieutenant in the gunroom.

"Sir, I need to speak with you," he said.

"Very well, Jonathan," Greene said. "What can I do for you?"

Reed looked around. "Is Mr. Tenpenny about?"

"No," Greene replied. "He is ashore. What's this about?"

Reed took a seat and told his story to the premier—how he'd discovered the discrepancy in the cocoa bags and confronted the purser about it, only to be brushed off. He told of McCleary's inquiries and was gratified to see that Greene was as surprised as he himself had been.

"You suspect that the purser is smuggling cocoa ashore to sell for his own profit?" Greene asked.

"It seems more and more likely that such is the case, sir."

Greene rose and went to the door of the gunroom, where he passed the word for McCleary. He resumed his seat but said nothing until McCleary arrived and came to attention.

"At ease, Mac," Greene said. "Mr. Reed has told me about your inquiries on his behalf. Do you have anything to add?"

"I do, sir. I spoke to two of the petty officers who took the cocoa ashore. Both of them said it wasn't Mr. Tenpenny who had them load the bags and gave them the address ashore. It was Altman, sir." Altman was a hand in Mr. Rivkins division.

Greene looked at the table. "So, Tenpenny has an accomplice? No matter. Mac, I have a job for you. Very quietly, I want you to find the sergeant-at-arms. Take him with you to the purser's cabin. I want you to bring me his ledger and order books."

"Aye, sir."

After the Cornishman was gone, Greene turned back to Reed. "We need to see what his books say. Do you still have the manifest you were using?"

"Aye, sir," Reed said. "It's in my cabin."

"Bring it to me."

Reed fetched it and handed it to the premier. Greene scanned the document, and Reed pointed out the numbers for the cocoa.

"Mr. Reed," he said slowly, "I want you to write me out a report. Start with your inventorying the stores and, for now, end it where you reported to me. Bring it to me as soon as you have completed it."

"Aye, sir." Reed rose and went to his cabin to write his report. Two hours later, he set his pen on his desk and sat back. He picked up the five pages of neat, tight script and went to find Mr. Greene. The first lieutenant was in his cabin, poring over the purser's ledger and order books.

"Ah," he said as he looked up, "there you are, Jonathan. Is that your report?" Reed handed him the five pages. "Thank you," Greene said. He set the report on the desk. "I shall read it in a moment. Mac has brought me the current ledger and order book, and I think we may have found what we are looking for. I have found an entry in the order book for eighty bags of cocoa, but the ledger only shows payment for ten."

Reed was confused. "But why would he make different entries?"

"Because most captains are only interested in the ledger. Tenpenny ordered eighty bags and paid for eighty—we know that because all eighty arrived—but he only entered ten in the books, which is what you found below. What he didn't count on was the manifest from the warehouse falling into your hands and your using that document to do your inventory. Normally, you would use one prepared by the purser from his ledger, yes?"

Reed nodded his head.

"There you have it," Greene said. He closed the ledger and picked up Reed's report. "Tenpenny's probably ashore making sure all his ill-gotten gain is safely hidden and on its way to England." Greene set the report down. "This looks good, Jonathan. If you hadn't done your inventory, the purser and his helper would have got clean away with it and divided a tidy sum between them, I'm sure. Order a marine guard on the purser's cabin. Nobody goes in without my permission."

"Aye, sir." Reed left to give the order and returned to find Greene gathering up his evidence.

"We need to see the captain," Greene said. "Ready?"

Reed swallowed hard. "Aye, sir."

They found that the captain was with the commodore. Greene asked to see Captain Brewer privately regarding ship's business, and Brewer made his excuses to the commodore. The three met in the gunroom, which Greene had ordered cleared, with a marine sentry stationed at the door to ensure they were not disturbed.

Brewer looked round. “It must be important, Benjamin. All right, what have you got for me?”

Greene cleared his throat. “Captain, I believe Lieutenant Reed has uncovered a smuggling operation aboard ship.”

“Smuggling?” Brewer asked in disbelief. “Smuggling what?”

“Cocoa, sir.”

“Cocoa.” Brewer repeated.

“Yes, sir.”

Brewer wondered if this were a joke, but quickly decided it could not be. And indeed cocoa was a valuable commodity, if not as sought after as tobacco. “Let’s hear it.”

Greene told his captain the entire story, and the farther he got into his tale, the more serious the captain’s face became. By the time Greene finished presenting his evidence, Brewer’s brows were furled in anger.

“Show me the books,” he ordered.

Greene did so, pointing out the different entries in the order book and ledger. He also showed the captain the manifest from the warehouse in Rio that Lieutenant Reed had used for his inventory.

“Has Mr. Tenpenny returned to the ship?” he asked.

“Not yet,” Greene replied.

“Benjamin, send Mr. Rivkins ashore with a marine escort to find Mr. Tenpenny and bring him back aboard,” Brewer ordered. “Also, have the sergeant-at-arms find Mr. Altman and clap him in irons until we get this thing sorted out. I don’t want him hearing about it and running.”

"Aye, sir." Greene came to attention and left on his errand.

Reed stood there while the captain read through his report. A few moments later, Brewer noticed him.

"Sit down, Mr. Reed," he said without looking up. "I shall be through in a moment."

Reed took his seat, breathing as softly and quietly as he could. Finally, the captain sighed and dropped the report on the table. He lowered his chin to his chest and began to massage the bridge of his nose with his thumb and forefinger.

"Can I get you something, Captain?" Reed asked. "A drink, perhaps?"

"No, nothing, Lieutenant, thank you," the captain answered without looking up. "I'm just thinking." A few moments later, he rubbed his face with both hands and looked up. "No matter what happens with this, Mr. Reed, I want you to know that you have done very well. I shall be pleased to say as much in my report to the commodore and the Admiralty."

"Thank you, sir."

An hour passed before the door opened and Mr. Greene entered.

"Mr. Rivkins is returning," he said with some satisfaction. "He has the purser. I left orders for him to be brought here."

Brewer nodded.

Greene sat beside his captain. "Sir? Might I suggest coffee?"

Brewer looked up. "Yes, thank you."

Greene looked at Reed and nodded. Reed called to the steward for three coffees.

Winfield brought the steaming cups and set them on the table. Reed thanked him.

Ten minutes later there was a knock on the door, and the marine sentry admitted Mr. Tenpenny and his escort.

"Mr. Tenpenny, as ordered, sir," Rivkins said formally.

"Thank you, Lieutenant," Brewer said. "Leave two guards; take the rest with you. Dismissed."

"Aye, sir." Rivkins indicated that the two marines closest to the purser were to stay. The rest followed him from the room, and the sentry closed the door.

"Mr. Tenpenny," the Captain said, "do you know why you were summoned back to the ship?"

The purser's eyes darted to Reed, seated at the captain's left, and he swallowed hard.

"No, sir."

Brewer nodded at the expected answer. "Talk to me about cocoa."

The purser played it off. "Cocoa, sir?"

"Yes. Mr. Reed reported to you a discrepancy he had discovered. Have you investigated?"

Tenpenny shifted nervously. "I was in the process of doing so when Mr. Rivkins informed me that you had ordered my return to the ship, sir."

"I see," Brewer said. Reed noticed a menacing tone in his voice now. "Will you please inform me as to what you have discovered so far?"

The purser shook his head. "I have nothing to report as yet, Captain."

"Ah." Peril and warning were now plain to hear in the captain's voice. "You informed Mr. Reed that you purchased some cocoa for yourself, with your own funds, and shipped it home to England for your family, did you not? What ship did you put the bags of cocoa in?"

"*Liverpool*, Captain. She sailed for home yesterday."

Brewer picked up Reed's report again. "And that was ten bags, is that correct?"

"Aye, Captain."

"I presume you have the bill of sale," Brewer said without looking up, "indicating you paid for them with your own funds and not the ship's accounts?"

"I do, sir."

Brewer looked up at the purser. Death was in his eyes.

"And did Mr. Altman drop those bags off on his way to shore with the others?"

The purser's eyes grew wide. He said nothing. Brewer placed the order book on the table. Next to it he carefully laid the ledger and then the warehouse manifest beside it. Tenpenny closed his eyes and swallowed hard.

"Captain, I—"

Brewer cut him off. "If you have an explanation for this, Mr. Tenpenny, I should be glad to hear it now."

"It's not what you think, sir."

The captain's eyes gleamed with danger. "Really? Because *I think* you're smuggling cocoa to sell in Salvador and make yourself a pretty sum before you head back to England." The purser turned pale. "Well, sir?" the captain went on. "I am waiting!"

Silence filled the room. Brewer rose slowly. At his full height, he towered over the purser. Reed thought the effect must have been intimidating in the extreme.

"I despise a thief, Mr. Tenpenny," Brewer said slowly. "I have a good mind to give you six dozen lashes for your crimes."

The purser nearly fainted. He clutched a chair back for support as he made his plea.

"Six! Captain, please! That would kill me!"

The captain was unmoved. "It is what you deserve, sir, make no mistake! However, I will have mercy on you, Mr. Tenpenny. You will be given two dozen lashes. Mr. Altman will receive one dozen for his part in your scheme. I will also ask the commodore to order you both returned to England in HMS *Creole,* to be discharged dishonorably from His Majesty's Navy upon arrival."

The purser stood as straight as he could while still leaning on the chair for support.

"Captain, please!"

Brewer would have nothing to do with it any longer. "Sergeant, clap him in irons! Defaulters at eight bells."

The miserable purser was led from the gunroom in irons. Brewer leaned forward, hands on the table, trying to regain his composure. It was several moments before he was able to resume his seat.

"Mr. Greene, we shall need a replacement," he said.

"I have already looked into that, sir. Petty officer Franks ran a successful grocery before he was pressed. I think he will do as the new purser until we can replace him officially, or he has a chance to get his warrant."

"Then the job is his for the duration. See that he is instructed in his new duties. Oh, and be sure he is front and center when justice is administered to his predecessor."

CHAPTER THIRTEEN

Captain William Brewer had no sooner dismissed both Greene and Reed and retired to his cabin in the gunroom when a midshipman arrived with a note from the commodore, asking if the captain would be pleased to join him for supper. Brewer had been in the service long enough to know that an invitation from a superior officer was more like an order than a request, so he dressed appropriately and presented himself to the marine sentry outside the cabin door at the appointed hour.

He entered after the sentry announced him and found the commodore standing before the desk, looking at Brewer's library on the shelf mounted on the bulkhead above. He turned at the sound of his guest's footsteps.

"Ah, there you are, Captain," the commodore greeted him. Turning back to the bookshelf, he said, "This book you have on Washington... Is that the same man who led the American army in their revolution and then became their first president?"

"It is, sir," Brewer answered.

"I've heard amazing stories about him. I have often wondered if they're true."

"Feel free to borrow the book, sir," Brewer offered. "It was interesting reading."

The commodore took the book off the shelf and leafed through it.

"Thank you; I believe I shall," he said, and set the book on the desk. "Would you care for a drink, Captain?"

Brewer nodded. "Thank you, sir."

Hardy smiled. "Alfred! Open that bottle of cognac I brought aboard, will you?"

The trusted servant appeared in the pantry door. "At once, Commodore."

The commodore turned and went into the dayroom. "Let us sit, Captain."

Brewer followed his host, and by the time they took their seats under the stern windows, Alfred had arrived with two glasses of dark nectar on his silver platter. Each officer took one, and Hardy thanked him.

The commodore watched him go. "I will say this privately to you, Captain—you can thank your lucky stars you extracted that promise from me before I met Mr. Thomas."

Brewer smiled. Both men sipped their drinks.

"Tell me," Hardy said, "what was it that pulled you away so precipitously earlier today?"

"My officers discovered a case of smuggling aboard, sir. I have dealt with it, but I would like to request the two men involved be sent to England for court-martial and dismissal from the service."

"I see," Hardy said. "What was the item involved?"

"Cocoa, sir."

Hardy stared. "Excuse me, but I do not wish to misunderstand you. You did say *'cocoa'*, yes?"

"I did, sir."

Hardy sat leaned back, threw his head back, and laughed. Brewer sat there feeling slightly embarrassed.

"Please forgive me, Captain," Hardy said when he calmed down, "but to lose one's career and possibly one's very liberty over *cocoa* struck me as possibly the most absurd thing I've ever heard. I presume you have satisfied yourself as to the guilt of the perpetrators?"

"I have, sir; the purser ran the scheme, and he had one hand helping him."

The commodore picked up his drink and took a long, slow draught as he considered what his captain had said. Brewer recognized the look and sat back to wait.

"I believe," Hardy said eventually, "that we can settle this amongst ourselves, Captain. I can find three post captains to sit on a court-martial panel. We can try these brigands ourselves and send them home on the slowest, dirtiest ship we can find."

Brewer hid his smile behind his glass. "As you say, sir."

"Good. I shall write out orders to the captains I have selected. They shall report the day after tomorrow for the trial. Have your first lieutenant speak to the accused and give them the option of having counsel appointed for their defense."

Alfred appeared to call them to the table. The two officers stepped out to find the table decorated with a gorgeous roast goose, meat pie, peas, and pudding. Brewer stared.

"Sit, Captain," Hardy urged him. "I brought these from *Creole*. Don't worry; the sloop *Retribution* is scheduled to arrive any day with supplies for the squadron."

Brewer inhaled the aromas appreciatively. "I still find it hard to believe that the Brazilians allow us to purchase supplies in Rio, knowing they will be brought to Salvador to sustain our squadron."

Hardy grunted. "It's Pedro's way of buying off King George. He knows the prime minister and the government are on his side, but he also knows that the king favors Portugal. He's hoping to placate the king so we don't take a more active role in the conflict." He helped himself to some of the goose. "The problem for the emperor, of course, is Cochrane. That renegade can't restrain himself, no matter what the consequences. He proved that when he went after your sloop in the Caribbean. If he decides to attack English shipping or, God help us, a Royal Navy ship escorting a merchantman, the government may have no choice but to side with the king and enter the war on the side of the Portuguese."

Brewer considered the implications. The British fleet was not what it had been during the Napoleonic wars, but it was still more than capable of blockading the main Brazilian ports. But there was the problem of the many British tars who were sailing under Brazilian colors. Should there be a break with Brazil that led to open warfare, in a great many instances Englishmen would be firing on their own countrymen.

Brewer shook his head and resumed his meal.

Life continued apace for HMS *Phoebe* and her crew. Drills were conducted daily to prevent the crew from losing their edge, and they were constantly cleaning and polishing so that the appearance of the ship would be worthy of a commodore's flagship.

That didn't mean that they were not overjoyed to see HMS *Talavera* finally arrive in the harbor. The proud, new seventy-four slid majestically into port and was guided to her berth by a pilot.

The next day, the commodore transferred his flag to the newcomer. In the afternoon, the crew cheered when a boat from the new flagship made her rounds, delivering mail to every ship in harbor. Brewer remained in his cabin, sitting in his day cabin and sipping a glass of wine. Nevertheless, he leapt to his feet when the knock finally came and the marine sentry announced the first lieutenant. Greene strode into the room, smiling and holding up three letters, which he handed to his captain.

"Thank you, Benjamin."

The premier nodded and departed. Brewer took the letters to his desk. He noticed his hands were trembling as he scanned the outside sheet and put the letters in order. He broke the seal on the oldest one and read.

> My Husband,
>
> How strange it is, and how wonderful, for me to write those words. I have waited my whole life to do so, and I am thrilled that you are the one who will receive them. I have never known such happiness as I did during those two weeks we spent at the cabin, alone and together.
>
> I eagerly await your return. Lady Barbara informed me that you are well versed in taking an evening stroll. In fact, she highly recommended that I

avail myself of your talents in that area. It is strange that I do not remember you mentioning that particular ability during our entire time together. Never fear, Husband, I shall not forget. I look forward to walking on your arm.

My father sends his greetings. His favorite joke now is how the number of eligible officers from His Majesty's Navy has dropped drastically since news of my marriage has become public. He says that he is concerned for my health or that I should perhaps be lonely without you now, for he has insisted that, while you are at sea, I should continue to live in his house as I always have. However, I believe it is he who fears being lonely. I do have an aunt who has taken up residence in Kingston, so if you can give me warning of when you are heading that way, I may be able to meet you there.

Brewer read the remainder of the letter slowly; it was filled with declarations of her love for him and promises that she would wait for him forever. The second letter, written a week after the first, was filled with more of the same, but it was the third letter, written ten days after the second, that got his attention.

I do not know how to tell you this, my husband. I have waited until I was sure, but I hope you are sitting down. We are to have a child in the spring! The doctor is sure. He told me he thought he could detect a little heartbeat when I saw him two days ago! I hope to hear it when I see him next. This leads us to another problem: What do we name him? Or her? We never talked about that. Please write me immediately with your suggestions!

Stunned, Brewer sat back in his chair, the letter slipping from his fingers to the desk below. A baby? Now? He felt a small surge of panic begin to grow in his stomach. All at once, he remembered Bonaparte talking about his son, the King of Rome, tears in his eyes. Bonaparte had said more than once that he would gladly accept exile under any conditions providing he could see his son again for only five minutes.

A son... I'm going to have a son, he thought over and over. *Or a daughter?* The thought startled him for a moment before he decided that a daughter would be fine with him. *As long as she looks like her mother and not me! Please, God, not that!* He laughed out loud in spite of himself.

"Sir?" Alfred's voice at the door startled him. "Are you all right, sir?"

"More than all right, my friend," Brewer said. He stood and held up the letter. "I'm going to be a father!"

"My congratulations, Captain!" Alfred said.

Just then there was a knock at the door, and the sentry announced Mr. Murdy, the senior midshipman.

"Pardon the interruption, sir," he said formally, "but there's a signal for us from the flagship. *'Captain come on board.'*"

"Very well, Mr. Murdy. Acknowledge the signal, and have Mac ready the gig."

Brewer stowed the letters in his writing desk and made ready to go.

He stepped through the entry port of HMS *Talavera* to be greeted by her captain.

"Captain Brewer? Welcome to *Talavera*. I am Captain John Christopher."

"William Brewer." The two shook hands. "We're glad you finally arrived."

Christopher shook his head. "Unbelievably bad luck; worst I've ever seen on a crossing! We dropped off mail and personnel at Bermuda, then we were damaged in a hurricane northwest of Barbados. We limped into Port Royal for repairs. We left there only to become becalmed for ten days! The good Lord finally had mercy on us and sent a breeze just in time to save us from frustration and boredom! I tell you, Captain, I've never seen a crew so grateful to be moving in all my years of service."

"Well, we're here at last," Christopher said as they reached the door.

The sentry admitted them. Brewer was impressed. The commodore's cabin on *Talavera* was larger and even more stately than his stateroom on *Superb*.

The commodore stepped over and shook hands with his guest. "Good to see you, Brewer. I see you've met Captain Christopher. Come over here and sit down. How are you?"

"Honestly, I'm not altogether sure, sir," he said. "I've today discovered that I'm going to be a father."

"What's that? Good God, man, congratulations! Capital! Absolutely capital! When?"

"In the spring; that's what the letter said."

"Bascomb! Bascomb! Madeira for three. This calls for a toast!"

The commodore's steward returned and passed out the refreshment. The commodore raised his glass.

"To Mrs. Brewer! May she have a safe and easy pregnancy, and may she bring forth a healthy child. May both mother and child be there to greet their husband and father every time he returns from the king's service."

Christopher and Brewer raised their glasses as well.

"Here! Here!"

"Have you thought of any names yet?" Christopher asked.

Brewer shook his head. "That was one thing we never talked about."

"In honor of the occasion," Hardy said, "allow me to present my gift to the mother and father." He turned to Christopher. "Will you be so kind as to send a message to *Creole*. Inform her that her departure has been delayed for 24 hours. That way, Captain,"—he looked to Brewer—"if you can finish a letter to your wife tonight, *Creole* can take it straight to England for you."

Brewer raised his glass to the commodore. "Many thanks to you, sir, from my wife and myself."

"Not at all, not at all. I remember Nelson doing the same thing once; glad I have the chance to do it for one of my captains."

Christopher smiled at his fellow captain as he left on his errand.

Hardy drained his glass in a single draught. "Now, Captain, to business. I am sending you out on a patrol. Captain Christopher brought with him intelligence suggesting that Cochrane is about to step up his blockade enforcement, and I want a frigate out there to remind the Brazilians that English shipping is off-limits to them. You may cruise for two months, but no more. I may send a sloop out to bring you in sooner. The situation is moving much too quickly for me to leave a frigate out there indefinitely."

Captain Christopher returned. "*Creole* acknowledges the signal, sir."

"Good. We were just talking about the intelligence you brought regarding Cochrane."

Christopher nodded. "The Admiralty has picked up whispers that the good admiral is growing impatient with his Brazilian masters. If he follows his past pattern, it is entirely possible that he may act on his own, hoping to pull the Brazilian government along after him."

"When do I leave, sir?" Brewer asked.

"Within the week," Hardy said. "The next supply ship is due by then, and I want you fully provisioned before you leave. I will have your orders sent out to you within the next two or three days. Bear in mind they are subject to change right up to the moment you weigh anchor. Any questions?"

Brewer looked his superior in the eye and held his gaze. "What if I meet Cochrane?"

Hardy's face turned firm, authoritative. "Captain Brewer, you are hereby ordered not to engage a seventy-four with your frigate. You are also ordered to avoid engaging superior enemy forces. Is that understood?"

"Aye, sir."

Hardy rose, and Brewer followed suit. The commodore patted Brewer's arm affectionately.

"Don't worry, it shall be part of your written orders, so nobody can question you on it. His time will come, Captain. All you can do is pray the Lord allows you to be there when it happens. Nelson would have taken a shine to you, Brewer, but the times when Nelson got away with what he did before Trafalgar are long gone. Don't do anything foolish, and I shall back you all the way."

"Aye, sir."

Hardy put forth his hand. "Good luck to you, Captain."

Brewer took the commodore's hand, and then Christopher's.

"Thank you, sir."

It was three days later that *HMS Doris* pulled into the harbor, her arrival announced by the lowing of the cattle that crowded her deck. Signals went out from the flagship directing *HMS Phoebe* to the front of the line. Forty-eight hours later, *Phoebe* was fully provisioned and ready for sea. She sailed on the morning tide and made her course southwest along the coast. The orders sent to her by Commodore Hardy ordered him to begin patrolling the seas off Rio de Janeiro, as that was where Cochrane and the other Brazilian captains were taking their prizes.

As soon as the Brazilian squadron keeping watch on the harbor entrance dropped below the horizon, Brewer altered course to the south in order to get some sea room. All the time they went south, the captain himself stood at the fantail looking north. He was wondering where Cochrane was, and how he was planning to lay his hands on the Portuguese national treasure.

At last he wandered forward toward the wheel.

"Make your course sou'west, Mr. Sweeney, if you please," he said.

"Aye, Captain," the sailing master replied, and the quartermaster's mates manning the wheel complied.

"Hoping for prize money, sir?" Sweeney asked.

Brewer shrugged. "If we took a prize, what would we do with it, Mr. Sweeney? We can't take it into Rio. Taking it into Salvador means getting past the Brazilian blockade squadron. About all we can do at the moment is rescue English ships or escort them to safer waters."

Sweeney saw his captain's point and nodded. He changed the subject.

"I wonder if we'll meet Cochrane?" he said quietly.

Brewer said nothing, and after along silence Sweeney began to fear he had said something wrong. He made an attempt at an apology, but his captain stopped him with a gesture.

"It is I who should apologize, Mr. Sweeney," Brewer said somberly. "I was not ignoring you. In fact, you have asked the very question I have been asking myself. The last time, Cochrane had a frigate while I had only our little sloop-of-war. Now he has a brand new seventy-four to my frigate. Furthermore, he will most likely have support, while we are alone. Nevertheless, my original orders were to protect British interests *at all cost*. Make no mistake, should we find Cochrane in possession of an English ship, we shall most certainly challenge him, but I am by no means confident of the outcome."

Sweeney stood beside his captain and said nothing. In truth, he found it hard to argue with what he had heard. The captain would rightly risk his ship and crew to rescue British sailors and merchant ships from captivity, but he would not be able to justify, neither to Commodore Hardy nor later to the Admiralty in London, taking his ship into action against a superior enemy solely to seek revenge for what happened in the Caribbean. Too bad there wasn't a way to challenge a man to a duel using ships at sea instead of swords or pistols on land. Captain Brewer in his frigate against Lord Cochrane in his. Sweeney glanced sideways at his captain; the younger man was still staring out to the horizon and beyond.

Later, the midshipman of the watch approached the captain and saluted. "Begging your pardon, sir, but we're passing Rio's latitude. You said you wished to be informed."

"Yes, of course," Brewer returned the salute. "Carry on."

Brewer stared to the west for a time, wondering what he would find if he were to enter Rio. He knew that he could not, of course—his orders prevented him from doing so except in an emergency. He pressed his lips into a tight, thin line in an attempt to control his emotions. The really frustrating part was, he wasn't even sure why he was getting so agitated. He remembered how Bush had come to regret allowing his emotions to gain control of him in the Mediterranean, and he chided himself for daring to allow himself to take even one small step down that road. Brewer shook himself; anyone who'd seen the act might have mistaken it for a shiver. But he knew the difference.

He turned to his sailing master. "Mr. Sweeney, take us west until we're in sight of land. We'll patrol off the coast for a while."

"Aye, sir."

"Who has the watch?" the captain asked.

"Lieutenant Rivkins, sir." It was Greene who'd answered.

"Very well, he has the deck," Brewer said. "I shall be in my cabin. Call me if we sight anything."

"Aye, sir," Greene answered.

The premier watched his captain descend below deck before strolling over to the wheel where Mr. Sweeney was talking with the quartermaster.

"Do you have a moment, Mr. Sweeney?" Greene asked.

"Certainly, sir."

The two men made their way to the fantail, out of earshot of the crew.

"I'm worried about the captain," Greene said.

"In what way, sir?"

Greene leaned against the fantail and crossed his arms over his chest.

"I'm not exactly sure. Remember how he was for a while in the Caribbean, that fixation he had on finding El Diabolito, getting his revenge? I'm beginning to wonder if he isn't falling into the same condition regarding Lord Cochrane."

Sweeney leaned against the rail. "Has he said anything?"

Greene shook his head. "No, not really. It's more a feeling I get from watching him—the set of his shoulders when the subject comes up, the way he went after the *Valdivia* off Peru. I've even heard rumors that he went toe-to-toe with Cochrane aboard the flagship and Hardy had to step between them."

"Good God!" Sweeney exclaimed under his breath. "Where did you hear that?"

Greene just looked at him and shook his head discretely. Sweeney got the message: don't ask, and keep it to yourself.

The two men stared at the deck in silence for several moments before Sweeney spoke softly.

"Thank God Cochrane's got a seventy-four."

"Do you think that will stop the captain?" Greene asked somberly.

Sweeney considered this, then asked, "So, what do we do?"

Greene shrugged. "There's nothing we *can* do. He is the captain, after all, and he hasn't done anything to show that he is unfit for command. What he *is*, Mr. Sweeney, is a proud man who feels himself humiliated by Cochrane's actions in the Caribbean, and if he gets the opportunity, he may try to even the score."

Sweeney studied the mountain of sail above the deck.

Greene leaned in again. "Please, do not misunderstand me, Mr. Sweeney," he said softly. "I do not expect the captain to act rashly or to put the ship or crew in danger unnecessarily. I do not believe he would cross that line, no matter how much he personally would like to." He straightened up again and crossed his arms over his chest, resting his chin between a thumb and forefinger. "Still, it concerns me that he has this cloud over him."

"Is there anything we can do?" Sweeney asked.

Suddenly, Greene's eyes opened wide and his brows rose as a thought hit him. "Maybe not we ourselves, but I believe there is someone who could." He beckoned for the midshipman of the watch.

Captain Brewer was in his cabin, staring at a blank piece of paper which he hoped would magically transform itself into a letter to his wife but had thus far been extremely uncooperative. He was vaguely aware of the presence of Alfred. The faithful servant had offered him coffee or a beverage twice in the last three bells—both refused rather curtly—and now had taken up a post just inside the pantry, presumably to polish the silver, but where he could keep his captain under discreet observation. Brewer ignored him and stared at the blank page on the desk before him.

He had been aware of the growing frustration within himself for three days now. The seed had been planted during the confrontation with Cochrane aboard *HMS Superb* and had been growing ever since. Cochrane had humiliated him in front of his crew in the Caribbean, first by forcing him to carry that letter to Hornblower, followed every mile by *Valdivia*, and then by attempting to destroy him as he fled toward Jamaica. He hadn't realized until long after the battle with the *Valdivia* the full extent of the measure of satisfaction he'd gleaned from that encounter. It was as if one aspect of honor had been satisfied.

He frowned at the paper. He could not remember being so sensitive with regard to his honor in all the time before he'd assumed command of a King's ship. He sighed heavily and sat back, his eyes never leaving the empty page. He could not remember—indeed, could not imagine—Bush displaying similar feelings to what he was enduring now. Nor Hornblower, for that matter. Perhaps they were just better at hiding their feelings than he was. If so, it was a skill he needed to master.

There was a knock at the door, and the sentry announced the doctor. Spinelli stepped in and surveyed the situation, nodding to Alfred, still at his post with a concerned look on his face. It was clear to the doctor that things were every bit as bad as the first lieutenant feared. The doctor stepped up to the desk and looked over his captain's shoulder.

"Well," he deadpanned, "at least your spelling is improving."

"Adam," Brewer said heavily as he looked up at his friend, "if you've come to cheer me up, you've picked a bad time."

Spinelli pulled a chair over and sat down. "I disagree, sir. It seems I've come at the most opportune moment. What is bothering you so, Captain?"

Brewer still stared at the blank page on the desk. "What makes you think something is bothering me?"

The doctor sat back indignantly. "William, if you wish to be left alone, just say so. But do not insult my intelligence or mock my concern with such a question."

Brewer looked at the doctor, taking in the firm set of his jaw balanced against the concern that was so evident in his eyes. He rubbed his face and sighed.

"I apologize, Adam," he said, "but there is really nothing you can do for me."

"What is it, William?"

Brewer stared at the desk for several moments before whispering a single word.

"Cochrane."

"I see," the doctor said quietly. "Alfred? Coffee for two, if you please. Thank you."

Brewer said nothing, and Spinelli waited while Alfred prepared coffee. He placed two cups on the desk and withdrew, all without a word. His eyes met the doctor's and conveyed a sense of hope.

"William," Spinelli said after the servant was gone, "drink this. Now, tell me what happened aboard HMS *Superb*."

Brewer looked glumly at the doctor, then at the cup. He picked it up and blew on the rim before taking a tentative sip.

"His usual best," he said as he set it down. "Would you care for a game of chess, doctor?"

"Delighted," Spinelli replied.

Brewer rose and retrieved the set. Spinelli drew white. The board was set up, and the game began. The first several moves were made in silence. It wasn't until the doctor pulled off a spectacular move and took his opponent's rook that the ice was broken.

"You asked about *Superb*, Adam," Brewer said as he played. "Cochrane was already there when I arrived, and it wasn't very long before he brought up the battle with *Valdivia* in the Pacific."

"He brought it up?" Spinelli asked. "Even though that ship was trying to recapture an English whaler?"

Brewer shrugged. "It didn't seem to matter to him. Remember, he has a seventy-four now, so I suppose he didn't care about being polite. Anyway, I explained to the commodore that we had recaptured the whaler, and how I gave *Valdivia* a choice between coming after us and pursuing the whaler. I made it plain that we did not attack until after it was clear that they were going for the whaler."

"And what did Hardy say?"

"He approved. Not that his opinion mattered in the least to Cochrane, who was getting angrier by the moment. I think that thirty years ago he would have challenged me to a duel." Brewer moved his knight. "Check. He tried to get Hardy to punish me."

Spinelli took the knight with a bishop. "Whatever for?"

"The attack on the *Valdivia*," Brewer replied. He moved a pawn. "Check."

The doctor moved his king. "And what did the commodore say?"

"That he was going to commend me in his report to the Admiralty." Brewer moved his rook.

Spinelli smiled. "I bet Cochrane loved that." He moved his queen the length of the board. "Checkmate."

Brewer frowned and sat back in his chair, still studying the board. "Yes. I'm afraid he made it clear—to me, at least—that when we met again at sea, there would be a reckoning."

Spinelli leaned forward. "William, don't worry about it."

"The game? You got lucky and took advantage of my distractions, sir."

"No, not the game. I mean Cochrane. You were in the right with *Valdivia*, Hardy even said so. Cochrane knew it as well. This isn't the same as El Diabolito."

"I know."

"Then let it go, Captain. You'll be doing yourself a favor."

The captain was spared having to respond when a knock at the cabin door was followed by the sentry admitting Mr. Midshipman Dye.

"Begging the captain's pardon," he said as he came to attention, "Mr. Rivkins sends his respects and says we've sighted a sail to the northeast."

"Thank you, Mr. Dye. My compliments to Mr. Rivkins; I shall come on deck directly."

"Sir!" The midshipman came to attention again and was gone.

Brewer rose and grabbed his hat. "Duty calls, Doctor."

Both men headed for the deck. Brewer accepted a glass from Rivkins, who met him as he arrived.

"Report, Lieutenant."

"Sir, we have sighted a strange sail bearing northeast. Per your standing order, I immediately altered course to intercept and notified you at once."

"Thank you, Lieutenant." He lifted his head and said to the deck at large, "I have the deck! All hands make sail!"

Rivkins bellowed the orders, and the hands ascended to the yards. The sky quickly disappeared from view, hidden behind the mountain of canvas that now filled the atmosphere above the deck. Every man felt the ship leap forward beneath his feet

"Mr. Rivkins, I'm going forward," Brewer said. He was met by Mr. Greene coming up on deck. Without breaking stride, the captain said, "Mr. Greene, you're with me."

Greene grabbed a glass and walked swiftly to catch up to his captain. He found him at the bow, his glass already to his eye.

"What do we have, sir?" Greene asked.

Brewer studied the sail they were fast approaching. "We are closing on a ship, Benjamin. So far, it seems to be alone, although we know nothing about nationality or purpose yet. It should be hull-up in the next few minutes."

"Deck there!" the lookout soon called. "I can see her now! She's an English merchant ship!"

"Is she alone, lookout?" Greene bellowed.

"Aye, sir! Her course is WNW!"

Greene turned to find his captain still studying the merchantman. There was a scowl on his face.

"Beat to quarters, Benjamin."

"Aye, sir." Greene turned aft. "Beat to quarters!"

The drumbeat began in earnest and the crew rushed to their stations. Eight minutes and thirty seconds later, HMS

Phoebe was ready for battle. All eyes were on the captain now, and he was once again studying the newcomer.

"Run out the larboard battery, if you please," Brewer said as he closed his glass. "She may be manned by a prize crew."

"Aye, sir!" Greene saluted as his captain headed aft.

"Mr. Sweeney," Brewer said when he reached the quarterdeck, "reduce sail and bring us across her stern. Half pistol-shot."

"Aye, sir." Sweeney grabbed a speaking trumpet and began to issue the appropriate orders. Hands went aloft again, and soon the frigate slowed noticeably. Mr. Greene approached.

"The name across the stern reads *Beverly*."

"Thank you, Mr. Greene," Brewer said. He picked up a speaking trumpet and stepped over to the rail. "Ahoy, *Beverly*! Heave to! Prepare to receive my boat! Heave to!"

Someone on *Beverly's* quarterdeck waved a hand in acknowledgement, and moments later hands were observed scurrying up the shrouds to take in sail.

Brewer turned. "Heave to, Mr. Sweeney. Mr. Greene, take some marines and a boarding party and head over there. Take Mr. Reed with you; send him back with a preliminary report for me."

"Aye, sir," Greene said. He touched his hat and left the quarterdeck. Thirty minutes later he was standing on the deck of the *Beverly*. An officer approached.

"I am Thomas Black, master of the *Beverly*," he said.

"Lieutenant Greene, first lieutenant of His Majesty's frigate *Phoebe*. If you'll pardon me, Mr. Black, I need to search your ship." With a nod, Greene dispatched three teams of marines and tars to search the merchantman.

"What is the meaning of this, sir?" Black demanded. The outrage in his voice caused Reed and two tars with him to draw their pistols. Greene stopped them with a gesture.

"Mr. Black, I need to satisfy myself that this ship is not under the control of a prize crew. Once I am convinced of that, we shall talk."

Black stood back and fumed at the affront. Within fifteen minutes, the teams were all back on deck and reporting to Greene. Black saw Greene dispatch another officer back to his ship before coming to join him.

"I really must apologize," he said, offering his hand, which Black accepted after a moment's hesitation. "We had to be sure you had not been captured by a Brazilian privateer. Where are you bound?"

"My orders were to sail for Rio," the master said, "but just before we sailed we heard rumors that Rio might not be a friendly place for an English ship by the time we got there, so I decided to make for Salvador instead. I figured we had a better chance of finding the Royal Navy there."

Greene nodded. "Good idea." He shrugged. "Well, almost a good idea. When we left Salvador there was a Brazilian squadron blockading the harbor."

Black shared a concerned look with a man Greene presumed to be the mate.

Black turned back to Greene. "What do you suggest?"

Greene said, "I must report to my captain. Instructions will be sent to you. Stand by for now."

Black agreed and went to inform his crew. Greene gathered his boarding party and departed *Beverly*. When he arrived on board *Phoebe*, he went straight to the captain's cabin. He found Brewer sitting at his desk, working on his log.

"Well, Benjamin?"

"The ship is the *Beverly*, sir," Greene began. He gratefully accepted the seat indicated by the captain. "Master's name is Black; he says he was on the way to Rio but decided to divert to Salvador. His cargo is food, medicines, and coal."

Brewer wondered what orders the Salvador port blockade would follow. "Where is he now?"

"I have him standing by on his ship."

Brewer rose and stepped into his day cabin, where he began to pace back and forth before the open stern windows. Greene sat and waited.

It didn't take long. Brewer ceased his pacing and resumed his seat. His brow was still furrowed, indicating to Greene that he had not arrived at a fully satisfactory decision. He looked expectantly at the captain.

"Let's invite Master Black to dine with us, Benjamin," Brewer said. "I have one or two ideas that seem possible to me, but they depend upon Black being a man who can maintain his nerve. Alfred! There shall be three officers for supper tonight. Can you manage?"

The servant closed his eyes, mentally reviewing his inventory. "It can be done, sir, although it may not be the fanciest meal."

"Thank you, Alfred," Brewer said. "Turn of the second dog watch?"

"Aye, sir."

"Good," Brewer said. "Mr. Greene, send the invitation, if you please. Tell Mr. Black we shall send a boat for him. Now

I must beg some privacy to finish my log and write a letter to my wife."

Alfred's fare that evening, while not what he served to admirals or to Commodore Hardy a few weeks before, still drew commendations from their guest. Afterwards, Brewer, Greene, and Mr. Black retired to the day cabin to smoke cigars.

"Mr. Black," Brewer was saying, "I think it might be a good idea if you would allow us to accompany your ship to Salvador."

"How do you plan to get past the blockading squadron, sir?" Greene asked. "They will surely want to stop and search the ship. I can't imagine Cochrane allowing medicines and coal to proceed."

"They are destined for British concerns, Captain, I assure you," Black hastened to add.

"Yes, I'm sure they are, Mr. Black," Brewer reassured his guest. "But as Mr. Greene has intimated, that fact won't matter to the Brazilian squadron. They can claim they believe it is destined for out Portuguese allies and confiscate it—and *Beverly* as well."

At this, Mr. Black became vociferous in his objections. Brewer raised a hand for silence.

"I have given the matter much thought, and it seems to me," he said deliberately, "that we may have to simply run the gauntlet. Mr. Black, how's your nerve holding out these days?"

The two ships approached Salvador as the sun was going down. HMS *Phoebe* was leading *Beverly*, both ships sailing under plain sail on a northwesterly course. Captain Brewer was pacing on the lee side of the quarterdeck, while Lieutenants Greene and Rivkins stood with Mr. Sweeney beside the wheel.

"How far to Salvador, do you think?" Greene asked.

When Sweeney deemed they were no more than twenty-five or thirty miles from Salvador, Mr. Greene ordered Mr. Rivkins to beat to quarters.

Activity exploded to the beat of the drums, and Greene reported their progress to his captain.

"Very good, Mr. Greene." Brewer accepted a glass from a hand with a nod of thanks. "Any sightings as yet?"

"None, sir. Do you think we might get by undetected?"

Brewer scanned the horizon. "No, I don't. Cochrane will have trained his captains too well for that. We should be fine, provided we can get *Beverly* the start she'll need. Are the rockets ready?"

"Aye, sir, awaiting your signal."

Brewer lowered his glass, concern written all over his face. "I have decided one thing, Benjamin—if you want to say one good thing about war, it's this: you don't have to worry about creating an international incident."

"Deck there!" cried the lookout in the mizzen tops. "Ship of the line coming over the horizon off the starboard beam!"

Brewer and Greene moved quickly to the starboard rail, where telescopes revealed a fast-growing field of white on the horizon coming straight at them. A minute later, the ship changed to a westerly course in an attempt to cut them off. The change in course gave them a better look at the sails of the newcomer.

"Looks like a seventy-four, sir," Greene said.

"So it does," Brewer replied a bit testily, mentally chastising himself for allowing his nerves to show.

Greene saw his captain's eyes narrow in concentration as he sighted on the ship.

"There! She's making all sails!" Brewer exclaimed. "Mr. Sweeney! All hands make sail! I want every stitch she'll carry! Mr. Dye! Send a signal to *Beverly* to make all sail and head for Salvador!"

"Aye, sir!"

"Deck there!" It was the mizzen lookout again. "Two sails on the port quarter!"

Brewer and Greene looked at each other.

"Let's hear you, lookout!" Brewer called.

"The first one's a brig or sloop, sir," the lookout cried. "The second one could be a frigate. She's hidden behind the first one at the moment, sir."

Greene strode the deck, peering through his glass first at the approaching seventy-four, then the two ships on the opposite beam, trying to decide which was the more immediate threat.

"Deck there! The second ship is definitely a frigate! Both ships making all sail!"

Greene saw that Brewer was still studying the new sighting. A moment later, he walked back to the starboard to study the seventy-four more closely. Greene joined him.

"Do you notice anything strange?" Brewer asked, indicating the ship of the line. Greene remained silent, so his captain continued. "There's no admiral's broad pennant flying from her mast."

Greene looked again and saw at once that his chief was right—the pennant that had flown from the *Dom Pedro I* was absent. "So, Cochrane's not on board?"

"Apparently not," Brewer said. He lowered his glass. "Benjamin, check and see if any pennants are flying from our friends on the other beam."

Greene touched his hat. "Aye, sir."

He was back shortly and reported, "None in sight, sir."

"So," Brewer said as he pushed off the rail, "I think we may safely assume that Cochrane is not on any of those ships. That changes things for us, Benjamin. I believe now is the time to be bold and pray that none of those ships are commanded by competent English captains who have left the king's service for money." He studied both threats for a moment. "Which one do you think is closer?"

"The seventy-four looks closer, sir, but I believe the other two will be upon us first."

Brewer nodded. "I agree. Load the guns and run them out. Mr. Sweeney, put me port aft of *Beverly*!"

He stood on his quarterdeck as his ship took up a position between *Beverly* and the two approaching ships, which had run up Brazilian colors. The approaching frigate had altered course to starboard a little after seeing *Phoebe's* new position, angling for a chance to rake the English frigate's stern. Brewer smiled. *Not today, my friends.*

He snapped his glass shut and walked over to the wheel.

"Mr. Sweeney," he said, "I want you to reduce sail slightly so we drop back toward those ships. At some point, I expect the frigate to turn hard-a-starboard to try to rake our stern. At that moment, I intend to turn hard-a-larboard and deal with the brig before turning back and attempting to rake the frigate's stern."

"Aye, sir," Sweeney said. "And the *Beverly*?"

"I think she will be able to beat the seventy-four into harbor, but if she doesn't, we'll have to assist her, so we must be swift. Get on it, Mr. Sweeney."

"Aye, sir." The sailing master picked up the speaking trumpet and began issuing orders, and the captain soon felt his ship begin to slow. He saw his first lieutenant approaching from the starboard rail.

"Anything on the seventy-four?" he asked.

"No, sir," Greene replied. "The ship does not appear to have cleared for action. As long as she does not open fire, *Beverly* may make it into the harbor."

Brewer updated his premier on his plans. "If we can pass close enough to the brig to unleash the carronades, we may get lucky and put her out of action with one broadside. However, I don't want to waste any more than one pass on her, or the frigate may have time to turn back on us."

Greene eyed the two approaching ships. "The timing may be tricky."

Privately, Brewer agreed, but all he said was, "This is what we train for." A thought struck him. "You know, Benjamin, when this is all over and we return to Jamaica, we should see about getting several cases of good wine for the crew to celebrate."

"I look forward to it, sir."

"Good," the captain said, patting his friend on the arm. "Now, let's see about luring these two flies into our spider's web."

It took twenty-eight minutes for the Brazilian frigate's captain to decide the time was right for him to make his move. As soon as Brewer saw her men scrambling up the shrouds and her bow begin to swing around to starboard, he sprang his trap.

"Now, Mr. Sweeney! Hard-a-larboard!"

"Aye, sir!"

The quartermaster and his mates turned the wheel over as hard and as fast as they could. HMS *Phoebe* responded and came around quickly. The brig was not even with *Phoebe* yet, so Brewer pounced on her unprotected bow.

"Mr. Sweeney!" he cried, "Take us across her bow. Half-pistol shot, if you can!"

"Aye, sir!"

Brewer went to the waist. "Mr. Rivkins! We are about to cross the brig's bow! Fire as your guns bear!"

"Stand by the carronades!" Greene bellowed.

Brewer's maneuver caught the Brazilian ships by surprise. The frigate tried to reverse her turn and ended up in irons as her British counterpart bore down on her consort. HMS *Phoebe* drew across the brig's bow and her guns erupted, 32-pound carronades and 18-pound cannon spewing death and destruction on their vulnerable target. The broadside was disciplined, guns firing in twos or threes as they bore true, the overwhelming majority of the shots striking either flesh or wood, sending deadly splinters across the deck that cut down even more of the crew. The poor ship staggered off to port as the British sailed past.

"Hard to larboard, Mr. Sweeney!" Brewer called. "Now for the frigate. Mr. Greene! What's the seventy-four doing?"

"Course unchanged, Captain!" Greene shouted. "She's run out her guns!"

"Let's hope Mr. Black doesn't lose his nerve," Brewer said.

HMS *Phoebe* came around the wounded brig. Brewer was tempted for just a moment to rake the ship's stern as they passed, but he decided that the ship was out of the fight. They cleared the brig's stern to find that the frigate was just barely moving in her fight to come out of irons.

"Mr. Sweeney!" Brewer shouted as he turned toward the wheel. "Take us across her stern!" He ran to the waist and called below. "Mr. Rivkins!"

The lieutenant appeared. "Sir?"

"We are going to rake the frigate! Ready the larboard battery! Stand by to fire!"

"Aye, sir!"

Brewer stepped back and watched their approach with interest. Their foe was catching wind now, but not fast enough to escape the devastation he was about to unleash.

He stepped to the waist. "Stand by, Mr. Rivkins."

"Ready, sir."

Just as Brewer was about to give the order to fire, a rogue gust of wind caught both ships, causing *Phoebe* to roll and pushing the Brazilian out of the line of fire.

Brewer fought to regain his balance and quickly realized what had happened.

"Mr. Sweeney! Hard to larboard! Mr. Rivkins! Fire!"

The ship turned and Rivkins' broadside caught the enemy frigate squarely in the starboard quarter. While not as devastating a blow as raking the stern would have been, it also was not quite enough to prevent the Brazilian from responding in kind.

The enemy broadside swept across the Englishman's deck and upper works. Brewer himself was knocked to the deck by the force of a passing ball that hit Midshipman Drake squarely in the chest. Brewer saw him vanish in a blood-colored cloud. He regained his footing and tried his best to ignore the cries of the wounded. He saw the ship was continuing on her turn to port and staggered to the waist.

"Mr. Rivkins! Starboard battery! Run out and fire as you bear!"

"Aye, sir!"

Brewer turned to see Greene and Sweeney struggling with the wheel; two of the quartermaster's mates were on the deck at their feet, one missing his head. The captain turned away and made himself focus on the enemy. It looked like one of the older twenty-eight gunners Britain had built in significant numbers in the late 1790s and early 1800s—12-pounders, most likely, but very nimble ships if handled correctly. He grunted; the Admiralty had probably sold it to the Brazilians rather then put it up in ordinary. Brewer shook his head, hoping that the ship wasn't manned by Englishmen.

"Mr. Sweeney!" he called. "Give me some distance! Mr. Rivkins! Reload both batteries with round shot! We shall try to pound her at long range!"

"Aye, sir!"

Brewer paused to watch as Rivkins gave instructions to Lieutenant Reed. Each lieutenant headed for a different battery. The captain couldn't help but remember Rivkins as a midshipman on the old *Lydia*, drifting aimlessly and most likely heading for a wasted life of alcoholism and wantonness. Fortunately, he had allowed Brewer to take him under his wing, as it were, and now the captain considered him a fine officer who might well earn his own flag one day.

Sweeney had straightened HMS *Phoebe* on a course away from the Brazilian. Brewer went to the wheel and was relieved to see the bodies had been removed, and two new mates were manning the wheel.

"Mr. Sweeney, turn us around," the captain said with more calm than he thought he possessed at the moment. "I want to take her down the starboard side at long range."

"Aye, sir." The sailing master moved off to begin issuing orders.

Brewer looked to his first lieutenant.

"The quartermaster?"

"Below, sir. He took splinters in the shoulder and upper chest. His mate Perkins was the one killed."

The captain nodded dully as his ship came around to face the enemy again. The Brazilian was turning much more slowly than he'd expected and he wondered if *Phoebe* had managed to damage the enemy's steering somehow.

"Watch out, Mr. Sweeney—those ships were nimble, as I recall. He may try to dart in on us to close the range."

"Aye, sir."

The minutes passed slowly as the ships closed on each other. There was no pretense, no maneuver, just a straight-out fight at what Brewer fervently hoped was a range too great for the Brazilian's armament to respond effectively. Brewer was struck by an idea and turned to his premier.

"Benjamin," he said, "have all the carronades load with chain. I intend to fire with the starboard battery, then reverse course and fire another broadside with the larboard. After that, I intend to close on the frigate, hopefully from the stern or at least the quarter. If we can get close enough, we can use the carronades to devastate her rigging."

The two ships continued to close. The Brazilian fired first, her shot falling short. Brewer took this as proof that the enemy captain was not a former king's officer. He walked to the waist.

"Alright, Mr. Rivkins! Fire!"

Eighteen 32-pounders went off. The sound was deafening, the smoke blinding.

"Lookout!" Brewer cried. "Let's hear you!"

"Several hits, sir! Can't rightly tell the damage yet!"

"Mr. Sweeney, reverse your course! Mr. Rivkins! Stand by larboard battery!"

"Standing by, sir!" came the reply from below.

The ship came around until she was running parallel with the Brazilian frigate again. Brewer judged his moment carefully.

"Now, Mr. Rivkins! Fire!"

Again the deafening roar of 18-pounders split the air, and again the smoke forced the officers and men to listen to the lookout for the outcome.

"Hits again, sir!"

"Hard to larboard, Mr. Sweeney. Cut across her stern at half-pistol shot."

"Aye, sir!"

Brewer looked around and saw the signals midshipman, Mr. Dye.

"Mr. Dye! Take a glass and run forward. I want to know what happened to *Beverly* and what that seventy-four is up to."

"Aye, sir!"

As the *Phoebe* made her turn, she ran out of the smoke from her broadsides, and Brewer was able to get a better view of the damage they'd inflicted. He could see that his foe's starboard side had taken a terrible beating, and a lucky shot had carried away the frigate's spanker.

"Sir!" Brewer turned to see Dye rushing toward him. "*Beverly* looks like she's made harbor, sir, but now the seventy-four's heading our way!"

Brewer headed forward, calling for Greene to follow. The two reached the bow and saw at once that the midshipman's report was true.

"What now, sir?" Greene asked.

"We'll pass astern of the frigate and head out to sea with all sail set. We can outrun the seventy-four and lose her completely after nightfall. Then we sneak past her in the dark and make for Salvador."

"And the frigate?"

Brewer shrugged. "With *Beverly* safely in the harbor, there's no more reason to fight. If she leaves us alone, I shall leave her alone."

Sadly, it was not to be. As HMS *Phoebe* went to pass, the frigate opened fire with any gun that might possibly bear. Brewer ordered the starboard carronades to fire, reducing much of the frigate's rigging aft of the main mast to shreds.

"Call all hands to make sail, Mr. Greene," Brewer said. We need to stay ahead of that battleship until night cloaks us."

The seventy-four crowded on sail, but, even damaged as she was, the English ship was swift enough to outpace the larger ship. Darkness fell, and Brewer directed the ship to be darkened, making her practically invisible under the cloudy night sky. Brewer ordered course changes to the north and then the west, and the dawn found them safely navigating the harbor entrance to Salvador.

CHAPTER FOURTEEN

Captain William Brewer stood on the deck of his frigate and watched the pilot direct her to a berth. His eyes were red and bleary, and he craved sleep, the result of staying up all night writing his report for Commodore Hardy. His vision had blurred a couple of times towards dawn. In any case, the report was ready and waiting, along with the mail for the boat from the flagship.

In the mail bag was his letter to Elizabeth. He begged her for news on her condition, how the pregnancy was going, and what names she liked for the child. For reasons which at this moment he could not fathom, he found himself hoping this first child would be a girl, graced with her mother's beauty, but not necessarily her mischievous nature. He was startled out of his daydreams by the voice of his first lieutenant.

"Captain?" Greene was saying. "The pilot has departed, sir."

"Oh, thank you, Mr. Greene," Brewer said.

"Captain?" It was Lieutenant Rivkins calling from the rail. Brewer walked over. Rivkins handed him a glass and indicated some ships on the far side of the harbor. "Looks like the Portuguese fleet arrived while we were away."

Brewer put the telescope to his eye and tried to concentrate. He counted one seventy-four, three frigates, four sloops or brigs, and ten merchant ships that presumably had brought supplies and reinforcements. He turned briefly and looked toward HMS *Talavera* and wondered what the commodore thought of all this. He turned back and studied the Portuguese squadron in more detail. The ships looked old compared to the newly bought or built ships of the Brazilian navy, and he doubted the king of Portugal had hired veteran British sailors to man his ships, or had an admiral like Cochrane to lead them. If the Brazilians could mass anywhere near the same number of ships and Cochrane was on the scene, Brewer considered the results of any battle a forgone conclusion.

"Boat approaching!"

"It's from the flagship, sir!"

Brewer dragged himself from the rail and surrendered to his body's cry for sleep.

"See that the mail and my reports get to the boat when it arrives, Mr. Greene," he said, unable to keep the weariness out of his voice. "I'm going to get some sleep before anything else demands my attention."

It seemed to Brewer that he had barely closed his eyes before he was awakened by a firm hand shaking his shoulder. He reluctantly opened his eyes and allowed the face of his coxswain to swim into focus.

"Mac?"

"Sorry to wake you, sir," Mac said. "Signal from the flagship, sir. The commodore wants you."

Brewer groaned as he struggled to sit up. “The commodore? Dear God. Very well. How long have I been asleep?”

“A bit over four hours, sir.”

Brewer moaned and rested his head in his hands. “Feels more like four minutes.” He sat up and inhaled deeply. “Acknowledge the signal. I shall come up on deck as soon as I have dressed. Call away the launch.”

“Aye, sir.” Mac stood and was gone.

The captain closed his eyes for just a moment to gather the will to rise and dress. He sniffed, and cracked one eye open. There was Alfred, standing before him with coffee. Brewer smiled and accepted the cup.

“Thank you, Alfred,” he said. “You are a lifesaver.”

The harbor waters were calm during the passage to the flagship, but Brewer could not shake the sense that a looming crisis was behind this summons.

He was met at HMS *Talavera’s* entry port by the commodore’s flag lieutenant, Mr. Lincoln, who saluted smartly.

“Welcome aboard, Captain. If you’ll follow me, please? The commodore is waiting.”

Brewer returned the salute and followed his guide in silence. Moments later, he was admitted to the commodore’s great cabin. He found Commodore Hardy standing in the day cabin talking with Captain Christopher and a foreign officer. Each man had a glass of wine in his hand.

“Brewer!” Hardy said. He broke away from the others to shake Brewer’s hand heartily. “Come in! You know Captain Christopher, and this is Governor General Madeira de Melo, commander of the garrison of Salvador." Hardy turned to the Portuguese officer. "Sir, allow me to present Captain William Brewer of His Majesty's frigate *Phoebe*."

The general bowed. Brewer returned the gesture and looked to Hardy.

"We are discussing the immediate future of Salvador," the commodore said. "Please, gentlemen, be seated. Captain Brewer, allow me to bring you up to date with regard to current events. In the past few weeks, the Brazilian armies surrounding Salvador have made significant gains in the hills to the west and south of the city to say that Salvador is now under siege. The governor general has come to seek our advice on how to proceed, should the need arise to evacuate Portuguese interests from the city."

"I see," Brewer said. "Are we awaiting the arrival of their naval commander?"

"He is under my command," the governor general said firmly.

Brewer looked to the commodore, who asked, "Governor, how long can your forces hold out, considering the supplies and reinforcements that your naval forces brought?"

The governor shifted uneasily in his seat. "That depends, Commodore. Can we count on your squadron to assist us in breaking the blockade the upstart's navy has set up outside my city?"

The commodore shook his head. "I'm afraid that goes against the orders I have received from the Admiralty. My orders are to refrain from getting involved in a fight except to protect British interests and property. I am not allowed to take sides in your war."

The governor leaned forward, his forearm planted firmly on his knee. "And yet, have you not already done so, Commodore? Did not your young captain here do so even yesterday, when he attacked and disabled two Brazilian ships?"

Brewer bristled. "That was in defense of an English merchantman, sir!"

The governor waved Brewer's objection aside. "I doubt your Admiral Cochrane will see it that way."

Brewer nearly reacted to that as well, but the commodore raised a hand.

"Admiral Cochrane belongs to the Brazilian navy, sir. I suggest you remember that, especially on board my ship."

The governor made a deprecating gesture. "My apologies, Commodore. I meant no offense. But I tell you now, Commodore, without Britain's active intervention, Salvador will fall, and Brazil will have won its independence."

Brewer was not surprised when Commodore Hardy did not reply to this. British interests would be best served by an independent Brazil, which theoretically would open up vast markets to British exports.

"Are you able to evacuate all who wish to leave," Hardy asked at last, "should that become necessary?"

The governor stared at the commodore before darting a swift glance at Christopher. Then he lowered his head to stare at the deck. When he saw that, Brewer realized he was looking at a defeated man.

"I am not sure," de Melo said without looking up. "The entire garrison will be evacuated, of course, but many of our people have lived here for generations and do not wish to leave. I have warned them that there is no guarantee of what will happen after we are gone and the Brazilians take over, but they are willing to take the risk. There is another convoy to aid in the evacuation, made up of nearly empty ships, which should be arriving within the month, if the Brazilians will allow it to enter the harbor."

"I don't see why they wouldn't," Christopher offered. "Why would they object to letting you leave?"

"Because of the treasury," the governor said quietly.

The three British officers shared a quick look.

"Pardon me, Governor," Christopher asked in a low voice, "but may I ask how much treasure we are talking about here? How many ships will you need to take it back to Portugal?"

The governor general looked at the deck for several moments, as if trying to decide whether or not to divulge the information. His British hosts heard him sigh heavily and saw his shoulders shake.

"The treasury consists mainly of gold and silver, coins and bars of each. We have two ships in the harbor now that can carry 1,000 tons, and ten more are coming with the evacuation convoy. The Brazilians have been told they are necessary to evacuate the population who wish to return to Europe."

Captain Christopher pursed his lips, and a low whistle escaped.

"I had no idea we were talking about so large a sum," Hardy said softly, "or that many ships to move it."

"Commodore," Brewer interrupted, "I have just remembered something that I failed to put in my report, and I believe it is important. When we fought our way into the harbor yesterday, the last ship we eluded was the *Dom Pedro*

I. Sir, she had no admiral's broad pennant flying from her masts."

Hardy stared in surprise. "You don't say? I don't suppose you saw it flying from any other ship in the squadron?"

"No, sir."

"Well, well," Hardy said, as he crossed his arms over his chest.

"Excuse me," de Melo said, "but what does this mean?"

Christopher turned to him. "It means Admiral Cochrane was not with the blockade squadron."

The governor general turned back to Hardy. "This is good for us?"

"Yes," Hardy said, "provided we can move while he is gone. How soon can you have the treasure loaded after those other ships arrive?"

The governor seemed to take on new life. "The additional ships are expected in six days. Once they arrive, the loading can commence at once. At this moment, to our knowledge the Brazilian forces surrounding the city do not have a direct view into the harbor. Should they gain one, we will only load the treasure at night, so that it will be more difficult for them to see what is loaded onto what ship. The negotiations with the Brazilians for the peaceful evacuation of the city are almost complete. I have received permission from my king to surrender and bring our people home. I will ask that Admiral Cochrane be informed of the surrender terms and that he be ordered to comply with them completely."

"I'm not sure how much weight that will carry with Cochrane," Hardy said dryly. "Have the Brazilians mentioned the treasure at all?"

"Not specifically," de Melo said, "although three times now, Admiral Cochrane has stressed the requirement that we can only take personal items with us when we leave. All else must be left behind."

Hardy shrugged. "Well, we'll just have to press ahead and see what happens. Governor, do you have a plan for smuggling the treasury back to Lisbon?"

De Melo spread his hands. "Commodore de Campos has suggested that we send the warships out first, and then, while they are engaging the blockade squadron, the merchant ships with the people and the treasury will make a run for the open sea and then for Lisbon. Under no circumstances would they stop for any reason."

Captain Christopher looked pleased. "Actually, that doesn't sound too bad of a plan. What say you, Commodore?"

"Good as any," Hardy said, "given the ships available and the fact that they have no intention of returning. The danger will come if one or more of the Brazilian warships spot the second group of ships and break off to engage them. Of course, there's every chance that Cochrane will be concentrating every available ship outside this port. What's our latest estimate of the Brazilian Navy's strength?"

The Flag Captain was well informed. "The latest reports put them at possibly five ships of the line—definitely two seventy-fours—eight to ten frigates, mostly 28-gunners bought from us, as it happens, plus an unknown quantity of smaller ships: sloops, brigs, luggers, and the like."

"And what ships did Commodore de Campos bring?" Hardy asked.

"One seventy-four, three frigates, four smaller vessels—corvettes, I think they call them—and ten merchant ships, two of which the governor says are thousand-tonners."

"Thank you, Captain," Hardy said to Christopher. He turned to de Melo. "What forces are supposed to accompany the other ten ships?"

"I am not sure, Commodore," the Governor confessed. "Our navy was decimated by the French occupation of our country."

"Sir," Brewer said, "I doubt that Cochrane or whomever he left in command of the blockade squadron will allow any Portuguese warships to enter Salvador, certainly not a seventy-four."

"I agree." Hardy said. "What if we got word to the squadron and had them stop somewhere out to sea, between 200 and 250 miles Northwest of Salvador, and ordered the merchant ships to head for that rendezvous? They should make that by the end of the second day at sea."

"Everything depends on how well the Portuguese warships engage the blockade squadron," Christopher said, addressing the governor directly. "If Cochrane is not present at the battle, your forces may be able to engage them long enough for most, if not all, of the merchantmen to get away. But if Cochrane is present, I think he will see through the scheme and order some of his fastest ships to break off and pursue the merchantmen."

"Perhaps some of the Portuguese corvettes should sail with the treasury ships?" Brewer suggested.

"Perhaps," Hardy cast an approving look Brewer's way. This was a sensible suggestion, as it put the corvettes to good strategic use. "Governor," he said firmly, "we need to speak to Commodore de Campos."

De Melo rose "Very well, Commodore. I shall give orders for him to report to you tomorrow. Please keep me informed about your plans."

Hardy's deep voice was a rumble when he replied, "Remember, Governor, I have no plans. We are simply trying to assist your commodore in his plans for a evacuation."

"Yes, yes, I remember," De Melo said, "but I still have hope. Farewell, gentlemen."

Captain Christopher escorted him to the entry port and returned. Hardy offered Madeira.

"Tell me, sir," Brewer said, "do you really think we'll be able to stay out of it?"

Hardy accepted a glass from the steward and took a seat beneath the seventy-four's great stern windows. "Those are our orders, Captain," he said. "Of course, events will dictate our actions. Should I order you to stay in harbor, just to be safe?"

Brewer grinned. "That won't be necessary, sir." He accepted a drink and sat on the commodore's left as Captain Christopher sat down on his right. The three men drank their wine. Finally, Brewer asked the question that had been bothering him.

"Do you think that the Portuguese have a chance of success?" he asked.

Christopher shrugged. "Personally, I think it depends on whether or not Cochrane is there."

Brewer looked to the commodore. Hardy shrugged. "I tend to agree with Captain Christopher."

Brewer raised the glass to his lips.

"And our involvement?" he asked from behind the glass.

Hardy's eyes darted to his young captain and back to his drink just as quickly. Brewer glanced to Captain Christopher just in time to see his eyes go from the commodore to the glass in his hands. Brewer drank his wine and waited for the commodore.

"Our orders say no," Hardy said in a low voice.

"Does the Admiralty know what we suspect about Cochrane and the treasure?"

The commodore shook his head. "No, I haven't told them that."

Brewer lowered his glass. "Do you still believe it's true?"

Hardy drew a slow, deep breath, held it for a minute, then let it out just as slowly. His eyes never left the dark liquid in his glass.

"Yes."

"Do we not have an obligation to act in order to prevent the admiral from acquiring the treasure?"

Hardy stiffened visibly in his chair, and Brewer thought for a moment that he had gone too far.

"Captain Brewer," Hardy said, "this squadron is not my personal property. We operate as much as possible under the orders of the Admiralty in London. I suggest you remember that if you wish to rise any higher on the captain's list." He paused to drain his glass and to rein in his temper. "That being said, I am open to suggestions."

At that moment, there was a knock on the cabin door and the sentry admitted the midshipman of the watch. The lad entered the room and came to attention.

"Mr. Simmons' respects, sir, but there's a boat approaching from a ship bearing an English flag that has just entered the harbor."

Captain Christopher straightened. "What do you mean, 'a ship bearing an English flag'?"

"Mr. Simmons does not believe it to be an English ship, sir. But it is flying the Union Jack."

Christopher glanced at Hardy; the commodore shrugged. The captain turned back to the midshipman.

"My compliments to Mr. Simmons. I want a marine guard at the ready. Whoever boards from that boat is to be escorted here."

The midshipman came to attention. "Aye, sir!" He turned and marched smartly out of the cabin.

They had time to finish their wine before the sentry knocked on the door. All three rose to their feet. Two marine guards marched in and stepped back to admit a tall, well-knit man in civilian dress. It was the Brazilian admiral himself.

"Admiral Cochrane," Hardy said, "what an unexpected surprise. Will you have a drink? Bascomb, a glass for our guest. Please, Admiral, sit with us and share madeira."

Brewer settled himself quietly as Cochrane took a seat opposite Hardy and accepted a glass from the solemn Bascomb. Cochrane raised his glass and toasted his host before taking a drink.

"Ah!" he said. "Excellent. I apologize for the unorthodox means of my arrival, but it is necessary that I speak with you, Commodore, and I did not think the governor general would welcome the *Dom Pedro I.*"

Hardy resumed his seat. "No, I don't suppose he would. What can I do for you, Admiral?"

Cochrane raised his glass again. "Very well—to business, then. Commodore, I wish to know what your orders are regarding the evacuation of the Portuguese from Salvador."

"My orders are my own, sir," Hardy said calmly, "and you may rest assured that I shall follow them to the best of my ability."

Cochrane's expression was cool and appraising. "Then let me tell you *my* orders to the squadron blockading Salvador. Every ship attempting to leave the harbor is to be stopped and searched. Evacuees are permitted to take nothing but their personal effects. Any ship that does not stop will be fired upon."

"*Every* ship?" Hardy said. "And where does that leave my squadron, sir? Or any English merchant ships sailing for home?"

Cochrane smiled. "That is up to you, sir."

The commodore's face became an unreadable mask. He studied the admiral with eyes that were hooded.

"I think I can safely tell you, Admiral, that neither the ships of my squadron nor any English merchant ship leaving Salvador will submit to being boarded and searched."

"That is your final word?" Cochrane asked.

"It is."

The two men stared at each other, and then the admiral drained his glass and rose. Hardy and the captains followed suit.

"Thank you for the excellent wine, Commodore," the admiral said, settling his hat upon his head. "Until we meet again!"

Cochrane glanced at Captain Christopher, ignored Brewer completely, and left the cabin. The marine guards followed.

Hardy stood there, with his back to his friends and arms crossed over his chest, staring at the cabin door. Brewer glanced to Christopher, but the flag captain indicated they should remain silent and wait the commodore out.

Finally, Hardy dropped his arms to his sides and turned to his companions.

"Well, gentlemen, it seems that we are not going to be allowed to sit this one out."

Christopher shook his head. "It seems not, sir."

Hardy strode about the day room. "Christopher, we need to speak to Commodore de Campos, and I don't trust the governor to remember to have him visit us. What say we send him a nice, social dinner invitation? Perhaps for tomorrow night? What frigates have we left in the harbor at the moment?"

Christopher looked to Brewer and smiled. "Only HMS *Phoebe*, sir."

Hardy nodded with a grin. "Of course. Captain Brewer, you are also invited to dinner tomorrow. Say, the turn of the first watch? Good. Now, gentlemen, I have some planning to do."

Back aboard *Phoebe*, Brewer invited Mr. Sweeney, Lieutenant Greene, and Dr. Spinelli to join his for supper that night. Then he went below and informed Alfred that he would be away the next night, and to request a supper for four that evening.

In his cabin, he sat down at his desk and eyed his bookshelf longingly, but in the end he decided to write a letter to his wife. He drew out paper, pen, and ink and began.

My Dearest Elizabeth,

I am writing to you from the harbor at Salvador, Brazil, the last remaining Portuguese outpost in the country, and not for much longer, I'm afraid. The forces of the Emperor of Brazil have laid siege to the city, and the new Brazilian navy has blockaded the port. Never fear, beloved, I am safe aboard a king's ship. Commodore Hardy's orders from the Admiralty are to stay neutral in the conflict.

My prayers are with you and the child. I have given the matter of names some thought; see what you think of these. (Allow me to say from the start, that if we have a boy, I want you to promise me that you will not, under any circumstances, name him Horatio! I love his lordship, and I owe him much, but there are limits.) I have thought that David, Benjamin, or John would be good candidates for a boy's name, while Mary, Emma, or Abigail would be fitting for a girl. When the time comes, if I am not with you, name the child as you see fit; I only care that you are both there for me to love. Only please notify me immediately of the event. I want to know who I have waiting for me at home.

In the doorway, Alfred cleared his throat to get his captain's attention.

"Sir, your guests will be arriving momentarily."

"What? Already?" Brewer took out his pocket watch and opened it. He hurriedly signed the letter, closed and sealed it; Mac would see that it went out with the next mail bag. He packed away the writing implements in his writing desk and then stowed that in its corner. Then he retreated to his day cabin to welcome his guests.

Per his previous arrangement with Alfred, the four men were immediately seated for supper. Mac, acting in his capacity as steward once again, entered the room with a platter piled high with chops, which he set carefully in the center of the table. Following that was a big bowl of stewed potatoes and a smaller one of young carrots in butter sauce. Pudding came after that, along with fresh hot bread and preserves.

"Gentlemen," Brewer said from his seat at the head of the table, "Much has happened this day. Eat hearty; we have a lot of work to do tonight."

The feast disappeared rather quickly, and the grateful partakers retired to the day room for port, cigars, and scheming.

"Now," Brewer said once they were all ensconced in the day cabin with glasses of port and smoking cigars, "to the business of the evening. No doubt you wish to hear about the meeting aboard the flagship. Then I need your advice regarding our plans so that I can have something practical to submit to the commodore when he asks. When I arrived, the commodore was already entertaining the Portuguese governor general of Salvador. The city is under siege and negotiations are under way for the evacuation by sea of all those who wish to leave, along with their personal effects. The Brazilians are very particular that *nothing else be removed from the city*. The reason for this, gentlemen, is that when the Portuguese royal court fled from Napoleon's invasion in 1807, they brought along with them their country's entire royal treasury and deposited it here, in Salvador. That treasure has grown to such a size that it will take more than ten thousand-ton merchantmen to take it back to Lisbon. Naturally, the Brazilians want to get their hands on it before it leaves their country."

"Is the blockade squadron strong enough to prevent the treasure from leaving?" Greene asked.

"Our intelligence says that the Brazilian forces are stronger than the Portuguese squadron in the harbor, but not by much. And there are additional Portuguese forces on the way here, escorting the merchantmen needed to remove the treasure."

"What are the Portuguese plans, sir?" the doctor asked.

Brewer took a deep drag on his cigar and blew a cloud of smoke upward before replying. "The governor general wasn't very forthcoming. Under pressure from Commodore Hardy, he said that his commodore wanted to attack the blockade squadron with his warships, then send the merchant convoys out under cover of the battle. Hardy suggested that word be sent to the warships escorting the approaching merchant shipping that they heave to at a certain point and wait for the evacuation convoys to escort them back to Lisbon."

Mr. Sweeney and Greene nodded in appreciation. The doctor sat silently, a thoughtful look on his face.

"Not a bad plan, really," Greene commented.

"That was my thought as well," the captain said. "My concern is that Cochrane may see through the scheme and detail off some of his smaller ships to intercept the convoy and retake the treasure."

"And the commodore's position?" Sweeney asked.

"Commodore Hardy's position is that the British squadron is under orders to stay out of any direct conflict. As you may imagine, that answer did not please the governor general."

"So, what happened?" Spinelli asked.

"Commodore Hardy wishes to confer with the Portuguese commodore—a man named de Campos—and has issued an invitation for him to dine on the flagship tomorrow"

Sweeney leaned forward. "And Admiral Cochrane?"

"The admiral wanted to know what the commodore's orders were from the Admiralty regarding the evacuation. Of course, Hardy refused to say. Cochrane then informed us that his own orders to his squadron were that every ship leaving the harbor was to be stopped and searched. No exceptions."

It was the doctor who broke the silence that lay heavily in the room.

"And those that refuse to stop?"

"They will be fired upon. No exceptions."

"So," Greene said quietly, "it looks as though we are in it after all."

"So it would seem," Sweeney agreed.

"I want to know if you gentlemen have any thoughts I might present to the commodore."

The captain saw his first lieutenant and sailing master look to each other and smile. When they turned back to him, it was Mr. Greene who spoke.

"I think we may have an idea or two for you, Captain."

Captain William Brewer sat in the stern sheets of the launch on his way to the flagship. The meeting in his quarters had lasted long into the night. The only real question now was, how aggressive was Commodore Hardy willing to be?

The plan Brewer intended to present was a variation on the Portuguese commodore's plan. The Portuguese naval forces would advance from the harbor first and engage the Brazilian blockade squadron just before dusk. After the battle was joined, Commodore Hardy in *Talavera*, along with *Doris, Beaver,* and *Conway*, would escort the evacuation ships out to sea and set course NNW for the waiting Portuguese ships of the line. When night had fully fallen, Brewer in *Phoebe* would leave the harbor with the treasure fleet and steer SSW in an effort to break out into the South Atlantic. Once clear of the battle area, he would lead his convoy east and then northeast to St. Helena when he thought it safe. Once the commodore had turned his charges over to the Portuguese squadron, his squadron would make for St. Helena to escort the treasure convoy back to Lisbon.

If the ploy succeeded, the Brazilians would see Commodore Hardy leave Salvador and pursue him with whatever ships they had available, leaving nothing to spot or challenge his own convoy when it sailed under cover of darkness.

It was a good plan, all right. Now, all he had to do was convince two commodores to agree.

The dinner was over, and Brewer and the other guests followed their host into the commodore's great cabin and took their seats around the room. Bascomb, Commodore Hardy's servant, passed drinks around to everyone before withdrawing. Hardy made a toast to open the meeting proper, and then everyone took seats.

"Commodore," he said to de Campos, "does the governor general know you are here?"

"He does indeed, Commodore."

"And did he give you any instructions?"

Brewer saw a small smile creep over the Portuguese commodore's features. He was a tall, thin man with a dark, Mediterranean skin tone. His eyes were black and his hairline had receded in a manner not unlike that of Bonaparte the last time Brewer had seen him, complete with the wispy comb-over atop his head. Brewer judged him to have connections, possibly royal ones, but he also felt that this was a man who had bothered to learn his profession along the way, much like Hornblower's brother-in-law, the Duke of Wellington.

"The governor did call me into his office," de Campos said. "Let us just say that he has agreed in principle to abide by whatever plan we agree upon here."

Commodore Hardy's eyes flashed appreciation.

"Gentlemen," he said, "we have two goals. First, to safely evacuate all Portuguese citizens who wish to leave Salvador before the Brazilians take possession of the city; second, to deny possession of the Portuguese royal treasury to the Brazilians in general, and Admiral Cochrane in particular. The reason we are having this meeting here, on my flagship, is due to Admiral Cochrane's statement, made in this room in front of Captains Christopher and Brewer as well as myself, that English ships, both Royal Navy and merchantmen, would be stopped and searched leaving the harbor. The British government will not stand for such insolence. In light of this, I have decided to act in support of the Portuguese evacuation of both her citizens and her gold.

De Campos raised a finger and stroked his jawline. "I am not sure it is much of a plan, Commodore. My thought is that my squadron will seek out battle with the blockade squadron. The merchant shipping will endeavor to slip out and away in the confusion."

Hardy nodded. "Yes, that is the plan the governor told us. I am unsure of its chances for success if the admiral is present. We have talked it over, Commodore, and we concluded that Admiral Cochrane might smell a trap and hold back some of his smaller warships to intercept your merchantmen."

De Campos listened and thought for a moment before speaking. "And if he were not there?"

Hardy shot a look to Christopher. "I'm afraid, Commodore—unless you know something that I don't—that we must presume the worst: that Admiral Cochrane will be present on his flagship when your forces leave the harbor."

Brewer leaned forward. "Sir, I have an idea."

Hardy was a commander who listened to his officers. "Yes, Captain?"

Brewer looked from Hardy to de Campos, and counted off points on his fingers as he spoke. "The idea to engage the blockade squadron is a good one. Whether Cochrane is there or not, we must make the Brazilians dance to our tune. First, we initiate the engagement one hour before the sunset. Second, after the battle is joined—say, just about dusk—Commodore Hardy in *Talavera,* along with most of the British squadron, escorts the merchantmen carrying the evacuees and their possessions out of the harbor to the waiting Portuguese forces. Cochrane, if he is present, will surely be expecting a ruse of some kind; he will jump on this convoy to stop and search it."

"And we should allow that?" Christopher demanded, looking affronted.

"The search won't matter, because there will be nothing there for him to find," Brewer said. "In fact, the longer he takes with that convoy, the better we shall be pleased, and here is why. Third, two hours after that convoy has left, when it is full dark, HMS *Phoebe* and perhaps one other ship will escort the treasure convoy out of the harbor on a SSE course. Their destination will be St. Helena and then Lisbon."

The room was silent for a moment. Then Hardy picked up his glass, and spoke.

"I couldn't help but notice, Captain," he said, "that you saved the escorting of the treasure fleet for yourself."

"Well, sir, I believed the Portuguese would expect the flagship—and yourself—to be guarding the most important cargo, and to them that's the treasure."

The commodore took a drink, and Brewer thought he saw a smile covered by the action.

"Captain Christopher?" Hardy asked. "Your opinion?"

Christopher looked hard at Brewer for a moment before answering. "I believe the plan has much to recommend it, sir, especially the attempt to sneak out the first convoy after the battle has occupied the attention of the blockading squadron. That is exactly what Cochrane would expect us to try, and he will have to react to it. I wonder, however, if we aren't being a tad *too* clever."

"How so, sir?" Hardy prompted.

Christopher leaned forward. "Wouldn't a man like Cochrane *expect* us to try to fool him like this?"

Brewer started to answer, but Hardy stopped him with a gesture. "I suppose it is possible, Captain. Do you have a better idea?"

Christopher sighed heavily. "It seems to me simpler to reinforce Commodore de Campos' squadron with our squadron to make sure the Brazilian warships cannot intercept the merchant shipping when it leaves the harbor."

"Now *that* is something a man like Cochrane would expect us to try," Brewer said. Christopher shot him a look, which Brewer dutifully ignored.

"Gentlemen, please," Hardy interjected, retaking control of the meeting. "Commodore de Campos, what do you think?"

The Portuguese officer tapped his chin thoughtfully. "I like the plan on first hearing, Commodore. I am concerned that our people may be in danger if the Brazilians come after them."

"But they would have been in danger under your original plan as well, Commodore," Christopher said. "Under this plan, at least the Royal Navy will be there to protect them."

"True." De Campos shrugged.

"Anything else?" Hardy asked.

De Campos shook his head. "I don't think so. Have we made contact with the incoming Portuguese ships?"

"Yes," Captain Christopher said. "A sloop pulled into harbor in the night. The additional transports should be here within a week. Three Portuguese seventy-fours and five frigates will be waiting for the evacuees at the meeting point to escort them the rest of the way to Lisbon."

"What about the treasure convoy?" de Campos asked.

Brewer leaned forward. "After turning their convoy over to the Portuguese ships, Commodore Hardy's force will make its way to St. Helena to provide escort for the treasure fleet back to Lisbon. Our thinking is that the Brazilians will think twice about attacking a British escort."

De Campos considered the plan. In truth, it had much to recommend it, other than the fact that it left Portuguese forces wet-nursing the refugees while the British got the honor of escorting the king's treasure home. He sighed and took a long, slow drink of his wine to cover his displeasure. He had not been entirely truthful with his British hosts. The governor had indeed called him into his office earlier that very morning, as soon as he'd heard about the invitation. At first the governor had forbidden him to go, and the argument which ensued between them had been as loud as it was volatile. When he finally walked out of the office, three hours later, his instructions from the governor amounted to one sentence: *Make sure the British sail with us.*

He set his glass down on the table, knowing that the only way to carry out his governor's instructions was to swallow his pride and agree to their plan. He put on his best diplomatic face and looked up.

"We shall follow your plan, Commodore," he said formally. "I look forward to toasting its success in Lisbon with the finest port that Portugal has to offer."

The last of the transports arrived six days later, and the work of loading the evacuees' belongings began immediately. This was carried out from dawn to dark; but after night fell, the work switched to a different part of the harbor, where the treasure was loaded carefully and quietly onto its designated ships. Every effort was made to conceal this activity from the Brazilian forces besieging the city. Some of the supplies to be evacuated were loaded onto the treasure ships during daylight hours; this was to ensure that the Brazilians had no cause to wonder why certain ships were apparently not being used in the evacuation.

Plans were carefully laid and adjusted and remade for each of the three forces that would sail. Timing was critical. If Commodore Hardy's convoy sailed before Commodore de Campos had the blockade squadron fully engaged, it would be too easy for the Brazilians to break off and have enough ships to harass or follow the convoy. If Brewer's treasure convoy sailed before it was pitch dark, or if one of its ships went off course and was seen by a Brazilian ship, Brewer's small force, consisting of his frigate and two luggers, could be overwhelmed and the treasure lost.

Hardy's convoy was the decoy, although there was some question—still unanswered when the convoy eventually sailed—as to how much resistance should be offered by the escorting British warships before any inspections were allowed. A Royal Navy escort boasting a seventy-four simply did not step aside and allow the ships it escorted to be searched. When Brewer was present during discussion of this question, he tactfully remained silent; after all, he didn't want the commodore to "offer" him any advice on how his own group should proceed.

Finally, the loading of the goods was complete and it was time for the evacuees to board their transports. The trouble was that the loading of the treasure had not quite kept pace, and there was still several hours' worth of work left to be done. To buy time, the governor general sent a message to the general of the besieging Brazilian forces, stating that to make sure nothing unnecessary was taken on board, he, de Melo, was ordering an inventory of all items loaded aboard the transports, which he would duly share with the Brazilian general. The general promptly wrote back, thanking the governor on behalf of his emperor! This trick gave them the time they needed to finish loading the gold.

CHAPTER FIFTEEN

The afternoon sun was well on its way to setting, and a nervous William Brewer paced his quarterdeck. Everything was in readiness; the evacuees—all 12,000 of them—were aboard their transports, along with their belongings. Thirty-one ships would be escorted by Commodore Hardy in *HMS Talavera*, along with frigates *Doris* and *Hannover* and a handful of smaller ships. Brewer's own convoy consisted of eighteen large merchant ships, filled to the brim with the Portuguese royal treasury, the escort being made up of Brewer's own *HMS Phoebe* and two luggers to round up strays like sheep dogs on the downs. The Portuguese squadron under Commodore de Campos stood ready at the harbor's entrance. De Campos had one seventy-four, four frigates, two brigs, and some smaller ships with which to attack the blockade squadron.

Every captain on the quarterdeck of his ship waited for one man—Commodore Hardy. He was the one who had to give the order to sail. Once given, the three groups had to sail in sequence, allowing sufficient time to pass between, or surprise would be lost. Twice in the past three days, the Brazilians had sent a small ship to try to spy out the harbor, but each time the harbor defenses had discouraged the vessel from sailing too close.

Brewer didn't think the Brazilians could report anything other than the presence of the Portuguese naval squadron at the entrance to the harbor. That alone would have warned the blockaders that a breakout was imminent. Brewer was fairly sure that Cochrane was in communication with the armies besieging the city. He shrugged his shoulders and continued to pace, but he was slightly encouraged by the strengthening wind in his face.

He turned at the end of his stride and saw Mac standing quietly off to the side, as he had been since Brewer had come up on deck. He held Brewer's hanger with his sword and a brace of pistols, ready for his captain when the ship sailed from the harbor and into the unknown. Brewer was thankful once again for his presence. He knew, as well, that when the battle was eventually joined, Mac and Alfred would guard his back. He smiled for just a moment at the thought.

He glanced skyward as he made his next turn and noted the position of the sun. The only group that had to sail before sunset was Commodore de Campos' squadron. They had to have enough light to seek out and engage the Brazilian ships blockading the harbor. It was vital that every Brazilian ship be brought to battle, or else some would be left free to intercept the other convoys that would sail. Brewer thrust his chin back down onto his chest and waited for the signal. He knew that there were easily a dozen lookouts and officers who had telescopes to their eyes at that moment, all trained on the same thing—the mainmast of HMS *Talavera*.

"Sir?" It was Mr. Greene. "The signal's been raised on the flagship."

"Portuguese have acknowledged, sir!" Mr. Rivkins called.

Brewer ceased his pacing and walked to the rail to watch the battle squadron sail. A knot was forming in his stomach. A good many of the men sailing with de Campos would not come back alive; that number would be even higher if Cochrane were out there. They were sacrificing their lives to give their countrymen safe passage back home to Lisbon. Brewer had never been asked to make that kind of sacrifice. Even in the Mediterranean, he'd never felt any of them were one-way missions. Now he watched as brave men sailed, knowing full well what lay ahead. He felt his back stiffen, almost of its own accord, to honor those who went to do their duty.

It wasn't very long before gusts of wind brought back the echoes of the battle, the sounds of cannon fire a long distance away to go with the glimpses of light that danced on the horizon. Brewer stood alongside Greene and Mr. Sweeney at the rail, watching. He had no idea how long he had been there when Mr. Murdy approached.

"Begging your pardon, sir," he said as he touched his hat, "but the night signal has just been raised on the flagship."

"Thank you, Mr. Murdy," Brewer said. He and Greene turned to see the triangular signal of lamps blazing high over *Talavera*'s deck. Greene touched his captain's arm and pointed to the leading Portuguese transports. They had acknowledged the signal and were raising anchor. One after another, the ships got under way. HMS *Doris* led them out. By the harbor's light, Brewer and Greene could see their decks lined with men and women staring back at the land. None of them made any sound that he could hear; there was no cheering to be returning to Portugal, there was only silence behind the normal workings of the ships. They stayed in their places, looking for the last time at what had been their homes, right up to the moment that the dusk swallowed them as they left the harbor.

Several ships had not yet cleared the harbor when a bright flash illuminated the horizon and caused everyone on the deck of HMS *Phoebe* to look out toward the battle. Then came the sound of an awful explosion, and an accompanying blast force smote them. The blast was strong enough to push them back a step or two, and when they recovered all they could do was stare with mouths agape. There was no doubt in anyone's mind what had happened.

"A magazine, no question," Sweeney said.

"Undoubtedly," Greene replied, "but whose?"

"From the force of it," the captain said, "likely a seventy-four; it would take a ship that big to produce that kind of blast over that distance."

The question is, whose seventy-four?" Sweeney said.

No-one could answer.

The entire enterprise now took on a more serious, more deadly tone. Brewer pulled out his watch and noted the time that the last ship in Hardy's convoy disappeared into the night. Now the wait began until he could order his own ships to sea. He went to the lee rail and gazed up at the night sky and the stars beginning to show.

On his signal, the luggers would depart and search the area to the southeast. If they encountered Brazilian ships they were to send up flares, warning the convoy of danger. If they found the way clear they were to scout ahead, and *Phoebe* would escort the treasure ships out of the harbor and away on a SSE course. This would be held throughout the night. In the morning, the luggers would round up any stragglers, and the entire convoy would change course to the east. They hoped to see nothing but empty seas until the time for the final course correction, which would take them to St. Helena, where they would wait for Commodore Hardy's forces.

Brewer desperately wanted to know what was happening with the battle. It had been going on for nearly two hours. He knew Commodore de Campos' orders were to engage Brazilian ships as long as there were any afloat that could possibly interfere with the treasure convoy. Brewer lowered his gaze to the horizon. He still saw intermittent flashes of cannon fire, although the darkness would make it relatively easy for a ship to disengage and disappear. He pulled out his watch and noted that forty-five minutes had passed since the last of Hardy's ships had sailed.

"Mr. Greene," he called, "have Mr. Dye signal the luggers to sail."

"Aye, sir." Greene touched his hat and was gone.

The luggers should take no more than thirty minutes to determine if there were any Brazilian ships to the southeast. Brewer had been concerned at first about the lugger's ability to find the enemy in the darkness, until he'd hit upon the obvious—he sent the luggers out with orders to have their lights fully lit. Any Brazilian ships within sight would be drawn to them like moths to a flame. The luggers were equipped with red rockets that they could fire in the event they could not escape from the enemy. Lookouts on HMS *Phoebe* and in the forts had been briefed on keeping a sharp eye out for the rockets.

The thirty-minute deadline passed without incident. Brewer checked his watch to be sure before turning to Lieutenant Greene.

"The second signal, if you please."

"Aye, sir."

HMS *Phoebe* led eighteen treasure ships out of Salvador and onto their south-southeastern course. Thirteen of the ships in the convoy were the huge thousand-tonners, loaded with the king of Portugal's gold. Brewer's plan was to keep his frigate to the north of the convoy, trying to stay between it and the battle. To that end, he reduced sail once out to sea and ordered running lights hung down the starboard side of the hull, hoping the treasure ships following him would see the lights and pass down *Phoebe's* starboard side as ordered. Four of the ships were seen from the deck as they passed the frigate; Brewer hoped the rest were just off in the darkness.

The night passed quietly enough. Brewer caught a few hours' sleep and was again on the deck with the rising of the sun. He stepped up on deck, and in the predawn mist identified Lieutenants Greene and Rivkins in conversation with Mr. Sweeney and the quartermaster.

"Good morning, gentlemen," he said.

All touched their hats to a chorus of "Good morning, sir."

"I am about to send extra hands aloft as lookouts, sir," Greene volunteered. "Right now, we have three transports and one lugger in sight."

"Thank you, Mr. Greene." Brewer turned and surveyed the conditions. He could barely make out the shapes of the ships through the haze. "Pass the word for Mr. Dye, if you please."

The signals midshipman presented himself and saluted. "You sent for me, sir?"

"Yes, Mr. Dye. Signal the lugger to begin a search to the south for the missing transports. After that, signal the transports to form up on us, course southeast."

"Aye, aye, Captain."

He was back in ten minutes. "All signals acknowledged, Captain. The transports are turning to follow."

"Very good, Mr. Dye." Brewer accepted a glass from a nearby petty officer and began to scan the horizon. The transports were indeed closing in on the frigate, and he watched as the lugger dipped below the horizon to the southwest and disappeared. An hour later, two more transports appeared over the horizon from the south and joined their formation. Two hours later, a cry came from the lookout.

"Deck, there! Sails approaching from the southwest!"

Brewer and Greene met at the rail, telescopes raised to their eyes.

"Can you make them out?" Greene cried.

"Looks like a lugger and six transports, sir!"

Several minutes passed before Mr. Dye called out from the mizzen shrouds.

"I can make them out now, Captain! It looks like HMS *Hawk* leading six missing transports!"

"I agree, sir," Greene said. "That means HMS *Falcon* is searching for seven transports."

Brewer lowered his glass. His mind raced as he tried to figure out where the missing transports could be. He turned to his first lieutenant.

"Order Mr. Dye to signal the transports to join our convoy. Have him signal *Hawk* to search to the southwest for the missing transports. Tell them we shall hold a southerly course for six hours before turning east."

"Aye, sir."

"Mr. Sweeney, as soon as those transports have joined us, the entire convoy shall change course to the south."

"Aye, Captain."

Sweeney turned to the wheel.

The quartermaster smiled as he approached. "So, t'would seem that the captain doesn't trust the Portuguese transport captains not to run us over, wouldn't you say?"

The sailing master looked at him and shrugged. "Would you? Stand by for the turn south."

The quartermaster laughed as he turned his attention back to the wheel. His mates shared a knowing look and smile; it was plain what they thought of merchant captains.

The trip south passed slowly. Brewer spent every minute of the six hours on the quarterdeck, much of it pacing back and forth along the lee rail. He was trying not to worry about the missing transports. Every captain knew his ultimate destination as well as the approximate course planned for the convoy as a whole. His step faltered as the idea of a mutiny on one of the treasure ships entered into his mind for the first time. He had to admit that the presence of that much treasure combined with the solitude of a dark night would make a tempting opportunity for an unscrupulous individual. Brewer sighed and continued his pacing. He had no time to chase down the transports, not while the results of the battle were unknown to him—Cochrane could be searching for him at this very minute.

He noticed his first lieutenant standing off to the side and ceased his pacing.

"Excuse me, sir," Greene said, "but you wanted to know when the six hours were up."

"Yes," Brewer replied. "Thank you, Benjamin. Signal the convoy. Course due east."

"Aye, sir," Greene touched his hat and went to pass the order on to Mr. Dye and the sailing master.

The captain considered resuming his pacing, but he found himself frustrated by a growing feeling of helplessness. Instead, he made his way to the fantail and stared out over the waters toward the sou'sou'west, trying to will the missing transports and their escorting luggers to appear. He knew the captains of the luggers, Willingham of the *Hawk* and Benson of the *Falcon*; his impression when he'd met them aboard the flagship and then later during the final briefing on board *Phoebe* had been favorable. Good men who were good at their jobs. Now, staring out over the empty waves, he hoped he was not wrong.

He heard a throat discreetly cleared, and he turned to see Alfred and Mac standing there. Alfred was holding a tray containing a plate with a few slices of cold ham and a cup of tea.

"You didn't come down to eat, sir," Mac said. "We thought you might be hungry."

Alfred said nothing the entire time, his eyes meeting and holding those of his captain, his compassion and care obvious in his gaze. Brewer nodded his thanks as he picked up a hunk of ham and his cup. To his surprise, he found he was indeed hungry, and the contents of the plate disappeared in short order. Alfred came to attention briefly before retreating below deck; Mac knuckled his forehead before following.

There followed two hours of alternating periods of pacing and staring, none of which did anything to lessen the captain's growing sense of helplessness and failure. Brewer was about to descend to his cabin to update his log when the call finally sounded.

"Sail ho!"

The cry came from the lookout in the mizzen tops. Every eye on the quarterdeck turned in that direction.

"Where away?" cried the First Lieutenant.

"Sou'west, sir!" The lookout pointed.

Brewer and Greene moved swiftly to the fantail and raised their telescopes to scan the area. They found the small but growing patch of white on the horizon.

"Lookout!" Greene cried again. "Let's hear you!"

"Looks like three ships, sir! Maybe four!"

Brewer tensed at the news and immediately chastised himself for not keeping better control over himself. There was nothing to do for the next hour or so but wait. The pacing resumed.

"Deck there! Sails look like a lugger and four transports!"

Brewer's heart leapt as he dashed to the rail to see for himself. This time it was easy to distinguish the smaller sail ahead of several larger ones. He turned to Mr. Greene.

"Raise the recognition signal!"

"Aye, sir!"

Brewer watched the approaching ships in anticipation as the signal was hoisted. Within minutes, Greene was at his side.

"It's the *Falcon*, sir, with four of the missing transports."

Brewer let out the deep breath he had been holding. That left three still missing, along with the *Hawk*. He closed his glass and handed it to the midshipman of the watch.

"Well," he said. "Mr. Greene, let us have Captain Benson over for a drink, shall we?"

Lieutenant Jason Benson, captain of His Majesty's lugger *Falcon* stood respectfully in the day cabin of HMS *Phoebe*, a glass of Madeira in one hand and the other behind his back. He was a full head shorter than Brewer and thin as a rail; one got the impression after meeting him that his energy was all spirit, not of his body. In fact, his personality reminded Brewer of what Bonaparte's must have been like as a young officer at Toulon.

"It took us much of the day to round up our strays," Benson said. "We were an hour or so into our journey to find you when we ran into the *Hawk*, and Captain Willingham told us of your course deviation. My sailing master and I put our heads together and worked out a course to intercept, and here we are."

"You've done excellent work, Captain," Brewer said, "and I shall be pleased to note as much in my log and in my reports to Commodore Hardy. For now, I want to place *Falcon* one mile to the southwest of the convoy. I want you to run all your lights during the night; hopefully one or more of the missing ships will see you and close to investigate. The convoy of course will be dark. I will place *Phoebe* one mile to the north of the rear of the convoy. I think that's the best place to intercept any Brazilians who may be looking for us."

"And if they do find us?" Dr. Spinelli asked.

"We shall try to outrun them," Brewer said. "I know, I know, but it may be possible if the ships that find us suffered damage in the battle outside Salvador. If that doesn't work, I shall signal for the convoy to take up a new course of SSE. Captain Benson, you will lead them on a long, parabolic course to St. Helena."

"And you, sir?" Benson asked.

Brewer held the man's eyes. "HMS *Phoebe* will give you as much time to get away as we can. We will catch up to you at St. Helena."

Benson met his host's gaze a moment longer. "Aye, sir."

"Sir," Greene said, "what about *Hawk* and the missing transports?"

Brewer smiled grimly and drained his glass. "Let's hope we see them at St. Helena."

The convoy proceeded uninterrupted for the next two days. Brewer split his time between pacing the quarterdeck and playing chess with the doctor in his cabin. He hadn't wanted to at first, but once he started he found that it occupied his mind and saved him from hours of useless worry. It was during just such a game on the afternoon of the second day that their monotony was relieved.

Brewer advanced a rook, a move which managed to surprise his opponent. The doctor sat up and stared.

"William," he said, "have you lost your mind?"

Brewer ignored the challenge. "You play your game, doctor, and I'll play mine."

Spinelli shrugged and bent over the board again. He moved a bishop, taking his captain's knight and putting his king in check."

"If you still have a game," he said under his breath.

A knock on the door preceded the sentry's admission of the midshipman of the watch. Mr. Henry marched up to his captain and came to attention.

"Yes, Mr. Henry?" Brewer asked without taking his eyes from the board.

"Sir, Mr. Rivkins sends his respects and wishes to report a sail on the horizon."

The captain's eyes snapped to his midshipman. "Where away?"

"To the nor'west, sir."

Brewer nodded, and his eyes went back to the game. "My compliments to Mr. Rivkins. Tell him I shall come on deck presently."

"Aye, sir." The midshipman came to attention again and was gone.

"Cochrane?" Spinelli ventured.

Brewer shrugged. "No way to tell yet. If she's Portuguese, she'll close on us. If she's Brazilian, she may close or she may well sit out there and keep track of us to bring reinforcements. In any case," he paused to move the rook again, "let's go see. Checkmate."

He strode from the room, leaving the doctor to stare at the board. It was only when he was alone that the doctor smiled and followed his captain from the room. He made it to the quarterdeck just in time to see the captain take a glass from a petty officer.

"Lookout! Let's hear you!" Brewer called.

"Looks to be a brig, sir!" came the reply.

"Do we go after her, sir?" Rivkins asked from his side.

The captain lowered his glass and stared out at the horizon. "Do you remember a mutual friend from the Mediterranean, the British Envoy to Naples?"

Brewer looked over his shoulder just in time to see a twinge of embarrassment on his lieutenant's face.

Rivkins said, "Yes, sir," and moved away. The premier took his place, touching his hat to his captain.

Greene nodded toward Mr. Rivkins. "Sir?"

Brewer put his glass back to his eye. "We were escorting a brig taking the British Envoy to his new post at Naples when we were lured away by a sail on the horizon." He lowered the glass and turned to his friend. "When we made it back, the brig was gone. It had been taken by Barbary pirates while we were off chasing their lure."

"Ah," Greene said.

"Deck, there! The sail's leaving!"

Brewer studied the horizon and saw the strange sail was turning to head back the way it came.

"What course, lookout?" Greene called.

"Nor'east, sir!"

Greene sighed. "Think she's gone to get Cochrane?"

"What else?" The captain handed his glass to a midshipman. "So. The time has come, I think. Signal the convoy. *Falcon* is to lead the convoy to the southeast and around to St. Helena. They leave immediately."

"Aye, sir," Greene said. He touched his hat and moved off, calling for Mr. Dye. The doctor, who had been hanging back, stepped up.

"So," he said, "now we settle things for the Caribbean, eh?"

Brewer looked at the doctor through hooded eyes, his mind recalling all the threats Cochrane had either made or implied since Hornblower had rescued him from the admiral's vengeance. He shrugged and turned to the sea. His friend stood beside him, silent and steady, a rock at his back he could utterly rely upon.

"Thank you, Adam," he said quietly.

The doctor nodded his acknowledgement; nothing else was needed between them.

The captain walked over to the wheel, where he was met by the first lieutenant and the sailing master. Both men touched their hats at his approach.

"*Falcon* has acknowledged the signal, sir," Greene said. "Captain Benson is making sure all transport captains understand their orders. He reports they should be on their way within the hour. Less, if the transport captains respond swiftly."

"Good," Brewer said. "I want them below the horizon before the Brazilians return."

Forty-five minutes later, he stood at the fantail and watched as the convoy sailed away. He stayed there until the last transport had dropped below the horizon and safely out of sight.

"Orders, sir?" Greene asked.

"Steady as you go for now." Brewer saw the look of surprise on his premier's face. "Come now, Benjamin; we don't want to make it too hard for the Brazilians to find us, do we?" He looked to the clouds. "It's nearly supper time; will you join me, Benjamin?"

Greene bowed. “An honor, Captain.”

Brewer smiled and led the way below deck to his cabin.

“Alfred!” he called, and the servant appeared. “There will be another officer for supper.”

“Very good, sir.”

Brewer moved to the bottle of Madeira that was on his desk and poured each of them a glass. He handed one to Greene and indicated that they should sit in the dayroom.

“I want to make my intentions known to you first, Benjamin,” the captain said. “After we eat, we shall invite some others in for a counsel of war.”

Greene held up his glass in salute. “I take it we are to be the rear guard.”

“To be plain,” Brewer said after a swallow, “yes.”

Greene’s glass went higher in a there-you-are gesture, and the two men drank. Brewer brought the decanter and refilled their glasses.

“I am operating,” the captain began, “on the worst-case scenario: that the unknown sail was that of a Brazilian brig and that it disappeared to find what was left of their blockade squadron and direct them our way. We have no way of knowing what forces the Brazilians will have left to throw at us, but it is safe to assume they must have *some* forces available, or they would not have sent out the brig to scout for us. For the present, I intend to hold this course. It is what they expect us to do, and it is where they will look for us first. I expect them to come at us from the northwest or perhaps the north, although for the sake of argument I suppose it is possible that Cochrane will figure out our destination from our course and rush ahead to stand in our way. In any case, we will engage as many as we can in order to give the convoy as much time as possible to get away. I gave Captain Benson orders stating his complete authority to take whatever actions or course he deems necessary to get the convoy to St. Helena safely. The only thing we can now give him is time."

After supper, Brewer passed the word for all officers to report to his cabin. Brewer wasted no time in making the situation known to all.

"Gentlemen, we have been spotted by a brig of unknown nationality. I am working on the assumption that the ship was Brazilian and has gone to contact what's left of the blockade squadron and send them our direction. I have ordered *Falcon* to take the treasure fleet south on a parabolic course to St. Helena. We will proceed on our present course in the hope of intercepting the Brazilian force if it comes after us. Any questions?"

Brewer unknowingly held his breath. He watched as each man digested the news. Some, Brewer knew, felt their worst fears now confirmed. Lieutenant Reed looked as if he were trying to hold himself together; the captain remembered being in the very same position once. Mr. Rivkins stared at the ceiling. Brewer wasn't worried about him; he remembered how he'd fought in the Med and knew he would be all right. Others, older and battle-hardened, took the news almost in stride. Mr. Sweeney and Lieutenant Greene shared a knowing look, a determination to do their duty. The doctor sat calm and collected, but Brewer knew that his mind was racing, going over lists of supplies he had on hand for dealing with the casualties that were sure to come. It was Captain Enfield of the marines who finally broke the silence.

"Will you want my sharpshooters in the tops, sir, or on the deck to repel boarders?"

Brewer let his breath out. They would be fine. HMS *Phoebe* would do her duty. The remainder of the evening was spent discussing tactics based on various scenarios that might arise. When he finally dismissed them, he felt much more confident than he had earlier in the day.

Two days later, a knock on his cabin door roused Brewer from his reports. Mac opened the door and admitted Mr. Murdy, the senior midshipman.

"Yes, Mr. Murdy?" Brewer asked.

"Mr. Reed sends his respects, sir," the midshipman said. "He begs to report a sail coming over the horizon from the nor'nor'west."

"I shall come immediately."

"Report, Mr. Reed!" he called as soon as he was on deck. He nodded his thanks to a petty officer who handed him a glass.

"Sail bearing nor'nor'west, sir!"

"Let's hear you, lookout!"

"Definitely more than one, sir!" the lookout called back. "Might be the brig leading a frigate!"

Brewer found them, but they were still hull-down to the horizon. He lowered the glass and looked around. Lieutenant Greene was studying the horizon; Mac and Alfred were armed to the teeth and holding his weapons ready for him.

"Benjamin," Brewer said quietly, "beat to quarters, if you please."

Greene tucked the glass under his arm and touched his hat. "Aye, sir." He picked up a speaking trumpet. "Beat to quarters! All hands! Beat to quarters!"

The *rat-a-tat-tat* that rang out sent the crew to their work. Brewer knew the deck beneath him was being readied for the fight, his own quarters disappearing in the conversion. The sharpshooters went to their positions, and the gun crews readied their pieces to load and run out.

"Deck there!" shouted the lookout. "There're four ships! Looks like the brig is leading a frigate! The other two're either brigs or sloops—I'm not certain! They're piling on sail, sir!"

Brewer watched as the fields of white heading toward him grew with the added sail. The frigate turned to port in an attempt to get ahead of them and cut them off.

"Sir!" It was Mr. Greene. "I see a broad pennant flying from the frigate!"

It took Brewer only a moment to confirm his premier's report. Admiral Cochrane was letting him know that he was out there. The brig had not altered course, so very soon *Phoebe* would cut across her bows. The other two smaller craft were still on the far side of the frigate. He turned to Greene.

"I want all carronades in the larboard battery loaded with grape and the 18-pounders with grape over ball. Have the entire starboard battery load with ball."

Greene touched his hat and proceeded to issue the orders.

"Mr. Sweeney! I want to put a broadside into her as we pass. With good shooting and a bit of luck, we'll disable her before she can damage us. As soon as we do that, I want to haul around to port and put a broadside into the frigate. Then we will turn to starboard and put another into her as we cross her stern. After that, we can deal with the other two ships."

Sweeney took a moment to digest the plan, then he nodded. "Aye, Captain."

"Good," Brewer said. Next, he took his hanger and sword from Mac and buckled it around his waist. Alfred handed him his brace of pistols.

"Thank you both," he said. "Stay close."

Greene returned, and Brewer briefed him on the plan. The captain walked over to the waist.

"Mr. Rivkins!"

The lieutenant appeared and touched his hat.

"Are you ready?"

"Aye, sir. Larboard battery loaded with grape over ball, the starboard with ball. Awaiting your orders."

"Very good," Brewer said. "Run out your guns and stand by!"

Brewer took his position on the quarterdeck by the rail, watching the brig approach. As the two ships neared, he could see activity on the brig's deck. The Brazilians were taking in sail, fearing a collision with the English frigate. Brewer smiled as he walked over to the waist. He looked down to find Mr. Rivkins standing there. Brewer nodded, and Rivkins ordered the larboard battery to stand by. The captain looked back to the brig, timing it just right. He looked up the deck to be sure that he had the attention of Lieutenant Reed forward and Mr. Greene at the quarterdeck carronades. He looked back to the brig, now at point-blank range.

"Fire!" he roared.

The broadside exploded from HMS *Phoebe*. Rivkins had ordered his battery to fire in two sections, the second five seconds after the first. Brewer appreciated the precaution; a brig is not a very big target. The quarterdeck carronades were able to traverse sufficiently to fire at the target along with those on the fo'c'sle.

Brewer didn't wait to survey the damage to the brig. He turned to Sweeney.

"Hard to larboard!"

The quartermaster's mates at the wheel put it hard over, and the captain felt his ship begin to come around. He turned to give the order for Rivkins to run out the starboard battery, but he turned to find the enemy frigate running her own guns out. Cochrane had beaten him to the punch.

"Down!" he cried. "All hands, down!"

He dove to the deck. The light from the Brazilian's broadside barely beat the sound across the waters, but it was the iron that did the damage. Brewer lay as flat as he could with his arms over the back of his head. Despite his warning, he heard the screams of men who'd been unable to obey in time, but he forced himself to wait until he was sure it was safe before he lifted his head.

He rose and saw that *Phoebe* had managed to complete her turn before the broadside hit. Brewer ran to the waist.

"Mr. Rivkins, report!"

The lieutenant appeared. "We have some guns out of action, sir. We are getting them back into service as quickly as we can."

"Run out every gun you can in the starboard battery and fire!"

"Aye, sir!"

"Mr. Reed!"

"Here, sir!" came the reply from forward.

"Fire!"

Brewer turned to the quarterdeck carronades and found that their captains were standing by. They fired at his direction.

"Sir!" Mr. Greene cried, "The Brazilian is closing!"

"Mr. Sweeney! Hard to larboard! Take us around the brig!"

"Aye, sir!" The sailing master tossed the body of a quartermaster's mate out of the way and took the wheel himself as he put it hard over.

Brewer looked around the deck and surveyed the damage to his ship. He counted three carronades from the starboard battery out of action. He saw Mac and Alfred staggering back to their feet. He couldn't begin to count the casualties. The deck aft of the waist was littered with body parts and injured men being helped below. The rigging looked to be in good shape.

As for the brig, her foremast was down, and her deck looked like a slaughterhouse. *Phoebe*'s 18-pound shot had penetrated her sides and exploded several canon. But now the Brazilian frigate was heading to the other side of the brig, hoping to catch *Phoebe* as she rounded the brig from aft.

"Mr. Sweeney!" Brewer called. "Hard to starboard! Take us about! All hands make sail! Mac! Take the wheel!"

The big Cornishman jumped to the wheel and helped Sweeney put it hard over to starboard. Brewer felt his ship leap forward as the wind filled the additional sails.

"Mr. Sweeney, I want to run down those other two ships while the frigate is making her way around the brig. If we can put those two out of action, then the treasure convoy should be safe."

"And the frigate?" Greene asked.

"Oh, I don't think the convoy will be the first thing on the admiral's mind now that he knows I'm on this quarterdeck," he said softly, a smile at the corner of his lips. "Do you?"

Brewer turned to his first lieutenant. "We've got about most of a half-hour before we overtake those two ships. Make a quick tour of the ship and get me a damage report, including casualties. Have the carpenter check for any holes below the waterline. See if the bosun needs to make any repairs."

"Aye, sir." Greene touched his hat and headed forward.

"Mr. Sweeney," Brewer said, "I'm going forward. I'll take Mr. Dye to carry messages. Mr. Dye, you're with me."

"Aye, sir," said the youngest midshipman.

Brewer made his way forward as quickly as he could, taking care not to slip on the blood that pooled in several places on the deck. When he arrived at the bow chasers, he was pleased to find Mr. Dye still only a step behind him and clean.

Brewer raised his telescope to his eye. From here he was able to identify the ships as sloops carrying all sail in an effort to get past him and look for the convoy. The near one looked like a 16-gunner, probably 8-pounders judging by the size of the gun ports he could see. Even damaged as Phoebe was, the sloops were no match for her.

Lieutenant Greene arrived. "Begging your pardon, sir."

"Yes?" Brewer turned to his premier. "Report, Mr. Greene."

"Three carronades of the starboard battery are out of action, one on the fo'c'sle and two on the quarterdeck. Mr. Rivkins reports that four of the starboard battery's 18-pounders are also out of action. They are trying to repair the damage. The carpenter reports no holes below the waterline that he could find. He is on the gun deck helping get the 18-pounders back into action. And Mr. Knight says that he and his mates will 'keep the old girl moving for you, sir.'"

Brewer grunted. He dropped the glass and turned to Greene.

"They're splitting up. Benjamin, I'm going aft. We're going to stick to the nearest one. I want you to stay here and take command of the bow chasers. I'm leaving Mr. Dye with you to run messages between us. Let me know when you think you're in range. I want to put iron in her as we pass. If we can disable her, we will have time to deal with her consort before the Brazilian frigate can catch up with us."

"Aye, sir."

Brewer made his way aft. He stopped at the waist.

"Mr. Rivkins!" he called, and the lieutenant appeared.

"Sir?"

"We're going after the near sloop. I want your guns loaded with ball. Shoot for her hull."

"Aye, sir."

Brewer continued aft and found Mr. Reed on the quarterdeck, assisting with the damaged carronades.

"Mr. Reed," he said, "we're going after the sloops. Load with grape and stand by."

"Aye, sir."

By the time Brewer had joined the sailing master and given directions, the enemy frigate was just clearing the brig and setting a course to intercept them. He turned back in time to see the sloops split, the near one heading south while the far one went southwest.

"Now, Mr. Sweeney," the captain said. "Give me a course to take the near one down our starboard side. As soon as we've put our broadside into her, alter course to larboard to intercept the second sloop."

"Aye, sir!"

Brewer looked aft to the Brazilian frigate, now settled down for a stern chase. She bore every stitch of canvas she could carry—as did *Phoebe*. He only hoped she wasn't a better sailer than his ship.

Midshipman Dye appeared and saluted. "Mr. Greene sends his respects, sir, and says he thinks he can reach her now."

Brewer took a quick look forward to judge the distances for himself. Satisfied, he turned back to his midshipman.

"My compliments to Mr. Greene he may fire when ready."

"Aye aye, sir!" Dye said. He knuckled his head and went forward.

Brewer rubbed the bridge of his nose to try to ease the tension. Mr. Sweeney saw this and asked, "Captain? Are you all right?"

"Fine, Mr. Sweeney, thank you. Do you know who I suddenly find myself missing ?"

Sweeney shook his head.

"Mr. Short." He pointed to Mr. Henry. "Mr. Henry! Take a glass and find a spot in the mizzen shrouds! I want a report on all shots by the bow chasers!"

"Aye, aye!"

The lad grabbed a telescope and found a spot about halfway up the shrouds where he made his perch secure and pointed his glass forward. Sweeney smiled. Small, agile, and full of energy, Mr. Short, midshipman on HMS *Revenge,* had been famous for being forever in the shrouds with a glass, reporting unbidden on everything from the weather to an enemy's whereabouts. He had not transferred from *Revenge* to *Phoebe* back at Port Royal.

The boom of the bow chasers firing sounded on the quarterdeck. Brewer and Sweeney looked to the midshipman in the shrouds.

"One off the port quarter, another twenty yards short!"

Two minutes later, the guns fired again, and Henry was on it. "A hit! A hit! The other missed to starboard by ten feet."

"Right!" Brewer snapped his glass shut and picked up a speaking trumpet. "Lookout! Let's hear you! What's happening on the sloop?"

"She's still holding course, sir!"

The bow chasers fired again.

"Two hits, sir!" Henry shouted.

"Sloop's drifting a bit to starboard, sir!" the lookout reported.

"That's it!" Brewer said. "Pass the word to Mr. Greene to cease fire! Mr. Sweeney, I want to pass their larboard quarter at half-pistol shot."

"Aye, sir! Altering course three points to larboard!"

Brewer walked to the waist. "Mr. Rivkins, run out the starboard battery and stand by!"

"Aye, sir!"

Brewer turned to the carronades. "On my order, Mr. Reed."

"Aye, Captain!" Reed ran forward to command the fo'c'sle carronades, leaving the quarterdeck guns to fire at the captain's command.

Brewer watched the sloop, gauging the distance. He waited until about two-thirds of the battery bore on the larboard side of the sloop before giving the order.

"Fire!"

Every gun in the larboard battery went off as one. The effect on their target was devastating. The deck and gun ports—the entire larboard side of the sloop aft of the foremast—vanished in a cloud of smoke, blood, and splinters. Brewer looked back and stared as *Phoebe* sailed out of the smoke. He had never seen such destruction wrought by a single broadside in his life. The sloop was visibly settling into the water by the larboard quarter. Brewer saw no one alive on the deck at all. A few of the crew were trying to leave the ship from the lower deck, hanging on to any debris large enough to help them stay afloat. Brewer hoped they would have time to come back and help.

Sweeney altered course to starboard to set the intercept course for the second sloop. But she had witnessed the destruction of her consort and wanted nothing to do with the British frigate. She made a long, sweeping turn to larboard which was intended to bring her back toward her own frigate. Brewer immediately saw the danger to his ship; if he tried to cut across the turn, he would deliver his ship to the guns of the approaching Brazilian frigate.

"Mr. Sweeney," he ordered, "intercept course. But wait for the word."

Sweeney held his captain's eyes for a moment before nodding. "Aye, sir."

Brewer walked to the waist. "Mr. Rivkins!"

The Lieutenant appeared and saluted. "Sir?"

"In a moment we are going to turn hard-a-port to try to cut off the remaining sloop. I want the starboard battery loaded with grape over ball. Wait for the word to fire on the sloop as we pass. I want the larboard battery loaded with grape; we may get a chance to send a broadside over the bows of the frigate. You may run out when loaded, but wait for the word to fire."

Next, Brewer turned to his first lieutenant."Mr. Greene, load the larboard carronades with ball, starboard with grape. Load and run out. Wait for the word to fire."

"Aye, sir."

Brewer stood beside Sweeney near the wheel, trying to take in simultaneously the sloop bearing away to his larboard and the frigate approaching from the stern. The sailing master and quartermaster's mates stood by silently, waiting for the word. Finally, the captain turned and said,

"Now, Mr. Sweeney."

The sailing master touched his hat to his captain, then turned to the mates at the wheel and nodded once. The mates immediately put the wheel over hard to larboard. HMS *Phoebe* straightened up on an intercept course, aiming slightly ahead of the fleeing sloop to cut her off.

As soon as they steadied up on the intercept course, Brewer looked back to the Brazilian frigate. As expected, she, too, had turned to larboard in an attempt to close on his ship. He studied the distances carefully, gaging the wind as best he could as well as the relative speeds of all three vessels. It seemed inevitable that the frigate would soon get a clear shot at *Phoebe*, and if he didn't maneuver, it would be the most devastating shot of all: directly up the stern. He made his decision. He had to disable the sloop in order to safeguard the treasure convoy.

"Steady as you go, Mr. Sweeney. I want to make our pass at half-pistol shot."

"Aye, sir," Sweeney said. He stood stolidly behind the wheel. "Steady as we go. Half-pistol shot."

Brewer went forward. At the bows he found Lieutenant Greene watching the sloop.

"Report, Mr. Greene."

Greene called over his shoulder, "The sloop is bearing to starboard and attempting to flee, sir."

"Can you reach her with the long nines?"

"I believe so, once her course straightens up, sir."

"Load and run out, Mr. Greene."

He stood back and watched as Greene directed the operation. He sent word back to Sweeney to fall in behind the sloop as it changed course. Fifteen minutes later, Greene announced he was ready to try.

The roar was deafening, but the wind carried the smoke away quickly. Both shots hit the water about twenty yards behind the sloop. The craft immediately reversed course, steering hard to larboard until she was heading back toward her British pursuer. Brewer was just about to warn Mr. Rivkins to ready the larboard battery when the sloop unexpectedly healed over to larboard again and crossed their bow. Brewer had turned to send an order to Sweeney when the sloop let loose her broadside. Waves of grape spread death and mayhem over the deck. Brewer saw his first lieutenant go down as he himself was slammed to the deck with a sharp pain in his arm. Right after he hit the deck, he felt the ship heel over as though the wheel had been put over hard to larboard, and he knew Mr. Sweeney was trying to avoid a collision with the sloop. A few moments later, he heard the starboard battery fire. He could only put it down to some officer on the quarterdeck who'd seen him fall in the broadside and ordered Rivkins to fire.

Brewer staggered to his feet and looked around. There were several dead and injured on the fore part of the deck. He raised his eyes to see the damage wrought by their broadside on the sloop. One mast was down. The ship was drifting off to starboard and seemed down by the starboard quarter.

"Captain!"

Brewer spun at the cry and almost fell when he was hit with an overwhelming feeling of dizziness. He steadied himself and staggered over to where one of the men was leaning over the crumpled form of Lieutenant Greene; he knelt beside him.

"How is he?" the captain asked.

"Looks like he's hit in the upper chest and right shoulder, sir," the man said. "He's still breathing."

Brewer carefully felt his friend's neck and felt the weak pulse before forcing himself to rise cautiously to his feet. "Get him below to the doctor. You two, help him."

The two hands responded at once, and Brewer watched as the three men carried the first lieutenant below deck to the doctor. Only when he was out of sight did the captain make his way aft, trying his best not to stagger.

He arrived on the quarterdeck and paused to lean against one of the carronades. Mac spied him and immediately came over.

"Sir!" he said, "You're hurt! Let me look at you!"

"Not now, Mac!"

The coxswain caught his captain's eye. "At least let me put a bandage on it, sir. To stop the bleeding until the doctor can see you."

"Very well." He leaned back on the carronade and allowed Mac to take his coat. Only then did he notice Alfred standing on the other side, pulling bandages out of his coat pocket.

Mac cut the captain's sleeve off at the shoulder and examined the wound. "Nasty gash. Looks like a deep graze, sir; I don't think it hit the bone. Let's get you bandaged up proper."

Between the two of them working on him, it didn't take long. He objected to the sling when Alfred offered it, but he accepted it in the end. He had to admit, it did take the pressure off his shoulder.

"Thank you," he said. "Stand by."

"Mr. Sweeney," he called as he went to the wheel. "What's our situation?"

"Minor damage to the ship, Captain," came the report. "Mr. Knight and his mates are already working on splicing a couple of cables that were cut. No additional guns out of action. I have no word on casualties yet."

"Mr. Greene was hit in the chest and arm. He was taken below to the doctor."

For a moment, Brewer thought that his sailing master was about to offer his condolences in the midst of a battle, but Sweeney merely nodded and watched the bosun and his mates at work. That was when he heard it—the cry every captain dreads.

"Captain!" The terror in the voice caused Brewer to spin—nearly falling in the process—to see the Brazilian frigate closing, altering course to cut across their stern.

"All hands down! All hands..."

Brewer was hit nearly simultaneously by two sensations. One was the concussion of the frigate's broadside, a powerful blast of heat and wind. The other actually hit him an instant before the broadside, knocking the wind out of him and slamming him to the deck. His head spun, and his ears rang. He felt a weight on him that made it hard to breathe. He did not realize until Mac shook him gently by the front of his shirt that he was being spoken to. His ears were ringing. He nodded his acknowledgement, and Mac helped him to his feet.

"Sorry for the tackle, sir," Mac said. "Are you hit?"

"I don't think so," Brewer said slowly, "but I think it would hurt less if I were. Thank you, Mac."

Mac grinned sheepishly. Behind him, Brewer noticed one of the captains of the quarterdeck carronades come up and speak to Mr. Sweeney. The sailing master immediately went to the fantail and looked over the side at the rudder. Brewer excused himself and followed.

"You're right, sure enough," Sweeney said to the gun captain as he arrived.

"Report, Mr. Sweeney," Brewer said.

"Captain, Edwards here said he heard a loud crack after the frigate went past," Sweeney said. "He looked over the fantail and then came to tell me. Captain, the rudder's gone."

Brewer looked over the fantail. He had to see for himself, though he knew from how the ship had started to drift that his sailing master was speaking the truth. He straightened up and thought desperately for a way out of this.

"Where's the frigate?" he asked.

"She's gone around the sloop, sir," a midshipman answered.

"Probably to observe the damage before coming back to deal with us," Sweeney said. Brewer nodded.

"Pass the word for Mr. Rivkins," Brewer said.

"That frigate will figure out our damage when they come around the sloop and we're still on this course, sir," Sweeney said.

The second lieutenant appeared. "Damage report, Mr. Rivkins," Brewer said.

"We got hurt when he raked us, Captain," the young lieutenant said. "He must have been loaded with grape over ball. I lost ten killed outright, and double that in wounded, plus five guns out of action."

Brewer took it all in, and it added up to trouble. "Order Mr. Reed to take command on the gun deck. Mr. Greene has been hit, and I need you up here. Our rudder's been shot away. Is there any way to drag one or two of the guns to fire astern?

"None, sir."

"That's it, then," Sweeney said.

"Pass the word for Mr. Murdy." Brewer stared at the deck and took in a deep breath, then exhaled slowly. He raised his head when the senior midshipman arrived. "Mr. Murdy, take command of the fo'c'sle guns, including the long nines. Our rudder's been shot away. You have my permission to fire at any enemy ship that comes within range of any of your guns. Do your best to keep them at a distance."

"Aye, sir." The man knuckled his head and was gone.

"Mr. Rivkins," the captain continued, "please pass the word to Mr. Reed that he is to fire at will if any enemy ship presents itself."

"Deck there!" It was the lookout calling. "That frigate's clearing the sloop!"

Sweeney stood beside the captain, the very picture of frustration and helplessness. "All he's got to do is stay out of range until he can work his way behind us and rake our stern until we surrender. We're sitting ducks."

"Our mission will be a success," the captain said. "The treasure ships will get away."

"Of course, sir," Sweeney said stiffly.

"Sir?" It was Rivkins, standing beside the rail. "Looks like he's figured it out. He's reversing course, probably heading back around the sloop so he can come out behind us."

That's what I would do, Brewer thought.

"Sail, ho!"

The cry from the mizzen tops startled the captain, as it was literally the last thing he expected to hear; or so he thought, until he heard the next report.

"Three ships, sir, from the sou'west!"

For a brief moment, Brewer was afraid that the missing treasure ships and lugger had appeared. Sweeney had a glass to his eye and reported differently.

"Sir?" he said in disbelief, "I recognize the lead ship! It's the *Amazone*! Admiral Roussin and the French squadron!"

"What?" Brewer forced himself to stand and move to the rail. He took Sweeney's glass to see for himself. "Thank you, Lord," he whispered.

The Brazilian frigate reversed course again and sailed off to the north, away from the approaching French ships. This proved to Brewer that, broad pennant or no, either Cochrane was not aboard that frigate, or he was wounded and no longer in command. Brewer wasn't sure which he wished for more.

He handed the glass back to the sailing master. "Heave to, Mr. Sweeney. I am going below to speak to the doctor."

"Aye, sir."

The sickbay was dimly lit and smelled of blood, and worse. Brewer made his way carefully, trying to speak a word or give a reassuring touch to any of the wounded who were conscious. He waited until the doctor was finished with his current patient before he approached.

"Well, Adam?" he asked quietly. "What's the butcher's bill?"

"Twenty-nine dead," the doctor said wearily as he wiped his hands. "Most of those deaths caused when our stern was raked. Twenty-six injured, but I'm not sure whether three of those will see the morning." Spinelli noticed the bandage on Brewer's arm. "What happened to you? No, don't tell me, let me guess: your personal nurse was doing my job again, wasn't he? Well, sir sit down. Let me look at it."

Brewer sat and winced as the doctor untied the bandage. "I got it at the same time Benjamin was hit. How is he?"

The doctor didn't answer. He pursed his lips and sucked his teeth as he examined his captain's wound. He tossed the old bandage in the barrel and reached for a clean one.

"You should be fine in a few days. As for Mr. Greene, he was not so lucky. The shot in his arm broke the bone, while the shot to his upper chest cracked his shoulder blade and broke his collarbone before heading downward and barely missing his lung. I managed to get the bullet out, but we have to watch him carefully. Infection in the chest could kill him."

"Can I see him?"

Spinelli shook his head. "The surgery was hard on him. I gave him as much laudanum as I thought he could handle for the pain. He's asleep now, and I'd rather not wake him."

Brewer nodded slowly, then grimaced as a wave of nausea swept over him. "Of course. Please let me know when he wakes up."

"Aye, sir. What happened up there?"

Brewer looked around the sickroom, seeing the many men who had died or been injured to protect the Portuguese convoy. "Remember how our French friends missed our party with El Diabolito? Well, this time they showed up, and in the nick of time, too."

Brewer made his way out of the sickbay and headed for the deck. On the way, he ran into Mac.

"Alfred and me'll begin putting your quarters to rights as much as we can until we get to port, sir, if that's all right with you. Also, Mr. Rivkins said that I should tell you the *Amazone's* hove to and is sending a boat."

"Thank you, Mac," Brewer said. "Carry on. I'll head to the deck."

By the time he got there, the boat from the *Amazone* was just arriving, and very soon he was shaking hands with Captain de Robespierre.

"You showed up just in time, Captain," Brewer said. "Thank you."

"It is our pleasure, *Capitaine*," de Robespierre said. "My admiral asks if there is anything we can do for you?"

"Our rudder is shot away. Can we get a tow to St. Helena?"

The Frenchman bowed. "But of course, *mon ami*. I also have been instructed by my admiral to ask you one very important question."

"What is it?"

"Admiral Roussin wishes to know if your cook has survived the battle?"

Painfully, Brewer began to laugh.

THE END

About The Author

James Keffer

James Keffer was born September 9, 1963, in Youngstown, Ohio, the son of a city policeman and a nurse. He grew up loving basketball, baseball, tennis, and books. He graduated high school in 1981 and began attending Youngstown State University to study mechanical engineering.

He left college in 1984 to enter the U.S. Air Force. After basic training, he was posted to the 2143rd Communications Squadron at Zweibruecken Air Base, West Germany. While he was stationed there, he met and married his wife, Christine, whose father was also assigned to the base. When the base was closed in 1991, James and Christine were transferred up the road to Sembach Air Base, where he worked in communications for the 2134th Communications Squadron before becoming the LAN manager for HQ 17th Air Force.

James received an honorable discharge in 1995, and he and his wife moved to Jacksonville, Florida, to attend Trinity

Baptist College. He graduated with honors in 1998, earning a Bachelor of Arts degree. James and Christine have three children.

Hornblower and the Island was the first novel James wrote, and it was the first to be published by Fireship Press. He has self-published three other novels. He currently lives and works in Jacksonville, Florida, with his wife and three children.

If You Enjoyed This Book

Please write a review.

This is important to the author and helps to get the word out to others

Visit

PENMORE PRESS

www.penmorepress.com

All Penmore Press books are available directly through our website, amazon.com, Barnes and Noble and Nook, Apple iTunes, Kobo books and via leading bookshops across the United States, Canada, the UK, Australia and Europe.

BREWER'S LUCK

BY

JAMES KEFFER

After gaining valuable experience as an aide to Governor Lord Horatio Hornblower, William Brewer is rewarded with a posting as first lieutenant on the frigate HMS *Defiant*, bound for American waters. Early in their travels, it seems as though Brewer's greatest challenge will be evading the wrath of a tyrannical captain who has taken an active dislike to him. But when a hurricane sweeps away the captain, the young lieutenant is forced to assume command of the damaged ship, and a crew suffering from low morale.

Brewer reports their condition to Admiral Hornblower, who orders them into the Caribbean to destroy a nest of pirates hidden among the numerous islands. Luring the pirates out of their coastal lairs will be difficult enough; fighting them at sea could bring disaster to the entire operation. For the *Defiant* to succeed, Brewer must rely on his wits, his training, and his ability to shape a once-ragged crew into a coherent fighting force.

BREWER'S REVENGE
BY
JAMES KEFFER

Admiral Horatio Hornblower has given Commander William Brewer captaincy of the captured pirate sloop *El Dorado*. Now under sail as the HMS *Revenge,* its new name suits Brewer's frame of mind perfectly. He lost many of his best men in the engagement that seized the ship, and his new orders are to hunt down the pirates who have been ravaging the trade routes of the Caribbean sea.

But Brewer will face more than one challenge before he can confront the pirate known as El Diabolito. His best friend and ship's surgeon, Dr. Spinelli, is taking dangerous solace in alcohol as he wrestles with demons of his own. The new purser, Mr. Allen, may need a lesson in honest accounting. Worst of all, Hornblower has requested that Brewer take on a young ne'er-do-well, Noah Simmons, to remove him from a recent scandal at home. At twenty-three, Simmons is old to be a junior midshipman, and as a wealthy man's son he is unaccustomed to working, taking orders, or suffering privations.

William Brewer will need to muster all his resources to ready his crew for their confrontation with the Caribbean's most notorious pirate. In the process, he'll discover the true price of command.

BREWER AND THE BARBARY PIRATES

BY
JAMES KEFFER

It is said that a man is grown by his past, and so it was with William Brewer. Before he took command of HMS Defiant in a hurricane and before he hunted pirates in HMS Revenge, Brewer endured a crucible of fire that molded him into the legend he became. Fresh from the tutelage of Napoleon Bonaparte on St. Helena, Brewer signs on for a cruise under Captain Bush in HMS Lydia to the Mediterranean to battle the Barbary Pirates. Here Brewer learns to fight, but he also learns what it means to command men in battle and what it takes to order men to their deaths. Their enemy is a Scottish renegade who is responsible for the deaths of dozens of his fellow sailors over the years and the selling of hundreds of Europeans into African slavery. Along the way, Brewer is introduced to new heroes and new devils. He also receives sage advice from no less than the Duke of Wellington himself. In the end, Brewer has to use all he's learned – not to mention going beyond all that – to save HMS Lydia from total destruction at the hands of pirates.

PENMORE PRESS
www.penmorepress.com

Midshipman Graham and the Battle of Abukir

BY

JAMES BOSCHERT

It is midsummer of 1799 and the British Navy in the Mediterranean Theater of operations. Napoleon has brought the best soldiers and scientists from France to claim Egypt and replace the Turkish empire with one of his own making, but the debacle at Acre has caused the brilliant general to retreat to Cairo.

Commodore Sir Sidney Smith and the Turkish army land at the strategically critical fortress of Abukir, on the northern coast of Egypt. Here Smith plans to further the reversal of Napoleon's fortunes. Unfortunately, the Turks badly underestimate the speed, strength, and resolve of the French Army, and the ensuing battle becomes one of the worst defeats in Arab history.

Young Midshipman Duncan Graham is anxious to get ahead in the British Navy, but has many hurdles to overcome. Without any familial privileges to smooth his way, he can only advance through merit. The fires of war prove his mettle, but during an expedition to obtain desperately needed fresh water - and an illegal duel - a French patrol drives off the boats, and Graham is left stranded on shore. It now becomes a question of evasion and survival with the help of a British spy. Graham has to become very adaptable in order to avoid detection by the French police, and he must help the spy facilitate a daring escape by sea in order to get back to the British squadron.

"Midshipman Graham and The Battle of Abukir is both a rousing Napoleonic naval yarn and a convincing coming of age story. The battle scenes are riveting and powerful, the exotic Egyptian locales colorfully rendered." - John Danielski, author of *Capital's Punishment*

The Distant Ocean

BY

PHILIP K ALLAN

Newly returned from the Battle of the Nile, Alexander Clay and the crew of the Titan are soon in action again, just when he has the strongest reason to wish to abide in England. But a powerful French naval squadron is at large in the Indian Ocean, attacking Britain's vital East India trade. Together with his friend John Sutton, he is sent as part of the Royal Navy's response. On route the Titan runs to ground a privateer preying on slave ships on the coast of West Africa, stirring up memories of the past for Able Sedgwick, Clay's coxswain. They arrive in the Indian Ocean to find that danger lurks in the blue waters and on the palm-fringed islands. Old enemies with scores to settle mean that betrayal from amongst his own side may prove the hardest challenge Clay will face, and a dead man's hand may yet undo all he has fought to win. Will the curse of the captain's nephew never cease to bedevil Clay and his friends?

Printed by BoD™in Norderstedt, Germany